PRAISE FOR ANA HOLGUIN

"[Ana Holguin is] an author I know is going to become a lot of readers' new favorite."
—Alicia Thompson, *USA Today* bestselling author of *The Art of Catching Feelings*

"Ana Holguin has all the makings of a must-read romance author."
—Zoraida Córdova, *USA Today* bestselling author of *Kiss the Girl*

Up Close & Personal

"Graced with a charmingly complex pair of protagonists and written with both a sharp sense of humor and great insight into the challenges living with anxiety can present, Holguin's deliciously fun debut both entertains and enlightens." —*Booklist*

"Charming, witty, and tender."
—Abby Jimenez, #1 *New York Times* bestselling author of *Say You'll Remember Me*

"Wow! Rarely do I read debut novels this good! Chock full of delightful charm, deep insight, and a romance you will be rooting for with every bone in your body."
—Mia Sheridan, *New York Times* bestselling author of *Archer's Voice*

"From the mental health representation to the heartwarming and hilarious friend group, there was just so much to love in this swoony romance.... I lived inside this book the whole time I was reading it, and loved every minute."
—Alicia Thompson, *USA Today* bestselling author of *The Art of Catching Feelings*

"An extremely charming slow-burn romance that asks us to dig past first impressions and get vulnerable to get to the heart of who we are."
—Zoraida Córdova, *USA Today* bestselling author of *Kiss the Girl*

SECOND CHANCE DUET ♪

ALSO BY ANA HOLGUIN

Up Close & Personal

SECOND CHANCE DUET

ANA HOLGUIN

FOREVER
LARGE PRINT

This book is a work of fiction. Names, characters, places, and incidents are the product of the author's imagination or are used fictitiously. Any resemblance to actual events, locales, or persons, living or dead, is coincidental.

Copyright © 2026 by Ana Holguin
Reading group guide copyright © 2026 by Ana Holguin and Hachette Book Group, Inc.

Cover design and illustration by Nicole Medina
Cover copyright © 2026 by Hachette Book Group, Inc.

Hachette Book Group supports the right to free expression and the value of copyright. The purpose of copyright is to encourage writers and artists to produce the creative works that enrich our culture.

The scanning, uploading, and distribution of this book without permission is a theft of the author's intellectual property. If you would like permission to use material from the book (other than for review purposes), please contact permissions@hbgusa.com. Thank you for your support of the author's rights.

Forever
Hachette Book Group
1290 Avenue of the Americas, New York, NY 10104
read-forever.com
@readforeverpub

First edition: March 2026

Forever is an imprint of Grand Central Publishing. The Forever name and logo are registered trademarks of Hachette Book Group, Inc.

The publisher is not responsible for websites (or their content) that are not owned by the publisher.

Forever books may be purchased in bulk for business, educational, or promotional use. For information, please contact your local bookseller or the Hachette Book Group Special Markets Department at special.markets@hbgusa.com.

Library of Congress Cataloging-in-Publication Data

Names: Holguin, Ana author
Title: Second chance duet / Ana Holguin.
Description: First edition. | New York : Forever, 2026.
Identifiers: LCCN 2025045387 | ISBN 9781538756904 (trade paperback) | ISBN 9781538756911 (ebook)
Subjects: LCGFT: Romance fiction | Fiction | Novels
Classification: LCC PS3608.O484237 S43 2026
LC record available at https://lccn.loc.gov/2025045387

ISBNs: 9781538756904 (trade paperback), 9781538756911 (ebook), 9781538782637 (large print)

For Ida, and all the eldest daughters with big dreams

Chapter One

MY LIFE HAS always been loud.

Car horns, the group of tourists talking behind me in a language I don't understand, Vanessa Carlton's "A Thousand Miles" booming from some guy's open-top convertible—it's happening now on the corner of Forty-Second and Tenth, but it's all the same to me. My childhood home was like this up in the Heights—fewer honking cars, but roughly the same amount of people talking—and so was my dorm at Juilliard. The sounds thrum through my veins. I love it.

I do not, however, love being late. I glance down at the phone clutched in my hand: It's 8:38 p.m., which means I will be, at best, fifteen minutes late for dinner with my old college friend Rebecca. It had been ambitious of me to say yes to her invitation, knowing I had a late-afternoon recording session booked for another round of yogurt advertisements. At least this jingle would be streaming on all major platforms; even if I wasn't personally inspired by yogurt, this exposure would go national.

Before the crosswalk signal changes, I type out a quick text.

> **Celia**
>
> So sorry, running a few min late!

She responds right away with a picture of a martini in a low-lit restaurant accompanied by a smiling emoji. Okay, she's fine.

For a moment, I feel a twinge of panic when I remember this morning: a notice stuffed into my mailbox from my property-management company, stating their intent to raise all rents in the building by 10 percent starting in the New Year. That letter alone had almost been enough to derail my entire day, but then an email came in from one of my clients, letting me know they were "going in a different direction" for their next commercial, so they wouldn't need me next month after all. I can read between the lines just fine; this was another job lost to AI music, if you can even call that garbage *music*.

Problem is, they're not the first clients I've lost to that AI bullshit. They won't be the last, either. Anything to save a buck, right?

More than anything, I wanted to wallow in my tiny apartment today, the first and only place I've ever been able to call just mine in my entire New York life. After years of living with roommates of all varieties, it was only a couple of years ago I found a place I could afford on my own. Month by month, I've scraped by on my modest ad contracts, with just a tiny savings safety net to catch me should I stumble.

But I had a studio session booked and a corporate giant counting on me to deliver, so I had no choice but to shove those initial worries aside and get my ass to work. Now that I'm done for the day? Now, I can worry—about the fact that there is no way I'll be able to afford my apartment in just a few months, about a corporate world that dehumanizes the lifetime of work I've put into being a professional musician and composer every time they generate some soulless thirty-second blob of sounds, about every little extra cost that won't go into my savings account should I have to move. Costs like this dinner with an old friend, which I probably should have canceled.

The last of the cars whizz through the yellow light just as it turns red and the crosswalk switches over to the Walk signal. It's too late to cancel now, so a combination of curiosity and anxiety spurs my legs faster than normal until I'm very nearly running down the sidewalk. My mind's preoccupation with my personal financial and career doom fizzles with each pound of my sneakers on the cement.

Despite this new life trajectory, I'm looking forward to seeing an old friend.

It's been years since I last spoke to Rebecca in person; the last time I remember seeing her was at her Goodbye New York party (which she threw for herself, naturally). Ever since, she's been out in LA, hustling hard toward her dreams of being a music supervisor on the biggest of movies. To my knowledge, she's been widely successful—her Instagram and IMDB pages are proof of that. We've remained friendly over the years, swapping DMs and comments on social media. There've even been a few catch-up email threads started and later abandoned as we both got busy.

By the time I pull open the door to the cozy Hell's Kitchen restaurant, I'm sweating. I spot Rebecca immediately; despite the aesthetic changes she's made in the last few years, her sharp expression and jet-black hair haven't changed. For a second, I hover near the door, watching as she sips her martini while typing one-handed on her phone. Nostalgia rolls over me in a wave.

God, are we really in our thirties now? Where the hell did the time go?

Before the hostess can approach me, I weave through the tightly packed tables to where Rebecca is seated along the far wall. She looks up at my approach, her diamond nose stud twinkling in the candlelight, and her red-painted lips pull into a wide smile.

With some difficulty, she manages to scoot back from the table and meet me halfway for a hug. "Celia! Girl, it is *so* good to see you!"

"You too, Rebecca," I reply, the scent of her sandalwood perfume enveloping me in its own kind of embrace.

She steps back from our hug and holds me at arm's length. Shamelessly, she gives me a thorough once-over; I can feel her gaze slide over my outfit, taking in all the changes that have occurred in me over the last… "God, how long has it been?" I ask out loud. "Like, four years?"

"It'd be five years this December," she replies. "You look good, girl. Love that you're still wearing the hoops."

She releases me. On instinct, I reach for the gold hoop earrings I've worn since the day I got them for my high school graduation present. Occasionally, I'll swap them out for something nicer when the event calls for it, but Rebecca is right—these earrings are my signature. Always have been, always will be.

We both take a seat at the table and I grab one of the laminated menus to glance over. "Sorry I'm late. Recording ran over today. Had some trouble getting the mixing right."

"All good," she says with a wave of her hand. "Honestly, I'm just happy to be back in the city. Every time I come back, I remember how much I miss it here."

"Yeah? How's LA treating you?"

Her answer is suspended on her lips when our server appears. I opt to follow her lead and order whatever it is she's drinking. When he leaves us, Rebecca settles back into her chair, flips her long hair behind her shoulders, and lets out a gusty breath. "It's good. Ruthless, but good. Everything they say about it is true."

"So it really is a plastic, life-sucking cesspool?" I ask with a wink.

Normally, I wouldn't be so brash with an old friend I hadn't seen in years, but Rebecca is a part of my fondest memories from college. Like me (and everyone else), she'd entered Juilliard determined to prove herself. But where Rebecca differed from our peers was in her forwardness; so many of the elites that made up our musical circles spoke in riddles and passive-aggressive undertones designed to make you second-guess yourself. That was a truth I had a hard time learning as an outsider, but Rebecca? She went toward everything headfirst, with brutal honesty and sheer determination as her best weapons, forsaking the pampered, private school upbringing she'd experienced.

At my Tinseltown insult, she laughs. It's still the same loud, boisterous honk that I remember. "Yes. As you can imagine, I fit in quite well there."

"Give yourself some credit. You give as much as you can take." I narrow my eyes to take a closer at her face, searching for any sign of said plastic, but there's none that I can see. She looks just like the eighteen-year-old girl who hooked her arm in mine one summer evening and declared we were friends. "You look great, by the way."

She smiles deviously. "Good. The best work is the kind you can't see."

"Wow, I sure have missed your honesty," I say with a laugh.

For the first time all day, I'm not thinking about my rent increase, my lost jobs, none of that. I'm just politely thanking the server as he drops off my martini, relishing the immediate burn of gin and vermouth on my tongue when I take a sip, and listening as Rebecca orders a few small plates to share. When our server disappears again, she shakes her head and rolls her eyes. "Sorry," she says. "I shouldn't have ordered for the table without checking with you. Did you develop any food allergies in the last however many years?"

"No. Don't worry. I'm glad to see some things haven't changed."

"Yeah, I'm still a bossy bitch, aren't I?" she asks, mostly to herself. Her sharp expression softens slightly as she considers this; in the romantic, muted light of this restaurant, she looks wise beyond her years.

"You say that like it's a bad thing. You know I've always loved that about you."

My compliment brings her wandering eyes back to our table. She hits me with a shrewd look, her light eyes rimmed with kohl that lends itself well to her new, slightly edgy look. "I have to be this way now with the egos I deal with every day. But enough about me. How are you? What are you up to these days?"

I blow out a sigh strong enough to make the candle flame dance in the middle of the table. "Oh, I'm good. Still trucking along."

"Are you still composing? You said you

came from the recording studio today, yeah?" she asks, her tone filled with genuine interest.

At this, my heart twists. The barest truth is that yes, I'm still composing—except it's not at all the work I'd planned to do. While jingles for advertising campaigns technically count as composing, they aren't the grand scores I'd envisioned writing as a doe-eyed baby musician in the hallowed halls of one of the world's finest music schools. Worse still, I've been doing this for *years*—spinning my wheels while dredging up creativity for banal platitudes about yogurt and power tools. The only respite I get comes from writing music for aspiring talent. That's all I have to sustain the part of me that yearns to create something really meaningful.

Despite a decent roster of advertising clients and the writing credits I've managed to accumulate, no one in film wants me. I couldn't even get a callback for assistant or mentorship opportunities—not since the first one ended thanks to budget cuts, a tale as old as time in the arts. My professors' recommendations helped initially, but they only got me so far. Years of rejection have jaded me. I've since stopped reaching out.

But I owe Rebecca honesty. That's what bound us together as friends in undergrad; during Ear Training I, our friendship went to the next level when I whispered that she was flat rather than humiliate her in front of the class. Ever since, we've had each other's backs.

"Yes and no," I finally reply, not even bothering to hide the resignation in my tone. "I compose for ads, but that's about it."

Her well-manicured brows furrow as she takes a sip of her drink. "But I heard Lady Osborn's last album. You did drums for that, didn't you?"

Right, the jazz artist I'd collaborated with last year. I'd written the percussion book and performed it for Lady Osborn's latest release. "Yeah, I do some of that here and there. It's corporate America that pays the bills, though."

Rebecca eyes me shrewdly again, her gaze raking over me in that *almost* judgmental way. It's almost as if she can hear what I didn't say—that the advertising clients are no longer enough to pay said bills, at least the ones that aren't dropping me for their stupid computer music. My skin prickles with awareness while my stomach does a funny little swoop; it's nerve-racking enough, outwardly admitting my professional standstill while my classmate soars through her chosen field (thanks, in part, to the connections of her entertainment-lawyer dad). If she'd wanted to, Rebecca would have made a fine composer, but that's not what called to her. With her eye for detail and her combined passion for both music and images, she'd always known she wanted to be a supervisor and editor.

And here she is, kicking ass at it.

"Well, I have to say, this is good news for me," she says after a long beat. "As nice as it is to see you, I came here with an agenda."

There it is, hovering just out of reach—the reason my friend from all those years ago texted me out of the blue.

"Oh?" I ask as I try (and fail) to contain my obvious interest.

But our conversation stalls as the first round of food arrives: a dish of oysters, accompanied by plates and wedges of lemons in ceramic ramekins. Both of us grab a shell, Rebecca reaching forward to clink them together, before she says, "Bottoms up!"

When we're both done with our first, she leans forward to place her hands on the table. This simple change of her body language heightens the tension that's got my heartstrings pulled tight. "So anyway," she starts, "this is both a personal and professional dinner. I'm working on a big project now—something really cool—and our composer just dropped out."

My eyebrows raise in response. "I'm listening."

"It's Chris Ross's first foray into TV. I worked

with him last year on that space movie. He's doing a series for Limelight's streaming studio called *Lineage*. It's this intense drama about a rich family and the spouses that married into it." She pauses to finish her drink. "Everything was good to go until Gustav Schneider had to drop out due to health issues. We're already shooting, so we're kind of fucked."

My pulse ratchets up at these names. Ross is among the top directors in Hollywood; his movies are produced by the biggest studios, his career littered with awards and accolades. As for Schneider, there is no bigger name in film scoring. Well, perhaps one—but I prefer not to think about him much after dealing with his son at Juilliard.

I can barely find my voice when I ask, "Is Schneider okay? What are you trying to say, Rebecca?"

"Yes, yes, Schneider will be fine. He just needs to take some time off. What I'm saying is that I talked Ross into taking a chance on a more junior composer. We kind of don't have a choice, considering how tight our timeline is. He agreed, but on one condition—he needs *two* composers, if he's going to take someone green."

"Oh."

It's all I can manage. Suddenly my denim-colored chambray shirt feels too heavy, the material too hot for this cramped restaurant. I'm aware of every single part of my body—from the ends of my curly hair to my toes pressing against the tips of my Nikes. This is the closest I've ever gotten to my dream. My *real* dream, of telling a story with music that doesn't exist to sell something to someone. It could be the start of the career I'd always envisioned for myself—and possibly the solution to my recent financial woes.

After years of rejection, I'm scared to believe it's real.

"Why me?" I find myself asking.

"Why not you?" Rebecca scoffs. "You were the best composer in our class—no, don't even argue with me on that. You approached it with this, like, almost psychotic gleam in your eyes. You are *good*, Celia. Plus, you'll get me in the editing process. I'm pretty damn good at my job."

It's funny, the feeling that comes over you when you realize: *This is it. This is the moment I've been waiting for.* All the rejections, all the unanswered calls and emails, all the shitty jobs I've had to take just to keep going—this is where they led me. Right here, to a small table for two in Hell's Kitchen, sitting across from a woman I've known since we were little more than girls. It's a warmth that spreads over me, settling somewhere low in my stomach.

"Yeah. Okay." As reality starts to sink in, I nod. "You said Ross needs two. Who's the other composer?" In an uncharacteristic move, Rebecca bites her bottom lip. The red lipstick she's wearing doesn't smear when she licks her lips, clearly uncertain. This is enough to bring my nerves back. "Spit it out, Rebecca."

"It's Oliver Barlowe."

And just like that, my mood plummets.

Rebecca notices. She leans farther forward, her entire chest pressed into the table. "Listen, Celia. I know you two were weird in undergrad, but he's not as insufferable as he used to be. I've run into him a few times over the years. We've kept in touch. He's still the same guy, but he's different now. He's less..."

"Horrible?" I offer. "Pretentious?"

"I was going to say 'stuffy,' but that works, too."

"Why would he even do this? Can't he use Daddy's name to propel his career forward?"

That I even have to ask this question grates on my nerves. As the son of Robert Barlowe—the living legend who has been scoring films for decades—Oliver no doubt has his pick of jobs. His dad has been collecting awards like they were trinkets while maintaining a hold on Hollywood's most prominent film directors since we were toddlers. Of course, Oliver's nepo-baby status wasn't enough to make me hate him when we first met as teenagers all those years ago. He did that on his own, with his personality.

My blood boils at the thought of working with him.

"Believe it or not, he doesn't," Rebecca says. The earnest look in her eyes irritates me. "Oliver ran away to London about the same time I went to LA. He's mostly been writing commissioned pieces—things for the ballet, modern dance, shit like that. He did a couple of indie films in the last few years, but that's not enough. Ross needs to know he's got a safety net with a duo, even if one of them comes from a legacy. He *hates* when there's behind-the-scenes drama, which is ironic considering the types of stories he tells, but it's true. He doesn't have time to hand hold or coddle anyone. If anything jeopardizes his production, he puts an end to that shit right away."

Taking a second oyster from the dish, I buy myself some time as I knock it back without any lemon. This is quite the predicament;

to be offered the chance to work with someone like Chris Ross, who has the experience to guide a massive project like this, is remarkable. Without a doubt, this is a career-making opportunity. One that could change the course of my life forever.

Rebecca is handing me the chance to make my lifelong dreams come true, but Oliver Barlowe is attached. Does that make it a nightmare, then?

I shake my head to clear my thoughts. "When do you need a decision by?" I ask. Taking on a project like this would require a complete immersion; there would be no time for anything else. A full season of music can be anywhere from four to eight hours of completed composition; the amount of time it would take to craft, score, and polish that much music is nearly unfathomable. I would have to eat, sleep, and breathe this score for the next few months.

Which means that I would have to eat, sleep, and breathe alongside Oliver, too.

Rebecca lets loose a breath. "Tomorrow. I looked at your portfolio on your website. It's good. Good enough that it will convince the decision-makers that you can handle the workload. Chris will want to meet with you to make sure you're not, like, a weirdo or a liability, but the job is as good as yours, Celia."

The look in her eyes—pleading, prodding, hopeful—says what we both don't bother to speak aloud: that she needs me to do this. That she's putting her own reputation on the line to recruit Oliver and me. That this is the opportunity of a lifetime. It's the big break that everyone dreams about and so few get.

"I'll let you know by tomorrow afternoon."

Even when the words leave my lips, I already know what my answer will be. Because even though Oliver Barlowe and I have a complicated history at best, there is *no* man in this world that will keep me from my dreams. I've worked too hard for too long. I can't walk away simply because I don't like someone. I've done my time in the trenches, writing catchy tunes to accompany such riveting products as the latest cat food. Not only that, but I literally *can't* afford to say no—not with a rent increase hanging over my head and no new ad job lined up.

Film scoring—really, any production work in movies and TV—used to be a certified boys' club. But now Rebecca has a key, and she's invited me in.

**FROM: Celia García
<celia@celiagarcia.com>
TO: Ann Martin <ann.martin
@talentfirstagency.com>
DATE: Thursday, August 13 at
11:14 PM
SUBJECT: Job opportunity?**

Hola Ann,

It's been a while! How's the family? Are you summering in Rhode Island again this year?

I might have a gig coming up in film. An old friend of mine from Juilliard tapped me for it. I still have to decide if I want to do it, meet with the producers, etc. Before I commit, I wanted to see if you had any interest for my composition work lately? Don't want to cross any wires or anything!

Cheers,

Celia

**FROM: Ann Martin <ann.martin@
talentfirstagency.com>
TO: Celia García
<celia@celiagarcia.com>
DATE: Thursday, August 13 at
11:39 PM
SUBJECT: RE: Job opportunity?**

Hello Celia!

So nice to hear from you. Everyone is good here, we're spending our days in the sun here in Newport. How is life in the city?

In terms of interest in your work, things are quiet. We're seeing an overall decrease in composition/score work across the board here at the agency (with the obvious caveats). I still believe in your talent and skill just as much as I did when I signed you seven years ago! This career is all about persistence and tenacity. If you have anything new to add to your portfolio, please send it my way. I'd love to send it around and put some feelers out there on your behalf.

All this to say, if you have interest from your college connections—GO FOR IT!

Best,

Ann

Chapter Two

I STARE AT THE email from my agent for longer than necessary. My phone screen starts to darken, but I tap it to keep it from going to sleep. Reading her response over and over again only solidifies the fears that started curdling in my stomach as soon as Rebecca and I hugged goodbye on the sidewalk with a promise that I'd be in touch tomorrow.

If I'm honest with myself, my email to Ann was my last-ditch effort to find a way forward in this career in a way that doesn't involve Oliver Barlowe. But now it's clear there *is* no other way. To keep at my passion, at the one thing I know how to do, I have to take this job. Turning it down would be putting the final nail in the coffin of my forever dream.

Even though I'm lying on my bed, my stomach drops. I toss my phone on the opposite pillow, let out a heavy sigh, then pull myself to sit. I force myself to take a drink of water from the bottle on my desk. I should not have had a third martini.

Now that my decision is made, even if only with myself, a whole new set of fears takes root somewhere in my gut. I stare at my humble home studio shoved against the wall next to the bed while my pulse pounds in my ears. So far, I've made do with what I could afford (and had space for); this primarily consists of a powerful computer with the software needed to orchestrate, a full keyboard plugged into said computer, and a handful of sound mixers, most of which I acquired secondhand from friends. Thankfully, every job I've taken has granted me access to professional recording studios to create the final product. But to compose a full score on my home setup? It would be impossible.

When was the last time I wrote for a full

orchestra? Oh, right—two years ago, when I was hired for a luxury perfume commercial. But that was for a reduced group. No more than twenty-five musicians.

When was the last time I wrote music for dialogue? Well, if you counted ad jingles...all the time.

When was the last time I touched an instrument other than a keyboard or drums? God, it's been years.

When was the last time I even played the *drums*, my first love and the reason for my entire existence in the musical world? It's been at least a month, when I sat down at my father's club and pounded away on the house drum set.

That in itself is a problem—as a New Yorker, space and privacy are limited in the best of times. Outside of my parents' compound in Washington Heights, I've never lived in a place where having a drum set wouldn't get me promptly kicked out of the building. Although, if I don't take this job with the show, I might have no choice but to leave this building anyway.

I start to pace. Every creak of the hardwood floors underneath my bare feet is an echo of my own heartbeat as I wonder if I even have the talent to pull this off. Even through the fog of three strong drinks, the reality of my situation becomes clearer with each step.

I am so unprepared for this.

But then again, Oliver is involved. Could we pull it off? Could we work together after the last time we saw each other and all the years since?

There's only one way to find out.

♪

Within minutes of opening my eyes the next morning, I text Rebecca that I'm in.

She responds right away, the chime of the notification cutting through the rare moment of quiet, if you can call it that. My upstairs neighbor is already vacuuming, and my downstairs neighbor is watching *Good Morning*

America on full blast. Still in bed with the muffled ambient noise of other people's lives as the soundtrack, I rub the sleep out of my eyes and stare at her text.

> **Rebecca**
>
> Hell yeah! The crew gets into NY Monday to prep for the next leg of the shoot. I'll set up a meeting with Chris asap. Monday? Can you come to the Limelight offices?

I don't need to look at my calendar to know I'm wide open.

> **Celia**
>
> Tell me the time and address and I'll be there

A thought occurs to me then, just as the response bubbles ripple on my phone screen.

If I'm going to meet the great Chris Ross and convince him that I'm good enough to do this job, I should probably meet with Oliver first. It's been nine years since we last saw each other. Our parting wasn't exactly pleasant.

> **Rebecca**
>
> Perfect. I'll make sure Chris sees your portfolio. Will send you mtg deets over the weekend.

My fingers hover over my phone screen. I know what I need to do. To start this professional relationship off on the right foot—to start over, really—I absolutely need to make some sort of peace with Oliver. Yet I can't ignore the dread that's only heightened by the fact that the guy who lives above me has transitioned from vacuuming to running on his treadmill. The heavy *thunk thunk thunk* of his feet isn't an even rhythm. It drives my percussion brain bonkers.

I haul myself out of bed and brush my wild postsleep hair out of my face. Standing in the center of my small studio apartment, clad in my underwear and old Juilliard T-shirt, I grip my phone while my heart pounds. My palms are damp with perspiration by the time I type out a response.

> **Celia**
>
> Great. Can you send me Oliver's contact info?

When Rebecca replies with a number I don't recognize—of course, with the original 212 New York area code—I decide that's the perfect time to set my phone down and brush my teeth.

So I do—I brush my teeth, fix myself a cup of coffee, then fold and put away the clean laundry that's been sitting in a basket for three days. I look around my apartment in search of something else to do that's not the one thing I don't *want* to do, but there's nothing. I cleaned last week. My sheet music is organized and filed away under my desk. Even my kitchen pantry is tidy and neat. Underemployment will do this to a person.

After finishing the last bit of coffee, I roll my shoulders and take a deep breath. My phone is where I left it on my desk. No new emails, no messages.

It takes me several tries, but finally I craft a message that's worth sending:

> **Celia**
>
> Hi, is this Oliver Barlowe? This is Celia García.

He leaves me on read for hours.

During that time, I go on a long walk, headphones in, and pretend I'm not looking for new messages every time I change songs. To soothe my nerves, I listen to the very first score that made me fall in love—an action-adventure blockbuster from my childhood—even though it was written and conducted by none other than Oliver's father, Robert Barlowe. The soaring French horns send goose bumps skittering across my skin despite the anxiety coursing through me.

By the time my phone dings with a new message, I'm home, showered, and double-checking that the portfolio and media kit on my website are current (they are). I jump at the sound. I force a deep breath before looking at it.

> **Oliver**
>
> Did Rebecca give you my number?

My face contorts into a frown. Yeah, there he is. Another text comes in from him.

> **Oliver**
>
> Hi, by the way. Good to hear from you.

I frown even harder. *Is* it good to hear from me? Sure doesn't seem like it.

> **Celia**
>
> Yeah Rebecca gave me your number. I thought we should connect before this potential meeting with Chris Ross.

There. Let him understand that this outreach has a purpose, and that I would never text him if it weren't for this job we're meant to do together.

He leaves me on read long enough that I consider double texting him just to be annoying, but I distract myself by scrolling Instagram.

> **Oliver**
>
> I hear the meeting is happening Monday. We don't have a lot of time. What are you doing tonight?

I set my phone down and stare at the blank wall behind my computer. He's right; we should meet sooner rather than later. But the fact that I'm going to have to give up a Friday night—probably the first of many—to work with Oliver Barlowe is a hard pill to swallow.

When I tell him that I can meet him, I let out a groan.

At least I washed my hair today.

**FROM: Dr. Riccardo Costa
<riccardo.costa@Juilliard.edu>
TO: <Freshman Bachelor of Music Listserv>
CC: Rachel Hill
<rachel.hill@Juilliard.edu>
DATE: Monday, August 5 at 4:13 PM
SUBJECT: Invitation—Optional Freshman Social, Thursday August 8, 6:00 p.m.**

To our incoming freshmen,

I trust that this email finds you well and that you are enjoying the last few weeks of summer. Ahead of the official move-in date, I and a few other faculty members wanted to invite you all to an optional social gathering, to be held Thursday, August 8, at 6:00 p.m. We will convene in room 105 of the Juilliard School main building, located on the first floor.

This will be an opportunity to meet some of your peers in an informal setting. We will provide snacks and drinks and hopefully some good conversation! If you are not yet in New York or are unable to attend, please do not worry. This social is entirely optional. If you plan to join us, please email my admin assistant, Rachel, cc'd here so that we can plan for food and beverage.

On behalf of the entire Juilliard music faculty, we look forward to welcoming you all at the new-student orientation later in August.

My best,

Dr. Costa

Head of Undergraduate Music

Assistant Dean of the Music Division

Chapter Three

THIRTEEN YEARS AGO

THE AIR HAS an unseasonable chill to it for early August, so much so that I'm grateful I grabbed a cardigan out of my closet before leaving my house. Well, technically my parents' house now—in just a few days, my official residence will be the very same dorms I just passed. Butterflies fill my stomach at the thought. Despite the tour I did in the spring, not to mention all the daydreams that have occupied my mind since I was, like, twelve, I still can't believe I made it. I'm going to *Juilliard*.

Which is why, when I got that email from Dr. Costa, I literally screamed and then planned my outfit. A social event just for those of us who could be here early? There was no way in hell I was going to miss that. This is my chance to make a good impression with the faculty before everyone else settles in. If there's one thing I'm good at—besides percussion—it's being social.

The thick gray clouds overhead threaten to ruin the black dress and green cardigan my mom ironed this morning. As I step toward the door to the school's main building on West Sixty-Fifth, a crack of lightning illuminates the glass facade, followed immediately by a rumble of thunder. Rain starts to fall in earnest just as I duck inside. Gracias a Dios, I made it without ruining my hair and clothes.

I stare at the Post-it note I've had clutched in my hand the entire walk-train-walk commute here: "Juilliard School, room 105, first floor." I didn't trust my phone to pull up the email from Dr. Costa, so I came prepared with my own instructions. Which is a good thing because there's, like, no one around. I pause in front of the big staircase and pretend to adjust the purse on my shoulder (Dooney & Bourke—a graduation gift from my sisters). In the quiet of the cavernous space, I can hear the soft murmur of talking coming from somewhere to my right. I follow the sound until a glass wall comes into view. There's a handful of students like me inside, along with Dr. Costa and Drs. Adams and Kendrick, whom I remember from my auditions and interviews. Everyone is scattered among tables and chairs. There are pizza boxes, a platter of cookies, and a bunch of canned drinks on a table against the far wall.

My heart races. My dad has reminded me, time and time again, that you only get to make a first impression once. Sure, there's a whole bunch of official new-student orientations coming, but this is different. This is *voluntary*. And I busted my ass to be here.

I roll my shoulders, smooth my curls quickly, and head inside with all the confidence I can muster.

When I step through the open door, several people turn to look at me. Most of them are students, none of whom I recognize. This surprises me because I figured at least some of them would have been on my campus tour. But no. I remember to smile just as Dr. Costa breaks from his conversation with another student.

"Ah, welcome! It's Celia, isn't it?" he asks from where he stands halfway across the room.

I have to keep myself from wincing when he says my name wrong, like *Cee-lee-uh* instead of *Cell-ee-uh*. He looks just like I remember him from all my auditions and interviews, with blond hair where he isn't balding, a soft belly tucked inside a gray button-down and dark slacks, and frameless glasses perched on his nose. I don't think I'll ever forget exactly what this man looks like. I was beyond terrified when I first met him.

"Hi, yes, that's me," I reply. "Good to see you."

"So glad you could make it." He smiles at

me, and then I'm hit with the same confused and terrified feeling I experienced during my first round of auditions. His smile seems so genuine, but this man—the head of the entire undergrad music program—holds the keys to my future. "Please, do come in and help yourself to snacks and such."

I look around at the ten or so students perched on tables and chairs. No one is eating. They all have the same high-alert expression on their faces. "Thank you, sir."

One of the students sitting at a table near me stands up and extends her hand to me. She's fair skinned, with dark hair that's pulled back into a ponytail, her blue eyes bright as we shake hands. "I'm Rebecca. Trumpet and brass performance."

Oh, so that's how we're doing it. "Celia," I reply, using the correct pronunciation of my name. "Percussion, but I'm majoring in composition."

"Nice." She nods with an impressed smile. "This here is Blake, Chloe, and Anthony."

That's how I'm folded into a group of four fellow first years. Right away I notice that Anthony is very cute, with dark hair to match his dark eyes and an inviting, warm smile. Everyone seems to have approached this voluntary mixer with a much more casual attitude than me; all the students are wearing some combination of jeans, T-shirts, and shorts. There's a fleeting moment of self-consciousness when I realize this, but I shake it off as Chloe tells us about growing up in France and studying vocal performance at the Paris Conservatory (she's a soprano with big opera dreams). My mom always told me it's better to be overdressed than underdressed.

More students trickle in. After a while, everyone relaxes enough to start on the food. Rebecca and I are standing near the snack table, cookies in hand, when someone new enters the room, causing a flurry of activity. We exchange a brief glance before craning our necks to see who is creating such a stir.

My heart rate picks up as I consider the

possibilities—is it a famous Juilliard alumnus? Maybe the dean of the whole school? Some kind of celebrity? It's impossible to tell because the professors flank them right away, blocking them from view.

"Any idea who that is?" I whisper to Rebecca.

She shrugs. We both wait. The chocolate chip cookie is really good.

Eventually the crowd parts enough and I see him—a guy, definitely around my age, wearing a full gray suit complete with a purple paisley pocket scarf. His light-brown hair is messy, almost as if he just rolled out of bed or never learned how to brush it. My brows pinch together in confusion before I can stop myself. Who is this person? Why is a freshman wearing a full formal suit? Did he sleep in it?

Most importantly, why is everyone so excited to see him?

Aside from the over-the-top outfit, he looks young. Like, so much so that I'm wondering if he's one of those child prodigies starting college at sixteen or whatever. But then, what sixteen-year-old wears a suit to an informal social hour? What *eighteen-year-old* does that?

Most of my questions get answered when Rebecca dusts her hands off and whispers, "Oh. That's Robert Barlowe's son, Oliver. I heard he got accepted into Harvard, Yale, Berklee over in Boston, all of them. Guess he chose to come here."

"Robert Barlowe, like the composer with two Oscars?" I murmur back, but no one is paying attention to us anyway. "I didn't know he had a son."

Rebecca's eyes widen as she looks at me. "How did you not know that?"

A bunch of pieces click into place then: First, that most of these students know each other, or at least know *of* each other. Blake and Rebecca had mentioned going to the same music camp in the summers growing up; Chloe and Anthony's parents are both professional dancers, so they were always in the same circles. This world—it's small, and I've only just discovered it. I'm an outsider looking in. Literally.

Oliver Barlowe looks over in our direction, and I watch as he and Rebecca exchange head bobs to say hello. So they know each other already, too. Oliver's gaze flicks to me. I fix my face into the most pleasant, chill smile possible as we stare at each other. His expression remains completely blank until his attention is pulled away by Dr. Costa, who is animatedly asking how his dad is, where they spent the summer, and who knows what else.

That's how it goes for the rest of the night. Nearly everyone flocks to Oliver, who is so soft-spoken that I can't even hear him talk despite my best efforts to eavesdrop. I do get to spend some time talking to Dr. Kendrick, our main composition professor, and manage to impress him when I tell the story about the famous salsa musician Ruben Rivera playing at my family's club over the summer.

At the end of the evening, when people are starting to say their goodbyes, I find myself standing near the now-empty snack table, alone and unsure of myself. The night wasn't a total bust—I did meet my peers and get some face time with the professors—but Oliver's arrival sidelined everyone, including me. Even now, he's standing in the middle of four people, arms crossed, silently watching the conversation move around him. It's like everyone has already decided he's the star. The world is orbiting around him.

I feel someone's arm loop through mine, and I startle slightly before looking to my left. Rebecca is there, the two of us now linked together. She glances at Oliver, then back to me, before she says, "I think you and I are going to be good friends, Celia."

She says my name the right way. I didn't realize how much tension I was holding in my shoulders until they relax of their own accord. I squeeze her arm and smile at her.

"Me, too."

When I look back toward Oliver, I find his eyes on me. He doesn't smile. Neither do I this time. We never say a word to each other that night.

50 ♪ Ana Holguin

DEADLINE EXCLUSIVE:

Chris Ross to Make TV Debut with *Lineage* Ordered by Limelight & A24

BY LISA MORRISON, TV EDITOR MARCH 20

Limelight, in partnership with A24, greenlighted Academy Award, BAFTA, and Golden Globe winner Chris Ross's first ever TV show, *Lineage*, a prestige drama about a wealthy New York family that controls one of the largest media empires in the world. Golden Globe winner Luke Tudor (*Today & Tomorrow*) and three-time Emmy nominee Erica Stewart (*Clash*) are attached to star.

Speaking exclusively to *DEADLINE*, Ross said, "I've wanted to do TV for a long time, but it had to be the right story. *Lineage* is perfect for this format. It gives us more time to explore these characters and their dynamics." Adam Simmons, who recently won his third

Academy Award for best original screenplay with *Underneath*, wrote the script. Ross will serve as executive producer and showrunner, teaming up with longtime collaborator and fellow Academy Award winner Gustav Schneider* on the music.

Limelight ordered up eight episodes. It's expected to stream in the spring of next year.

*EDITOR'S NOTE: At the time of this article's publication, Schneider was set to compose the score. He has since dropped out, citing scheduling conflicts. Ross has not yet named a replacement.

Chapter Four

OLIVER SUGGESTS THAT we meet at a café in SoHo that evening, so I do what any reasonable person does: Google the hell out of both it and him. The place we're meeting seems nice. It's one of those places that's a coffee shop by day but at night serves wine and finger foods that arrive on boards instead of plates. It's casual and cute.

Oliver himself, however, is much more difficult to pin down. I'd already figured out that he does not have an Instagram, but there are basically no photos of him on the internet. Even his IMDB page has a placeholder avatar where his headshot should be. His name produces a ton of results, most of which echo what Rebecca already told me; he's been working steadily, doing small-budget movies and writing for ballets and midtier symphonies. But perhaps the most interesting thing I learn is that when I search for "Oliver Barlowe," Google asks me, *Did you mean Robert Barlowe?*

I have no idea what to expect when I emerge from the subway that evening, clad in one of my favorite summer dresses, hair clean, face made up. The effort I put in—I'm telling myself it's an armor to protect myself from all the uncertainty I'm facing. When I pause to check my reflection in a glass storefront, I have to admit that I look good. This blue dress hugs my curves in all the right places. My curls are holding strong against the humidity of the summer.

When I pull open the door to Jean's Bistro, I scan the place for the man of the hour. It'd be a lot easier to find him if I had any idea what he looks like these days. I have no choice but to scrutinize every white guy around my age.

One man looks like he *could* be Oliver—if he'd gained weight and lost most of his hair—but he doesn't look up when I approach. So, not him.

I adjust my tote bag on my shoulder and wander deeper into the café, which is a lot bigger than it looks from the outside. The walls are papered with pale pink-and-white stripes. It smells like coffee and fresh bread, though most patrons are drinking wine as they talk among themselves or work on their laptops. Tired of awkwardly making eye contact with every stranger I see, I'm on the verge of pulling my phone out of my bag and just calling Oliver when I hear my name coming from somewhere behind me.

"Celia?"

I whip around, surprised at the correct pronunciation. What I find is a man standing next to a table, looking so unlike the boy I knew that my mouth drops open in surprise.

Gone is all the softness of youth that held Oliver in a viselike grip when we knew each other before. Now his face is framed and sculpted by delicate lines, with cheekbones so sharp they look like they could cut glass. Still, one thing that stayed soft is his mouth—which looks almost too big for his face now, with a full set of lips that preside over a clean-shaven jaw like some kind of king.

He's taller than I remember, too. I have to crane my neck to look up at him, which isn't unfamiliar to me; I take after my mother in that regard, who is the shortest of the Garcías, clocking in at just over five feet, two inches. But he is *wider* than the gangly-limbed kid I remember. He's not built like a bodybuilder or anything—he's just filled out now.

Honestly, if it weren't for his midnight-blue blazer—a much nicer version of what he used to wear—I would have kept walking. He looks so different that I wouldn't have recognized him otherwise.

"Oliver?" I finally respond. "Wow. You look different."

"So do you." His voice is still soft and

gentle, just like I remember it from before. But his face—that is a *change*. He used to be so closed off and cagey that I could never get a read on him, but now his brown eyes are open and bright as he looks at me. He's not exactly smiling, but he's not scowling, either.

I don't know if what he's saying is true. I've remained largely unchanged since college, unless you count the plushness that developed over the years as a result of a very sedentary job. My hair is still the same rich, dark brown, kept long as usual; my style has evolved somewhat over the years, except for my signature items, like the gold hoops. If anything, I've evolved into a better version of myself. The best so far, actually. Somewhere along the course of my twenties, I lost the will to care about the things people usually consider flaws; so what if I have dimples on my thighs, so what if there are lines in my skin that mark my growth? I like to think I carry myself better because I deposited that emotional, vain baggage exactly where it belongs: the trash.

It hits me then—that I'm supposed to greet him in some way. We know each other, despite a rough exit and a nine-year absence from each other's lives. We were never friends. Now we're going to work together.

Do I hug him? Shake his hand? Can I get away with avoiding it altogether? God, I hate how uncertain he makes me feel.

I settle for the latter, extending my hand toward him, which he shakes with a quirk of his eyebrow. His skin is cool and soft, save for the scruff of calluses on his pinkie and thumb. The marks of a dedicated pianist.

On closer inspection, his hair is the same color: a light brown, just like his eyes that are giving me a thorough once-over. He did manage to tame his hair somewhat since we were in school. It's still shaggy on top, but he must have seen a proper barber because the messiness is much more artful than I remember.

It looks like he constantly runs his hands through it.

When our hands separate, he motions to the table he was occupying previously. There's a white paper cup already there, sitting next to his cell phone and a pair of tortoiseshell-rimmed glasses. Since when does Oliver Barlowe wear glasses? "Shall we? Or do you want something to drink?" he asks.

"No, I'm good," I reply as I take my seat opposite him, slinging my tote over the back of the chair. I really have no need for caffeine, especially when I'm this nervous. I can hear my pulse in my ears, bright and staccato.

There's a lot riding on this meeting—both of us are determining whether we can work with each other, all while navigating the ghosts of dislikes past. There is no doubt in my mind that Oliver basically hated me in college, but the question remains: Can both of us move beyond the mutual animosity from when we were younger?

I dredge up some of the hospitality I've

been taught all my life and ask, "How have you been? It's been, what—like, almost a decade?"

He considers this for a moment, his mouth pressed into a flat line, those full lips pulled between his teeth. "I can't believe it's been that long," he says finally. "I've been well. I was working in London until last year. I've only been Stateside since May."

I brush past my own annoyance at this—how nice it must be to hop between countries. "Rebecca mentioned you were living there. What brought you home?"

He clears his throat before answering. "A breakup."

"Oh," I say, trying to mask my genuine surprise. Prior to that declaration, I'd never given much thought to Oliver's romantic life. He never dated anyone in college, as far as I knew. I don't know his sexual orientation.

As if reading my mind, he adds, "My girlfriend and I parted ways amicably. It was just time for me to come back."

I don't miss the way his eyes flicker over me, assessing the reaction I'm working very hard to mask. "Oh." Scrambling to find something more substantive to say, I add, "I'm sorry to hear that—but you said things ended amicably, so I guess that's good. Right?"

The corners of his lips tug up, as if he's fighting a smile. "Right. And you? How are things?"

If I'm understanding him correctly, that morsel of information about his breakup was his olive branch. He's trying to find common ground with me, to establish some sort of baseline in a tentative truce. But to be vulnerable with Oliver, to share with him that this job we're mutually gunning for is the key to solving my professional and financial woes?

Hell no.

Instead, I shift in my seat, letting the ambient noise of the café fill the space between us for a moment. My fingers tap the table, finding the rhythm of some song piping in from the speakers. "Things are good. Staying busy, you know."

"Good." He nods, takes a sip of his coffee, and crosses his long legs under the table. "So, this meeting on Monday—what has Rebecca told you so far?"

"Just the basics, really. The show is a drama about a rich family. Chris Ross's first TV series. A big deal, et cetera et cetera. Limelight is throwing a lot of money and weight behind it according to *Deadline*."

"Yeah, I saw that article, too," he says. "I've never met Chris Ross. Have you?"

This comes as a surprise to me; I would have assumed that Oliver had encountered him at some point, given his close connections to Hollywood bigwigs. "Nope."

"It's my understanding that this is sort of an informal interview and pre-pro meeting all rolled into one. Well, technically it's just a production meeting since they've already started filming." His gaze goes distant for a second while he collects his thoughts. "I'm writing up some questions about the show and his process, but beyond that, I don't know what to expect."

I twist around in my seat to pull a notebook out of my tote, dangling it in the air for a moment before dropping it back into my bag. "Yep, same. Homework for the weekend."

"Have you done a TV show before?" he asks, and even though he sounds genuinely curious, I bristle at my own lack of experience.

"No. Have you?"

"No." He finishes off his coffee as he contemplates something behind me. I resist the urge to turn around and look. "I've only done a couple of smaller budget movies. Never something of this magnitude. I spoke to a friend who did all four seasons of *The Man in the Tower* and he said it's pretty grueling. There's a lot of music to write for eight hours of screen time."

I find myself nodding along as his gaze slides back to me; these thoughts have already occurred to me. "Makes sense that Ross would want two composers in Schneider's place. If we do this, it will be all-consuming."

At the word *we*, his lips part just briefly.

He recovers quickly, the look of surprise—or was it disdain? It's so hard to tell with him—replaced by the cool, careful mask I remember from college. "Yes. I have some thoughts on how we can accomplish this and where we can work."

My face flushes at his presumption. I want to tell him that I have ideas, too, that I know where we can do this. The lie is half formed on my tongue when I open my mouth to speak.

But I reel it in before it has a chance to escape. The fact is I have no idea where the two of us could sit for hours on end, with all the resources we need at our disposal, as we plow through a massive project. Instead, I simply ask, "Oh?"

"My family has a studio. It has everything we could possibly need—"

At the mention of his family—meaning his

dad—I try to straighten my spine and recross my legs to make myself look less small. What happens is I accidentally kick him and the table in the process, effectively cutting him off as the table skids on the hardwood. Also, I probably bruised his shin.

"Sorry, I didn't mean—"

"Ah, sorry—"

We speak over each other while he grabs the table to keep it from falling over. I'm so off-kilter and embarrassed that I don't even ask why he's apologizing. I'm the one who just nailed him in the leg with my shoe.

"I'm sorry," I repeat. My face is on fire. "Tight space."

"It's fine. Really."

When his eyes meet mine, I see he's blushing, too. Pink blooms on his cheeks. It forces me to notice a smattering of freckles across his nose and the planes of his face.

I wish I had ordered a big glass of wine.

"So you were saying something about your family?" I say, scrambling to move past whatever awkward thing just happened between us. "Why are you doing TV anyway? Isn't film more your thing?"

He blinks, surprised, before replying, "It's my dad's thing, not mine."

"Oh. When we were in school, that's what you said you wanted to do, so I just assumed..." I trail off and finish with a half-hearted shrug.

"Things change, Celia," he says, eyes sharp, voice low and not particularly warm. "So, we are in agreement, then? If all goes well with Ross tomorrow and we do this, we'll work at my family studio?"

Seeing no other option—at least not one that's free—I chew my bottom lip. Oliver notices; his eyes drop to my mouth before darting away to his now-empty coffee cup. "Yeah. Okay. If we get this job, that's what we'll do."

"Great. I'll see you Monday."

He rises to stand and I follow suit. We exchange another stilted handshake before he gathers up his things and disappears into a crowd of people that have gathered near the entrance. As he walks away from me, I notice that he's wearing a full matching suit—and that he has a paisley pocket square dangling out of the brown leather messenger bag he's carrying.

Rebecca was right; Oliver isn't as stuffy as he used to be. He's more conversational now, overall a little less arrogant. At the very least, I think I can work with him for the foreseeable future, if only for the sake of my career.

But despite what he just said to me, seeing that outfit (even on his adult body) complete with a matching pocket square, I'm reminded: Some things never change.

SECOND CHANCE DUET ♪ 67

Client: YUMMIES CAT FOOD
Title: PICKY EATERS
Job No: 5490
Length: 30s
Platform: Streaming & TV
Voiceover Artist: Erin Campbell
Music: Celia García
Date: August 14

VIDEO	AUDIO
We open on a cat sniffing a bowl of food. It turns its nose up at it and walks away.	MUSIC: Sad solo violin
The cat sits in a window, looking out at the street.	**Life is HARD**
The cat is now winding through its owner's legs, meowing.	**Especially when it seems like no one is listening to you**

The owner pets the cat and points to the food.	MUSIC: Sad violin builds
The cat turns away from the food. It doesn't want it.	**For those picky eaters in your life, give them what they want**
[cut to] YUMMIES WET FOOD SPECIAL MIX on the counter	MUSIC: Shift to upbeat, happy strings
Owner places bowl of YUMMIES WET FOOD SPECIAL in front of the cat. It starts to eat right away.	**YUMMIES WET FOOD SPECIAL—perfect for the ones who are hard to please**
[cut to] Owner and cat snuggling in the kitchen, YUMMIES WET FOOD SPECIAL box behind them	MUSIC: Fun and happy

Chapter Five

THE FOLLOWING MORNING, I exit the 181st Street subway station and am immediately assaulted by brilliant sunlight. Summer has returned for one last hurrah; the air is already sticky and sweet with the smell of pastries wafting over from the Dominican bakery just down the block. The scent carries me the three-block walk north, to the strip of street the neighbors have taken to calling Calle de García in homage to my family name.

It didn't used to be this way. When I was young, my family jammed itself into the small top-floor apartment in what had once been a brownstone. All five of us lived there: my parents, my two younger sisters, and me, split unevenly among the three little bedrooms. My father's salsa club, Besos, has always been a part of our lives; located just down the street from our home, it was where I practiced both piano and drums after school when my mother wasn't teaching piano lessons to the neighborhood kids. It wasn't until I graduated from my very expensive college (even with the need-based financial aid and a handful of student loans to accompany my family's help) that my parents bought the entire building when it went up for sale. That wouldn't have been possible without the help of well-timed inheritances from my abuelos. These days, the bottom two units are rented out to families a lot like ours.

Now, we have some generational wealth to our names. Not bad for a bunch of second- and third-generation immigrants.

But I'm not headed to the apartment today; at 10:00 a.m., I know exactly where to find my father. I'm not surprised to find the side door to Besos is unlocked at this hour, given the deliveries usually arrive in the morning. When I enter the club, I find it's dark, quiet, cool—a little unsettling, considering how lively and loud it gets in the evenings. All the chairs have been flipped up and set on top of the tables. The stage in the far corner is empty, save for the instruments and microphone stands littering the raised platform. My footsteps echo on the tile floors as I peer toward the bar, but there's no one there.

I adjust the bag on my shoulder as I call out, "Papi?"

There's a ruckus in the kitchen, hidden by the swinging doors. A clatter of metal slices through the silence, followed by swearing in jumbled Spanish. Smiling to myself, I follow the noise and push through the double doors to find my father collecting a bunch of silverware off the floor.

"Bendición," I try again, biting back a laugh.

It's clear that I scare the shit out of him. From his position on the floor, his entire body tenses before he looks over his shoulder, eyes wide, until he realizes it's just me. "Ay, dios mío, hija," he says with a hint of exasperation. "You trying to give your old man a heart attack? Dios te bendiga."

I shake my head and bend down to help him gather the remaining silverware, tossing handfuls into the plastic tray as I go. "What happened here?"

"The new dishwasher left these in the machine overnight. When I lifted the tray out, the handle broke," he says. He points to the plastic handle on one side of the tray, which has clearly snapped in half. "Now I have to run them through again."

We finish up quickly. This time, my father lifts the big tray of now-dirty cutlery from the bottom before placing it into the commercial dishwasher and loading it up with detergent. Once the machine kicks to life, he wipes his hands on his well-loved jeans and turns to face me. A familiar grin stretches across his face, etched with gentle lines of age that only make him look brighter, warmer. As if he's a star, just entering the prime of its life.

In a way, he is. My father has only gotten better with age—not only as a parent, but also as a friend, a business owner, and a community member. José García is well-respected in Washington Heights.

Oliver Barlowe may have the legacy of his father, but I have mine, too.

"What brings you home today, hija?" he asks as he envelops me in a hug.

When we pull away, I find the anxious knot that formed over the last two days has lessened a little. "I need your advice."

"Ah, one of *those* visits," he says with a wink. "Come on, let's make some coffee."

I follow him back through the double doors, to the club floor, where he slips behind the bar. I take a seat on the other side, directly in front of the espresso machine, and drop my tote bag onto the empty stool next to me. Immediately, I'm overwhelmed by the comfort of such a simple, familiar action; I've done some iteration of this a million times in my life. My sisters and I spent countless afternoons here, with them doing homework at one of the four tops while I practiced at the drums or piano. That is, until one of them couldn't take the pounding anymore and forced me off the stage.

Loud. Life has always been loud here. I've always loved it.

Today, however, it's quiet, save for the rumbling traffic outside and the clicks and whirrs of the espresso machine. Sunlight filters in through the slanted blinds, illuminating the dust motes that flit through the air like hundreds of tiny dancers. They're not unlike the real dancers that come here night after night, their bodies writhing and twisting to the rhythms of the salsa bands that play here regularly.

My father sets a fresh café con leche in front of me before taking a sip of his own. "What's going on, hija? Everything okay?"

His dark eyes—an exact mirror of my own, from the color of our irises to the rounded shape—hold a poignant concern as he looks at me. I take a sip of my coffee before I answer him. "Yeah, everything's good. I had dinner with a friend from college the other night. You remember Rebecca? The one with the black hair? She played trumpet."

My heart twists at the half-truth about my overall state of affairs. I don't want to tell my father about my financial and career troubles, not after my family sacrificed so much to put me through school to begin with. He's always been so proud of me, fully present for every milestone I hit, even when I first moved into my own place. That's the kind of celebration that urban parents living in an expensive city can understand. If he even caught a whisper of my rent increase and financial instability, he would offer to help.

But I'm the oldest kid—in my thirties, no less—and I can't bear the thought of that conversation. Of failing my parents and sisters in setting the example. Pressure cloaks my shoulders, neck, and chest.

In the few seconds that my father scans his memories, searching for any tangible mentions of Rebecca, I make a mental promise to myself: My family can never know just how close I am to falling behind. To failing. My pride may not be my best asset, but at least I'll know that whatever happens next is *my* responsibility.

"I think so. ¿Qué pasa?" he finally asks.

"Well, she moved out to LA a few years ago and has been working as a music supervisor and editor. That's someone who helps finalize the final score and soundtrack for a film." I hesitate for a beat, wondering if I should explain this further, but decide to charge ahead. "Anyway, she offered me a job. Chris Ross is making a TV show—a big-budget one—and they need a composer."

My father's eyes go wide, his mouth slack as he comprehends this. If there's anyone in my life who understands what this means—what it could *potentially* mean—it's José García III. He's the person who took me to my first movie, where I became so enamored with the music behind the family action-adventure story that we went out and bought the CD immediately after. He's the one who taught me how to read music and play the drums. He's the reason I practiced as hard as I did. He's the one who kept me on track when adolescent woes about boys and school drama threatened to derail me.

Both of my parents sacrificed a great deal so that I could attend Juilliard.

"Hija…" The word is barely a whisper, as if he can hardly believe it. After all this time, *here* is the exact opportunity we'd both been waiting for. "That's the guy who made that time-travel movie I didn't understand, no?"

I nearly choke on my coffee as I struggle not to laugh. "Sí, the same one."

"Celia, that's great news!"

Always my cheerleader. I can't help but smile at his genuine enthusiasm, at the pride radiating from his smile, at the way he slaps his hand on the bar top in triumph. It's almost enough to make me forget about all the worries that plague me. But as exciting as this is, I came here for some perspective, too. "Well, there's a catch," I caution. "Ross will only take someone junior if he gets two composers."

This doesn't faze my father at all. He simply shrugs, undeterred by this news. "So? You work with someone equally as great as you, and then BAM! Muñequita's dream comes true."

His enthusiasm and term of endearment choke me with emotion. I'm on the verge of crying into my café con leche when I say, "Maybe. But the cocomposer is Oliver Barlowe."

"The one who dressed like an abuelo?" my father asks. At this, I can't help but laugh while I nod. "Well, so what? Even if he's still a mierda, it's nothing you can't handle."

I knew I complained about Oliver when I'd come home on weekends and breaks during school, but the fact that my father can recall him so easily surprises me a little. My family only met Oliver in person once, after a performance. I still cringe whenever that memory pops into my mind—like right now—because it could not have gone worse.

My father's confidence in my ability to handle assholes lifts my spirits a little. Still, there's that anxious knot in my chest and the pressure threatening to smother me. "I can handle Oliver, papi, but I'm worried." I have to take a deep breath to steady myself. "What if I'm not good enough? What if I can't do this? What if I fail?"

"Hija, you *won't* fail. You are *more* than good enough." The lightness is gone from his voice now. He reaches across the bar to take both of my hands in his, leaning forward as he does. Rough fingers scrape across my wrists. "You've been making music since before you could read. This is in your bones. We didn't name you after one of the greats for nothing, you know."

"Celia Cruz was a salsa artist. This is playing with the big dogs, with the—"

He dismisses my argument with the shake of his head. "So? Life isn't a dress rehearsal, hija. It's the real performance. This is the moment you've been waiting for."

"I know, I just…I don't even have the tools to do this, you know?" I start. "I actually saw Oliver yesterday, and he said we can use his family's studio, but I haven't even worked on—"

"Celia, stop." He shakes my hands to bring me back down to earth. "You have the talent and skill to pull this off. Your friend Rebecca knows this, I know this, your mother and sisters know this. You're getting ahead of yourself. You're the only thing standing between yourself and your dream right now."

I find myself nodding as he speaks. This is it—the pep talk, the pull-it-together moment I needed. It doesn't erase the lingering feelings of self-doubt that remain in my chest, but it helps alleviate some of the immediate pressure. Hearing my father echo my own beliefs—that this is *my* moment—was what I needed.

"Thanks, papi. You're right. I know you're right."

He releases my hands and cups my cheeks, just like he did when I was little. The action makes me feel small as much as it makes me feel big—like I'm still his little girl who did a good job at her second recital, proud in a way that only comes from dedication and hard work. Although my father and mother both gave me the gift of music, they also gave me this: the perseverance to keep going, even when it feels hard.

When he releases me, we each polish off our lukewarm coffee. I glance over my shoulder at the stage where I spent so many hours of my life and feel a tug somewhere low in my belly. "You mind if I play for a bit?" I ask when I turn around to face him.

"Be my guest, hija."

I answer his smile with my own before hopping off my stool. As I meander through the tables, I'm overwhelmed with a feeling of déjà vu so strong it nearly knocks the wind out of me. For a brief moment, my steps falter, but then I'm climbing the small set of stairs onto the raised platform, weaving my body through the microphones and music stands until I'm seated at my usual stool.

That sense of déjà vu doesn't dissipate when I grab the drumsticks and twirl them between my fingers. It's bold enough that I'm almost having an out-of-body experience. But there's something grounding me, keeping me tethered to this place that feels more like home than anywhere else in the world.

When my foot taps the bass drum pedal, I realize this is true—that making music *is* home, and it's where I'm meant to be.

Today 3:13 PM

Celia — *3:13 PM*

Hey I know it's Saturday but we should probably run our questions and research by each other right?

So we don't end up doubling our efforts here Or looking like assholes in the meeting

Oliver — *3:46 PM*

Yes

Celia — *3:48 PM*

Great. Obvi I want to know more about the story. I tried finding more info online but it's just the same press releases
I feel like that's most important

> **3:49 PM**
> Also his process, how he likes to work

> **3:51 PM**
> wdyt?

Oliver   4:37 PM
wdyt? What does that mean?

> **Celia**   4:41 PM
> it means "what do you think"

SECOND CHANCE DUET ♪ 85

Today 7:14 PM

Oliver 7:14 PM

Oh

Yes I think it's important we ask these questions. I also want to know more about their visual ideas. I want to know what they envision for the audience to see and how our music might accompany that so see/hear are in harmony

Celia 7:20 PM

wow you're like really smart. did you go to a really good school or something?

Today 8:33 PM

Oliver 8:33 PM

lol

> **Celia**   *8:36 PM*
> do you know what that means?

> *8:37 PM*
> sorry that was an asshole thing to say, meant it as a joke

TODAY 10:01 PM

> **Oliver**   *10:01 PM*
> Better to be an asshole now versus in the meeting

> **Celia**   *10:04 PM*
> lol true

Chapter Six

LIMELIGHT STUDIOS HEADQUARTERS are in Union Square, just a few subway stops (and a fifteen-minute walk) from my apartment in Hell's Kitchen. But Monday brings heavy rains and thick humidity, so I opt to splurge on a cab. Normally, my personal budget is tight enough as it is with student loan payments that I forgo these kinds of expenses, but I can't show up to a meeting with Chris Ross looking like a wet dog. I try not to think about my rent increase, about how much I *need* this job to survive, as I stare at the ticking meter on the dashboard of the taxi and swipe my card in the machine.

After dashing into the lobby, I totter to a stop in my heels. I'm nearly ten minutes early, yet Oliver is already here, looking like a dapper professor in a suit so nice it has to be custom tailored, but today's color palette consists of grays and black. We almost look like a matching set, considering I opted for the simplest form of professional attire: all black, head to toe, minus my signature gold hoops.

His head is buried in his phone, those tortoiseshell glasses perched on his nose, so he doesn't notice me when I approach him. "Hey," I say quietly, trying not to draw any extra attention to myself in the lobby of executive-looking people. Oliver doesn't hear me, or maybe he just ignores me, so I inch closer to him. "Um, *hello*?"

He startles ever so slightly—a hitch of his breath, his eyes flashing up to meet mine. He slides his phone into a leather messenger bag draped over his shoulder before answering. "Hi. Sorry."

"When did you start wearing glasses?" I ask, flabbergasted by how good they look on his adult face, which is still so jarring to see after years of knowing a different version of him.

"A year ago maybe? Just one of the joys of getting older. All that glaring I did as a kid caught up to me."

I had expected a nonresponse from him, so the self-deprecating remark throws me off. "Oliver, did you... did you just make a sorta joke?"

When he frowns, a line forms between his brows. "Is that so shocking?"

My phone dings; it's an automatic calendar reminder that we have five minutes until the scheduled meeting. "Yes, but we'll have to dissect that later. Let's head upstairs."

Together we check in at the security desk, where we are given little plastic temporary badges that allow us to enter the rest of the building. We take one of those ultrafast elevators up to the twenty-third floor; it's one of three in Limelight's possession in this building alone. The ride up is spent in silence. For my part, I'm trying to manage my nerves, to prevent excessive sweating, to maintain an even rhythm of breathing despite the roaring heartbeat in my chest.

This is it: my shot at my dream job.

When the elevator doors open to another mini-lobby, Rebecca is waiting for us. She's leaning against the receptionist's desk, her dark hair pulled back into a tight bun, her eyes on her phone, fingers flying as she types. It's not until Oliver and I are standing right in front of her that she looks up.

"Sorry," she mutters as she slides her phone into her back pocket and stands up straight. "Good to see you guys. How are you?"

When her full attention is on us, the hope in her eyes is clear. Her gaze flits back and forth between us; it's assessing, yes, but there's no denying that she's happy that we're both here.

"Good, thanks," I offer first. "You?"

"Good. Busy." Rebecca blows out a stressed-out breath. "This other project that I'm working on is taking forever to wrap up and it's killing me."

"You're doing that superhero movie, right?" Oliver asks.

"That's the one. It's fun, don't get me wrong, but it's a *lot* of work." She shakes her head briefly. "Anyway, we're down the hall in a conference room. Chris is finishing up in another meeting, so he'll be in shortly."

She gestures toward a long hallway and we follow her. As we walk, I take it all in: the all-black ceiling, furniture, and walls, the glass-encased conference rooms, the can lights overhead that make the whole place feel more like an art gallery and less like a corporate office. There's a sort of quiet buzz that fills the space up. It's the sound of people talking, phones ringing, glasses being set on desks. While it's a far cry from an actual movie/TV set or recording studio, it still fills me with an overwhelming sense of joy.

I'm here. I made it this far.

Rebecca leads us into a glass-walled conference room with views overlooking a cloudy NYC skyline. "Take a seat wherever you'd like," she says. "Waters are for everyone. I'll be right back."

She disappears back into the hall, presumably to retrieve whoever else is needed for this meeting. I take a seat next to Oliver and grab a bottle of water from the center of the table. There's something about being in this room, on the precipice of such a huge opportunity, that has caused my mouth to completely dry out.

"Nervous?" Oliver asks as I down half the water in two gulps.

I really don't want to let this man see me ruffled, so I settle for a modicum of honesty. "A little."

He says nothing in response. I chance a glance at him to find his lips are pursed; this is the look I'm familiar with, the sort-of frown he wore a lot in college. He taps into his phone and seemingly ignores me.

With the door shut, the conference room is quiet. Silent, even. I hate it, the absence of any noise. Oliver doesn't make a peep as he stares down at his phone screen, his body angled in such a way that I can't catch a glimpse of what he's reading.

Then, out of nowhere, he says, "Don't be."

"What?" I ask, equal parts confused and startled by his words cutting through the quiet.

"Nervous," he replies as he turns to face me. When our eyes meet, I can't decipher his expression—there's no trace of emotion anywhere. "You shouldn't be nervous. You're quite competent."

"Competent." My dumbfounded echo of his word choice hangs heavy between us.

He closes his eyes briefly and lets out a small sigh. "I just mean that you can do this. You were always so…"

His words taper off as he pinches the bridge of his nose. My heart is practically tripping over itself at the mention of our history—this is not the time or place to dredge that up. Matter of fact, I hope we never do. But at the same time, curiosity burns through me. I *need* to know how he's going to finish that sentence.

"I was always what?" I ask, forcing my tone to stay breezy, even as one eyebrow raises.

His cheeks flush with color, the contrast highlighting his freckles again. His mouth opens as if to speak, but whatever he was about to say dies on his lips when the door to the conference room swings open. Rebecca walks in, followed by a series of people. Immediately I recognize Chris Ross, with his gradually graying wavy blond hair and expressive blue eyes. The minute he enters, his presence fills the space entirely. He's not a particularly big man—I'd put his height somewhere in the middle of Oliver and me—but he carries a sort of magnetism that draws all matter directly to him. It's a symptom of a man at the top of his game.

Oliver and I rise to stand at the same time. I straighten out my own blazer just to have something to do with my hands while I plaster a smile on my face. As Rebecca maneuvers toward a chair, she gives me a subtle wiggle of her eyebrows: *Good luck.*

"This is Celia García and Oliver Barlowe," Rebecca says as she motions to the two of us. "Celia and Oliver, this is Chris Ross, showrunner and executive producer, along with John Marshall, who will be working as director of photography, and Damian Delacorte, who is also producing."

There's a flurry of hands as we all greet each other. Each time I lock eyes with the men I'm introduced to, I commit their faces to memory. Aside from Ross (who is easy to remember considering how much he is photographed), there's John, with his wild white hair and grizzled face, and Damian, with a shock of red hair and a smattering of freckles across his nose. They seem nice enough; both offer me tentative smiles as we all sit down at the conference table.

"So," Chris says by way of greeting. His

voice is loud and booming. "Rebecca tells me you all went to school together?"

Oliver beats me to it. "Yes. We were in the same class at Juilliard."

"Juilliard kids, huh?" John asks. "Where are you both from?"

"New Yorker, born and raised," I reply. This is a strategic answer; after spending several hours Googling Chris Ross, I know that he is also a New Yorker by birth. I'm hoping this will earn me brownie points.

It does. Chris's head cocks to the side as he looks at me. "The Bronx?"

"Close. Washington Heights."

"Huh. I spent a lot of time in and around the Heights growing up. I had an uncle who lived in Highbridge."

"You an NYC kid as well?" John asks as he looks at Oliver.

"Not really. I was mostly raised in LA," Oliver replies. I have to quickly mask the look of surprise that no doubt registers on my face;

I had no idea Oliver grew up on the West Coast. Outwardly, he is the antithesis of California cool. He looks like he was born and raised in an uptight academic lecture room, or maybe a concert hall.

"Makes sense, given who your father is." This from Damian. "How is your old man? It's been a while since I've seen him."

"He's well, thank you."

I don't miss the way Oliver's shoulders tense at the mention of his father. As casually as possible, I lean in my chair to get a better look at him. There's a rigidity to the set of his jaw, offset by the beating of his pulse under his ears. I had no idea Daddy was such a touchy subject for him.

"As I mentioned before, I think Oliver and Celia would make a great team for *Lineage*," Rebecca says. I shoot her a look of thanks for getting the conversation on track. "Between the two of them, their catalogue is impressive, and I can personally attest to their talents.

They were the very best in our composition practicums in school. Everyone was jealous of them."

"Including you?" Chris asks with a smirk.

"Me most of all," Rebecca replies.

Chris shifts his attention to Oliver and me, his big blue eyes darting between our faces. "Rebecca made sure I looked at your portfolios. There's good work there. Obviously, we're going at this a bit backward—normally you two would have read the script by now and we would have had some calls to discuss your ideas." He pauses, shifting his weight in his chair as he crosses one leg over the other. "Unfortunately, we don't really have time for that, so let me tell you both a little about the story. Feel free to ask questions as we go along."

And so, Chris launches right into it; he paints a vivid picture of the Moore family, a cluster of wealthy East Coast elites that built their fortune establishing and later controlling one of the largest media companies in the world. The heart of the story—the real drama—has to do with the adult children of Jonathan Moore and how far they're willing to go to get what they want.

It's a far cry from cat-food commercials. The thought of telling this story through music lights me up in such a way that I'm practically vibrating in my seat.

Oliver and I lob questions back and forth at them. John explains his ideas behind the color palette for the project (deep greens, browns, and blues to accentuate the old-money feel of it all). On the subject of budget, Chris cuts Damian off by stating, "I want a full orchestra. Whatever you need." We discuss characters and their respective actors. Damian alludes that the studio would like to explore a second season, but Chris gives him a look that says, *We'll see*.

The more we talk, the less nervous I feel. Oliver and I play off each other well; our weekend text preparation allows us to communicate in such a way that I feel like I'm starting to understand what they want. I have no doubt in his abilities to do this. He's scored a handful of films, after all.

But me? I'm still a little unsure, especially since this show is set in a world that I don't know *at all*. I grew up in a middle-class household and I'm on the brink of losing an apartment I rent, not own. Everything I'm wearing was plucked straight off the rack at Zara and H&M. They're talking about filming in Monaco, for fuck's sake. I've never even been to Europe.

I glance at Oliver, speaking softly but confidently in his beautiful suit, and realize—*I need him for this*. He belongs here and always has. The thought curdles in my stomach, but I have no choice but to smile and nod and continue taking notes.

When I ask about the timeline for the project, Chris sits up a little straighter in his chair. "So, here's the deal: We just wrapped the LA sequence and start the New York shoot this week. Usually, I like to have music on set. Not the full score, but I'll need something soon. A theme or two to get me started. I can't do temp music. It fucks up the whole process. As shooting progresses, we'll send you footage so you can keep moving. By the time we wrap, the score should be close to done. That's when Rebecca will enter the picture, and we'll all collaborate as we work toward picture lock. So I'd say... probably December or January for recording the score?"

Despite the aggressive deadlines he's proposing, I find myself saying, "No problem," at the same time Oliver says yes.

"Great. Then welcome to the team."

For the remainder of the conversation, I seem to exist outside of my body. There's talk of contracts being sent to agents, of scripts being emailed to Oliver and me by the end of the day. While I understand that there is fine print to sort out—yes, I very much need to get paid for this job—I'm floating on cloud nine.

I did it. I'm here. I'm actually going to score something other than jingles that sell people shit they may or may not need. Not only that, but I'm going to make some *money*.

Not even an awkward elevator ride with Oliver can sour my mood. So what if I have to work with this man for the next few months? We did well in that room, almost like we were a team. If we stay focused on the work we're doing, then we'll be fine.

I'm still riding high when the two of us stride across the lobby to deposit our temporary security badges at the front desk. Outside the glass doors that look out onto the street, New York City is still a gloomy, rain-soaked pit of pedestrians running to get out of the downpour while garbage collects in puddles.

"That went well," Oliver says, pulling my attention away from the sidewalk and back to him. "Congratulations. This is a big deal for us."

I blink in surprise at his genuine words. "Yeah. It is. Congrats to you, too."

"When can you be ready to go?"

"You mean, start working?" I ask. "Well, I

can read the script as soon as they send it, so maybe end of the week?"

"I meant go to the studio."

My brows narrow as I stare up at him—didn't I just answer that question? "Like I said, end of the week. Thursday or Friday."

"You can be packed for a monthslong trip by Thursday?" he asks. As he pulls his glasses off his face and polishes them on the lapel of his blazer, I notice his cheeks have turned a brilliant shade of pink. He doesn't look at me as he places the frames back on the bridge of his delicate nose. "My family studio is in Boothbay Harbor."

And just like that, I crash back down to earth.

"What?" The word is almost a screech. I can't help it; my mouth drops open at the same time my stomach bottoms out. From inside my tote, I can feel my phone vibrating repeatedly as a rush of texts come in (no doubt it's the family group chat; everyone knows this meeting happened today). "You mean to tell me your family studio is in *Maine*?"

"Yes. It's our summer home. My dad was born in Ma—"

But Oliver doesn't even get the full word out. My whole body floods with a tingly, uncomfortable heat as I interrupt him. "Why didn't you tell me the studio is in another *state*? I can't up and move for, like, three months!"

"I got sidetracked," he says quickly. "At the café. I got sidetracked and forgot."

"*You forgot*," I reply, dropping my voice to a murderous whisper when I realize people are looking at us. "You can't be serious. I have nowhere to live in Boothbay Harbor and I can't exactly commute to Maine every day."

He hits me with an exasperated look before folding his arms across his chest. "Don't be silly, Celia. The house is big enough for the two of us."

A shriek of laughter escapes me. "No."

"No?" he repeats, his eyes wide in surprise.

"No!" The word bursts out of me, loud

enough that people in the building lobby turn to look at us again. Embarrassment washes over me in a wave, so I drop my voice again. "Oliver, this is ridiculous. I can't live *and* work with you for, like, three months."

He looks at me like *I'm* the one suggesting an unhinged plan. "Why not?"

I'm so close to listing out every single reason why this can't work. That we basically hated each other for years. That I haven't liked him since the day we laid eyes on each other and he couldn't deign to speak to me. That every time he ignored me or shut me out only made it worse. That I never forgot the night of the graduation party. But I have to salvage this; we have to maintain some level of professionalism, considering our agents are about to get contract emails that tether us to each other for months.

Instead, I take a deep breath, willing my face to stop flaming. "Because it's crazy. I have a life in New York. I can't just leave."

"Neither of us are going to have a life. This

show is going to consume us." He runs a frustrated hand through his hair, confirming my earlier suspicions about his disheveled locks. "Besides, what other option do we have? Do *you* know of any studio spaces we can rent for months at a reasonable price? My personal work setup can't accommodate two people."

I think of my own home studio, of how pitiful it is in comparison to what we'll need to get this done. There's no doubt in my mind that Robert Barlowe, legendary film composer that he is, has the best of the best tucked away in his summer home. In Maine.

There's no way I could come up with the kind of money that would be required to rent a studio space. I've seen the invoices billed to the customers I write for; rates are astronomical. The more I think about this—about all the logistical hurdles we're facing—anger strikes me hot and fast in the chest.

This is classic Oliver. He *would* withhold this crucial piece of information. He *would* assume that I'll uproot my life. He *would* presume that I will simply bend to his will. Some things never change.

But at the same time, he's right—we have no other option. It would be stupid of me to decline this invitation (if you can even call it that). Access to his father's studio is a leg up we both need.

"Fine," I say through gritted teeth. "I will go with you to Boothbay Harbor and I will be ready on Friday."

Before he can say anything else, I dash out into the soaked city with my head held high. The rain pelts me from all directions, but I hardly notice it. My thoughts go right back to that comment he made and what he didn't get to say—*You were always so…*

Maybe it's a good thing he didn't get to finish that sentence.

FAMILIA GROUP CHAT

Today 12:12 PM

Rosa — 12:12 PM
hellooooo it's been almost two hours??? any updates??

Amanda — 12:13 PM
chill hermana this could take all day

Rosa — 12:14 PM
YOU CHILL

Amanda — 12:15 PM
omg have you never been to a meeting before? they always run long

SECOND CHANCE DUET ♪ 109

Padre — 12:20 PM
Girls let your sister focus

Rosa — 12:21 PM
when have we ever done that lol

Amanda — 12:22 PM
no really

Madre — 12:30 PM
How do I turn off the flashlight on my phone?

Rosa — 12:32 PM
lmao

> **Amanda**   *12:35 PM*
>
> i just showed you how to do this, it's on your lock screen or in settings

> **Celia**   *12:40 PM*
>
> I GOT THE JOB!!!!!! 😭

> **Amanda**   *12:41 PM*
>
> I KNOW THAT'S RIGHT!!

> **Madre**   *12:43 PM*
>
> ¡Felicidades!

> **Padre**   *12:44 PM*
>
> Felicidades I never doubted this would happen

SECOND CHANCE DUET ♪ 111

Rosa — *12:44 PM*

WEPAAAAAAAAAAA!!! omg don't forget us when you're all famous

Amanda — *12:45 PM*

hollywoooooooood

Celia — *12:50 PM*

gracias gracias but actually no Hollywood

12:51 PM

I have to move to maine

Rosa — *12:51 PM*

WHAT

Amanda *12:52 PM*
???

Madre *12:53 PM*
¿Qué?

Padre *12:54 PM*
Por qué

Chapter Seven

"I SWEAR TO GOD, Celia, if you don't stop fidgeting, I'm going to ruin your hair on purpose."

My sister Rosa's steady hands grip my shoulders, forcing them to remain still. The metal curve of her scissors presses into me, even through the plastic hair cape draped over my clothes. "Sorry. I'm just nervous."

"I know, hermana, but you've got to *chill*."

I take a deep breath. My exhale sends a little puff of chopped-off hair flying onto the kitchen floor.

After learning that I would, in fact, be moving to Maine for the foreseeable future, I answered all the texts from my family as fast as I could until they unanimously demanded that I come home to tell them the whole story in person. Not that I needed much prompting. I was more than happy to jump on the train and spend an evening with them, considering I'm about to move seven hours away for the first time in my life.

Of course, I've been living on my own for a while now, but Midtown to the Heights isn't much of a jump. During my years at Juilliard, I lived in the dorms, but it was easy for me go home on weekends when I wasn't drowning in coursework. Since then, I've hopped from place to place, living with roommates (and, for a while, a former boyfriend), until I finally made enough to afford a studio apartment on my own. It's that same apartment I'm fighting tooth and nail to keep with this rent increase—a problem that is only partially solved with the paycheck coming my way. With our tight timeline and uncertain return date, there's no way for me to find a subletter.

But now I have to contend with the fact that I will not be a quick subway ride away from my parents and sisters, or any of my casual city friends for that matter. Which is why my mother, María, insisted on a big family dinner at their home, both as a celebration for this achievement and also as a goodbye. For the last three hours, all of us—my parents; my sister Rosa and her husband, Hector; and my sister Amanda—have been jammed into the same apartment I grew up in.

Dinner ended an hour ago, but the kitchen still smells of tostones, arroz amarillo con pollo, alcapurrias, and even the lingering sweetness of flan—a direct representation of my family's heritage, a delightful mishmash of flavors from the islands my grandparents came from. Not even the scent of floral shampoo and conditioner from my hair (washed while bent over the bathtub) can permeate the abundance of culinary smells lingering here.

There's only one person I trust with my hair, and that's my sister Rosa. I've always known it was a relief to my parents that my two younger siblings did not want to pursue an education as expensive as mine. Amanda was content to attend community college, where she earned her nursing degree. Rosa, ever the beauty queen, opted for cosmetology school—and so, the Rosa Kitchen Cut Special was born (for family and close friends only).

"Hija, will you be done by the holidays?" my mother asks from where she washes dishes at the sink.

"I don't know."

"What about my birthday?" Amanda asks while she dries said dishes with a hand towel. "It's my thirtieth. You can't miss it."

"I don't know, Mandie. You know I'll try."

My stomach—already full to the brim with food—sinks even further. As thrilled as I am about this job, I'm exhausted, too; the initial family celebrations quickly devolved into a game of "What about (blank)?" in which I had almost no answers. At this point, all I really know is that my agent is negotiating the contract, I've never been paid this much for anything in my life, and I'm already behind on reading the script, given the amount of laundry I had to do and errands I needed to run to prepare.

For his part, Oliver confirmed that the house will be ready by Friday—whatever that means. How does a house get ready, exactly? I've Googled the distance and town on my own, only to come to the sinking realization that Boothbay Harbor is farther than I thought it was. I've never even been to Maine. Most of our family's summer trips were spent along the Jersey shore, or, on occasion, in Florida or Puerto Rico. I've been to a handful of places on my own, but never Maine.

Through text, Oliver has also confirmed that he'll pick me up on Friday morning. Every time I think about being trapped in a car with that man for hours, my body buzzes with the need to expend nervous energy—which is exactly what I do now, by tapping my foot on the linoleum floor.

"Celia, seriously. I'm going to stab you with my scissors if you don't stop."

Rosa's warning is enough to make me pause. I'm so lost in my own thoughts that I hardly notice the *snip snip snip* of her scissors as she trims my dead ends. "Sorry! I can't help it!"

My dad ambles into the kitchen then, one hand rubbing his bloated belly while the other runs through his silver-streaked hair. He sidles up to where my mother stands at the kitchen sink. "Deja yo termino los trastes, mi amor," he says before kissing her on the cheek.

"It's okay, mi corazón, I'm almost done."

My heart contracts painfully in my chest; I'm going to miss this, all of this, from the big grand birthday celebrations to the small, everyday moments.

Yet I can't ignore the feeling that struck me during that initial dinner with Rebecca. It stayed with me, resonating deeply into my bones—that this is it, my chance at the life I've been imagining since I was a little girl seated next to her dad in a dollar movie theater.

I always knew success came with a price. I

guess this one is mine to pay. Pursuing your dreams is expensive.

When my hair is trimmed and mostly dry, the floor swept, and the dishes washed and put away, I corral my sisters in the kitchen and jerk my head toward the front hall. All it takes is one nod from me and they understand what I'm asking. On our way out the front door, we pass my mom, my dad, and Hector, who are all seated in front of the TV, watching the new season of their favorite telenovela. They say nothing to us as we slip out the door and into the cool, late August evening that smells of car exhaust and, inexplicably, roasting meat.

"Stoop chat or a walk?" Rosa asks as the three of us hover near the building entrance.

"Stoop chat, por favor," Amanda replies. "I just worked four straight twelves and me duelen los pies."

Even after all these years, the three of us assume our usual seats: I sit on the top step (an honor bestowed upon me as the eldest), while

Rosa and Amanda flank my sides a few steps down. The cement is cold and hard underneath my jeans as I settle in and lean forward to place my elbows on my knees.

Since we were little girls, this is what the García sisters have done. Whenever one of us (or all of us) was bored, restless, or upset, we parked ourselves on the building stoop. Sometimes we talked, told stories, or vented; other days we just existed, observing the happenings of our block or chatting with our neighbors. In the summers, we'd wait for the piragua man to roll by. We even sat out here in the winters, all bundled in our coats, hats, and mittens, until one of us couldn't stand it anymore or our parents dragged us inside.

It wasn't until I was twelve or thirteen—Amanda around ten and Rosa around seven—that we started walking. Just strolling, usually, in and around the residential streets of the Heights. We started doing it because walking had been my escape with my father; in retrospect, it was his way of making sure I wasn't neglected when two little sisters came along. But it also turned into a history lesson of our community, a safety lesson on stranger danger, and a way to clear my head. I've loved walking around the city ever since.

My little trip down memory lane ignites a question in me. "How long has it been since the last time the three of us sat out here?"

"I don't know. Maybe last year?" Amanda asks.

"No, I think it was the night before my wedding," Rosa says as she dusts a clump of my hair off her leggings. "That would have been about two years ago. We sat out here all night, remember?"

The memory of the three of us—accompanied by a bottle of illegally imported Cuban rum—makes me smile. "I remember until around midnight," I reply. "Then it starts to get a little blurry."

It came as no surprise to any one of us that Rosa was the first to marry, even though she is the youngest. She always had a proclivity for beautiful things, whether it was a set of fresh nails, a vibrant lip gloss, or a good-looking boy. When she met Hector as a twenty-one-year-old—with his sculpted muscles and charming smile that seemed to shine a little brighter whenever Rosa was near—it was clear that she had found The One. Amanda and I are a little slower to the game than Rosa.

Both of my sisters crane their necks to look up at me. It's the first time in a long time that anyone has had to do that; I'm short, they're short, my whole family is short. Looking at their faces, with their dark eyes and plush lips, is like looking at my own through a kaleidoscope—we are so clearly sisters, yet each of us is a little different from the next. Amanda's hair is straighter than mine, her face a little rounder; Rosa has my maternal grandfather's cleft chin and two dimples that appear when she really, truly smiles. I have none of these things, but we are all woven from the same tapestry. We are puzzle pieces meant to make an image whole.

"I don't know what I'm going to do without you guys," I say, willing my voice not to crack. "My whole life, both of you have either been up in my shit or a train ride away. What the hell am I going to do in Maine?"

"The years that we were all up in each other's shit, we nearly killed each other," Amanda says.

"Spoken like a true middle child." This from Rosa.

I snort. "Hey, we always figured it out. Everyone survived the years we had to share bedrooms."

"Spoken like a true *oldest* child," Amanda chides. "Who also had her own room the longest."

Rosa narrows her eyes as she surveys me, the wings of her black eyeliner creasing ever so slightly. "Is this about leaving us, or having to work with him? I remember how much you used to hate Oliver."

"Didn't we use to call him Professor Pendejo?" Amanda asks.

A groan escapes my lips when I rub my hands over my face. "Ugh, sí, we called him that, among other things. Dad says he dressed like an abuelo."

This earns a genuine laugh from both of my sisters. "Do you remember how rude he was when we met him after your concert?" Rosa asks. "You tried to introduce him to all of us, and he just, like, blinked and walked away."

"Oh, I remember." It's those memories—especially that one—that almost kept me from taking this job. "I think he's less of a jerk now, but he's still the same guy."

What I don't tell my sisters is that he *looks* like less of a jerk now, too. Oliver's awkward college years, coupled with his odd sense of style, did him no favors in the likability department. Now that he's filled out (or, more accurately, grown up), the rest of him makes more sense. As if Oliver is whole now, no longer just the sum of his parts.

"Listen, Celia." Amanda pauses to stretch out her tired legs while she stifles a groan. "Do you remember how scared you were when you found out you got into Juilliard? You were so intimidated by all those fancy people, with their fancy clothes and fancy education and all that other fancy shit that rich people spend money on. But you still went and look how that turned out!"

Rosa nods enthusiastically while Amanda speaks. Her gold hoops, nearly identical to my own, bounce along her jawline. "She's right, hermana. Plus, it doesn't even matter where you work or what you do. You're always going to have to work with assholes. You remember how much I hated that bitch at my old salon?"

"Oh yeah. Wasn't her name Carol?" Amanda asks. Rosa shudders in response.

"You're right. Both of you are right. I know that." For what must be the thousandth time tonight, I take a deep breath. "It'll be fine."

Amanda puts a hand on my knee and offers

me a genuine, consoling smile. "We know. You'll be great. Besides, you're not going to be alone up there."

Just as I raise my eyebrow in question, Rosa chimes in. "Exactly. We're still going to blow up the group chat every day. You can't get rid of us that easily, hermana."

This reassurance from my sisters is exactly what I needed. Already my entire body feels a little lighter, my stomach a little less tense at the prospect of what lies ahead of me. I scooch down two steps so that I'm seated on the same level as them. Wrapping an arm around each of their shoulders, I pull them into a hug, relishing the familiar comfort of my sisters, my best friends, my ride or dies.

FACEBOOK MESSAGE FROM AMANDA GARCÍA

Thirteen years ago

> hermana
> when are u coming back to the house
> mom let me paint ur room. it's blue now. ALL MINE!!!!

> do u even care?

FACEBOOK MESSAGE FROM ROSA GARCÍA

Thirteen years ago

> it's so boring here without u. did u forget you have a family uptown

> is college really that hard? idk if i wanna go if this is how it is

> we never see you anymore

FACEBOOK MESSAGE FROM AMANDA GARCÍA

Thirteen years ago

> damn girl ur acting like u went to school in another country or something

> u haven't come home in weeks

FACEBOOK MESSAGE FROM ROSA GARCÍA

Thirteen years ago

> thx for coming to dinner. i miss u but im rly rly proud of u

> love u

Chapter Eight

THIRTEEN YEARS AGO

I KNEW COLLEGE WOULD be a big change, especially a conservatory with a reputation like Juilliard, but I wasn't prepared for this.

It's not so much the classes. Those are incredibly hard, don't get me wrong. It's everything that happens *outside* of the regular classes. To stay on top of my course load and to keep from looking like an idiot during everything from Music History to Ear Training to Composition, I have to spend almost every spare second either in the library or practicing. And it's not just percussion that I have to keep working on—so much of what we cover in our classes all comes back to the piano.

Every night, I'm here, in the practice rooms, on one of 250 Steinway pianos scattered around the school, working my way through an analysis of a long-dead composer whom I respect, sure, but holy shit, what were these guys on? I have to hear it to make sense of it. It's cute that I thought my twelve years of private piano lessons would set me up for success here. My hands can work their way through some of the most complicated time signatures and rhythms on a number of different percussive instruments—my school audition alone included snare, timpani, marimba, crash cymbals, and tambourine!—but the piano is going to be the death of me.

It's nearly 11:00 p.m. on a Wednesday night and I'm only halfway through this analysis of Liszt's *Liebestraum No.3*. I can't remember the last time I ate a proper meal and my eyesight is starting to blur. Even though the practice rooms are built to be as soundproof as possible, I can still hear snippets of my neighbors up and down the hall. A trumpet here and there, the flurry of a piccolo's scale, someone yelling just outside the glass door to my room.

I look at the sheet music in front of me, then at the notes I've scribbled in my notebook. Nothing makes sense anymore. Exhausted, I call it a night a few minutes early and pack up my things. Rebecca, Anthony, and I planned to meet each other to walk back to the dorms together, so this is as good as it's going to get. I'll come back here in the morning before practicum.

I find Rebecca and Anthony waiting for me near the end of the hall, by one of the larger practice rooms that houses a full concert grand Steinway. They both look as exhausted as I feel, with shadows under their eyes, the latter with his cello case dangling at his side, the former clutching her trumpet case to her chest. All three of us have backpacks slung over slumped shoulders.

"Ready?" I ask as I approach.

Both nod and glance in my direction before turning their attention back to the big practice room. Brows pinched in confusion, I look through the glass door to find Oliver hunched over the piano, wearing dress slacks and a button-down, completely oblivious to the fact that he's being watched. His fingers fly over the keys between rapid page turns of the music. My ears strain to identify the music, but I can't place it.

"What's he playing?" I ask.

Rebecca's eyes slide to mine. "Liszt. *La Campanella.*"

My stomach sinks. It's one of the most notoriously difficult piano études. Something I can't even fathom playing.

"He's double majoring," Anthony adds with a touch of annoyance. "Piano performance and composition. I thought Juilliard didn't even allow freshmen to opt in for a double major."

"They don't. Normally." This time it's my turn to sound annoyed. I wanted to double major in percussion performance and composition, but my advisor talked me out of it, citing the intense music and academic rigor required. Most students need an extra year to complete a double major, and I can't really afford four years at this school, let alone five.

Rebecca mumbles a distinct "fuck it" under her breath before opening the door to Oliver's practice room. He doesn't look up, doesn't even flinch as the sound spills into the hall. He just keeps on playing, solely focused on the music in front of him. If he's messing up, I certainly don't notice. All I hear is the bright radiance of the notes played at a brisk staccato pace. All I see are his long fingers flying up and down the keys while his head nods gently to the rhythm he must hear on his own.

Minutes ago, I was struggling through a different Liszt piece. One that is way less technically complex. A strange combination of envy and respect floods my system, warming my skin from head to toe.

Oliver Barlowe is hugely talented. That is an objective fact. It sucks, but it's true.

When he finishes, he looks over his shoulder

at the three of us crowding the doorway. His eyes find mine right away. He runs his hands through his already messy hair as we stare at each other.

Maybe I'm so tired that I'm hallucinating, but I could swear that he looks so...*sad*. Usually Oliver regards all of us—including me—with a cool indifference. I've never seen him look anything other than focused in classes, or just flat-out bored whenever he appears in a social setting, which is rare enough as it is. But tonight, he looks so *young*. His brown eyes are open and searching, like he's lost or something. A boy dressed in his dad's clothes, way out of his element. It does something weird to my heart.

And so, four weeks into the semester, I say my first words to Oliver: "You sound good."

"I fucked up the entire middle section," he replies flatly.

He shakes his head, turns back to the piano, and starts playing again. Rebecca, Anthony, and I understand we've been dismissed.

SECOND CHANCE DUET ♪ 135

DEADLINE EXCLUSIVE:

Chris Ross Brings in New Music Talent for *Lineage* TV Show with Limelight & A24

BY LISA MORRISON, TV EDITOR AUGUST 17

DEADLINE can exclusively report that Chris Ross has hired two music composers to score his first television show *Lineage*, which is currently filming in New York. An anonymous source shared that Oliver Barlowe, son of legendary composer Robert Barlowe, will partner with industry newcomer Celia García to write the music for the show.

"Everyone on the production team is so excited to see what these two come up with," the source said when speaking with *DEADLINE*. "It's high time we get some fresh musical perspective."

Oliver Barlowe has made a name for himself with multiple independent film credits and a slew of original works for the London Philharmonic, whereas García's career has largely been in corporate media. Industry vet Gustav Schneider was originally slated to work with Ross on the project but had to drop out, citing "scheduling conflicts."

Both Ross and studio heads at Limelight state that production is still on schedule, with a streaming date in spring of next year.

García is represented by Talent First Agency, Oliver Barlowe is represented by CAA, and Robert Barlowe is represented by WME.

Chapter Nine

I DON'T KNOW WHAT I was expecting to pull up in front of my apartment building at 10:00 a.m. on Friday morning, but it certainly wasn't this.

When the black Mercedes SUV rolled to a stop in a loading zone a few feet away from me, I ignored it initially. The hazard lights were a mere annoyance in my peripheral vision while I scanned the street for a more sensible car. A Camry, or perhaps a Volvo, as an indicator of the upper-class life. It wasn't until Oliver jumped out—dressed uncharacteristically casual in a pair of slim-cut jeans, a white T-shirt, and a pair of Wayfarer sunglasses perched on the bridge of his nose—and jogged around to the back that I realized this was his ride.

"Hey," he calls out to me as he pulls open the trunk door, which opens to the *side*. "Is this everything?"

Behind my own sunglasses, I gape at the sleek vehicle. I don't even glance at my own pile of luggage at my feet. The fact that I was able to fit most of my belongings—namely, clothes and toiletries—into one carry-on and one huge suitcase is a miracle on its own. But to ride up to Maine in a car this nice? This will be a revelation.

"Yeah. This is everything," I finally manage to say. My voice is barely loud enough to cut through the traffic noise, sirens, and Reggaeton music blaring from somewhere down the street. Together we load my mismatched luggage into the rear of the SUV next to his matching silver set.

I hop into the passenger seat and try not to gawk at the flawless tan leather interior. The car itself isn't brand new, but it's clearly been meticulously kept; there's not a single flaw in the dash or stain on the floor mats. Carefully, I set my tote bag onto the floor while clutching my bodega coffee in one hand; it would be humiliating to be the first person to make a mess in this car.

As Oliver taps off the hazard lights and throws the car into Drive, I can't help but notice the cords of muscles wrapping around his forearms. They tense and flex as he angles the steering wheel to veer us into the flow traffic. I've never seen him *not* in a blazer, at least not as an adult. The effect is jarring— I don't want to think of Oliver as a man, let alone notice the bits and pieces of him that are attractive.

Still, I find that I'm grateful I took the time to swipe on a bit of makeup this morning even though I'm dressed comfortably in leggings and a T-shirt. Makeup is something I normally do for me; I like the way I look with a bit of concealer, mascara, and some blush. For nights out, I'll add a little more—lip gloss, highlighter, whatever makes me feel good at the time. I don't do this for the male gaze, but I'm suddenly very aware that I am in close proximity to a male with a gaze. And will be, for months.

"Is this your G-Wagon?" I find myself asking, by way of distraction.

"Not exactly. I don't have a car in New York." He doesn't look at me when I ask this, instead opting to keep his focus on the chaos as he turns onto Broadway. "This car usually lives at the Maine house. It doesn't get driven much."

"How did it get here, then?"

"I flew up to get the house ready on Tuesday and drove it back."

For a brief moment, I'm so flattered that I'm speechless. He...flew to Maine to prep the house? And then drove the SUV down to New York, only to turn around and drive *back*? "Are you serious?" I ask after a long beat, followed by an immediate, "Why?"

Oliver does that thing he did before; he sucks both lips between his teeth, which effectively shuts his mouth into a single, tight line. Using my sunglasses as some guise of protection, I stare at him while he does this. If I didn't know any better, I'd guess that he was choosing his words carefully. As if he was hesitant to tell me the truth.

The silence between us stretches on for so long that I prompt him again. "Oliver?"

"Getting to Boothbay Harbor is kind of a hassle," he admits. "It's a bus to a train to a bus, or a plane to a bus, unless you hire a car service to pick you up in Portland or Boston, but that gets expensive. The house itself is on the outskirts of town. With all our stuff, I figured this would be easiest."

How annoyingly thoughtful. And selfless.

I move so that I'm facing forward and adjust my seat belt across my chest. Whoever sat here last was at least a foot taller than me. "Well, thank you. I'll pitch in for gas, obviously."

To this, he says nothing. The SUV is so expensive and well-engineered that the road noise is minimal, even as we crawl along in standstill traffic and the heart of NYC beats all around us. The effect is a muted, somewhat tense ride, during which I cautiously sip my coffee.

It's the quietest my life has been in a very, very long time.

Frankly, it makes me uncomfortable enough that I start subconsciously tapping my feet on the floorboard without rhythm. Oliver notices; he reaches forward to fiddle with the controls on the dashboard. Shortly after, the hum of the radio picks up, the SUV filling with the music of Bruce Springsteen.

"Have you made it far with the script?" he asks.

A breath escapes my lips in a gust. "No. I was so busy packing for this move that I barely got to page ten."

Just several hundred more pages to go.

"Same here." For a moment, I think that's all he's going to say, but then he continues on. "Do you happen to have it with you?"

I lean forward to pull a very thick stack of papers out of my tote. This is one of those errands that ended up being a time suck; I had the script printed and bound at a shop around the corner from my place instead of going to my trusted guy uptown. The intention was to make it easier to take notes on it, but after a long wait time and a miscommunication with the print tech, the whole trip wound up taking me two hours longer than I'd planned. Hence, only ten pages read so far.

After glancing at it, he does that thing again where he presses his lips between his teeth. "Would you be willing to read it out loud while I drive? If you'd rather not, I understand. Just figured since we'll be stuck in the car for hours, it would make sense—"

"Oliver," I cut in, interrupting him for the third time since our first meeting at the café. "It's fine. I don't get carsick or anything. I can read it. Where did you leave off?"

"Page five."

Gingerly, I set my coffee in the middle

console and adjust so that I can hold the script in my lap. This whole exchange has me a little off-kilter, so much so that I drop the papers twice before managing to angle them so I can read. In all the time I've known him, I can count the number of times I've seen Oliver flustered on one hand. To hear him ramble on while he asks for my help is endearing. Humanizing, even. Like a brittle piece of his cold, aloof exterior has cracked and fallen off. Just a tiny one, but it's something.

From this point forward, it's just the two of us—whether we're stuck crawling down Broadway or holed up in some house in Maine.

After turning the radio down, I clear my throat, flip to page five, and start.

♪

This is all I do—for three hours, I read out loud, while the towering buildings of Manhattan give way to the squatter, wider buildings of the suburbs. I try to keep it entertaining by mixing up my voice for different characters. Every now and then, I chance a glance at Oliver to see his sights set on the road, his lips pulled into a flat line. It's impossible to tell what he's thinking.

The tick of the blinker and the reduction in speed pull me out of the story and into the present. I dog-ear the page I was reading—somewhere in the midst of episode four—before closing it and looking around. Oliver has taken an exit ramp off the highway. In the distance, I see a gas station looming, its LED lights blaring at full blast even in the midday sun.

"We need gas," he says. Hearing a voice other than my own is so strange it nearly startles me.

"Yeah. Okay. I need water, too." This is true; my mouth is dry and my tongue feels like it's made of sand after reading out loud for hours.

We slow to a stop next to a gas pump a few minutes later. I'm quick to hoist my purse off the floor and fish my wallet out of my bag. "I'll get this one."

"Sure. Thanks." Without further preamble, Oliver flips a lever on his side of the car to open the gas cap and slides out of the SUV.

I follow suit. Stifling a groan, I stretch my legs and fill my lungs with fresh air. It's windy in Connecticut (or at least, I think we're in Connecticut), the landscape uninterrupted by the skyscrapers of NYC's concrete jungle. My hair whips around my face as I survey the gas pump. It's oddly colorful—the whole thing is a puzzle of vibrant blues and reds, with more buttons and nozzles than I expected. In the center of the whole thing, a D-list celebrity in a tiny TV pitches me the gas station's rewards system.

It occurs to me then that I don't know how to do this. I've only ever pumped gas once, when I was sixteen, on a trip to Florida with my family. Back then, we'd paid for the cheapest fuel with cash—it was a rental car, so no one really cared. I don't know what kind of gas a Mercedes takes, nor do I know when to insert my credit card. Do I do that before, or after I pump?

Shit. This is embarrassing.

"Oliver?" I ask tentatively, hoping he's still around. When he doesn't respond, I peer around the pump to find that he's nearly to the door of the gas station. The wind is lifting the hem of his T-shirt, exposing a lean set of hips and a strip of patterned boxers that peek out from under his jeans. I clear the dust from my throat and call his name a little more forcefully. "Oliver?"

He hears me this time and turns toward me. God, how silly I must look, standing here by a car worth more than I earned last year, clutching my wallet to my chest like it's a lifeline. But no matter how embarrassing this might be, fucking up his family's car by pumping the wrong gas incorrectly would be even worse.

As he jogs back toward me, he asks, "What's up?"

"I don't know how to do this."

His brows narrow, nearly disappearing under his sunglasses, as he stands next to me. "What do you mean?"

"I don't know what kind of gas a G-Wagon takes. I've only done this once before."

"You've only done this once before." His echo of my statement is full of wonder, like it never even occurred to him that a person would *not* know how to do this. But that's the reality of being born and raised in a city like New York, where public transportation is readily available and walking is a viable means of getting from point A to point B. I don't even have a driver's license; I never needed one. As I learned recently, Oliver grew up in California, where having a car is basically a necessity for survival.

Deeply annoyed, I don't say anything to this. I just stand there with my brows flattened in irritation, my wallet clutched to my chest, my tote bag slung over my shoulder, waiting for him to offer some kind of advice.

For a moment, he doesn't do anything at all; he just stares at me from behind his black sunglasses until his lips curl up, up, up enough that they've formed an actual, honest-to-god smile.

And then—he laughs.

It's the first time I've ever heard this sound come out of Oliver Barlowe. In all my years of knowing him, he's deprived me of this wonderful, throaty song, pitched in a rich baritone that resonates over the wind curling around us. It stuns me enough that I take a half-step back. This only makes him laugh harder. It's infectious, the way he clutches his side with one hand while the other runs through his hair. Soon I'm laughing, too—at myself, at him, at the absurdity of our situation at some random gas station on the side of the Connecticut highway.

When the giggles subside, Oliver patiently shows me how it's done (the card swipes first; the SUV takes premium gas). There's not a hint of condescension as he explains which buttons to press or how to trigger the nozzle so it automatically pumps. The whole thing is over in a matter of minutes, but the interaction lingers with me long after, when my purse is saddled with snacks and bottles of water and the car is whizzing down the road again.

Before I can resume reading, Oliver clears his throat, startling me. "Do you remember the other day when we were at the meeting with Chris, and you asked me what I meant when I said not to be nervous?"

"Yes," I say as I turn to face him with unabashed surprise. Not only do I remember this clearly, but I thought about it the entire twenty-minute train ride home, then on and off again over the rest of the week. *You were always so…*

"What I was going to say," he starts, then pauses, but I keep staring at him, observing as his cheeks flush. "I was going to say that you were always so good at it. Before, in college. At the music, yes, and with the people. I was never good at that—the people stuff. But you were."

My heartbeat echoes at the way the words come out of him, in cautious starts and stops. This is the last thing I expected him to say. I figured he would comment on the way I was always so forward and direct—or maybe bold, if he was feeling nice—but to *compliment* both my musical and people skills? And to make it a point to clarify the whole thing days later?

Maybe Rebecca was right. Maybe he has changed.

"Oh." This is a lame response, but it's like every other word has emptied out of my mind. I scramble for something more coherent as I shift in my seat to face forward. "I—well, thank you."

Out of the corner of my eye, I can see him nod curtly. End of discussion, then.

I flip open the script and continue reading aloud well into Massachusetts. Somewhere in the middle of the state, an accident causes traffic to snarl. It's late in the afternoon at this point and we're both hungry enough to succumb to the siren song of the Golden Arches. When we pull off the highway, I slip the script back into my tote—the dog-eared page tells me we're nearly halfway through the season—before tumbling out of the SUV onto wooden legs.

When we're both seated at a small table, two trays of familiar fried foods displayed in front of us, I find myself unable to look away from him. His sunglasses dangle from the crew neck of his T-shirt as he prepares his lunch-dinner: a burger and fries for him, an order of nuggets and fries for me. There's an indentation on the bridge of his nose where his sunglasses have sat all day. It's red, a little irritated, almost the color of the paper ketchup ramekins he orders neatly into a row at the top of his tray.

There's music playing in this McDonald's dining room, which would be empty if it weren't for us and the employee wiping down tables. Still, it's quiet enough that I can hear the hustle and bustle coming from behind the counter; the young employees are laughing and joking loudly about something, but not quite audibly enough for me to hear the details. It's strange, being in a place with this much noise, so close to another person, but hearing so little.

Just as Oliver takes a bite from a monstrous-looking burger, I ask, "So, what's the deal with the house?"

His gaze shoots to me as I pop half a nugget into my mouth—it's almost a glare or an accusation, but not quite. I've seen this look on him before, many times in college, as he stared at me from across the classroom or top of a piano. This particular type of heat in his light-brown eyes used to royally piss me off. But now it does little more than irritate me—just a slight ruffling of my proverbial feathers, enough to get a teeny, tiny rise out of me.

He finishes chewing, swallowing hard, before wiping the grease from his fingers onto a napkin. "What do you mean?"

I choke back a frustrated sigh. "I mean, like, anything at all. I have no idea what I'm getting myself into here."

"Well, it's on the edge of town, within walking distance of the waterfront," he says as he leans back into the hard metal frame of the chair. "Four bedrooms, four bathrooms, studio addition on the side of the house, small gym in the basement. It's fairly large. You'll have plenty of privacy."

"Okay, great." I pause to eat a fry. "And you said something about it being your family's house or something? You mentioned your dad was born in Maine?"

What I don't say is, *You tried to tell me your dad was born in Maine, but I cut you off.*

"Yes. It was his childhood home, until his family moved to Connecticut for work. They kept the cottage for summers, though. When his parents—my grandparents—passed, he got the house. I was thirteen, maybe fourteen, when my mom and dad remodeled it." He pops another fry into his mouth as a thoughtful look comes over his face. "Although, it would be more accurate to call it a complete gut job. It's not really a summer cottage anymore. They winterized it, added a bunch of rooms, updated everything, et cetera."

"And you spent your summers there? With your parents?"

"Every single one until I went to college."

Which was roughly thirteen years ago. "When was the last time you stayed at the house?" I ask, before adding, "Aside from this week."

"Around five years ago," he replies after consuming another fry.

"With your parents, or...?" I ask.

He wipes his hands on his napkin. "No, I was alone."

"Oh," I reply, clearly frustrated by how little he offers when I ask about his life. The mention of his mom and dad provides an easy opening, so I ask, "How are they? Your parents, I mean."

"Fine."

The single response, given so quickly, lands with a heavy impact that I don't understand. "Are you close with them?"

"No," he scoffs, then downs most of his soda.

When it's clear he's not going to offer any more information than that, I turn my attention back to my food. This is the most I've learned about Oliver's past outside of his musical capabilities *ever*, but the conversation feels so one-sided that it's more like an interrogation. I'm already tired from doing all the heavy lifting.

As we eat in silence, my mind works to connect the dots. Oliver's mentioned having two parents, but I don't remember seeing him with any of his family, not in the years we spent playing in the same ensembles or the day we both walked across the graduation stage. Because of his famous father (well, famous for our world), I'd never given much thought to Oliver's mom. It's possible that I met or saw her at some event but never registered who she was. Someone must have been there when he performed, right? At least for his graduation?

"Celia? Everything okay?"

Oliver's voice pulls me out of Juilliard's concert halls and back into the rural Massachusetts McDonald's. When my gaze meets his, I'm surprised to see a little *V* forming between his brows, his full lips pursed together just enough that they almost look like a pout. It's a look of concern—one brought on by my own listless frown. My stomach does a funny little swoop at this realization.

"What?" I ask, confused by so many things that I don't know where to start.

"I was just asking if your family still lives in the city."

"Oh. Yeah, they're still in the Heights," I reply absently, my mind hundreds of miles away from my own family's home. I push the mostly finished tray of food away from me.

I'm fully prepared to lie to myself that it was the nuggets that did that to my stomach, *not* the way Oliver is looking at me right now. Like he cares. "Sorry. Just wrapping my head around the fact that I'm moving into a house I've never seen before."

That isn't exactly true, but he gives me a tentative, small smile as he nods. As if he understands how that feels. I find myself smiling back at him without thinking about it.

I don't like lying to him. I don't like lying to *anyone*. But this is an act of self-preservation, one that is wholly essential to my own survival. Because under these harsh fluorescent lights, I have no choice but to wonder if Oliver Barlowe may not be who I thought he was.

LINEAGE — EPISODE ONE, "THAT ONE"

INT. — MOORE FAMILY SITTING ROOM   4

We open on EMILY and JAMES MOORE as they step into a private sitting room and close the door behind them. It's the kind of room no one ever uses, untouched and clean, decorated with expensive furniture.

> JAMES
> I told you he would come
> back from that trip
> either engaged, broke, or
> arrested!

> EMILY
> Well, he can't go broke,
> so you had a fifty-fifty
> shot of being right.

                    JAMES
                (laughing)
            Yeah, but engaged to a
            bartender? Could he be
            even more cliché?

                    EMILY
            I give it six months,
            tops. There's no way our
            brother makes it down the
            aisle.

                    JAMES
            Oh, I think he'll do it.
            I'll put money on that.

Chapter Ten

~

IT'S DARK BY the time we arrive at the house. The tree-lined driveway provides no insight into where we are. All I can see is a blurry outline of a building against a night sky. A floodlight activates when Oliver pulls up to the garage, so bright it's nearly blinding.

I'm out of the SUV as soon as he cuts the engine, desperate to stretch my legs. The last two or so hours of the drive have been devoid of any real conversation; once we lost daylight, I couldn't read from the script. Rather than talk to me, Oliver turned on NPR while I scrolled on my phone.

We remain silent as we grab our stuff out of the back of the car. I follow Oliver through a door, dragging my bags behind me, my nervous system on high alert as he calmly flicks on switches in a short hallway. I blink to adjust to the lights.

The house is *beautiful*.

We're standing in a den, a huge but comfortable room lined with bookshelves bursting with tomes, a squishy gray couch, and two wingback chairs that look as if they were pulled directly from a Victorian library. There's a staircase tucked into one corner and three different sets of doors.

"That's the studio," Oliver says as he sets his suitcases against a chair and points to a glass interior door. "The other two go to the back deck and the first-floor bathroom. That staircase leads to the owner's suite upstairs and downstairs to the basement. There's another bathroom downstairs. The other bedrooms have a separate wing."

A giggle bursts out of me. "A separate wing. Okay."

He glances back at me, one eyebrow raised. "I told you that you'd have plenty of space.

Do you want to leave your stuff here while you pick out a room?"

I nod and follow him deeper into the house, where he leads me to an enormous open kitchen, which is clearly meant to be the heart of it all. There's a marble island larger than my bed back home, plus a big dining room table off to the side made from real dark-brown wood. It opens to a living room decorated in soft creams and blues, complete with a fireplace and flat-screen TV. You could fit two of my Manhattan apartments in this living space alone.

"These stairs lead to the other bedrooms," Oliver explains as I trail after him. He continues turning on lights as we go up another set of ivory-carpeted stairs and into a long second-floor hallway. There are four closed doors up here.

"I feel like I'm in a carnival fun house." I can't help but huff out a shocked breath. "What happens if I pick the wrong one? Do I get pied in the face or something?"

"Yes, actually," he deadpans as he looks at me. "It's a family tradition."

When I laugh, a smile blooms on his face. Not a full one, but still, his eyes brighten and it looks like he stands a little taller. Like he's proud or something.

Warmth spreads across my skin. I ignore it, too overwhelmed to process what that means. "Which room should I take?" I ask instead.

"Whichever you'd like."

He stands in the hall while I open the various doors and poke my head in. One leads to a bathroom with a buttery yellow theme, while the other three lead to said bedrooms. Each one has a distinct but related color scheme, which seems to be "coastal forest chic"; there's a pale-green room, a soft-blue room, and a creamy-white room. They're all decorated with lovely touches like gauzy curtains, landscape paintings, and comfortable furniture, but they're absent of any personal mementos. No family pictures, no posters of favorite childhood movies, no old soccer jerseys in shadow boxes mounted to the wall.

"Which one was your room?" I ask.

"The green one," he replies. "If you want to take the owner's suite, you can. I'll take my old room."

"No, it's fine. I like the blue room, but where is your stuff? You said you spent your summers here as a kid. I want to see some Oliver baby pictures."

"I came out of the womb just like this," he says, his tone tinged with what I think is slight bitterness, but I don't miss how his face reddens when he diverts his gaze to the circular window over the stairs.

"I'd believe that if I hadn't witnessed your glow-up," I reply with a smile. "I knew you at eighteen, remember?"

"How could I forget?" he asks distantly, but the question isn't really directed at me. It's barely a whisper said to the night sky outside. He beelines for the stairs, careful not to brush against me in the hall, leaving me standing there awkwardly, framed by a bunch of open doors.

"Make yourself comfortable," he calls as he descends from view. "I'll bring your bags up."

His abrupt dismissal cools me off immediately. All of a sudden, I'm aware of how chilly it is in this big house. I clutch my arms to my chest as goose bumps raise all over my skin.

Oliver delivers on his promise while I'm in the upstairs bathroom. I can hear his footsteps as he drops my stuff into the blue room, then again as he retreats downstairs. That night, I never go back downstairs.

♪

When I open my eyes the following morning, it takes me a full five minutes to remember where I am.

Brilliant sunlight streams in through the French doors to the left of my bed, bathing the entire room in a glow so bright it's nearly blinding. Squinting through sleep-dusted eyes, I realize that I did not close the thick navy curtains before climbing into bed last night. They hang to the side of the doors that lead to the small Juliet balcony, framing the picturesque view. I can just make out the green canopy of trees and bright-blue sky beyond the metal railing.

Grumbling to myself, I haul my tired body to a sitting position and glance at my phone. It's just after 10:00 a.m., meaning I slept in much later than intended, but I decide then and there to give myself some grace for this. I stayed up super late to finish reading the script, then struggled to fall asleep for what felt like hours.

When my teeth are brushed and my face slightly more awake from a splash of cold water, I run a comb through my unruly hair and change into the first athleisure outfit I find in my suitcase. This is my half-hearted attempt at maintaining some professional boundaries between myself and my new roommate. It would be utterly bizarre to face Oliver in my old pajamas on the first day.

The house is silent on my way downstairs, save for the songbirds chirping in the woods outside. I head straight for the kitchen, where I'm delighted to find a bag of fresh coffee grounds next to a stainless steel machine that looks like it can make any number of caffeinated beverages. It takes me a second, but I figure out how to brew a small pot of coffee, then explore the kitchen while the machine gurgles to life.

In the new light of day, I take in the space with fresh eyes. It occurs to me that everything in the house—from the kitchen appliances to the built-in bookshelves flanking the fireplace—is spotless. There isn't a hint of dust or dirt anywhere that I can see. Even the sheets on my bed were clean last night; everything, including the blankets, smelled freshly laundered. How long did it take Oliver to get this house ready by himself? Was he running around here for hours trying to get an empty house fit for two people?

My questions are answered when I see a

handwritten note affixed to the side of the fridge with a Harvard magnet:

Amelia (cleaning)—207-455-1090
John (gutters/yard)—207-455-8512
Fred (fireplace)—207-577-1466
Pete (piano tuner)—207-901-2294
DO NOT CALL BOB, ONLY PETE

Oh, that it explains it. This house, his family—it comes with an outsourced crew. That is not a life I know.

When I pour myself the first cup of coffee, I hear it—a creaking sound, almost a squeak, coming from somewhere *not* in the kitchen. The rest of the house is so quiet the sound seems abnormally loud. My ears strain to identify it, but short of recognizing that it's got something to do with wood flooring, I come up short. It's not the sound of a house settling; it's too measured, almost rhythmic, in the way the wood whines.

It has to be Oliver doing something,

somewhere in this house. Either that or we have a very specific type of ghost. I'm almost afraid to find Oliver doing some kind of weird morning what have you, but I'm too curious to resist. With my coffee mug clutched carefully in my hand, I tiptoe out of the kitchen, across the expensive-looking rug in the dining room, and down into the den. This room leads to the three-season porch that wraps around the part of the house that faces east. Last night, I didn't bother to look out in the dark, but I can see it clearly now through the French doors. It's a sprawling, ambling sort of outdoor room, airy and open, encased by mesh screens to keep the bugs out.

In which Oliver is currently in a downward-dog position, ass up, fingers and toes spread on a yoga mat, while he stretches his feet.

This is the last thing I expected to see.

Transfixed, I stare at the flexing of his shoulders, courtesy of the blue workout tank top he's wearing. He's facing toward where I hover on the other side of the door, so I have a clear view of the slope of his back. His bottom half is clad in a pair of gray shorts; I can't really see his legs at this angle, but I *can* see the pert globes of a tight, round butt as he lifts and lowers one foot at a time.

Oh no. Oliver Barlowe has a *very* nice body. I should not be noticing this.

He shifts, his body angling forward as he gracefully lowers himself into a push-up position. When Amanda first started working as a nurse full-time, she became deeply invested in yoga; it was her preferred form of stress relief. I was often dragged to a class alongside her. I'm familiar enough with the practice to know that he's about to chaturanga his way into up-dog, which means that he'll be facing me.

I should really turn away. It would be very, *very* weird for him to find me staring at him like this.

But my curiosity about this development—about *why* Oliver does yoga and *when* he started and *why* he is so sweaty right now—causes a hesitation just long enough to doom me. He does exactly as I expect; he shifts forward, his spine and shoulders rolling until he's posed like a seal basking in the sun. When his eyes find me hovering in the shadows of the den, he loses focus and drops from the position.

I blush so hard my cheeks could light the whole house on fire.

Scrambling, I turn away from the porch and bust my ass back into the kitchen. I've only taken two sips of my coffee so far but I'm wide awake now, my heart pounding in my chest as I flit around the kitchen like a lost hummingbird. I can hear the doors to the porch open, then the click of the latch as they close. Bracing myself, I position myself at the sink, which overlooks the front yard of the house by way of a big window. I try to focus on the bees buzzing around a leafy bush full of vibrant yellow flowers, but I can't. My thoughts are consumed by how *awkward* I just made our first morning as roommates/colleagues.

Not to mention how good he looked all sprawled out on his green yoga mat.

"Hey."

I whirl around at the sound of his voice. He's standing on the other side of the kitchen island, his chest moving with labored breaths. There's a dusting of pink across his high cheekbones, though I can't tell if it's from yoga-related exertion or my voyeurism. I know, beyond a shadow of a doubt, that my face is still flushed with heat.

"Hey." It comes out higher-pitched than I intended.

For several long seconds, we stare at each other. Oliver keeps his focus on my face, but I'm still grateful that I took the time to change out of my pajamas. A pair of opaque black leggings and a hoodie is better than a holey Juilliard T-shirt and my underwear.

Because I'm an extrovert who can't handle silence, I say, "I didn't take you for a yogi."

"I'm not," he replies. "A professional, I

mean. I've only been practicing for a few years. I usually do it after a workout."

"You worked out?" I blink. "This morning?"

"Yeah, in the gym downstairs. The yoga—I do it after. It's good for my back."

"Your back?" I ask, struggling to process this new knowledge of Oliver's lifestyle.

"I have terrible posture," he says as he rubs a hand along the back of his neck. "Too many years hunched over at a piano."

He did have terrible posture when we were younger. Even when standing, he curled into himself, as if he could somehow make himself smaller if he tried hard enough. Maybe that's why he's so much bigger than I expected—not only does he exercise now, but he ironed out the wrinkles that used to make him look crumpled.

"Oh. Well, I didn't mean to interrupt you." It's my turn to do something with my hands, so I tap my fingers on the coffee mug I'm clutching. "Sorry."

He clears his throat as his hand drops to his side. "I see you found the coffee. I didn't have time to do a full grocery run, but I got the basics. We'll have to go to the market at some point in the next couple of days."

"Yeah. Okay. No problem."

His gaze dips down my body, then darts away to the window behind me. It's fleeting, the way he looks at me, but I don't miss it. I have to stop myself from running away from this awkward exchange. Finally, after a long beat, he drags his eyes back to me with what looks like a concerted effort.

"Do you want to take a look at the studio? I can show you around, if you want." His tone is pleasant. Helpful, even.

I nod, relieved that he's not annoyed that I made this morning so weird. "That'd be great."

He leads me through the den and to the half-wood, half-glass door we only glanced at last night. As soon as he lets me in, a gasp escapes my lips. I clutch my coffee to my chest, right next to my thundering heart. It's *magnificent*.

There's an enormous multiscreen computer against a partition, with a built-in keyboard and desk full of various sound mixers. It faces an internal window that looks out over an honest-to-god sound booth, complete with a small baby grand piano, a drum set, and a handful of microphones that dangle from the ceiling. There's even a glockenspiel and a set of bells tucked away against one wall.

Even the lighting in here is nice, with soft overhead cans that emit a gentle, comfortable glow. The walls are a blond wood, so the space still feels bright despite having no windows. It puts my paltry home studio to shame.

A rush of gratitude overwhelms me for Oliver—for him even having access to this kind of place, and for his insistence we come here. This is better than anything I could have ever secured for us in the city. At the same time, I'm overwhelmed by something else that makes my head spin in a pleasant, dizzying sort of way. It's the salt-and-spice scent of his skin, still a little sweat slicked from his workout.

I shake my head to clear my thoughts and look over at him. He's standing next to me, hands on his hips, as he surveys the computer setup. He reaches down to push a button, and all four screens come to life.

"So, this is it," he explains. "It'll take a few minutes for this to boot up, but you're welcome to play anything in here."

"Thank you." The sincerity in my voice must catch his attention. He looks back at me with furrowed brows, so I add, "Seriously. Thank you. This is amazing."

"It's—well, yeah." His face softens, almost like he's relieved. "You're welcome."

I smile as he stumbles over his words. All these years later and he still doesn't know how to take a compliment or a bit of gratitude. But unlike before, I find it more endearing than annoying.

"So how's this work?" I ask. "Should we take turns in here, or sit down together, or...?"

He blinks rapidly, as if caught off guard by my questions. My own uncertainty multiplies as he drags a hand over his face and then through his hair. His jaw muscle tenses when he folds his arms across his chest. My own spine stiffens in response.

I thought these were normal—if not slightly forward—questions to ask of a creative partner. We have to figure out how to compose together, right? Is the thought of working alongside me so terrible that he's clenching his teeth? If so, then why did he ask me to stay here with him?

All of a sudden, I'm eighteen years old again, already self-conscious as an outsider at Juilliard, feeling the sting of Oliver's rejection when I invited him to join our study group. His reaction had been so similar then—an icy kind of shock, followed by him literally fleeing from me in a hallway, as if I wasn't worth the words. That was worse than any verbal "no thanks."

Slowly, Oliver shakes his head and directs

his gaze to the door behind me. "I should shower," he says quietly. "And organize my notes on the script."

I swallow hard and force myself to return to the present. "Okay. Well, you know where to find me."

Two hours later, Oliver comes back downstairs dressed in a pale-yellow linen button-down and jeans, smelling of classic soap as we pass each other in the hall. He heads into the studio as I scrounge up a brunch made of buttered toast. When I'm done eating, the door to the studio is closed. All I can see through the glass panes of the door is the curve of Oliver's spine as he hunches over the computer desk. I can't bring myself to go inside and join him.

SPRING CONCERT

Juilliard
Wednesday, April 29, at 6:00 p.m.
The Juilliard Orchestra—All Levels

Berlioz	*Roman Carnival Overture*
Shostakovich	Symphony No. 9
Stravinsky	Suite from *The Firebird*

Featuring Oliver Barlowe on piano

This concert is performed in partial fulfillment of the requirements for the Bachelor of Music degree.

Chapter Eleven

TWELVE YEARS AGO

BY THE TIME the concert is over, I'm sticky with old sweat. My black dress clings to my skin as I set my mallets on the marimba and start gathering up my sheet music. The stage lights are hot, and there's no doubt in my mind that my curly hair now consists primarily of frizz. The audience's applause flowing over the stage makes it all worth it—even if it's just our families and friends.

Disheveled appearance aside, the night couldn't have gone better. It was my first performance with the Juilliard orchestra after playing with the Lab all year, which is where most first years get their bearings. Myself and two other percussionists—a junior named Aaron and a senior named Bo—ran the pit. After rehearsing all semester, we played beautifully together, weaving around each other through pieces by Berlioz, Shostakovich, and Stravinsky. The last one is my favorite.

Aaron, Bo, and I congratulate each other on a job well done and set to work packing up our instruments. The other students start filtering off the stage to retrieve their cases. I'm eager to get everything wrapped up and find my family. It's the first time they've ever seen me play with the Juilliard orchestra, since my holiday concerts were a much smaller group, and I can't wait to talk to them about it.

Some thirty minutes later, I'm inching through the throngs of people in the halls outside of the Sharp Theater. I get pulled in different directions by my friends—*Celia, come meet my mom!* and *Oh, Celia, this is my big brother I was telling you about!*—coming from every which way. I smile and wave and shake hands and give hugs to people I've heard about all year. The entire time, I scan the crowd for the four faces I really want to see.

Finally, I spill out of the masses and into the main lobby of the building. Standing off to the side near the glass walls that overlook the exterior grounds are my dad, mom, and both sisters. I head straight for them but get hijacked by Anthony and his parents, who pepper me with polite questions about how I found myself at Juilliard.

I manage to extract myself after a few minutes and turn to see my family waving at me. They're dressed in what my mom always called church clothes, even though we aren't religious outside of the major holidays. Their nice shirts and pants are ironed. My mom has her dark hair swept back in an elegant twist. Every single one of them is beaming.

"Hija!" Dad exclaims as I rush over to them. "That was *magnificent*."

My mom smooths my hair and cups my cheeks before I swat her hands away. "Madre, please," I whisper, too proud to let my friends see me being doted on.

"Sorry," she replies. "I'm just so proud."

"Honestly, that was cool as hell," Rosa says, hands on her hips.

"*Language*," my dad cautions with flattened brows.

Amanda bumps her shoulder against mine. "Yeah, I knew you were good, Celia, but not, like, *that* good. That was next level."

"Thanks." I'm smiling so hard my cheeks are starting to hurt. "Kind of amazing that everyone up there is still a student, right?"

My dad shakes his head. "Barely even adults and you're all up there sounding like pros."

"Are you sure that guy on the piano is a student?" Rosa asks. "He was really going for it out there."

Amanda nods. "Way better than anyone else I've ever seen play at any of the thousand concerts we've been to." My mom tuts, so Amanda adds, "Sorry. Your students are good, but you saw him up there. That was, like, something else."

Out of the corner of my eye, a figure hovers in my periphery. I turn slightly to see Oliver standing by himself. His eyes are on the crowds still milling around in the halls. He must be waiting for someone.

"Yeah, actually. That piano player is right there," I reply, then lower my voice to a whisper, forcing my family to lean in so they can hear me. "His dad is, like, famous in our world. Some people say he got the solo tonight because of that, but... I don't know. You saw him play."

"Famous?" Rosa asks with both eyebrows raised. "Would I know who he is?"

"No," Amanda answers for me, and I can't help but snort. We both know that Rosa's knowledge is more *general pop culture* and less *niche classical music world*.

"Is he a friend of yours?" my mom asks as her eyes slide to the boy in question.

"No," I scoff. "He's not anyone's friend, really."

"Hija," my mom chides, and I already know what's coming based on her scolding tone. "Don't be so rude. That's your classmate. You should introduce us. Be nice to him."

I want nothing more than to argue with her, to tell her that Oliver is a snob who thinks he's better than the rest of us, but I know from the way she has her hands on her hips that there's no point in trying. If I don't call him over, she'll march right over to him on her own. María García has been an elementary teacher my entire life; no one is going to be excluded or forgotten, not on her watch.

With a heavy sigh, I turn and call out, "Hey, Oliver!"

His attention snaps to me. I wave at him to tell him to come over here. His eyes go wide, like he's a deer in the headlights. I wave again, this time with a little more passion. Slowly he starts to make his way over to where I'm standing with the rest of the Garcías. He stops just outside of the semicircle my family formed and gives me a quizzical look.

"Oliver, this is my family," I say as brightly as I can, extending my hands out toward the people who look just like me. "My dad, José, my mom, María, and my sisters, Amanda and Rosa. Everyone, this is Oliver. He played the piano tonight."

"Nice to meet you," my mom says as she smiles at him.

"Great job up there," my dad adds.

"Yeah, you were great." This from Amanda.

"Are you really only in Celia's grade?" Rosa asks. "Like, you're eighteen or nineteen or whatever?"

Oliver says nothing. He just stands there in his all-black suit, blinks several times, and swallows hard enough that I can see his throat work. An uncomfortable, tense quiet settles over our group while everyone waits for him to respond. I knew this wasn't going to go well.

I have no choice but to break the silence

myself. "Yeah, Oliver is in my year. It's the first time they've ever had a freshman pianist play the *Firebird* at the end-of-year performance."

My dad nods encouragingly at Oliver as he says, "Well, it's obvious why. You've got a real talent."

Oliver looks at all of us, one at a time, his brown eyes closed off and cold. Finally, he mumbles something that might be a "thank you" or something else, but I can't tell. With that, he darts away from me, from my family, and disappears out the exterior doors and into the gathering night. Humiliated, I stare after him for several long, stunned seconds.

Oliver really is *that* rude.

My cheeks heat as I turn to look at the confused faces of my family. Next to me, Rosa giggles, which causes Amanda to laugh, which then forces my mom to pinch both their arms with a frown on her face. Reckoning with the sting of another Oliver dismissal—of my whole family this time—is something I never want to experience again.

"I tried to warn you," I mutter finally.

My dad shrugs. "Can't win them all. What do you say we go get some food, huh?"

All four women give a resounding yes. Together, the five of us step out onto the streets of New York City and wander down the block. We eat, laugh, and talk at an Italian restaurant until they kick us out some four hours later. That night, my dad coins the term Professor Pendejo.

FROM: Chris Ross <cr@eyeproductions.com>
TO: Celia Garcia <celia@celiagarcia.com>, Oliver Barlowe <oliverb@gmail.com>
DATE: Sunday, August 23 at 2:12 AM
SUBJECT: music?

got anything for me to chew on? a theme? even just a lick of something?

c

FROM: Oliver Barlowe <oliverb@gmail.com>
TO: Chris Ross <cr@eyeproductons.com>
CC: Celia García <celia@celiagarcia.com>
DATE: Sunday, August 23 at 2:27 AM
SUBJECT: RE: music?

Hi Chris—not yet. Expect something this week.

Oliver

Chapter Twelve

TWO DAYS AND four peanut butter sandwiches later, I break.

I blame a picture that Rosa sent to the family group chat. It's an enormous platter of sashimi from a new place that just opened around the corner from the apartment she shares with Hector. It overwhelms me with homesickness—for my family, yes, but also for the sheer convenience and choices I took for granted in New York. What I wouldn't give for a take-out order of anything other than sandwiches or eggs.

After interrupting Oliver's yoga session, the two of us have been orbiting each other like moons physically unable to get close. The studio is our planet. We take turns sitting in there, the soundproof door to the den firmly shut, as we try to work out some kind of beginning to this score. The learning curve of a setup different than my own has me further behind than I'd like to admit.

It was during one of my solo studio sessions that I noticed the shelves on the wall behind me. In a brainstorming moment, I spun my chair around and browsed the built-ins, noting the variety of books, metronomes, and various odds and ends that fill up the space. On the center of the top shelf was Robert Barlowe's first (of several) Academy Awards.

This does nothing to quell the impostor syndrome that manifests as burning anxiety. Chris's late-night email reignited that fire—we owe him something worthwhile, something *good*, like, yesterday. Problem is that Oliver and I are doing little more than coexisting in this house, let alone working together.

Aside from polite good mornings and "You can have the studio now," Oliver and I don't really speak to each other. In fact, I don't really say anything out loud at all. The family group chat remains in constant rotation, but text threads are different. When Oliver is cloistered away in the studio, the house is practically silent. The soundproofing on that room is remarkable. On more than one occasion, I catch myself tiptoeing on the stairs or in the kitchen, as if my very presence is an affront to the placidity of this place.

Even my outdoor strolls around the property are so different from my walks around New York that I might as well be on a different planet. I've discovered a few short walking paths that weave around the house and yard but haven't been brave enough to take the ones that lead up the hills and into the woods. Out here, there are no honking cars, no one blaring music through open windows, no strangers yelling into megaphones about god knows what. It's just me, the birds, and the bugs—which serve as a deterrent from staying outside for too long.

At the very least, I've finished reading and

digesting the script. The printed pages are filled with in-line notes and tabs that mark dialogue that resonated with me. The visualization of the story is there in my mind, even if I can't seem to get it out of me and onto the keyboard.

But this afternoon, I'm not thinking about music, or Chris's email, or Maine's foreign silence, or any of the characters in *Lineage*. I'm thinking about how hungry I am and how much I don't want to eat another fucking peanut butter sandwich. When I trudge downstairs and head directly for the studio, visions of pasta, steak, and Cheetos dance in my head.

I don't even bother to knock before I wrench open the studio door. "Can we go to the grocery store?"

Oliver's fingers drop from the electronic keyboard that feeds directly into the main computer monitor before he swivels around in the chair to face me. He eyes me over the rim of his glasses, gaze snaking over my body. "Now?"

"Yes. Now. If I see one more peanut butter sandwich, I'll scream." The first installment of my contract payment hit my bank account and I am *hungry*. After many exploratory Google Maps searches, I've learned that the closest store is not within walking distance to the house. I need the car—and by extension, Oliver's driving skills—to get there.

He sighs as he stands, his hands roaming over the front of his khakis to smooth out wrinkles. One thing I've learned about Oliver in the last few days is that he is the type of person to wear khakis unironically. He usually looks like he walked straight out of a J.Crew advertisement, complete with linen button-downs and boat shoes without socks. Here, he's less Professor Pendejo and more classic East Coast WASP.

I, however, am much more casual. It's technically still summer here in Maine, but the days are much cooler than the concrete jungle we left last week. I find myself pulling sweatshirts over my jeans and tank tops or wrapping a cardigan around my sundress frequently. Today, I'm wearing a simple gray T-shirt and old denim cutoff shorts. I'll definitely need a jacket once the sun sets.

When we're back in the SUV, Oliver deftly navigating us out of the attached garage, guilt starts to simmer in my chest. I was short with him today, essentially demanding that he take me grocery shopping. After all he's done to get us this far (not to mention, having access to the house to begin with), he didn't deserve my impatient outburst.

"I'm sorry for snapping at you earlier," I say as I adjust the sunglasses on my face. "I'm just in the red, and I'm not known for being calm when I get to this point."

"In the red?"

Oh, right—he has no idea what I'm talking about. "It's a system my sisters and I made up based on hunger levels. If you're in the green, you're good. If you're in the yellow, you need to get some food in you in the next thirty to forty-five minutes. One hour, tops. If you're in the red, shit starts getting dangerous. It helps us avoid unnecessary fights."

The corner of his mouth tugs up. "And you're in the red now."

"Yes. Not your fault, though, so I'm sorry."

"Apology accepted."

I fall silent as he drives us down the main road into town. This is the first time I'm actually seeing Boothbay Harbor proper; every day since our arrival has been spent at the house, which is surrounded by dense woods, allowing for ample privacy. Now, I'm finally seeing the charm of an East Coast fishing town. It's undeniably cute, with its sloping lawns and white houses with blue shutters that dot the highway along the water.

It gets even more adorable the farther we drive into town. The homes give way to businesses, of which there are many—everything from multicolored shanties advertising a local fish fry to art galleries make up the main drag. It's still tourist season here, so there are plenty of people meandering on the sidewalks in the abundant sunshine. When I roll down the window, I find the air is tinged with the smell of salty ocean and fish, far more than it is at the house.

Oliver pulls into the parking lot of a local grocery store and cuts the engine. "I'll get this round of groceries," I tell him before hopping out of the car and shutting the door. "It's the least I can do."

I'm pleasantly surprised to find he doesn't argue with me. He just shrugs and continues toward the entrance to the store. There's a bit of an imbalance between us here, one that I'm determined to rectify as much as I can. I'm living in his family's house rent free, using the technology and instruments purchased by his father's success, and the man has no choice but to drive me around. My financial woes may not be solved forever, but the least I can do is pay for groceries and gas.

When I pull a green shopping cart from the stall inside the store, I hesitate, wondering if I should go it alone and find him at the register. This is one of those gray areas we struggle to navigate—we're roommates, yes, but we're also colleagues, not to mention our uncomfortable history. I'm no stranger to coexisting with roommates, but with Oliver, it's different. He's so quiet and reserved, unlike most of the people I've shared a home with. Does he like to shop alone? Does he want some space? Do I?

Damn. I knew this was going to be hard.

He's wandered a few feet ahead of me at this point, but he glances back to where I stand near the entrance, white-knuckling the shopping cart. His brows knit together as he stares at me. "You okay?"

I take this as a sign that he wants to shop together, so I push the cart toward him. "Yeah. I'm good."

And so, we shop together, wandering through the tightly packed aisles, collecting an assortment of groceries as we go. Every item Oliver deposits into the cart unveils a new layer of his psyche; I never would have guessed he eats pre-popped popcorn or that he prefers Double Stuf Oreos like me. He likes the expensive jelly with the French name. We both prefer sourdough bread and Honeycrisp apples.

When he deposits a package of Haribo gummy bears in the cart, I can't help but comment on it. "I didn't know you had a sweet tooth."

His eyes slide to me, then to the gummy bears, then back to me again. "We all have our vices," he replies with a small shrug.

I offer him a smile, which he only half returns before he turns around and continues down the aisle. There is a strange sort of comfort in knowing that Oliver has a weakness. Even if it's something as tame as sugar.

Though this grocery store is small, it's decently stocked, except for the one small section labeled "ethnic foods." To Boothbay Harbor, ethnic means big-brand mild salsa, ramen noodles, soy sauce, tortillas, and British tea bags. With a sigh of resignation, I grab a few items that I can use to make some iteration of comfort food before steering the cart toward the deli counter.

When we get to the liquor section, I'm pleasantly surprised to see him load not one, not two, but three bottles of wine into the cart. I add another for good measure, and then we head to the cash register.

It's not until we're back in the SUV, the trunk full of groceries and my bank account with a considerable dent in it, that I dive into the trail mix I just bought, my mood considerably lighter than when we left the house. It's this good mood that ignites an idea in me, so I turn toward him, watching his sharp profile as he turns back onto the main drag.

"I have an idea," I say, my tone light now that there's a promise of food variety in my life. "I'll make dinner tonight. How's baked trout sound? I can use some of that fresh dill we just bought."

The change in his expression is almost imperceptible, but I catch it—the way his mouth flattens and his jaw tenses. "I can't."

"What?" I ask, not bothering to hide my stunned expression. "Why not?"

"I don't like seafood."

"Wait—what? Like, you don't eat any fish? Not even shrimp?"

His frown deepens. "I'm allergic to shellfish, so I guess I just never developed a taste for any of it."

I don't know whether to laugh or scream. Considering I just spent a lot of money on a variety of fresh, locally caught fish, I'm inclined to do the latter. He said nothing as I loaded up in the meat-and-seafood department. He said nothing when I paid for enough fresh fish to feed a family of four for several nights. Didn't even think to mention it, even though we're currently residing in a fucking fishing town.

I force my voice to be calm as I ask, "Why

didn't you say anything when I bought all that stuff?"

He's quiet for so long that I wonder if he's just going to ignore my question entirely. I shove a handful of trail mix into my mouth and fix my eyes on the world outside my window, seeing nothing as we cruise down the road. Fine—this is fine. We can barely talk to each other about what to eat, and somehow, we're supposed to work closely together and turn something in to Chris this week? Great. Just great.

"I didn't think it mattered," he finally says, quietly, almost like he's embarrassed.

I turn to gape at him. "Why wouldn't it matter?"

"Never mind," he mumbles. "Forget I said anything."

I want to argue with him. I want to press him on why he won't answer, or actually, I want to ask him why he barely talks to me at all except for that one time we texted all weekend. I've seen him hold lengthy conversations. He was so good in that room with Chris, John, and Damian. He is a functional, capable adult—I know this because I've *seen* it.

I also know that I'm still in the red, and that this snack is barely tiding me over until I can sit down and eat a proper meal. If I open my mouth right now, I'm going to say something I'll regret later. Instead, I just sigh and start to pick through trail mix in search of chocolate.

At least we bought wine. We're going to need that.

SECOND CHANCE DUET ♪ 205

**FROM: Dr. David Kendrick
<david.kendrick@Juilliard.edu>
TO: <Twentieth-Century
Composition Course Listserv>
DATE: Monday, August 25 at 8:16 AM
SUBJECT: Welcome back**

Hello students,

I hope you all enjoyed your break. It was a pleasure to see so many of you at our summer concert series. The talent in this group is immense.

I like to think of your sophomore year as the true start of your composition coursework. In this class, you'll be challenged to think about music in ways you never have before. I have no doubt in your abilities and look forward to seeing you rise to the occasion, as all Juilliard students do.

My office hours this semester are Tuesdays and Thursdays from 3-5 p.m. Feel free to come by any time during these periods if you have questions.

If you'd like to get a head start, please visit the Lila Acheson Wallace Library and start at our collection of Iannis Xenakis's works.

Best,

Dr. Kendrick

Chapter Thirteen

TWELVE YEARS AGO

I FEEL LIKE I'M going to cry.
Dr. Kendrick surveys us from where he stands near the whiteboard, his blue eyes bright with a kindhearted mischief. This must be entertaining for him, watching all of us stare at him in various stages of confusion, or in my case, distress. We're barely a few weeks into the first semester of my cohort's sophomore year and his Twentieth-Century Theory and Composition class is already starting to break me. Whatever he just talked about for the last hour made no sense.

The stuff he wrote on the board, the examples he passed around? Fucking forget it. It doesn't even look like music. It looks more like the blueprint of a building than anything else, which I guess is the whole point considering the topic, but it doesn't help me understand it.

"What questions can I answer for you?" Dr. Kendrick asks. The whole class looks at him. The silence is deafening. "Right, so I know this is entirely new for most of you, which is why I'm pairing you up to complete this next assignment. Over the next four weeks, I want you to compose a piece of music for two instruments, using the twelve-tone matrix we just discussed."

I choke back tears. Next to me, Rebecca inhales a small gasp.

Dr. Kendrick paces at the front of the room with his hands behind his back. "Let's see— Rebecca, you work with Anthony. Blake, you're with Chloe. Nick and Siobhan..." As he adjusts his tie and continues pairing off members of our class, I prepare myself for what I know is about to come. There are not that many people in this class. Somehow, I already know who my partner is going to be before Dr. Kendrick even has a chance to finish with "Celia, you're with Oliver."

I wrench my gaze from my notebook filled with desperate scrawling to look at Oliver. He's across the room from me, looking uncharacteristically disheveled from how I remember him last year. He's not in a full suit this time; he's wearing a plain white sweater that looks especially soft with a pair of dark denim jeans. His hair is still a mess, but I can't blame him for that. I've also been running my hands through my hair in frustration all day.

We hold each other's gaze while Dr. Kendrick lays out the specifics for the assignment and when it's due. I hear the key bits—one month, two instruments of our choosing, look to Arnold Schoenberg for examples—but mostly I wonder what Oliver sees in me in that moment. Can he see how stressed and tired I am? Does he see the same dark circles that I do when I look in the mirror? Does it register that I'm one minor inconvenience away from having a total breakdown? It's impossible to say for sure with that cold expression on his face.

It takes me right back to the last time we spoke to each other—the end-of-year concert, when he was so rude to my family. I'd hoped I could make it through this school year with minimal Oliver time, but it seems I'm not that lucky. The stress of it all—the intensity of my academic workload, the fact that I have to work closely with him for the next few weeks on my weakest subject yet—causes tears to rise to the surface as I pack up my things. Swallowing hard, I force them down. I do not have time to cry right now.

I find Oliver waiting for me in the hall after class. In that moment, I decide to treat this like I'm ripping off a Band-Aid. I march right up to him and steel my spine.

"Hey, so," I start by way of greeting, "I feel like we should get started on this soon. I don't think this will be an easy assignment."

"Nothing is this year," he mutters, to my

surprise. I had no idea he felt the same way about our classes. He adds, "I have a piano session tonight until six, but I could meet you after."

"Sure. I'll be in Rebecca's dorm for the study group."

He blinks. "Oh."

The same study group that I invited him to join last year, which he declined by icing me out entirely. I wasn't worth the words then. Seems like I'm still not worth it now.

"So, yeah, that's where I'll be," I reply coolly. "You want to just come by there when you're done with piano?"

For a second, something in his face changes. He goes from the usual aloof expression to something else, something much more open. It's in his eyes—a softness, almost a sadness, that's distinct and unusual for him. It startles me enough that my heart skips a beat.

But then his expression shutters as he matches my indifference. "Right. I'll come to Rebecca's dorm when my lesson is over."

Then he turns on his heel and leaves me standing there, even more confused than I was a few minutes ago. That's saying something, considering I nearly cried in frustration in class. But I have no idea what just happened. Was Oliver Barlowe almost... *vulnerable* with me?

I shake my head to clear my thoughts. I don't have time for this. My stupid professional writing class starts in ten minutes.

♪

Rebecca, Anthony, Blake, Chloe, and I are all bordering on delirious. We're jammed into Rebecca's single-suite dorm; I've taken up residence on the floor next to Anthony and Chloe, while Rebecca and Blake sit cross-legged on the bed. There are open bags of Cheetos, Takis, and some kind of weird chickpea chips that Chloe brought strewn around the room. I think each of us has consumed at least two high-caffeine sodas over the last couple of hours.

A haunting, melodic chant in Latin emits from the CD player on Rebecca's desk. Next to it is a big stack of CDs, all borrowed from the library. We've been rotating different ones, testing each other and ourselves to name the piece, the major work, composer, and historical era.

I look at the notebook next to me. For this one, all I wrote down was *??????*

Anthony hauls himself up from the floor and hits pause on the player. The immediate silence feels strange. We've spent the last two hours submerged in music of times long since passed, and now I'm having trouble comprehending the fact that we are in New York City and that things like Cheetos even exist.

"I don't think I can do any more," Anthony complains as he rubs his eyes. "All this shit sounds the same now."

"Yeah, I think we maxed ourselves out," Rebecca replies with a groan. "If I hear *Iesus Christus* one more time I might lose it."

"Did anyone get that last one?" I ask.

"I think it was Hildegard von Bingen. Her *In Evangelium*," Chloe replies.

"Oh god, duh." I stretch out my legs and let them fall across Anthony's lap now that he's sitting with his back against Rebecca's bed.

There's a soft knock at the door, to which Rebecca yells, "Come in!"

Oliver appears in the open doorway. He looks like he did earlier in class—messy hair and all—except his sweater sleeves are pushed up past his elbows. His eyes go straight to where I'm half draped across Anthony.

"Are you ready to go?" Oliver asks of me.

"Hello to you, too," Rebecca chides.

His gaze flicks to her, then to everyone else in the room as I pull myself up to stand. "Sorry. Hey."

Blake snorts. "Were you in your studio lesson just now?"

"Yeah."

"How is it?" Chloe asks as she peers up at him and fiddles with her blond braid. "Being a double major, I mean."

"It's fine." Oliver sighs. "Hard, I guess."

"How'd you convince them to let you do it?" Anthony asks.

Out of the corner of my eye, I can see Oliver fidget impatiently while I pull on my shoes and collect my stuff. Selfishly, I take some comfort in seeing that Oliver is kind of an asshole with everyone. It's not just me.

"I applied and asked like anyone else would," Oliver replies flatly.

Anthony mutters a sarcastic "sure" under his breath. I look up just in time to see Oliver scowl; it seems he did not miss Anthony's implication that he gets special treatment. An awkward tension settles over the room, so I basically push Oliver out the door while calling out my goodbyes to the rest of the group.

"Where to?" I ask once we're safe in the hall. "My dorm is just down that way—"

"Actually, I have an idea," Oliver says, effectively cutting me off. He walks so fast I'm basically jogging to keep up with him. "Let's make a quick pit stop at Shakespeare & Co."

This is not what I expected him to say. I stop walking in surprise, my voice incredulous as I ask, "The bookstore?"

He stops, then turns to look at me, eyes bright. "Yes. Trust me."

I don't—but I go with him anyway.

♪

Half an hour later, Oliver dumps a bag of booklets onto the desk in his dorm. Like Rebecca, he has a single suite, but on another floor. Unlike Rebecca, his room is sparsely decorated. There's nothing on the walls, no posters or pictures taped up like the room I just left. It almost looks like a prison cell.

"Where did you get this idea?" I ask as I eye the space with caution.

"My piano instructor," Oliver replies. "I was telling him about the serialism assignment, and he said we could practice sudoku puzzles to help us understand the matrix process. That's what he did when he was in his undergrad."

That's the errand we just got back from—a quick trip to the bookstore down the street, where we bought six different sudoku puzzle books. It was weird seeing Oliver outside the halls of the school. Like my brain couldn't comprehend the fact that he could exist anywhere else—but there he was, striding down Broadway, head held high as we walked side by side in silence.

"My titi does these." I pick up a booklet and lean against the desk. "She's, like, really good at them."

Oliver only nods as he arranges his notes and textbook on the desk. When everything is set up, he cracks open a sudoku booklet and leans over to study it. I notice how big his hands are then, how long his fingers look spread out across the papers. No wonder he's so good at piano.

"This makes sense to me," he says after a long beat. He looks up at me then, eyes bright and a hint of a smile on his face, and I'm acutely aware of how close we are. "What do you say, Celia? Shall we try it?"

I've never heard him say my name before. It sounds beautiful coming out of his mouth, the way he took the extra care to say it correctly. I feel myself smiling back at him without even thinking about it.

"Let's do some damn puzzles, Oliver."

I may be a proud person, but I'm not too proud to admit that Oliver's suggestion helps me more than I ever expected. Four weeks later, we turn in a piece for piano and violin using a twelve-tone matrix. We receive full marks on the assignment.

SECOND CHANCE DUET ♪ 219

FAMILIA GROUP CHAT

Today **6:01** PM

Madre   *6:01 PM*

Hija it looks like there's a storm coming your way. Are you safe at the house?

Rosa   *6:13 PM*

omg you guys it's literally just going to rain

Padre   *6:16 PM*

Rosa por favor be quiet. Celia listen to your mother

Amanda   *6:44 PM*

it's already starting to rain in the city

> **Madre**   *7:00 PM*
>
> I know. Celia do you have supplies

> **Rosa**   *7:10 PM*
>
> what kind of supplies does she need for rain? she works inside all day

> **Padre**   *7:16 PM*
>
> Flashlights in case the power goes out

> **Rosa**   *7:17 PM*
>
> we have those on our phones

> *7:18 PM*
>
> mom can never figure out how to turn hers off

> **Amanda**   7:19 PM
>
> lmao

> **Madre**   7:25 PM
>
> Celia please answer us when you can. Love you hija

Chapter Fourteen

IN THE BLINK of an eye, I'm submerged into complete darkness. My hands freeze over the piano keys. For a second, I wonder if I just had some kind of stroke.

The fact that I'm even asking myself this question registers as a good sign, even if I'm completely blind. I've never experienced this kind of darkness before, where there isn't a single speck of light to guide me—no peek of streetlights from the other side of the curtains, no soft glow from the clock on my stove back at my apartment. With clumsy fingers, I grope my way along the top of the piano, where I left my phone facedown so I could concentrate. It lights up as soon as I flip it over. There are forty-two unread messages, plus an alert from the National Weather Service: *COASTAL STORM THREATENS NORTHEASTERN SEABOARD; HEAVY RAIN AND WINDS EXPECTED; TAKE COVER INDOORS.*

Well, that explains it. After cooking dinner for myself—yes, baked fish with rice, just for me—I locked myself away in the studio. I put my phone on Do Not Disturb so I could concentrate as I tried to write something interesting and moving enough to present to Chris this week. I guess this room really is soundproof; I haven't heard any signs of a big storm for the last two hours.

As I'm typing back a quick text to let my family know I'm okay, my phone warns me about my low battery. Three percent, to be exact. I sigh and pull myself up from the bench, then promptly whack my knee on the wooden leg of the piano. That'll leave a nasty bruise for sure.

With my phone's flashlight on full blast, I make my way out of the studio to find the rest of the house is just as dark. In the den, I can hear the rain pelting the exterior of the house and the wind howling like some kind of demonic dog. It's creepy enough that the hair on the back of my neck raises.

"Oliver?" I call out tentatively.

"Over here."

The glow of another phone flashlight appears as he rounds the corner from the living room and enters the kitchen. I can't see him, just the bluish orb of his phone as we make our way toward each other. I stub my toe on one of those big wingback chairs and mutter a stream of obscenities. I may not survive this night.

"You okay?" he asks as I bend down to survey the damage.

"I'm fine," I huff. "Do you have any real flashlights here? My phone is about to die."

When I look up, he's much closer than I expected him to be. He's hunched over on the floor with me, his long fingers splayed out against the rug next to my foot. Almost, but not quite, touching me.

"In the basement," he replies. "Stay up here, I'll be right back."

I'm certainly not going down into a pitch-black basement, so I cautiously pick my way over to the dining room. Just as I set my phone on the table, it dies completely. I find myself in complete darkness once again.

Oliver reappears a few minutes later, a real flashlight in one hand and a small black bag in the other. Now I can see he's changed out of his J.Crew outfit of the day and into something more comfortable; he's wearing a matching blue sweat set that looks so soft and cozy I almost want to reach out and touch it. It's nice to see him a little less put together than usual. It makes him feel a tiny bit more human.

"Candles, flashlights, matches, and batteries," Oliver says as he starts unloading the bag on the table. "Although I have no idea if the batteries are good anymore. They've probably been down there for ten years."

I pick up a big glass votive candle. "Wow, this isn't your first storm here, is it?"

"No. They happen somewhat frequently."

Together we light a few of the big candles and set them around the dining room table and kitchen counters. The flickering lights, combined with the storm that continues to assault the house with all it's got, makes me feel strange, like we're not on this planet anymore. Certainly not present-day, at least.

I look at my phone, dead on the table. "Well, now what?"

He looks around the room and shrugs. "We wait out the storm, I guess. Do you want some wine?"

Even though his question sounded cautious, I find myself smiling and nodding. "Now you're talking."

When Oliver pours for both of us, I realize that this isn't the first one for him—the bottle was open on the counter, his glass next to it, along with a book with a postcard shoved inside of it. As he hands me a glass of pinot noir, I ask, "What are you reading?"

"Oh." It's hard to tell for sure in the dim

light, but I could swear he blushes. "Just a memoir."

I take a sip and slide into a chair. "Do you read a lot?"

"Sometimes. Depends on how busy I am." He takes a seat opposite me. "You?"

"Not really." I scoff. "I'm more of a reality TV girl, but every now and then my sister will lend me something she really loved and I'll read that."

"You have two sisters, right? Both younger?"

I blink, surprised that he remembers this. "Yeah. Rosa and Amanda."

"They look so much like you," he replies absently, and I find myself curious about just how much wine he had before the power went out. We've never acknowledged that he's met my family—not even once in the years we spent working alongside each other in college. His eyes wander to the sea of darkness behind me, and I wonder if he's thinking about that night, too. How uncomfortable it was, how he snubbed us and ran off. Then his eyes slide to me as he says, "I'm sorry, by the way. About how rude I was when I met them. I didn't mean to be but I—well, I think I was nervous. But I never forgot that."

"Wow." The word slips out of me because I am genuinely shocked—that he remembers this, and that he's apologizing for it. I take a big gulp of wine to buy myself some time before adding, "Well, yeah. It was super awkward. But it's fine. Water under the bridge or whatever."

As soon as I say it, I realize that I mean it. I don't know if he's being honest about being nervous, but I do know that I don't want to hold this against him. Yes, Oliver seemed like a real snob that night of the recital, but what eighteen-year-old isn't an idiot in some capacity? There's a myriad of ways that Oliver and I didn't see eye to eye in undergrad, but I can let go of this one.

He smiles at me in a way that I've never seen before. It's a slow and gentle thing that takes its time. When it reaches his eyes, they sparkle in the candlelight. He's not wearing his glasses, so there's nothing between us, nothing at all, as we hold each other's gaze, me with a curious smirk and him with that soft curve of his lips.

That look does something to me that I do not want to think too hard about. I shiver. Take another drink of my wine. Then another.

"Water under the bridge," he echoes. "Thank you."

"Yep, sure," I blurt out, too fast to be casual but whatever; I blame the wine. "What about you? Any siblings?"

"No, only child. Isn't that obvious?" he asks, and the light sarcasm in his voice makes me laugh.

"Yeah, actually, it is. I've never met someone so solitary and quiet in my life."

"You get used to being on your own." He pauses to take a sip from his glass. "Though I do like your company, Celia."

It's my turn to blush. "Yeah?"

"Yeah," he replies, and something in his

eyes changes, but I can't put my finger on what it is exactly.

"Well, you're not so bad yourself."

In this moment, with the wine and the storm and the candlelight, it's true. This version of Oliver is different; he's not the talkative type that I know from having grown up with two little sisters who never once shut up in their lives, but he is open and curious. Nice, even.

"What were you working on just now? Before the power went out?" he asks.

I sigh and run my hands through my hair. "I have an idea for a theme for one of the characters. It's not quite there yet, though. I need a little more time to develop it."

"Will you play it for me?" he asks with an eagerness I've never heard before. "Tomorrow? Whenever the power comes back?"

I nod. To hear him so genuinely interested sends a trickle of warmth down my spine. I watch as he finishes his wine, then retrieves the bottle and pours us both another glass. In that moment, I realize two things about Oliver that fundamentally change the way I look at him.

First, he's not a snob. Not anymore, at least. Sometime in the last nine years, he's become almost friendly, but he is *shy*—to the point that he doesn't speak up for himself, which explains the shellfish miscommunication.

Second, it's not that he prefers to work alone, or is incapable of working with a partner, or doesn't know how to share—whatever reasoning I had built up in my head about why we're struggling to work together. It's that Oliver is so used to being on his own that he needs someone to extend a hand to him. He needs to be *invited*.

Tonight, the wine brought that particular wall of his down. It also opened my eyes so I could see him in a new light.

"Let's do it now." My heart races as soon as the words leave my lips. If he rejects me again, tells me no...

"Now?" he asks with wide eyes. Outside,

the wind howls hard enough that tree branches beat the walls of the house. There's a lump in my throat as I wait for him to say anything other than *no*. He takes a deep breath before adding, "Why the hell not? Grab a candle. Let's go."

The pressure in my throat dissolves when we both grab a candle and our wineglasses. My heart, however, continues to beat rapidly, even as Oliver slowly leads us through the darkness of the house and into the studio. I manage not to hit any body parts on the furniture.

As soon as the soundproof studio door closes, we're enveloped in a soft silence. There's no storm in here, nothing other than the two of us, the pinot noir, and flickering candlelight. We set everything on top of the piano before settling onto the bench. It's not quite big enough for two fully grown adults, so I can feel the heat of his body pressing against mine as we sit side by side.

My stomach does a funny kind of swoop

when I shift on the bench. At the same time, Oliver clears his throat.

"Show me what you've got so far," he says, his voice even lower and quieter than usual.

I place my hands on the keys in front of me. It takes me a second to gather my wits, thanks to the wine and the absolute rager going on inside of my chest. For reasons I can't explain, I'm nervous—more nervous than I've ever been in my life.

But when my fingers play the small lick of a melody I've written, they're steady. Because this? This I know how to do. Making music, writing it, playing it—it's my outlet. It's never once failed me.

When I stop playing, Oliver places one of his hands at the lower octaves of the piano. "That was C minor, right? Play it again, but slower." I do as he asks, slowing my tempo, while he works out chords with his right hand. When the musical phrase comes to a close, we do it again without prompting.

It sounds good—really good, but it's missing something. "Let me add some dissonance here," I suggest. "Again."

We play it again, this time a little different, but also a little more certain. It's strong enough that I'm able to focus on the music instead of the feeling of his arm brushing against mine. Over and over again, we play the same four bars of music, until something cohesive starts to form while Oliver makes subtle changes to the chords he plays with his hand.

"This is good," he says after the seventh or eighth pass. "We should record this on my phone before we forget it."

I know what he means; two glasses of wine have made the edges of my brain a little fuzzy. When he stands abruptly, our bubble bursts, a gust of cool air rushing around me when his warmth leaves my side. I stare at where my hands sit on the ivory keys as he steps out of the sound booth with one of the candles.

In the quiet, still room, I close my eyes and take a deep breath. For the first time since arriving in Maine, Oliver and I have made real, tangible progress—and it feels so, so good.

FROM: Celia García <celia@celiagarcia.com>
TO: Chris Ross <cr@eyeproductions.com>
CC: Oliver Barlowe <oliverb@gmail.com>
DATE: Friday, August 28 at 10:13 AM
SUBJECT: Lineage music

Hi Chris,

Sending over something that Oliver and I have been working on. It's just piano so far but we plan to orchestrate more. Let us know your thoughts when you can.

Cheers,

Celia

FROM: Chris Ross <cr@eyeproductions.com>
TO: Celia García <celia@celiagarcia.com>

SECOND CHANCE DUET ♪ 237

CC: Oliver Barlowe
<oliverb@gmail.com>
DATE: Friday, August 28 at 6:48 PM
SUBJECT: RE: Lineage music

i like this. lots of color in here. would like to hear it with strings

c

Chapter Fifteen

SOMETHING IN THE house changes.

The power comes back on, yes, so the next morning I wake up in my room with all the lights on. When I come downstairs, I find that Oliver has already been up for a while, as evidenced by the overwhelming scents of sugar and cinnamon that greet me as soon as I hit the first floor. He's fully dressed in jeans and a teal linen button-down, a dish towel draped over his shoulder as he flits around the kitchen; I'm wearing a pair of comfortable sweat shorts and a tank top.

"What is that incredible smell?" I ask in awe.

"Cinnamon rolls," he says simply.

"Did we buy some at the store?" I ask,

though I already know the answer—we didn't. I spent a good five minutes standing in front of the fridge case debating it, but ultimately decided not to because the cart was already overflowing. It's a small luxury I can go without.

He shakes his head as he checks the timer on the stove. His back is to me so I can't see his face as he replies, "No, but we did buy the stuff to make them from scratch. They'll be ready in a couple of minutes."

My jaw drops as my stomach rumbles. "You...made *homemade cinnamon rolls?*"

"Yeah." He turns to face me now, his brows lifted in question as he finally looks at me, like he doesn't understand why I'm struggling to comprehend this.

"Why?" The question comes out breathless. Cinnamon rolls are a pain in the ass to make. I've only ever done it once or twice in my life—which is enough times to know that the effort is rarely worth it, even though they're my favorite. If Oliver made them this morning, that means he's been at it for at least two hours.

As we stare at each other, his cheeks bloom with color.

"I saw you looking at them at the store," he says quietly. "You know I have a sweet tooth, too, so I figured..."

He peters out. The sentence hangs open-ended, like an invitation for me to fill in the blanks. I let out a shocked huff of a laugh and shake my head.

"You figured you'd make them on your own?" My voice is filled with wonder. "That's so...thoughtful. They're my favorite. Thank you."

He smiles just enough that it reaches his eyes, then nods. It's not a full *you're welcome* or *no problem*, but I'm starting to wonder if this is just how Oliver is. Maybe he's the type of person to show what he's thinking or feeling instead of saying it.

His cinnamon rolls are the best I've ever tasted. We eat half the pan that morning.

It's clear something between Oliver and me has changed—a subtle but undeniable shift, like the gravitational force between us switched gears so we're no longer orbiting each other. We can be next to each other now. Close, even.

And we are just that—physically close—in the days following our candlelight piano breakthrough. The email to Chris went out after we finished our delectable breakfast; his response gives us both the boost we needed to keep going. After Oliver and I celebrate this small win with a high five, I make it a point to tell him he's invited to join me in the studio anytime. That same evening, I find myself excited to post up in front of the studio computer and experiment with different sounds.

The door to the studio swings open, but I'm so dropped into what I'm doing that I hardly notice. It's not until I hear a chair dragging over the carpet that I tear my eyes away from the screen. Oliver sets a spare dining room chair next to where I'm seated and plops into it.

His cheeks are already pink when he asks, "Is this okay?"

"Yeah. Of course." The words come out of me in a weird high pitch I've never heard myself use before. I pretend not to notice that our knees are mere inches apart. "I was just playing with what we already wrote. Seeing if I could expand it with orchestration."

"Show me?" he asks tentatively.

Oliver pulls his glasses from the top of his head and sets them on the bridge of his nose. When he does this, he runs his hands through his hair. I smile at the action, all at once reminded of the boy I used to know who did this when he was at the piano; here is the man he became. Sitting right next to me, smelling like fresh soap and a hint of something fine and delicate. If he's wearing cologne, it's got to be expensive.

He catches me looking at him. Our eyes meet and he pulls his lips between his teeth—as if he doesn't know what to do with himself. A tingly sensation blossoms all over my skin.

It takes a lot of effort to turn my attention back to the computer. I drag the mouse back to the start of the phrase I'd been writing. I hit Play, and then sounds of half an orchestra fill the room for about ninety seconds.

My heart accelerates as soon as it finishes. The silence envelops the two of us again. "Well? What do you think?"

"I like it. It feels almost...melancholy," he says thoughtfully. "This is all for the character of Dahlia, isn't it?"

"Yeah."

He raises an eyebrow. "You resonate with her the most?"

"Well, yeah," I reply with a shrug. "She's the outsider who has no idea what she's getting herself into when Harrison brings her to meet the family."

"Don't sell Dahlia short," Oliver says with a smirk. "She catches on to their bullshit pretty quick. She refuses to let them play her."

I nod along as he speaks. My heart continues beating too fast in my chest. What he's saying—that's what I took from the script, too. We *agree* on something.

"Yeah, so I was thinking that it can transition into something more devious as the episodes play out." The words rush out of me so fast I can't contain them. "When we get to see her play the Moores at their own game."

As I talk, Oliver leans closer to listen. I can tell that he's focused on me completely—that *we're* zeroed in on each other, on the task at hand, on the act of creating something together. It's just him and me in the world right now. There is no one else, not even the hundreds of people who are making the same show we're discussing.

When our knees touch, neither of us pull away. Not for hours, until it's finally time to call it a night, well after midnight.

♪

The funny thing about this kind of collaborative work is that somehow, two people end up forming their own schedule. There's no one else here to make plans with, no one to meet at restaurants or coffee shops or even yoga classes that charge you a fee if you cancel. There are no requirements that we start at a certain time or limitations on when to eat certain meals. Breakfast becomes dinner. Lunch becomes handfuls of things from boxes eaten on the floor of the studio. Night is day; up is down. Oliver and I don't care—we're working together, and it's going *well*.

For the most part, that is. He disappears for an hour or two occasionally, but I don't press him on it. There are also stretches where we do little more than tinker away at the piano or shake a tambourine to a nonexistent beat. It's during one of those weird periods that Oliver looks down at me from the piano bench with a curious look on his face. I'm lying on the floor drumming a beat on my legging-clad thigh, but this is normal now.

"I think we need to change things up," he declares with authority.

I sigh. "Yeah. You're right."

"There's a hiking trail just off the back deck. Let's put some shoes on and get some fresh air."

"Hiking?" I haul myself to sit and raise my eyebrows. "I'm not really an outdoorsy gal. I'm what you'd call a city rat."

"Rats live outside."

"Not this one. This rat took up residence in a very nice building and has everything it needs."

He huffs out a half-laugh. "First of all, I'm not going to compare you to a rat. Second, we're not getting anything done right now and it'd be good to get some fresh air. Third, haven't you already been out walking?"

I brush past the initial surprise that he noticed my brief forays outside. "That's different than hiking."

"How so?" he asks, eyes narrowed, lips curled into a half-smile.

"Because it's flat," I reply with a roll of my eyes. "What time is it anyway?" I peer at my phone—it's 2:45 p.m. I have no real reason to fight him on this. "Fine. Let's go."

I'm about to pull myself to stand when Oliver appears directly in front of me, his hand outstretched. I look at it. For all the progress we've made in the last couple of weeks, this moment feels symbolic. Like it's more than just peeling me off the floor because this is the first time Oliver has invited me to do anything since we got here.

When our fingers touch, a jolt of something electric runs through me. He's warm—*so* warm—and his grip is strong. Those pianist fingers are long. Soft, too, except for the scrape of a few calluses.

I can't bring myself to look him in the eye for longer than a millisecond. I don't know what's happening to me and I don't know if I like it.

Once we both have our shoes on and sunglasses in hand, I meet him at the back door. He leads me outside in the breezy, cool afternoon. The fresh air kisses my face and I close my eyes to take the deepest breath I can.

When I open them again, Oliver is standing a few feet away near the edge of the deck, smirking at me. He looks so...stylish in that pair of black Wayfarers, light-wash Levi's, and a simple gray T-shirt that hugs his arm muscles. At least I'm wearing my cutest athleisure, a set of black leggings paired with a matching bra and a soft-blue shirt.

"Lead the way then," I say, not quite ready to admit this was a good idea, or that I like what I see.

He does, down the deck stairs and right onto a dirt path lined with enormous, leafy green trees and all kinds of grasses. The greenery waves at us in the light winds as we trek up a gentle slope. Birds call from every direction while the low buzz of insects hums around us. Normally the thought of all those bugs freaks me out, but today I hear it as something else. Like nature's own music.

From a few feet behind him, I watch as

Oliver sticks his hand out occasionally to run his fingers through the tall grass. His shoulders rise and fall when he takes deep breaths, especially when the climb steepens and we have to clamber over parts of the trail that got washed out in the heavy rains. I can feel my body heat with effort the longer we hike.

I can't deny that it's beautiful out here. The sun on my skin feels like a warm embrace. The edge of a chill from the breeze off the water is a welcome reprieve from the exertion. There's even a bunch of butterflies fluttering around.

The trail crests after a steep incline, then flattens out to offer a view of the harbor itself. We both slow to a stop to take in the sight. I'd gasp if I weren't winded.

"Damn," I whisper, genuinely impressed by the glittering waters below us, dotted with dozens of little boats. There's even a big lighthouse perched on the cliff across the water. "Okay, maybe this was a good idea."

"I'm glad you think so. Not so different from walking, right?"

His teasing words elicit a smile from me. "I mean, yes and no. When I walk in the city, it's never vertical like that last hill."

"Fair."

"The sun feels so pure out here." I pinch my shirt to shake out the sweat. "It never feels this intense back home."

"I should have brought water," he replies. "Wasn't thinking. Sorry."

I shrug as I peer up at him. "It's fine. I could have brought some, too."

He shakes his head and frowns. The actions are small, but I notice them. Maybe it's because I've been living and working in such close proximity to Oliver recently, but I'm starting to see that he's not the cold, impassive person I thought he was. He's expressive—sensitive, even—if you know what to look for.

"Hey," I say quietly. "It's really not a big deal. We'll turn back and hydrate at the house. I've just about reached my limit of outdoor time anyway."

"Right. Sorry."

"Are you always this hard on yourself?" I try to ask this as gently as I can.

"I'm naturally gifted at it, yes," he deadpans.

I use the shield of my sunglasses to keep an eye on him. Either my earnest question tipped him off or he's aware that I'm observing him, because everything about Oliver clams up. He holds himself so still as he looks out at the water below us, he could be mistaken for a statue.

Seeing him this way stirs up something new in me, something I haven't felt toward Oliver ever. I don't want him to shut down. What I want is to make him smile. One of the rare, real ones—not the half version he shows the world whenever the situation calls for it. I used to think that smirk of his was condescending, but I'm starting to understand just how much Oliver holds himself back.

I hedge my bets with a relatable joke. "I don't think it's possible to go to college where we did and not wind up with a complex like that."

He huffs out a half-laugh. "Maybe. You seem pretty well-adjusted."

"Oh, you'd be surprised," I mumble as I wrench my gaze down to the pebbles around my feet.

"What do you mean?" he asks, the tenderness in his voice winding its way around my heart.

I don't know how to explain all the pressure I'm under—the financial stress, the fact that I don't have another job lined up after this one, which adds to said financial stress, the fact that I feel like I can't tell my family because somehow it all feels like my fault, my problem to fix. The eldest daughter with big dreams isn't allowed to fail. Instead, I kick some rocks.

"This is a tough career," I say with forced ease. "Every no from the industry makes me feel like a flop."

"Hey." The bluntness in his voice forces me

to look at him. I can't read his expression with those damn sunglasses, but he's shifted to face me fully now, hands on his hips as he looks at me. "You said it yourself—this job is hard. You're not a flop. You're here, aren't you?"

I raise my eyebrows and fold my arms across my chest. "True. Just like we'll be fine without water, right?"

There it is—a *real* smile from Oliver, one that lights him up as he tosses his head back and laughs. I revel in the moment, the rich baritone of his chuckle, the roundabout way we relate to each other.

"Okay, point taken," he says, that sheepish grin still lingering on his face. "Shall we?"

I nod. This time, I lead us back down the way we came.

It's slower going on the way down, in part because I'm much shorter than him, but also because it's somehow trickier going down a hill than it is going up it. I'm also less experienced than he is on this trail—or any kind of trail—so I have to sort of pick my way down the dirt path. I try not to think about what Oliver must see or think about as he follows me.

Somewhere around the halfway point, I misjudge a step. My foot slides on loose rocks as my heart jumps into my throat. There's a terrifying, fleeting second where I think, *Oh shit, oh shit, oh shit, this is where I fall down the hill and die, this is why I don't hike*, but then I'm yanked back before I really tumble. Right into something hot, pliant, and firm.

Right into Oliver's embrace.

My face is pressed into his chest, his arms wrapped around me, my own wrapped around him as pebbles cascade around our feet. My heart remains in my throat, where it beats wildly, trapped between terrified of falling and recognizing that I'm safe. The scent of him overwhelms me immediately, that clean soap smell mixed with the tang of sweat permeating my very bones.

Neither of us speak. We stay that way for longer than needed. Just holding on to each other.

It's him who finally breaks when he asks, "You okay?"

The throaty timbre of his voice zings through me. I gulp. "Yeah. Thanks."

We release each other at the same time, but his hands skate over me, dragging across my waist until there's a few inches of space between us. I can't bring myself to look at him. But it turns out that doesn't matter.

I can feel the ghost of his touch for the rest of the day and well into the night.

LINEAGE — EPISODE SIX, "DON'T HATE THE PLAYER"

INT. HOTEL ROOM — NIGHT   361

WE RETURN to DAHLIA'S hotel room, where she sits on the bed. It's remarkably clean, like it's unlived in. The city skyline dazzles in the window. There is an incessant knock at the door.

          HARRISON (V.O.)
    Dahlia, please. I know
    you're in there.

She ignores him but looks distraught. The knocking grows more frantic. Her phone buzzes on the nightstand. It's a call from HARRY. The knocking grows so loud that she caves. A disheveled HARRISON bursts into the room.

             DAHLIA
    What the fuck is wrong
    with you? Do you want

someone to call the
police or something?

          HARRISON
     (quiet now but upset)
What did you expect, D?
That I'd be calm when my
fiancée basically moved
out of our apartment and
refused to answer my
calls?

He moves to touch her, but she flinches. He stops.

          DAHLIA
I told you I was done
playing their games. Your
family is psychotic. If
you won't back me up, then
I'm out.

Chapter Sixteen

THE MORNING AFTER the hike, I wake up to an email from Chris and the *Lineage* production team with download links of raw footage. I start watching them in bed, right off my phone, my heart racing the entire time. It's one thing to read the script and imagine how it will all come together visually. It's another thing to actually see the actors on a screen.

It also serves as a stark reminder that for all the work that Oliver and I have done over the last couple of weeks, there's still so much more to do. We haven't written anything that could serve as the show's main theme. We haven't fully orchestrated anything yet. We have some ideas, some phrases and some little licks of melodies, but if we're going to be ready to record with an orchestra by December or January, we have to get to *work*.

I tell myself that this is why I can't bring up the hike. I also tell myself that this is why Oliver shouldn't bring up the hike. When I find him at the kitchen island that morning, his white T-shirt and blue gym shorts damp with sweat as he stares down at his phone, I'm prepared to do anything necessary to steer the conversation away from yesterday afternoon.

"Morning," I say brightly on my approach. "Get a good workout in?"

He looks up and sets his phone on the counter. When he sees me, one eyebrow raises. "You're up early."

I reply with a noncommittal *mm* as I fix myself a cup of coffee. He's not wrong; I've proven that I'm not really a morning person since arriving here, so for me to be down here, dressed and ready at 7:30 a.m., is a surprise. He doesn't need to know that I had a restless night of sleep.

"I saw the email from Chris super early and started watching right away," I explain once I've had a sip of coffee. "Couldn't go back to sleep."

"The hardest working woman in show business," he says wryly, then asks, "Hungry?"

I snort and roll my eyes. "Hardly. But yes. Why?"

"I was thinking about making some pancakes?" The statement, phrased like a question, is innocent enough, but Oliver won't look at me. He keeps his eyes on the stove just behind me, as if this requires a lot of effort.

Nine years ago, I would have assumed it was because he didn't want to be around me. Now I understand how hard it is for Oliver to put himself out there.

"Yeah, okay," I say lightly. "I had no idea you were basically a chef."

"I'm not," he replies as he starts pulling bowls out of cabinets.

I sip my coffee before responding. "Just another one of your many talents, then?"

"Not exactly." He looks at me from across the kitchen island, hands on his hips. "This is a hard-won skill. I owe it all to a few cookbooks and many hours on YouTube in my twenties."

"The University of YouTube," I reply with a stoic nod. "The second best in culinary-arts education."

He quirks a brow. "Which fine institution is first?"

"My mom and her kitchen," I reply.

"She's a good cook?" he asks with a smile.

I beam at him. "The very best."

There—hike topic, avoided.

While he throws together pancakes from scratch, I sit at the kitchen island and sip my coffee. I bring up the *Lineage* scenes we received; turns out that I've watched more than he did. Even without any of the magic touches of editing—no color correction, no sound design, no music—both Oliver and I are blown away by the sheer scale and impact of it all. The sets and props alone are jaw-dropping:

palatial mansions, fleets of extremely expensive cars, helicopter rides across the San Fernando Valley. Not to mention the actors, who bring the fast-paced dialogue to life.

As Oliver sets a platter of golden, fluffy pancakes on the island, he says, "Did you know the actor who plays Dahlia is a Juilliard alum, too? She must have been a senior in the drama studio when we were freshmen, so I doubt we ever crossed paths, but still."

My stomach rumbles when the delicious smell of the pancakes overwhelms me, but I force myself to wait until Oliver has a chance to sit down. "No, I had no idea. I loved that other show she was in, *Clash*."

"I did, too," he says as he slides onto the stool next to mine. "Dig in."

I don't need to be told twice; it takes me no time to load up my plate. I've got a mouthful of buttery, syrupy goodness when Oliver casually adds, "You know, I sent in my audition packet for that show. Never even got a callback."

My mouth would drop open if it weren't full. I force the food down with a hard swallow as I swivel in my seat to face him. "Are you serious? I did, too. I mean, I didn't get a callback, either, but I'm shocked that you didn't."

That *I* didn't get a response is not that surprising. I'm almost used to it now after all these years. But to hear that Oliver, with the last name Barlowe, is also rejected with the same callousness that I am is a real shocker.

"That's showbiz," he says with a shake of his head. "Or something."

"Yeah, but you've been working," I say, still dumbfounded by this news. "And then there's your dad."

Oliver's shoulders tense the second I mention his father. I regret it immediately; he's made it clear enough that he doesn't like to talk about his family, for reasons I have yet to understand. But the surprise of learning that *Oliver Barlowe* didn't even get the courtesy of a formal no from a studio is enough to make me forget my manners.

"Believe it or not, having Robert Barlowe as a father is not the golden ticket you might think it is." Oliver's voice is low but clear as he talks. He keeps his eyes on his plate, cutting up his food as he continues. "I know it's opened some doors for me here and there, but I still have to have the talent and skill to back it up. Half the time, it seems like people are disappointed that I don't write the same way he does. If my style doesn't fit whatever producer's vision, then I'm out. Just like everyone else."

"I know. I'm sorry," I say quickly. "I didn't mean to imply you're not good enough on your own. I'm just surprised you get the same shitty treatment as me."

When he turns to face me, there is a distinctly sympathetic look on his face. "We all get shafted to some degree...but I do think you get it worse. That's just how this industry is."

"Yeah, and it's fucking stupid," I mumble into my coffee.

He laughs and nudges my shoulder with his. "It is stupid, until it isn't. What we're doing now is pretty fucking cool."

I look at him in time to watch him take a big bite of his pancakes. Now that he's sitting next to me, I can smell him, sweat tinged with clean soap just like yesterday, and I'm suddenly hit with a wave of gratitude so overwhelming I have to put my mug down.

"Thank you," I whisper. "For the pancakes, and for the reminder. Sometimes I think I get so caught up in how hard this all is that I forget to appreciate it when I should. Like right now."

He washes down his food with a swig of his own coffee. When his eyes land on me, those full lips of his curl into a small smile. "Anytime," he says softly.

Neither of us brings up the hike at breakfast. Not in the days after, either. We jump right back into writing—sometimes separately, but mostly together.

♪

Two weeks after whatever happened on that trail, Oliver and I are sitting together in the studio, knees touching as we're watching a scene from *Lineage* on one of the monitors. I can feel the place where his jeans meet my leggings everywhere in my body.

"Maybe low strings here?" Oliver asks over the two characters speaking. It's a tense scene between Dahlia and her future husband's sister, Emily. The back-and-forth between the two of them crackles with animosity.

I angle my head as I watch the two characters spar. "Maybe. Or maybe we don't put anything here at all. Wait until the next scene where it zeroes in on Dahlia. This conversation is so tense, you know? Sometimes it's good to let the silence do the heavy lifting."

"Hmm. You might be right." He sighs.

He shifts forward to pause the scene on the computer. This causes his thigh to rub against my leg. My breath quietly catches, but I'm saved from him noticing when an alert flashes across his phone screen. I can't see what it is from this angle, but all of a sudden, Oliver is jumping out of his chair as he mutters, "*Shit.*"

"What?" I ask, concerned. "What's wrong?"

"Nothing," he says quickly, but I can see the pink climbing across his cheeks—one of his tells, I've learned—as he shoves his phone in his back pocket. "I just—I have an appointment. I forgot."

My eyebrows shoot up as I lean back in my chair. "An appointment? Here, in Maine?"

"It's on Zoom." His chest deflates as he turns to look at me. My face falls when I see how flustered he is, especially when he adds quietly, "It's therapy. I go to Zoom therapy."

"Oh." I know this isn't an adequate response because he's looking at me in such a way that even I can tell he's scared I'll judge him for this. It's my turn to be unsettled as I shift in my chair and scramble for something to say. "I didn't know. I'm sorry. Not that I'm sorry you're *in* therapy, but I'm sorry for prying. I mean, it's a good thing, right? To want to better yourself, or whatever?"

I visibly cringe at the way that came out. The surprise of his reveal has me more off-kilter than I expected. He's watching me with an expression that's a mix of offended and confused. After shaking my head to clear my thoughts, I try again.

"I saw a therapist for a while. For a couple of years after graduation," I start. "I would have stayed with her for longer if I hadn't aged out of my parents' health insurance, but she really helped me in that stage of my life."

I know I haven't completely fucked this up when his lips curve into a smile. It's not one of those big, special ones I rarely see, but it's something.

"I'm glad," he says gently. "Mine helps me, too."

Then he disappears into the rest of the house, leaving me alone in the studio. This new glimpse into Oliver's psyche makes it feel like the inside of my chest is being wrung out. I try to turn my attention back to the monitor screens, but I see nothing. My brain is fried.

Whatever time it is, it's time to call it a day. I save our progress and exit the studio to find the rest of the house is quiet, the windows spattered by raindrops, and the world outside blanketed in thick gray clouds. It must be around dinnertime, then.

For lack of anything else to do, I pour myself a glass of wine and spend a significant chunk of time alternating between the family group chat and scrolling through my social media feeds while hunched over the kitchen island. Eventually I get bored and wander over to the living room bookshelves. They're tastefully filled with knickknacks like vases and expensive books about art. It again strikes me as odd that there are no family photos anywhere in this house. We could be in a very nice Airbnb for all the personal touches there are—minus, of course, the professional-grade music studio.

On the bottom bookshelf, tucked in a corner, are a handful of board games: Monopoly, Scrabble, Clue, and a chess set. Even though there's not a speck of dust, these games look like they haven't been touched since they were placed there. Based on the style of the boxes, that was probably the 1990s.

I crouch down and pull out Scrabble. The box is still sealed with the manufacturer tape.

"Hey."

Oliver's voice startles me. I almost fall backward onto my ass but manage to stop myself with one hand. I look over at where he stands near the kitchen, still dressed in the white short-sleeve button-down and pale-green chino combo from earlier.

"Jesus, are you a ninja or something?" I ask as I haul myself to stand. "How are you, like, silent when you move around this house?"

He shrugs as his eyes flicker to the board

game in my hands. "Where did you find that?"

"Right here." I point to the bottom bookshelf. "Why is it still unopened? It looks like it's been here for thirty years."

"It probably has been. I have no idea when we got that."

"Not a game family, then?" I ask as I turn the box over in my hands. The pieces rattle around inside.

He scoffs. "No."

This shouldn't surprise me, given that Oliver already told me he wasn't close with his parents, but there's something strange about the fact that they had these games to begin with. Like the Barlowes knew the kinds of things families often do together but never got around to actually doing them.

These boxes are just for show. They're props.

Here is another area where Oliver and I differ. My own family loves to play games—anything from the card game Brisca to Uno to Life. That's how we spent so many weekend evenings growing up, clustered around the kitchen table, yelling and laughing at each other in competition.

"Do you... wanna play?"

I don't realize how much I want him to say yes until he does. Not with his words, but with his expression, a slow grin that lights up his entire face. He gestures to the wine bottle I left open on the counter as I bring the game to the dining room table. I nod as if to say, *You know it.* He tops off my glass and pours one for himself without further prompting.

When we're seated across from each other, the game board between us, I look down at my letters and frown. I have a terrible set. I should have picked Clue instead.

"Ladies first?" Oliver asks.

I stare at my letters as I down a big gulp of wine. "Can I play in Spanish and English?"

"Only if I can play in French."

"Ugh. No." I glance up at him, surprised. "Are you bilingual?"

"I used to be," he replies as he sorts his letters on the tray. "I learned when I was a kid, but I find that I'm less proficient than I was since I use it less. Are you?"

"Yeah. My family speaks Spanish all the time."

He looks up at me then, and even behind his glasses, I can see genuine curiosity in his eyes. "You're close with them, aren't you? Do you miss them?"

"Yeah, but we talk every day, so that helps." I look around for my phone but remember that I left it on the counter. "The group chat never really stops."

"Good," he says before taking a sip of his wine. It sounds like he means it.

"Wait," I say as I hold up my finger—realizing this fun fact about Oliver is news to me. "Why are you bilingual in French? Or how?"

He blows out a long breath and leans back into his chair. "Why? I guess because it's what my parents decided when I was a kid. One day a French tutor showed up and suddenly I had French homework for the next eleven years. If you practice something enough, it sticks eventually."

"Allegedly," I mumble. "I still have nightmares about the strings practicums in college."

This makes him really laugh. We both take a long pull from our wineglasses.

"I think you're going to smoke me at this game," he says as he runs a hand through his hair. "I've only played Scrabble two or three times in my life."

I grimace as I look at my letters again. "Yeah, but you read a lot more than I do. My sister Amanda always crushes us when we play at home, and that girl goes through a book, like, every three days."

"You play a lot as a family?"

"Not as much as we used to, but we usually play a game or two around the holidays." My stomach bottoms out at the thought of possibly missing said holidays this year. I down the remainder of my wine and let the alcohol forget that feeling for me. "I swear, that girl will lay the most random combination of letters on the board and none of us will believe it's a word until we look it up."

I rise to grab the wine bottle from the counter. When I stand up, I feel the effects of it—the languid feeling in my limbs, the pleasant buzz floating in my brain. I refill both our glasses before sitting back down, this time keeping the bottle close.

"Ready to play?" I ask as I roll my shoulders.

Oliver raises one eyebrow as he gestures to the board. "Like I said earlier—ladies first."

We both take a sip from our glasses. The rain outside picks up. With a sigh, I put my best word on the board: D-I-R-T-Y.

He smirks as he lays down his own letters off my *Y*: T-H-I-R-S-T-Y.

I laugh. I can't help it. He does, too.

"Is this how we're going to play?" I ask as I

lean forward to rest my arms on the table, head cocked to the side as we stare at each other.

Oliver's gaze seems to burn right through me as he mirrors my body language until he's pressed all the way into the table. He takes a long, dramatic drink of his wine before he says, "You tell me."

I consider the weight of his words, the way he said them—like the ball is in my court. This is a dangerous game to play. But now that I've had almost two glasses of wine on a nearly empty stomach, I can do *this* version of Scrabble.

Off his word, I play W-E-T.

He runs his hand over his face as I shake a few more letters out of the bag. I watch out of the corner of my eye as he grips his chin. His cheeks are a brilliant shade of pink.

Heat zings all over my body. I thought I was getting chilly before in my denim cutoffs and old "I HEART NY" T-shirt, but I'm definitely not cold anymore.

He considers his tray of letters for a while before laying down C-R-U-S-H.

My stomach flips as I take another gulp of wine. The alcohol has unblocked the memory of his strong hands keeping me from falling, the smell of his skin and the warmth of his body pressed against mine on that hiking trail. All of it comes flooding back in a rush, overwhelming my senses. Clouding them.

My heart beats so loud I wonder if he can hear it, even with the storm outside.

And then I remember all the thoughtful things he's done for me since we came back into each other's lives: carrying my bags, making cinnamon rolls, not to mention offering up this house and spending a whirlwind few days getting it ready for our arrival. The fact that he flew up to Maine just to turn right around and drive fourteen hours round trip to pick me up?

I thought this game might verge on flirting, but is he...trying to tell me something? If he is, do I feel the same way?

When I pull my gaze from C-R-U-S-H on the board, his eyes are already on me. The look on his face is hard to read—intense with concentration, but I can't tell if it's because he's trying to communicate somehow, or if he just wants to beat me at this game. Our history makes me think it's the latter.

But then I realize we aren't even keeping score.

I look at my refreshed letters and consider my options. My heart is still racing when I lay down the word D-E-F-I-N-E.

Oliver takes a long, slow swig of his wine, clears his throat, and drags his hand across his jaw. I bite my lip and wonder if I just played the wrong move. Maybe I read into this too much. Maybe this is all just a board game between two former competitors, reunited and tipsy.

Just as I'm starting to regret ever pulling out that stupid box, he rises to stand and says, "I'd rather show you, if that's okay."

"Show me what?" I ask. My whole body feels like it's on fire.

"What I mean," he says, voice low as he rounds the table and steps closer to me. "Talking has never been my strong suit."

I look up at him from my seat, at the shoulders that grew so broad and strong, at one arm holding my chair in place while the other leans against the table, caging me in. I drink in all of who he is now—from the slant of his waist up to his chest—until I finally meet his gaze where he looms over me. His pupils are blown wide.

I'm shocked—*shocked* by what he's suggesting—but what shocks me even more is how much I want to know.

"Yes," I whisper. "Show me."

He moves his hand from the back of my chair to my hair. With agonizing tenderness, he runs his fingers through my long, wild curls. The sensation lights up every nerve ending in my body. Every thought, every question about what the hell is happening right now falls right out of my brain the second I feel his other hand do the same—lightly raking through my hair, until both settle to cup my face.

It's just me, in this body, and him, in his. No one else. The only two people in the world.

"Turn." His voice is rough with restraint. "Look at me."

Oh god. Those bossy commands used to fill me with rage years ago, but hearing it now, in this setting, in that tone of voice? Turns out that is an entirely different thing. I do as I'm told without hesitation, adjusting in my chair so I face him fully. He holds my cheeks in his hands as he lowers himself to his knees.

We're eye to eye now, and on instinct I open my legs to allow him to get closer. He leans forward so, so slowly that I try to meet him in the middle, but he keeps me in place with a gentle hold. Our chests rise and fall in tandem. Our shared gaze holds.

Oliver Barlowe on his knees in front of me. That is something I never even thought was a possibility in my life, yet here I am, heart racing, leaning into the touch of his hands, wanting more.

He runs a thumb over my lips as he says, simply, "You."

Finally, he closes the remaining space between us, and my eyes flutter closed at the same moment our lips meet. Sparks explode behind my eyelids at the softness of it, the lingering taste of pinot noir on his lips, the smell of him, clean and crisp, that expensive cologne I have yet to identify. My hands act of their own accord, threading themselves around his neck and into his messy hair, wanting to know what the rest of him feels like.

The slip of a tongue and I'm opening for him, heart racing, knees quivering, fingers snaking down his neck to explore more of him. We melt into each other with such ease that I wonder why it's never felt this way to kiss someone else before. But it doesn't matter because right now it's just us, and he's running one hand through my hair again while the other slides down my neck, stopping just short of my chest.

He breaks the kiss first with a small gasp but stays close, his forehead pressed against mine. As much as I want to look at him and see his face, I can't bring myself to open my eyes, nor can I manage to pull away. We're holding on to each other and I'm not ready to let go.

"Does that define it for you?" he asks softly.

"Oliver, I..." Words are impossible, because what the hell just happened? In the most literal sense of the question, my brain registers that he did, in fact, answer the prompt, and so I add a quiet, "Yes."

"Good."

He plants one last kiss on my lips—quick but intense—before slipping out of my grasp. It's only then that my eyes open, just in time to watch him grab his wineglass off the table and down the rest of it in one healthy gulp. His back is to me, so he can't see the stunned expression on my face.

There's no other word for it—I'm stunned that Oliver has a crush on me, and I'm just as stunned that the feeling is mutual.

SISTER GROUP CHAT

TODAY 8:13 PM

Celia 8:13 PM

why is no one answering my calls??

8:17 PM

hellooooo

8:25 PM

where the hell are you

8:41 PM

i've only been gone like a month and you've already abandoned me!!!!

> **Rosa** — 9:36 PM
> wow chill we just got out of the movies!!

> **Amanda** — 9:40 PM
> are you ok? answer your phone

> **Rosa** — 9:42 PM
> yoooo we're here now are you ok?

> **Celia** — 10:22 PM
> nvm I'm good, false alarm sorry

> **Amanda** — 10:25 PM
> you sure?? why aren't you answering??

> **Celia**   *10:33 PM*
>
> yes i'm sure, it's late and i'm tired sorry hermanas!! goodnight love you

Rosa   *10:34 PM*

wtf

10:36 PM

it's not that late?

10:38 PM

goodnight?? love you too i guess

Amanda   *10:41 PM*

love you sis, call me if you need anything

Chapter Seventeen

THE NEXT MORNING, it takes me all of two seconds after opening my eyes to remember what went down the night before, aka the hottest kiss of my life.

Right away, there's so much nervous energy coursing through my body that I clamp a hand over my mouth while I stretch out my legs in bed—in the same guest bedroom I came to last night, *alone*, after bidding Oliver a very dazed goodnight. Up he went to his dark wing of the house and up I went to mine. Alone.

I tried calling both of my sisters multiple times to talk through it while I shoved handfuls of trail mix in my mouth. When neither of them answered, I paced in my room, every centimeter of my skin alive with sensation, my mind racing a million miles per minute. I managed to calm myself when I popped my headphones in my ears and turned on some of Erik Satie's *Gymnopédies*. By the time they called me back, I knew that this wasn't something I was ready to share yet. Whatever happened between me and Oliver, we'd figure it out—just us.

In the watery gray light of a cloudy morning, I still don't know what to do next. Are we friends? Roommates? We're colleagues, yes, but are we on kissing terms now?

I roll over and groan into the plush pillow.

The longer I dawdle alone in this bedroom, the more awkward this is going to be when I do finally see him. Knowing Oliver, he's already gotten a workout in and is sitting at the piano. That didn't seem like it mattered before; we'd found a rhythm and a way to work *together*.

And now, we...what? Kiss sometimes?

I groan one more time for good measure

before hauling myself out of my bed and into the bathroom to brush my teeth. For a second, I consider changing into something nicer than my old gray sweat shorts and Juilliard T-shirt but decide against it. He's already seen me in my most basic clothes—what does it matter now?

When I appear downstairs, Oliver is in the kitchen, wearing a white T-shirt and a pair of blue-and-green plaid pajama bottoms, idly sipping his coffee while he reads on his phone. It's the first time I've ever seen him in real sleepwear. It only makes him more charming, seeing him a little undone with sleep-mussed hair.

He looks up and smiles when I approach the kitchen island. "Good morning."

"Morning." My voice is still scratchy from sleep.

"Coffee?" he asks.

"Please. Thank you."

He fixes me a cup just how I like it—cream, no sugar—without even asking me how I take it. So, he's been watching, noticing, cataloguing. More than I realized. My stomach somersaults as I take the first sip and realize that I know how he takes his coffee too: black.

"Have you been up long?" I ask, still a little off-kilter at seeing him in his pajamas.

"Not really," he replies. "My sleep schedule is a disaster."

I huff my agreement. "Tell me about it."

"Is it the bed?" A line forms between his brows, just above his glasses, as he looks at me. "You're welcome to try one of the other rooms—"

"No, no, the bed is fine," I say as I wave off the concern. "I'm the problem. I've never been good at keeping a sleep schedule. There are periods where I'll try to get better about it. You know, going to bed at a reasonable time, getting up early—that kind of thing. But it never sticks for me. I guess it's just that freelance life or something."

He nods as he takes a sip of coffee. "I know how that goes."

"Are you the same way, then?"

"Yeah, but I've never slept well." He purses his lips before adding, "Before you ask, yes, I've tried melatonin, Ambien, even weed gummies, all of it. Melatonin did nothing, Ambien made me a danger to society, and weed gummies just made me hungry and stupid."

"A danger to society?" I rein in a laugh. "What does that mean?"

"Well, the first time I took it I was in London. I woke up in the middle of Trafalgar Square the next morning with no recollection of how I got there. It was a twenty-minute walk from my apartment. The second time I tried it, I was back in New York, thinking that I'd be safer on home turf or something. I wasn't. I knocked on my neighbor's door so loudly that I woke him up in the middle of the night and he had to walk me back to my own place and put me to bed. I had no memory of this until I saw him the next day." He cuts me a sly look and adds, "It's okay. You can laugh."

I can't help the half-horrified chuckle

that slips out of me. "I'm sorry. That sounds terrible."

"It's fine. I always have this," he says as he raises his coffee mug and finishes off what's left.

That nervous, frantic energy that propelled me out of bed this morning intensifies as I watch him move around the kitchen to pour himself another cup of coffee. There's no denying that I enjoyed what we did last night—I can accept that. If the circumstances were different, if we weren't creative partners working together, if so much of my future weren't riding on this job...

Then I'd have no problem walking right up to him and kissing him again. Just to see if the first time wasn't a fluke.

But that's not my—*our*—reality. That much is clear when he looks at me, coffee mug in hand, with that careful mask back in place. Oliver is guarded again. So am I. An uncomfortable silence settles between us.

If there was a moment for us to talk about

the kiss, it's gone now. I take a sip of my own coffee before I say, "So. Lots to do today."

"Right." His response is short. Terse.

"I'm ready to get started whenever," I reply, trying for breezy, but mostly I sound out of breath.

Oliver's brow furrows ever so slightly. It's a blink-and-you-miss-it reaction to my awkwardness. Without a word, he turns on his heel and heads for the studio. I trail after him in silence.

It's going to be a very long day.

♪

After eight straight hours, we both agree it's time to call it. We drift off to our respective corners of the house and leave the giant proverbial elephant in the studio where it hovered over us all day. Alone in my bathroom, I shower, and for reasons I'm not yet willing to admit to myself, I shave my legs for the first time in a week.

I throw on a short pink summer dress

and admire my handiwork with the razor before finding Oliver downstairs, wearing dark jeans that fit him just right and another linen button-down, this one with light-green stripes. He's perched on the couch, his elbows on his knees as he scrolls through his phone, those full lips pulled between his teeth.

"I was thinking—" he starts to say, but stops short when he looks up at me.

Butterflies erupt in my stomach when his gaze drags up and down my body. My outfit isn't anything spectacular; it's just a simple cotton dress and my hair is still damp from the shower. But the way he's looking at me right now, with that quiet, dark intensity—you'd think I just descended the stairs in expensive lingerie.

"You've gotta be careful about that," I say with a smirk. "It'll get you in trouble."

"I'm aware," he mutters, then shakes his head and stands.

We stare at each other from across the living room. He's quiet for so long that I toy with the hem of my dress. His eyes track the movement.

The tension pulls taut between us. I hate it, the way it makes me feel so uncertain, the strange, heady combination of fear and desire that courses through me when I look at him, the weight of all my problems bearing down on my shoulders at the same time.

Finally, I blurt out, "Oliver, we have to—"

At the same time, he declares, "Let's go out for dinner."

"Oh." I blink. It seemed like we were about to have *that* conversation here, in the living room, but a restaurant works. I've missed eating out so much. Haven't stopped thinking about it since Rosa sent that picture weeks ago, honestly. "Yeah. That sounds good," I add.

His lips curl just enough that I would classify it as a smile. For Oliver, at least. "There's a brewery not far from here. Let's go."

It takes no time for me to grab my denim jacket, shoes, and purse. A few minutes later, we're tucked into the SUV, cruising down the twisty backroads surrounding Boothbay Harbor. The warm glow of sunset streams through the open windows, bathing Oliver in a golden light that makes him look so handsome that I can't help but sneak glances at him the entire fifteen-minute drive.

When we pull into the gravel parking lot, he cuts the engine. He's out of the car and pulling open my door before I even have the chance to unbuckle my seat belt. He offers me his hand to help me down, which isn't entirely necessary because I'm not *that* short, but I take it all the same. He lets me go the second I have both feet on the ground.

The place is busy, with nearly every table full, but we're seated at a small two-top near the bar right away. Oliver pulls out my chair before taking his own seat. These little displays of his affection—they're doing a number on me, now that I *think* I know what's going on. In all my years of dating and hooking up, I've never had anyone do these things so consistently. The last guy I was with—Drew, who lasted six months—never once carried my bags, let alone drove seven hours to pick me up.

Once Oliver is seated opposite me, I flip open the menu and ask, "Have you been here before?"

"Once, yes," he replies. "They had just opened the last time I was here a few years ago."

"Seems popular," I muse as I glance around at the sprawling restaurant packed with people. There are life preserver rings and pictures of the shore hung up on the walls; suddenly the name Hull & Keel Brewing makes sense. "People really love boats around here, don't they?"

"Well, it is a harbor town," he replies with a teasing half-smile.

Our waitress comes by a few minutes later, and we each order a flight of their beers and a burger. Oliver removes his glasses when she takes our menus and rubs the bridge of his nose. I pretend not to watch as he does this, but I'd be lying if I said I wasn't captivated by how well he's filled out as an adult. He is a *beautiful* man.

He's also a quiet one.

After a silent moment passes between us, in which his gaze lingers over various parts of my upper half, I'm on the verge of throwing my hands up and groaning in frustration over how confusing this all is. I think he must see this, because he clears his throat and leans over the table.

"Listen, about last night." His voice is so soft that I have to tilt forward to hear him over the ruckus of the restaurant. My spine is stick straight. I'm braced for impact as he continues. "I wanted to talk to you about it this morning, but I didn't know how. I still don't, to be honest."

"I don't either," I interject, like a plea.

He closes his eyes and blows out a breath. "I thought maybe it would be easier if we got out of the house, but now I'm not so sure. I didn't mean to make this weird, Celia. I just...I don't know. I wanted to be honest with you."

"I'm glad you were," I say as I take a risk and reach across the table to grasp his hands. His eyes fly open the second our skin makes contact. "I don't regret what we did. I really don't."

I watch as the tension eases from his shoulders. Almost everything about him softens in that moment, from his jaw to the fingers that had been bunched into tight fists against the table. I squeeze his hands gently in reassurance.

"I don't regret it, either," he sighs.

Our server drops by with our drinks then, forcing us apart. We both mumble a thank-you before I take a very generous drink of a wheat beer. Liquid courage or something.

I offer him a small smile. "I think it might be hard for you to talk about things and that's okay. I'm not asking you to, like, give me a monologue or something. But I *am* a talker, so maybe just listen for a second, okay? And then tell me what you think after?"

He inclines his head just enough that I understand him; it's his way of saying, *Yes, please go on.*

"Last night was—well, it was a surprise," I start. "A good one, for sure, and I really do like working with you. That's just my concern, though. This job we're doing together. We can't let this"—I pause to gesture to the open space between us as he narrows his eyes slightly—"get in the way of *Lineage*."

"It won't." He shakes his head sharply. "I know that. It won't."

I lean forward again so I don't miss any of his tiny but important reactions. "Okay. That's good. I think we can see where this goes, you know? You and me in that house, living and working together...we'll just take it day by day, yeah? But the work comes first. It *has* to."

Oliver is careful, *so* careful, to hold himself together as I talk. There's no flicker of anything on his face—no surprise, no sadness, nothing. It's not until he takes a long drink of his own beer that the facade starts to crack. The shutters behind his eyes open, finally letting me know that he's hearing what I'm saying.

"Day by day," he repeats carefully.

"This job..." The words dissolve on my tongue. I have no idea how to explain to him what's at stake for me. "It's just really important to me, okay? I need to know that I can do it. I need Chris to know that, too."

He angles his head in question. "You are doing it."

"We—" I point to him and then me. "*We* are doing it."

"It's a creative partnership, yes," he replies matter-of-factly. "But you bring a fresh perspective to it. You always have, even when we were at school. Your take on composition was always so new and compelling."

I raise my eyebrows. Like a moth to a flame full of compliments, I have to stop myself from melting into the table, because all I want is to be closer to him, to hear that someone who understands how hard this job is believes in me.

I shake my head to find some shred of my focus again. "Well, thank you. It's you, too, you know."

He sighs, more serious than ever. "I'm not talking about us working together. I mean you, specifically. You always had this unique take on everything from musicality to tempo. It's true of everything you've done in your career, too."

"My career," I repeat with a sigh. "What career? I had one internship with a small regional symphony in New Jersey after we graduated, and then nothing. I've been writing music for corporations. Literally selling people vacuums and shit."

He frowns and leans back in his chair. "You write percussion books for jazz. Legitimate artists."

"How do you know that?"

He takes a drink of his beer and flattens his brows. "The internet."

I cock my head and narrow my eyes. "You Googled me?"

"Well, yeah," he replies, and that telltale pink appears on his cheeks.

"I Googled you, too," I admit after a deep breath. "It's just hard. That's what I'm trying to say—I've been hustling for so long, trying to break into this industry, and now that I'm here, I'm terrified I'm going to fuck it up. I *need* this thing with Chris to go so well that I get hired for my next gig, because the corporate stuff is drying up. Not that that was ever what I wanted to do to begin with, but I need to get paid, you know?"

Even though he's nodding and placing a comforting hand over my own on the table, I know that he doesn't really understand what I'm saying. He can't. Maybe he's faced some rejection from the industry, but he already has a few film credits to his name and an IMDB page. Famous dad aside, he's been establishing himself for years. I saw that *Deadline* article about us. I'm the "newcomer"—the real risk in this situation, the one with the most to lose.

Like my apartment, and my will to keep going in a career when half the world is trying to replace me with AI while the rest just tells me no. That kind of thing.

"Celia, it *is* going well," he replies, his tone serious. "Chris's feedback has been all positive. We're making great progress. It's easy to get lost in a project this big, but that's why we're in this together."

"Together." I nod and swallow hard. "I just... I really can't blow this."

"You won't." He runs his thumb over my wrist in a gentle, reassuring touch. "You aren't."

"Then what about this?" I ask. "About us?"

It's Oliver looking at me this time, the full version of him, and for the first time I notice that his eyes aren't really brown. They're more green than anything, but I'd never know if I hadn't looked this closely. It makes me wonder what else I've missed.

"We take it day by day," he says, before bringing the back of my hand to his lips. "And the music comes first. Always."

When our food arrives, dinner becomes a much more lighthearted affair. The easy way we talk to each other about all the little things—from the book he's reading to my favorite show I haven't had time to watch—almost makes it feel like a first date. One of the rare ones that goes exceptionally well.

We walk out to the parking lot hand in hand. Instead of opening my door for me, Oliver kisses me senseless against the side of the G-Wagon, and my suspicions are confirmed—last night was *not* a fluke.

FROM: Student-Announcements-No-Reply <announcements@Juilliard.edu>
TO: Student Residents <meredith-willson-hall-residents@Juilliard.edu>
DATE: Monday, December 15 at 9:03 AM
SUBJECT: Reminder: Residence Hall Move-Out Day—Friday, December 19

Dear Students,

This email is to remind you that all students residing at Meredith Willson Residence Hall must vacate the dormitories by Friday, December 19, at 5:00 p.m. This is to ensure that facilities staff can perform critical maintenance work during the winter recess.

Your room assignments will remain the same when you return to campus on January 12. We thank you for your cooperation and look forward to seeing you all again in the New Year.

Should you have any questions, please reach out to your Residence Advisor.

All the best as you enter finals week.

Happy Holidays!

Juilliard Administration

Chapter Eighteen

ELEVEN YEARS AGO

THE WORLD OUTSIDE my dorm window is white. Pure white. Snow is falling so fast and thick that it's basically all I can see. There's no view of Lincoln Center today. Only the blizzard swirling about.

Not for the first time this week, I curse my luck at getting the worst possible slot for my practicum final, which is to say *the last slot*. Campus has practically emptied out for the winter recess. I'm definitely the last one in the dorm. On my walk back from Room 340, where I completed my very last final for Dr. Costa, I didn't see a single person, not even in the lobby downstairs.

With a sigh, I zip up my suitcase and drag it out the door and down the hall. Now that it's my sophomore year, I've gotten better about traveling light, even if I only have to take a subway to get home. At the end of my freshman year, I had no choice but to toss a bunch of my crap or give it away, because there was no way in hell I was taking three big bags on the C train. For the winter break, I can at least leave some of my stuff for next year behind, even if they won't let anyone stay here over the holidays.

The cleaning staff have already started working on my floor by the time I make it to the elevator, suitcase in tow. I cringe at the wet boot prints I left behind when I came this way earlier, then cringe again when I think about having to walk back through the snow to Columbus Circle. At least I don't have to fly to get home. I'm sure all planes are grounded in this weather and the airport must be pure chaos right before Christmas.

I zip up my coat and fix the beanie on my

head while the elevator descends. I emerge into the lobby, where not even the security guard, Bernie, sits behind the desk. It's completely empty. I can even hear the big clock ticking on the wall.

Just as I start to zigzag my way through the chairs and small sofas scattered around, I notice him. Sitting in front of the big window by himself is Oliver Barlowe. A black suitcase is next to him. He doesn't look my way even though my own suitcases' wheels are squeaking, loudly pronouncing my presence.

I hesitate a few feet from the door. Ever since our cursed matrix assignment, Oliver and I have struck a sort of silent, tentative truce. I still haven't forgiven him for being such a jerk to my family, but I am grateful for his help in our Twentieth-Century Composition class. We don't talk to each other, but we don't avoid each other, either. I catch him looking at me in class frequently, always with that same cold, unreadable expression. Sometimes I smile back at him as a thank-you for saving my ass with those sudoku puzzles. Once in a while, he'll smile in return.

What is he still doing here? I know he had his piano practicum early in the week because I saw him in the practice rooms every single night leading up to it, staying way later than anyone else. When he finished his exams, he never reappeared. There was always someone else in the room he liked best with the full concert grand Steinway. Over lunch earlier in the week, Anthony told me that he'd heard Oliver played Beethoven's Sonata No. 29 for his final. One of the most notoriously difficult pieces to play.

Curiosity gets the better of me, so I roll my suitcase over to where he's sitting. He's fully zipped up in a big black jacket with a fur-trimmed hood. His light-brown hair is, as always, a mess.

"Hey," I say, but he doesn't look over. "What's up?"

His whole body heaves as he sighs. "Not my plane out of here, that's for sure."

"Shit," I mutter. "Your flight was canceled?"

He nods but says nothing else.

"Where are you going?" I ask, because I don't have a clue as to where he would be headed for the holidays.

"Florida."

I have no idea what I was expecting him to say, but it certainly wasn't that. I pull my beanie off my head and blink in surprise. "Really? What's in Florida?"

"A cruise that leaves in the morning," he says quietly. "Airlines can't get me out until tomorrow night."

I observe as he watches the snow pelt the window from what seems like every direction. My stomach twists with something like pity, or maybe it's just empathy. I know that feeling of crushing disappointment where everything is out of your hands, but you still can't help but feel so bummed about it. Whatever Oliver's holiday plans were, they're going to sail off without him tomorrow.

"Shit. I'm really sorry."

He must hear the sincerity in my voice, because he turns to look at me finally, and it almost takes my breath away. Now that I've known him for over a year, I've seen Oliver in a number of scenarios: concentrating while performing or practicing, frustrated at himself or others for not getting something fast enough. But more often than not, he's stony faced and borderline rude. Today, though, he looks devastated. The sadness is mostly in his eyes. Like he's trying not to cry.

"Do you have somewhere to go? Somewhere to hang out for a night or two while the storm blows over?"

I know that I'm asking him this because the honesty in his expression is hitting me right in my big dumb heart. My dad always tells me that my sensitive, caring nature makes me a better musician because I feel so much that I can channel it into my playing. I never believed him before. But now, I'm looking at the guy who showed up to that social mixer and stole everyone's thunder, then didn't deign to speak to me or anyone else for basically the entire first year, but I can't bring myself to feel anything but tenderness for him. His holiday plans just slipped right through his fingers and now he's stuck in New York. Possibly alone.

"It's fine," he replies finally.

My brows pinch together. "Do you mean you have somewhere to stay? Because I'm pretty sure they're trying to tell us to leave."

Somewhere down the hall, a vacuum kicks on.

"I have somewhere to go, yes."

"Okay, well, good." A little wave of relief washes over me, because while I can feel for Oliver's sudden change of plans, I'm not yet at the point where I'm willing to invite him to spend Christmas with my family. If this had been Rebecca, or even Blake or Anthony or Chloe, I would have made the suggestion without hesitation. But Oliver? No, we're not there yet.

"We could go get coffee or something to kill some time," I offer instead. "Until you can go... wherever it is that you're going."

For several long, weird seconds, Oliver and I stare at each other. I could not tell you what he's thinking, not for a million dollars. Eventually he glances at the snow, then back at me. He shakes his head.

"Celia, I'm okay," he says with a smile so forced anyone could see right through it. "I promise."

I choose to not think about the little sting of rejection that hits me right in the heart. It doesn't matter because I don't really want to spend an hour or two trying to make conversation with the guy who, until minutes ago, had not spoken to me about anything not directly related to our coursework in eighteen months. My own family is waiting for me uptown, with the big Christmas tree in the bay window, decked out in lights and ornaments, radiator heat on full blast because my mom still refuses to be cold in her own home even after all these years.

"Okay then. Happy holidays, Oliver. See you next year."

"Happy holidays."

I jam my hat back on my head and turn to wheel my suitcase around. Before I know what's happening, Oliver is in front of me, stepping up to the door. Holding it open for me.

This time, when he smiles, it looks a lot more genuine. It even reaches his eyes, which still look a little sad as I pass by him, mumbling a surprised *thank you*. After I drag my suitcase down the ramp, I turn to look back, but I can't see him. The whole building is swallowed by the snow, and Oliver is still inside it, in the heart of the storm.

VOICEMAIL TRANSCRIPTION—
MONDAY, SEPTEMBER 21, 6:12 PM

Padre: "Hi hija, it's your dad. Just calling to see how you're doing. Haven't talked to you in a while and, you know, we think about you all the time, your mother and I. You know Michael, from down the block, the one with the little girl, Elisa? She must be about seven years old now. Well, he asked me if she could do drum lessons at the club in the afternoons because she wants to learn to play. Of course I said yes. She reminds me so much of you up there when you were small. I told them all about your job and you should have seen the look on her face. It was like Elisa didn't even know a girl could do all that. So I'm just real proud of you, hija. You work so hard and got yourself so far, but you never forgot where you came from. So just give me a call me when you can. Love you. Bye."

Chapter Nineteen

TWO DAYS LATER, I burst into the studio, mouth still full of cereal, chest heaving. While eating a late breakfast, I'd been listening to Oliver play the piano—variations on a theme we'd been working on for the last few days, over and over again, as he messed with modulations and style. He left the door to the studio open. I took it as an invitation.

Not that I needed it, because it all came to me in such a burst of inspiration that I would have kicked down that door if I had to. All because of my dad's voicemail that I finally listened to. His well-timed reminder of who I am, what I do.

Oliver whirls around on the piano bench at

my sudden appearance, eyebrows raised over his glasses. He looks especially J.Crew today in a cozy cable-knit sweater in a creamy-white color with a pair of khakis, while I'm in an oversize Yankees sweatshirt and leggings.

"Are you okay?" he asks. "You're not choking or something?"

I swallow my cereal and wave my hands. "No, no, no. I just had an idea. Where are the drumsticks?"

I scan the floor for where I left them last. Oliver does the same thing. I've been messing with them off and on since we found our groove, mostly tapping out rhythms on my leg, but I have yet to use them on the full kit in the room.

I find one under the piano and Oliver finds the other under his bench. He hands it to me with a curious smile on his face. My heart is racing as I practically skip over to the shiny black drum set in the corner.

"I'm going to play a steady four-four," I say to him over the tops of the tom drums.

"You come in with what you were just playing whenever you're ready."

He nods. I adjust my stool so my legs can reach the pedals and feel the sturdy weight of the sticks in my hands. I twirl my wrists once, twice, then a third time to warm up a little, and then I'm pounding away. Coming in hot, as they say.

It's an easy tempo—steady, simple, but effective, a cornerstone of contemporary percussion that all drummers learn when they're starting out. Oliver watches me closely as he listens. I feel the full weight of his focus for several bars even when my own eyes start to follow the hits of my sticks.

And then he starts to play.

It's the ostinato we wrote together—the theme we've been working on for days. Set against the rhythm of my drumming, it's completely transformed. It's no longer just a darkly beautiful, almost sad melody; it's something else entirely, unlike anything I've ever heard before. The emotion that Oliver pours into his playing is transcendent. Fuck, he is so gifted. My stomach bottoms out, as if I'm flying and caught a headwind that I can't control.

My instrument was the missing piece.

Oliver improvises a breathtaking bridge against the beats I'm laying for him. When the piece comes to a natural close, it's a little sloppy, but it's nothing that can't be fixed with time and practice. Silence swirls around us as I pull my drumsticks to my chest. My heartbeat is a wild, untamed thing while I watch Oliver take deep, steadying breaths before turning to look at me.

"Holy shit." The look on his face is hard to describe; it's heated, untamed but tense, almost frightening in the way it makes me feel, to see him all lit up like that. "That's it. That's the theme."

"I feel like I'm flying," I say, but it comes out like a laugh.

The tension in his face breaks when he

smiles wide. "I've never heard anything like that before. Chris is going to lose his mind."

"Can we send him a live recording of it? Do we have what we need to do that here?" I ask as I gesture vaguely to the rest of the studio with my drumsticks. "I don't think the computer version of it will cut it."

He's nodding before I even finish speaking. "Yes, I agree. We can write it out with the software, but it should be a live track. This studio has everything. We can do it here."

"Good. I can edit it. I'm good at that." Finally, my time composing and editing jingles comes in handy.

"Perfect." He turns slightly at the piano bench, hands poised and ready to play, but he keeps his eyes on me. "Can we run through it again? I want to work out the middle section."

"Yeah," I breathe. "Let's fucking go."

He grins at me, and I take my cue to start.

It takes us the entire day to lay out the track. Nine hours of work to edit one minute and forty-two seconds of music. We barely even pause to eat, opting instead to shove fistfuls of more dry cereal into our mouths at the computer.

Just as I hit send on the email to Chris with the file attached, Oliver sets a glass of wine on the desk next to the computer. I smile up at him to find he's got a glass of his own. I hadn't even realized he'd left me in here.

"A toast," he says. "To you and your talent."

I stand and raise my glass. "To us and *our* talent."

He rolls his eyes but smiles—a new one for him. At least he didn't try to fight me on the compliment this time. Not really.

We clink our glasses together. I close my eyes as I sip my wine. It's a beautiful, rich cabernet that he picked out during out last trip to the store.

"Delicious," I say.

The warm touch of a hand tucking my hair behind my ear causes my eyes to fly open. Oliver has moved closer, our bodies just inches apart. That heated expression is back on his face, but this time there's no tension to be found. The way he's looking at me now—it's all desire, from the blown pupils to the color spreading across his cheeks and the way he licks his lips.

"I know we agreed that work comes first," he says, his voice husky and low, "but it has, and now I want to focus on something else."

Heat floods my body as I run my hand up his chest. "If work comes first, then what comes second?"

"You do, Celia."

I gasp. My mouth drops open. Oliver may not be a man of many words, but damn does he choose some good ones.

He can tell that I like what I just heard because he smirks as he takes my wineglass and sets both of them on the desk. He grabs my waist just as I reach for his neck, and then he's bending for me as I push myself against him, our bodies and lips colliding in the same moment. There is no hesitation this time—it's just the two of us eager for each other, days after our first kiss.

And oh, I can tell he's been waiting for this moment. Oliver kisses me like a man starved, like his intention is to devour me, body and soul, like the world is going to end as soon as we break away. He tastes like the wine, but also just like *him*, that essence of who he is that I got to sample before, sweet but not without bite.

It's dizzying, the way his lips meld into mine, his tongue sweeping across my own as we learn the rhythm of each other's breathing. My fingers twist in his hair while his hands explore the curves of my body, daring to go further than before. He grazes my breast and I feel it everywhere, so much so that a moan escapes me, thrumming right through the both of us.

Oliver takes this encouragement in stride and palms me with such enthusiasm that I'm turned and backed against the desk. The hard wood juts into my lower back but I don't care,

I don't care about anything at all other than the way his skin feels when I run my hands down his body and back up to get underneath his clothes, splaying my hands wide over the hard surface of his abs while he gasps into my mouth.

I feel the tug of my sweatshirt and lift my arms without hesitation. There's a small part of my brain that acknowledges Oliver is about to see me in nothing more than the little cotton bra I wear around the house, but it quiets the moment his mouth finds mine again, then dips lower as he kisses my jaw, lower as he kisses my neck, lower as he kisses my clavicle, lower as he kisses the soft swell of my chest.

With my hands twisted in his hair, I look down at him, on his knees, worshiping my skin with his lips and tongue as his hands cup my breasts. My pulse pounds everywhere, but especially between my legs, that ache building at alarming speed.

Oliver Barlowe on his knees in front of me. Again.

"Hey," I whisper as I bend to tug at his sweater. "Your turn."

He murmurs something inaudible as he licks between my breasts. His mouth moves over to the left, his breath hot against my bra and my skin, and then he runs his tongue along the cotton fabric, and I have no choice but to rub my legs together and whimper. He must love that sound, because he does it again, this time with a little bit of teeth. My legs nearly buckle.

So, this is what it feels like to be on the receiving end of that intense, singular focus of his.

I give myself over to it, to the way he nibbles and breathes and licks his way to the other breast while his fingers shove up under the cup on the other side. I moan and writhe as he makes contact with my hard nipple. I don't realize how much I'm leaning into him until I feel my hair cascade over both of us like a curtain.

He looks up at me and the sight of him

with swollen lips and eyes drunk with desire almost takes the wind out of me. It's such a beautiful, devastating thing to see, this man letting go, showing me this side of him I never knew existed, worshipping my body after we made such beautiful music together.

His arms wrap around my back and pull me down toward him. I let him, my legs spreading as I straddle him, my chest spilling out of my bra, my arms draping over his shoulders as we find ourselves eye level with each other. Never in my life have I been looked at this way, this closely, like he sees all of me and wants it more than anything else. It's overwhelming to look at him and realize that I feel the same way.

I search his face as I reach down to pull his sweater off him. His chest heaves as he lets me pull it up and over his head, slow and careful to mind his glasses. And then it's the warm skin of his chest against mine, and my fingers tracing the freckles on his shoulders, the light dusting of hair across his pecs, my body filled with awe and wonder at how human and beautiful he is underneath it all.

I press a kiss to the hollow of his throat. When he moans, the sound goes straight to that ache between my thighs.

He turns us and lays me down on the floor gently, until my back is flush with the rug. With my knees bent, he holds them open with both hands and kneels between them. I drink in the sight of his toned torso, the curves of his strong shoulders, everything down to the bulge straining against his jeans. I can feel the heat radiating off my own skin as he stares down at me.

The look that passes between us says what we're both thinking—that whatever happens next changes things.

He runs his hands down my legs, stopping just short of my hips, and asks, "May I?"

Hearing that need in his voice silences the last alarm bells in my head—the ones warning me that if we get too involved with each other, things could get messy. What does it matter, really? It's just him and me here, the only two people in the world.

"Yes," I whisper, and then he peels my leggings off.

My heart is pounding in my chest, in my ears, between my legs, too, as Oliver runs a finger along the top of the black thong that matches my bra. Goose bumps erupt all over as I take a shuddering breath. I'm nervous, yes, but also dizzy with want, especially as I watch him lick his lips and run a hand over me, the only thing separating our skin the flimsy material of my underwear.

He leans back on his heels, pulls his glasses off, and sets them on the desk. Then he practically rips the underwear from my body as he lowers himself back down between my legs, this time all the way to his stomach. He kicks the desk chair out of his way and settles in so that he's perched on one elbow, face just over the rise of my hips so he can watch me.

He does just that when he slips a finger inside me. My eyes close and I gasp, reaching for something, anything, my hands landing on my own exposed chest. With light, teasing strokes, he explores me. My back bows and my body jerks with each pass of his finger.

Then there are two fingers, and is that another hand? There must be, because I can feel him inside of me while he somehow traces circles with perfect rhythm. He's working me in tandem but separate, those gorgeous hands of his capable of more than just creating music at a piano. Just like I thought.

An *oh my god* escapes my lips without me even thinking about it.

"Is that right?" I hear him ask in a throaty voice. "Look at me."

My eyes fly open as the pleasure starts to really build. The way he's looking at me, those eyes all hooded and dark, threatens to sweep me under right then and there. I'm panting as he bites his lip, shifting enough that he can plant a kiss at the crease of my thigh.

"Oliver..." His name is little more than a whimper. His response is a groan as his tongue replaces one of his hands. My back bows and my eyes close.

"Keep watching, Celia," he says between incessant, intense swipes of his tongue while one hand continues to work me from the inside.

I shake my head as pleasure surges through me. I can feel myself reaching the boiling point. I can barely handle it this way, with my eyes shut tight, my hips pinned into place by one of his hands, while his mouth and fingers work to unravel me completely.

"On your elbows," he commands.

This time, I listen. I pull myself up just enough to lock eyes with him, and oh fuck, he's right. This is so much more, to see him between my legs, and before I realize what's happening, the most mind-blowing orgasm of my life overtakes me in a series of waves so powerful I collapse onto my back.

He keeps going until he's wrung every last pulse and twitch out of me.

I stare at the ceiling with an empty brain.

My body is all I am—a body made of sensations and little residual aftershocks of pleasure that race along my skin. I couldn't form a sentence if I tried.

Oliver stretches out beside me and folds me into his arms. I throw a bare leg over his hip and press a kiss to his chest. I can feel the hard length of him pressing against his jeans and my body reacts of its own accord, straining to rub against it, to show him how good it feels between us.

"Celia," he whispers. "Wait, please."

I pause and pull back just enough to look at him with furrowed brows. "Let me. It's your turn."

"If you touch me right now, I'll…" He takes a shuddering breath and runs his hand down my mostly bare back. "Tonight is just about you."

I search his face for any signs that something is wrong, but I just see him, with flushed cheeks, swollen lips, and eyes still clouded with need. I cup his jaw and kiss him. I can taste myself on his lips.

"Are you sure?" I ask. "Because I want to—"

"I'm sure," he says. "Let me savor you."

Well, if that wasn't the exact right thing to say. My blood heats again and I swear he can tell, because he kisses me so intensely that my head spins. By the time his hand snakes down my body, the pressure between my thighs is already building again.

He shows me what those hands can do again. Two more times, actually.

FROM: Chris Ross <cr@eyeproductions.com>
TO: Celia García <celia@celiagarcia.com>, Oliver Barlowe <oliverb@gmail.com>
DATE: Wednesday, September 23 at 4:52 AM
SUBJECT: RE: Lineage theme

holy shit. I love it.

c

FROM: Rebecca Eagan <rebecca.eagan16@gmail.com>
TO: Celia García <celia@celiagarcia.com>, Oliver Barlowe <oliverb@gmail.com>
DATE: Wednesday, September 23 at 7:14 PM
SUBJECT: FW: Lineage theme

Hey! Chris forwarded me the theme you guys sent him. I can't stop listening to it!!!!

It's incredible!!!!! Damian is freaking out, he's sent me three emails about the show's intro with ideas already.

AMAZING WORK! I knew you two had it in you. Keep it up!

Rebecca

Chapter Twenty

~

IT'S DANGEROUS TO get a taste of something you enjoy. Take this job, for example—the work is hard, yes, but it's so rewarding. I love writing the music for a show that's bound to be really good based on all the footage we receive from set. I finally feel like I'm putting my expensive education to use. The automatic student loan payments that deduct from my bank account feel justified now that I'm telling a musical story with the skills and knowledge I spent my entire life working on.

And then there's *him*. Quiet, intense, immensely talented Oliver Barlowe, who gave me three orgasms in one night, then kissed his way across my body, dressed me, and walked me to my stairs. Like we were on some kind of date that involved my back on a rug and my boobs out. The same man who went right back to work in the days following because, as I said, the job comes first.

That doesn't stop me from thinking about him—that mouth, those hands—whenever my mind wanders. It takes all my effort to focus on the task at hand and score parts of cello, violin, bells, whatever. Now that I got a taste of that side of him, I want more.

Just like I want more work like this, and so I have no choice but to stay locked in on music and respect my own boundaries.

For his part, Oliver makes it clear that he wants more, too, even if we're heads down at the piano or computer 80 percent of the time we're not asleep. His touch is basically constant now, wherever we are. When we run out of food and make a trip to the grocery store, he holds my hand in the parking lot and finds any excuse to brush my hair out of my face or place a hand on the small of my back. Every time he does, a spark ignites somewhere inside me.

Day by day, I tell myself nearly a week after we defiled the studio rug. *We're taking this day by day, just like we agreed.*

But then we hit a lull. My drum idea, combined with Chris and Rebecca's enthusiastic response to it, spurred us into a frenzy of inspiration that neither of us were willing to compromise on. Those bursts of action always peter out, though, and so we find ourselves burnt out and tired, doing little more than plinking piano keys aimlessly and sighing.

"What time is it?" I ask, because I have no idea where my phone is, let alone what day it is.

"I don't know," Oliver mumbles. He's seated next to me on the piano bench and I can feel his posture wilting.

"I think we need to eat," I say.

He sighs. "Probably."

So, this is what Oliver looks and sounds

which means that neither of us have eaten since breakfast. I tap into Spotify and pull up some classic salsa music. Just hearing the familiar beats puts me in a good mood again, like I've carved out a slice of Washington Heights in this seaside Maine town.

By the time Oliver appears in the kitchen, I'm nearly done chopping the ingredients I need for dinner. I don't stop swaying my hips in time to the rhythm of the music when I look up at him from where I'm prepping at the kitchen island. It would be a crime to stop dancing when Marc Anthony is singing like he is now.

A quizzical expression forms on his face, one that's tinged with a cautious optimism. "What's all this?" he asks.

"Dinner!" I say brightly. "Pollo a la plancha, to be exact. I grabbed all this stuff last time we were at the store."

He gestures to the glass bottle of dark liquid on the counter. "Is that what the rum is for?"

like when he's beaten down. He's never let me see this side of him before, not really. A pang of empathy hits me in my gut. I'm tired, too. I can tell we're both in the red, as my sisters would say.

"Why don't I cook us some dinner? Or lunch, if that's what time it is?" I run a hand along his back. "Something you can eat."

He leans into my touch and closes his eyes. "You don't have to."

"No, but I *want* to," I reply, then kiss his cheek before sliding off the bench. "You just chill for a bit. Don't think about the music for a while."

He snorts but says nothing as I head into the kitchen. The fridge and pantry are fully stocked again—with way less fish than the first trip—and I made it a point to grab ingredients for the kind of food my mom would make for me. The homesickness still hasn't gone away.

My phone is on the kitchen island where I left it this morning. It is, in fact, dinnertime, apparently two different things? I don't know. I had to add in a sweetener to make it work."

"It's hard to mess up piña coladas." When my hands are clean and dry, I take a cautious sip from the glass. It's exactly as a piña colada should be—bright, crisp, refreshing, if not a little strong. The rum burns my throat on the way down in a pleasant sort of way. "It's good. You should be proud of yourself, Oliver."

He extends his own glass toward mine and we clink them together. "Cheers."

"Salud," I reply.

Our gazes lock as we each take a drink. He runs a hand over my hip and squeezes. Heat simmers in my veins. If both of us weren't so hungry, I'd take the rice off the stove half cooked and devour him instead.

I force myself to set my drink down and fire up the last of our dinner. Oliver sets the dining room table while I cook. Pollo a la plancha doesn't take long—especially when you're cooking on a powerful six-burner gas range with a cast-iron grill plate—and soon

"No, that's for piña coladas," I reply. "We're going on a little tour of the Caribbean tonight."

"Can I make the drinks?" he asks, and the earnest tone of his question makes my heart skip a beat. "I've never made piña coladas, but I can Google it."

I smile at him. "You've never made piña coladas, and I've only pumped gas twice in my life. We're even now."

He smiles back at me with full force, and it takes all my effort to return my focus to cooking. Out of the corner of my eye, I catch Oliver as he flits around the kitchen, pulling down glasses and retrieving items from the fridge and cabinets. He checks his phone repeatedly, as if he's determined to get this right. After a couple of minutes full of a screaming blender, a fresh piña colada appears to the side of the sink, where I'm washing my hands of food-prep germs.

"If it's terrible, tell me," he says from where he lingers at my side. "I had to use coconut cream instead of *cream* of coconut, which are the table is filled with platters bearing black beans, rice, chicken, and grilled onions.

"Piña coladas and salsa music," Oliver says once we're seated opposite each other at the table. "This really is a tour of the Caribbean."

"Arroz con gandules is really my specialty, but I don't have what I need to make it, so this will have to do."

As we take turns loading up our plates, he asks, "What's arroz con gandules?"

"It's a traditional Puerto Rican rice dish. My mom taught me how to make it."

I watch as he takes a bite. This isn't the first time I've cooked for him, but it is the first time I've made a family recipe while here in Maine. I want him to like it, probably more than I should.

"Delicious," he proclaims once he swallows. "Your mom taught you this one, too?"

My heart swells with pride. "She did."

"Then Mrs. García's kitchen really is the finest culinary-arts institution," he says with a smirk. "Without question."

For a while, we're content to just eat and drink while the music serenades us. It's the break we both needed after going full tilt for the last few days. By the time our plates are nearly empty and our drinks are gone, I can tell that Oliver is in a better place by the easy way he holds himself.

When we're both finished, he sets his napkin on the table and relaxes back into his chair. "Wow, I was hungry. Thank you for cooking. I had no idea I was in the red."

"I was, too," I reply. "But after growing up with two sisters, you learn how to spot signs of someone getting hangry."

I move to collect our plates, but Oliver stops me with a wave of his hand. "No, I got cleanup. You relax."

He pours us what's left of the piña coladas—a half-glass each, maybe—and gets to work in the kitchen. I sip my drink and try to catch up on the family group chat, which spent the last few hours discussing options for Amanda's upcoming birthday, but I keep getting distracted as I watch Oliver clean. Even though we've been in this house for weeks, doing some iteration of this same thing, it feels like something has shifted. The domesticity of tonight feels so intimate. More than it ever has before.

Maybe it's the rum, or maybe it's the fact that my heart feels like it's too big for my chest watching Oliver clean the kitchen, but for the first time, I can't help but wonder what the future holds for the two of us. If he'll be there when this job wraps up. If I want him there.

I shake my head to clear my thoughts. I can't go there yet. I can't get ahead of myself.

I down the last of my drink in one gulp and beeline for the kitchen. He's standing at the sink rinsing off some dishes, so I wind my arms around his torso and lean my cheek against his shoulders. I can feel the heat of his body through the impossibly soft fabric of his sweater.

He cuts the water and dries his hands with the towel I left on the side of the sink. He turns and wraps his arms around me. For a while, I'm content to revel in how beautiful his eyes are, to study the hues of green I never saw until recently. But then he leans down and kisses me with a devastating tenderness, and I feel that spark ignite again.

"What now?" he asks against my lips.

I kiss his jaw before asking, "Why don't you show me your bedroom?"

**From: Oliver Barlowe
<oliverb@gmail.com>
To: Celia García
<celia@celiagarcia.com>
(Draft email)
SUBJECT: (no subject)**

Hi Celia,

Not sure if you remember me, but it's Oliver Barlowe. We went to Juilliard together. It's been a long time but I just wanted to see how you're do

Chapter Twenty-One

~

THE OWNER'S SUITE is *massive*. It's beautiful, yes, with a bay window dressed by cream-colored curtains that overlooks the back deck and acres of land beyond it, pale-blue walls, and a big bureau made out of real, shiny wood. There are more doors up here; I can tell one leads to a bathroom because it's cracked enough that I can see the black-and-white tiled floors and a bit of a claw-foot tub. The centerpiece of the whole thing is an enormous king-size bed against the wall, complete with a sleigh-style frame, overflowing with pillows and blankets.

I drop Oliver's hand and walk into the center of the room. It's big enough that I could spin in circles with my arms out and not hit anything. I turn to look at where he leans against the doorframe, arms crossed over his chest, that intense look on his face.

"Well, you certainly got the best room of them all," I say. "My entire apartment would fit in here."

"I would have taken one of the guest rooms. I offered this one to you."

"It's only right you got this one. It's your family's house." I shake my head and glance around at the walls, which are devoid of any evidence that this place belongs to *any* family. No photos, no mementos, nothing—only framed paintings of stuff like boats and trees. "Is it weird for you to stay in your parents' room?"

He shrugs. "Not really. I don't think I set foot in here until I was sixteen."

I have to keep myself from frowning. I don't understand how that could be true—how could the only child of two functional adults never even see his parents' room? Where did he go when he had bad dreams or a stomachache? Who was there for him at night?

My skin grows hot under the weight of his stare. Before I can ask him any of the questions running through my mind, Oliver crosses the room in long strides, grabs my face, and kisses me. All my thoughts, fears, and worries evaporate the second I feel his lips against mine.

I wind my arms around his neck and melt into him. At the feel of his tongue, I open for him and tug at his hair. He groans in response. Something hard and insistent presses into my pelvis and it's as if that spark in my belly turns into a raging wildfire, hungry and needy for *more, more, more.*

Before I realize what's happening, he bends enough to scoop me up by the ass. My legs wrap around his waist on instinct as he carries us to the bed. My back hits the blankets and I bring Oliver down with me, unwilling and unable to let go of him with my legs.

Before, in the studio, we were slow with each other. Careful not to miss anything. This time, it's the opposite—we're frantic, chests heaving between hot, hungry kisses, hands scrabbling to remove articles of clothing. His sweater is the first to go. My shirt is next. Before I can even lean back onto the bed, my bra is off, the cool air rushing over my exposed skin in a wave until the heat of Oliver's bare chest presses against me.

He marks a trail down my body with his tongue and his lips. I wind my fingers through his hair and shiver from all the sensations zinging across my skin: the warm swipe of his tongue between my breasts, his mouth clamping over my nipple, his deft fingers making quick work on the button of my jeans. They're off in a flash, but before he can do anything with my underwear, I sit up and put a hand on his chest.

"Wait." I'm panting, my heart racing. "You first."

The way he looks at me, with every emotion on display on that gorgeous face of his—it cracks my heart wide open, to see him so bare like this. His eyes hold *everything* right now. Every feeling he never talks about, everything he sees and keeps and stores in that brilliant brain, it's all right there. Reflected back at me as he holds me captive in his stare.

He stands to let me undo his belt, then the button and zipper of his jeans. I fall to my knees on the plush rug and hook my fingers on his waistband. How much he wants this, wants *me*, is right there in front of my face, straining against the denim. My mouth waters and I swallow hard as I look up at him.

He runs a hand over his face as he looks down at me. The intensity behind his eyes could burn a hole right through the floor. My fingers tremble slightly as I pull down, and then Oliver is stepping out of his pants, and there he is, fully nude in front of me.

That ache between my legs throbs when I take him in my hand. I hear him mutter an "oh god" as he throws his head back. I stroke the length of him, slow at first, reading his body for cues, watching for what he likes best.

Me, on my knees, in front of Oliver Barlowe, thoroughly enjoying it—who would have thought?

His hands find their way to my hair as I settle into a rhythm that seems to do a lot for him. His hips buck and his breaths grow more sporadic, but his touch remains light. Not pushy, not demanding, just letting me know he's here with me, that he likes this.

It's only when I press my mouth to him that his grip in my hair tightens. He's holding me in place. I look up at him, my hands still full, my brows raised in question.

Our eye contact never breaks when he bends just enough to haul me to my feet. With my hands still full of him, he cups my face and kisses me with such passion that my eyes flutter closed. I can feel myself being inched backward until the back of my legs hit the bed. He guides me down with his hands until my back is flush with the soft duvet.

Then I'm shimmying up onto the bed and out of my pink underwear as he climbs over me. I'm kissing him everywhere I can reach—his arms, his shoulders, his neck—until he settles in the cradle of my pelvis. There we are, skin to skin, just the two of us, the press of our bodies and friction of it all driving that ache between my legs higher and higher.

He props himself on one elbow so that he can angle himself and snakes a hand down my body. His glasses are long gone now; there's nothing to hide how dark his eyes are as he slips his fingers just where I want them. My back arches on a gasp that he swallows when his lips find mine. My legs writhe as I rake my nails down his back, but it's not enough—I know what this tastes like, and I want *more*.

"Oliver." I slip my arms under and up so I can push the hair out of his face. His fingers pause their torture of me as I cup his face with trembling fingers. "Are we...?"

I don't even know what I'm asking him. Are we going to sleep together? That seems obvious because he's *right* there, I can feel it, but it's not enough; I might just explode from the anticipation. But what are we if we do this?

"Day by day," he says, his voice rough as he closes his eyes and rests his forehead against mine.

"Day by day," I echo, chest heaving. "Together."

"I have condoms."

I swallow hard. "I was tested recently. The results are on my phone. I have an IUD, too."

"I was tested, too," he says.

He climbs off me and finds our phones on the floor. It only takes a second for us to show each other the latest negative results on an app and then our phones are who knows where and he's back between my legs and my hands are in his hair and his are cradling my face and we both know what's going to happen.

Today, this day, it really is just us, and that's all that matters for now.

"Is this okay?" he asks between kisses, and I know that he's referring to the press of him against my pelvis. "I can get a condom—"

"It's okay. No condom."

As soon as I say it, I know how much I mean it. Somehow, we grew to trust each other this much. Enough to hand over all of ourselves to each other.

His lips find mine, then he's there, inside, and I'm gasping and he's panting and we're rolling and writhing and moaning. Every fiber of my being zeroes in on where we're touching, which is practically everywhere, but especially *there*, where I can feel that pleasure climbing higher and higher. Nothing in my life has ever felt as good as Oliver's hand gripping the curve of my waist as my teeth nip at that full lower lip of his, eliciting a throaty groan from him that ripples through me until it settles at that place deep in my core.

His name tumbles out of my lips just as he whispers a heavy "wait" and slips out of my grasp. I'm turned on my side and then he's stretching out alongside me, his chest to my back, the heat of him so overwhelming that every inch of my body sparks with sensation.

One of his arms sneaks under to band around my chest as he lifts my top leg up, over, and back, so it's draped over his and I have barely a second to think that I might detonate right there, at the way he's handling me, before I feel him again, and it starts all over.

Except this time, his hand slides down my torso, until it finds the place he knows I need to be touched. And *then* I'm overwhelmed.

"Like that?" His words are a caress across my neck.

The only answer I can give him is to moan his name.

"Fuck," he mutters. "Those noises, when you say my name. You have no idea what it does to me."

It hits me all at once, an orgasm so powerful it takes my breath away and ruins me for life. Those long, skilled fingers of his are relentless through it all and I know, distantly, that he's close, too, because his breath is rougher and the rhythm of his hips gets more and more frantic.

"Oliver," I whimper.

And then he comes undone. Completely.

I slide my hands over his—one on my pelvis, the other on my chest—and thread my fingers through his. He holds me so close to him it almost hurts, but I don't care. I'll hold on to him until I can't anymore.

TMZ EXCLUSIVE:

EMOTIONAL MOMENTS ON THE SET OF CHRIS ROSS'S NEW TV SHOW *LINEAGE*—ARE VIEWERS READY FOR THE DRAMA?

PUBLISHED SEPTEMBER 28TH AT 10:41 PM

TMZ has obtained exclusive photos from the set of Chris Ross's first television show, *Lineage*. Filming for the project has been kept tightly under wraps, with production spanning across multiple countries—until now!

Luke Tudor (pictured here) has a tense moment with costar Erica Stewart (also pictured) during an evening shoot earlier today. Despite the production crew's best efforts to keep them out of public eye for the scene, they were no match for New Yorkers. Luke and Erica were seen sparring for the cameras before Erica stormed off in tears. Someone get that girl some tissues!

Chris Ross (seen here in a black coat and black hat) is known for melodramatic films that are often awards-show darlings. From the looks of it, he's bringing that signature drama to the small screen. Will he be able to pull off this new venture? Only time will tell. *Lineage* is slated to stream as a Limelight exclusive in spring of next year.

Read more about Erica Stewart's rumored new beau, Haven Fitness founding instructor and star Mike Davis, HERE.

Chapter Twenty-Two

ALONE, IN THE harsh light of the bathroom, everything looks and feels different. My lips are swollen, my thighs are tender, and my hair is a disaster. I'm wearing one of Oliver's old Juilliard T-shirts, which is so long on me that it covers my underwear-clad butt, but I still feel more exposed than I did a few minutes ago when I was naked in his bed.

We slept together.

My heart races every time that thought thrums through me, which is about every other second that I spend standing at the marble counter of this very nice bathroom. The rest of my brain is occupied by how distinctly *not casual* it was, the way we trusted each other and let go of everything else. It was just us.

We slept together. And it was incredible.

The longer I hide in this bathroom, the weirder it will be when I go back to the scene of the crime, so I cut the faucet and take a deep breath, willing my heart to calm down. On the other side of the door, Oliver is seated on the bed wearing a pair of gray boxers and nothing else. His physique is lean but strong—not a "gym body," per se, but the body of a man who does go to a gym—and it really is something to behold. Butterflies erupt in my stomach when he looks over at me and smiles.

"I like you in my shirt," he says.

I fiddle with the hem of it. "It's very soft."

"Come here."

He reaches out for me. I couldn't resist the pull of him if I tried.

I step between his legs as we wrap our arms around each other. I wonder if he can feel the rapid beat of my heart when he presses his cheek to my chest. My fingers shake lightly when I stroke the back of his neck.

"Will you stay?" he asks, his voice quiet and small. "In this room with me tonight?"

I'm careful to hold in my surprise. Weeks ago, he invited me to this house, but that was for work. This is different. It's the first time Oliver has ever asked something of me, something that clearly means something to him based on the tone of his voice and the fact that he's burying his face against me.

Something shifts in me then. Maybe even breaks. I can't pinpoint what that feeling is, but I do know that I want nothing more than to stay with him. At least for tonight.

"Yeah." I keep my tone and my touch light. "I'll just go grab my toothbrush."

I feel him exhale against me. "I'll get it. Do you want anything else?"

"Maybe a glass of water?"

He pulls back, kisses me swiftly, and says, "I'll be right back."

He's gone before I can process that look on

his face—so uncharacteristically bright and open for him. In his absence, I glance around the room, amazed by what a mess we made in such a short period of time. The bed looks like a tornado ran through it. Our clothes are strewn about on the floor. My bra somehow ended up draped across the bureau.

I pick up our discarded clothes and pile them on a squishy white armchair next to the window. When I grab my bra off the dresser, a small picture frame comes with it, tangled up in the straps. It's small enough that I missed it before. I pull it free and find myself face-to-face with none other than a tiny Oliver.

He must be three, maybe four years old in this picture. His little pink cheeks are still babyish and round, so at odds with the blue suit and tie he's dressed in. He's smiling in that way only little kids do, with reckless abandon, not a single worry about angles or food in teeth or anything that we grow to be insecure about. He's so chubby and cute and innocent in this photo that tears well in my eyes.

The adult version of him appears in the doorway then, holding two bottles of water and my toothbrush. I look at him, then down at the picture, then back again. The smile on my face is enormous.

"You are so cute in this picture that I might cry. Literally."

He rolls his eyes, but in a distinctly playful way. "Oh god. Please don't."

"But look at you!" I'm practically screaming. "Your cheeks! Your scraggly bowl cut! That big smile!"

He shakes his head as he sets the waters and toothbrush on one of the nightstands. I bring the picture over to him and wipe the stray tear that managed to escape. He flattens his lips; I know he's trying to fight a smile.

"I have been looking for baby pictures of you the entire time we've been in this house," I say. "Do you have any idea how much this means to me? You were *extremely* cute. You look like you're ready to run your preschool in that suit."

"Well, you're wrong about one thing. I never went to preschool. Or any regular school, for that matter."

I look at him. "What?"

"I was homeschooled until I was sixteen," he replies as he sits on the bed.

In the thirteen years that I've known Oliver, he never once shared this piece of his history with me, nor with any of our classmates at school, who surely would have told everyone this over the gossipy meals we used to share. I feel like he's handing me a gift. One that I have to be very careful with when I unwrap it.

I climb over him and into the bed, stretching out against the mass of pillows and blankets. I prop myself up on one elbow and pat the empty space next to me. He slides in without hesitation, mirroring my positioning except for the hand he places on my hip.

"Tell me more," I say. "Please."

His brows furrow as he holds my gaze.

"That's it, really. My father's work required he split his time between LA, New York, and London. Before the digital age of film, he had to be physically present when picture lock was done, so off we went. Dad, Mom, Beatrice, and me. By the time I was sixteen, we settled in LA, so I spent two torturous years at a performing arts high school before going to college."

This is so much new information to me that I hardly know where to start. "Who's Beatrice?"

"She was my nanny," he replies, then hesitates, as if he's not sure whether to keep going. I'm desperate to hear more, so I wiggle closer to him until our bodies are flush. A wry smile stretches across his face when I throw my leg over his, but my trick works because he continues. "Bea is the one who raised me. She was there from the very beginning. She was even my homeschool teacher for my core subjects for a while, until I advanced enough that we brought in new tutors."

"What happened to her?"

"When my parents decided to settle in LA, she left us." His thumb rubs gentle circles on my hip. "I was old enough to fend for myself, and she was ready to start her own life."

The puzzle pieces that make up Oliver start to fall into place in my mind.

"Where is she now?" I ask. "Are you close with her?"

"Florida," he says, then rolls over just enough to grab his phone off the nightstand. "I just saw her and her family a few months ago. Here's us at Disney World together."

He taps into his photos and hands me his phone. I'm met with dozens and dozens of pictures of Oliver with a family of four that I've never seen before. Bea is easy to spot; she has bright-red hair and her arms around two kids who inherited her fair coloring and ginger hair. There's a boy and a girl who look to be somewhere between small kid and true teenager, with mouths full of braces and Mickey ears on their heads. Bea's husband is a stout, stocky-looking guy with dark hair and a beard. Oliver is in so many pictures with them, smiling and laughing and hugging in various places at the theme parks.

I zoom in on one where Oliver is standing with his arms around the kids in front of a bunch of palm trees. "Does your shirt say... *World's best uncle?*"

"Yeah. They made me that shirt." He smiles as I blink at him in surprise. "I think I have it with me."

A memory tugs at me as I keep scrolling through photos of him looking so at ease in Florida. Our sophomore year at school. The blizzard that set snowfall records.

"That one holiday break I saw you. In the dorm lobby." I look up at him over the phone. "You said you were going to Florida. Was it to see her?"

"We were supposed to go on a cruise with her whole family. It was a tradition for them, before she had the kids. I didn't make it that year, obviously." He sighs as he runs a hand through his hair. "Before, when you asked me if I was close with my family and I said no? That's not exactly true. Bea is my family, just not by blood. She's been like a mother to me since before I could walk."

I stare at him in amazement as I hand back his phone. "You're an *uncle*. To her kids."

"Basically, yeah," he says with a rueful smile as he sets his phone on the nightstand. "I was in my twenties when she had Bryce and Kelsey."

"Why does no one know this about you?" I ask as I grip his arm and give it a little shake. "Why didn't *I* know this about you?"

"No one ever asked," he replies, then shrugs, as if he didn't just say the most heartbreaking thing I've ever heard in my life.

I blink up at him and take in the look on his face. His jaw is relaxed, his eyes open and serene as he continues to trace small circles on my hip with his fingers. What he just said doesn't seem to bother him at all. Then again,

I guess it wouldn't if that's been his reality all his life.

I think back to that first social mixer at Juilliard—how half the room swarmed him to ask him about his dad, while the rest talked about him behind his back. Including me.

Shame slithers through my veins. I take refuge in Oliver's chest and curl into him until my head is tucked into the crook of his neck. He wraps his arms around me until we're so tangled up in each other I don't know where I end and he begins.

"For what it's worth, I want to know," I say, more to the warm skin of his shoulder than anything else. "I want to know everything I can about you."

He kisses the top of my head but says nothing else. For the rest of the night, I can't get that image of Oliver in his homemade "World's greatest uncle" T-shirt out of my head. It's the last thing I think about when I fall asleep in his arms.

♪ Ana Holguin

r/television • 12 hr. ago
Posted by wannabeaaronsorkin1
Limelight Teases Chris Ross's First TV Show 'Lineage' at Fall Fan Event
First look at Chris Ross's new show. Looks promising tbh
⇧ 4k ⇩   💬 212   ⇨ Share

AnonymousRaccoon8819 • 5 hr. ago
surprised we haven't heard more about this show considering they're filming all over the place. wonder if the studio was forced to put this out after the tmz article
⇧ 1k ⇩   💬 Reply   ⇨ Share

> **TangerineCream • 5 hr. ago**
> Ross always operates on a closed set. He runs a tight ship.
>
> **AnonymousRaccoon8819 • 5 hr. ago**
> i mean most sets are usually closed right? but we still get pictures when they're filming out in public places

TangerineCream • 5 hr. ago
Ross is different. I was a PA on set for two of his films. He makes studios fork over the money for extra security so his cast and crew don't get badgered by paparazzi or fans.

> **losangelista69 • 5 hr. ago**
> is it true he makes people sign a behavioral clause in their contract? i heard he fired someone for making a sexist joke to the costume dept or something
>
> > **AnonymousRaccoon8819 • 5 hr. ago**
> > ross ain't about to get caught up in the #metoo stuff lmao
> >
> > > **TangerineCream • 4 hr. ago**
> > > Yeah that's true. Honestly Ross's films were the best environments I ever worked in. If all sets were run like that I might have stayed in the industry longer lol. I'm out of the game now.

Chapter Twenty-Three

~

I T'S HOT. I wake up very, very hot.

Brilliant sunlight streams in through the big bay windows, the curtains still pulled off to the side. There's a heavy arm draped across my chest and a leg slung over mine. The fluffy white duvet is threatening to swallow me whole.

With one eye still closed, I peer around and remember where I am: the owner's suite of the house, with Oliver still fast asleep next to me. Or half on top of me, technically.

As carefully as possible, I reach for my phone on the bedside table. The time reads 9:21 a.m. There are forty-eight new text messages between the sister group chat and the one with my parents.

I can't help the sigh that escapes my lips when the events of last night come rushing back to me. Oliver and I slept together. It did not feel casual at all.

He stirs at my movement and I freeze, waiting. For what, I'm not sure—there's something deeply intimate about waking up next to someone. All of sudden, I'm afraid he'll regret what we did.

Do *I* regret what we did?

When the long sweep of his lashes flutter open, a crooked smile on his face the second his green eyes find mine, I realize I have my answer: No, I don't regret it at all.

"G'morning," he half whispers, his words still thick with sleep. "What time is it?"

"Almost nine thirty."

He blinks rapidly. "Really?"

"Yeah." I smile at the surprised tone of his voice.

"I slept through the night," he says, his voice filled with wonder as if he can't believe it. "I can't remember the last time I did that."

I brush a wild lock of hair out of his face. "You might have taken a trip into town. We'd never know."

"Oh, you'd know," he mutters as he pulls me into his chest. "You would have had to pick me up in the grocery store parking lot."

"I can't drive," I reply with a laugh.

"Desperate times calls for desperate measures," he replies, then shifts his hips and suddenly he's *there*, hot and insistent at my hip bone, igniting that spark in me all over again. "Maybe you're the solution to my sleep problems."

My body feels like liquid as I roll my hips against his. "You've been waiting for me all this time."

He tilts my head back to look into my eyes. I'm pinned in place by the intensity of him—searching, serious, and real. My hands slide up his chest. His heartbeat is a mirror of my own. In that moment, I feel something unfurl inside my chest, something delicate but undeniable, something I know will change me forever.

"I was, Celia," he replies, and then he kisses me with everything he's got and I know I'll never have to ask him—he's showing me that he doesn't regret it. Not one bit.

♪

A few hours later, I emerge from the shower in my own wing of the house. Oliver had Zoom therapy, which seemed like the perfect opportunity for me to overthink while washing my hair. That's exactly what I did. For a very long time.

Day by day, I remind myself while toweling off. We're taking it day by day.

I also remind myself that our work is not suffering at all. Whatever is transpiring between Oliver and me—it's not hurting the job we've been tasked with. Only in the privacy of my locked bathroom can I admit to myself that the personal stuff between us might actually be making the music *better*. As if the more we open up to each other emotionally, the more we create space for each other with our art.

I take a deep breath and run my hands over my face. It's fine. It's cool. It's just us, here in Maine. Work first. We're good.

My phone's ringtone slices through the quiet bathroom, temporarily halting my spiral. The name ROSA flashes across the screen. After tapping into the call, I press the phone to my ear and perch on the closed toilet.

"Hello?" I keep my voice low even though I'm alone.

"¡Hola!" my sister chirps. "Did I wake you up or something?"

"No," I reply. "What's up?"

"Why are you whispering?" Rosa asks. "Why are you being weird?"

I sigh and force myself to speak at a more normal volume. "I don't know. I'm fine, I promise."

"Okay, well, I'm going to come back to this, but first, I'm calling because I'm at your apartment to check on things, but I can't get your lock to work. What's the trick, again?" Rosa asks.

Oh, right. Even though I pay all my bills online like most people in this century, I still asked my sisters to check on my apartment every so often while I'm in Maine. "It's the dead bolt," I remind her. "It won't unlatch all the way if you don't force the handle up when you turn the key."

"Oh, that's right! Okay, hold on." I remain silent as I listen to Rosa's breathing, the jingle of keys, and the familiar whine of old hinges as my door swings open. "Okay, I'm in. Isn't New York real estate so funny? For just a few thousand dollars a month, you, too, can live in a shoebox with a door that requires ninja skills to open it."

"I consider it my home security system."

"How very silver lining of you," she replies. "Where's your mail key, again?"

"On the computer desk, in a little dish with a bunch of change."

Even through the phone, I can hear the creak of my old hardwood floors as Rosa crosses through my apartment. "Got it! So, how are you, hermana? You've been quiet in the chat lately and now you're being all weird."

"I am not being *all weird*," I grind out, but even when I say it, I know that it's not true. My sisters have always been able to see right through me, whether we were right next to each or miles apart. Rosa is the worst when it comes to keeping her mouth shut. If I try to barrel through this and pretend like I'm fine, she'll never believe it, and then she'll tell Amanda, and then Mom and Dad… "I'm just stressed. That's all."

It's not a lie, but it's not exactly the truth, either.

"About what?" Rosa asks over the *clomp, clomp, clomp* of her shoes on the stairs.

I bite my lip as I consider telling her everything—about Oliver, about the uncertainty of my career and finances, not to mention the lingering sense of self-doubt I've had since the minute I was offered this job. But I'm the big sister; I'm supposed to be the one who has it all together, the one who is there for *her*.

I settle on a topic that will not be news to her. "It's what we talked about on the stoop before I left. I just feel so out of my element here. It's going fine, I just...I want it to be great. That's all."

"I know, hermana," she replies, her voice soft. "I also know that it *will* be amazing, because *you* are amazing."

"Thanks." I smile as some of the tension eases from my jaw. "How are you and Hector?"

"Oh, we're good." Her voice switches to breezy. "Same old, same old here. Did I tell you that the salon finally agreed to pay for me to level up on my curly-hair certification?"

"No, you didn't tell me! That's great!"

I can hear the smile in her voice when she speaks. "Yeah, it'll be good for business, and the class is, like, two thousand dollars, so I'm glad I don't have to pay for it out of pocket. I learned so much at the first certification class, and there's not enough stylists that know how to cut curly hair the right way."

Thinking back on all the bad haircuts I'd gotten over the years before Rosa went to school, I reply, "No shit."

"Did you see what we're doing for Mandie's birthday?"

The familiar guilt of missing my sister's party hits me square in the gut. "You're going to dinner with a bunch of her friends, right? At that fancy place on the Upper West Side?"

"Yep. She wants to go bougie for the night." The echoes of the stairwell end as Rosa reaches the hallway that leads to the mail room. I can envision it all in my head, the building I've called home for the last two years, just from the sounds alone. "But you know we're just going to end up at Besos, drinking with Mom and Dad."

"Hey, speaking of—I had her gift shipped to Mom and Dad's place." This was a task I completed a few nights ago, posted up in my bed and unable to sleep. "It should already be wrapped. Can you make sure she gets it before the dinner?"

"Sure. What did you get her?"

"That Louis Vuitton tote she's always wanted."

My sister clicks her tongue. "Daaaaaaamn," she says. "You can miss my next birthday if that means you're going to get me a nice-ass purse."

"Very funny," I reply as I roll my eyes.

"Okay, I've got your mail. Doesn't look like there's anything important here." There's a pause on Rosa's end. I can't hear it, but I can practically feel her sorting through the stacks of envelopes, her long, sparkly nails separating out the multicolored papers. "Coupons for Ulta, some political junk, Best Buy coupons, more coupons from restaurants... Damn, what a waste of paper. Oh wait," she adds. "There's something from your building here. One second."

Panic flares through me and I surge to my

feet. "No need to open that one. I already know what it says."

But even as the words leave my mouth, I can hear the tearing of paper on the other end of the line. Silence hangs between us as Rosa no doubt scans the letter from my building management company. Finally, after what feels like forever, Rosa asks, "Your rent is going up? Did you know about this?" Frozen in equal parts embarrassment and horror, I say nothing. She continues on, her voice laced with concern. "This letter says it's the second notice. Damn, hermana. Can you afford this on your own? Your rent was already insane."

"I'll be okay," I manage to say, despite my voice threatening to break. There's no point in telling her I've looked at other places online; the options are grim, but she doesn't need to know that. "I'm good for another few months with this TV money."

"Mierda," she breathes. "This is more than what Hector and I pay in the Heights with our mortgage, and we have *two* incomes. And two bedrooms."

"I know."

"What are you going to do?" she asks as the stomping of her feet on the stairs resumes.

"Keep hustling," I reply. Which is the truth—if I'm going to keep up with the rising costs of living, I have no choice but to keep trying. "The connections I'm making with this job are important. If I can leverage this show into my next gig, I'll be fine."

Even though Rosa mumbles, "Right, yeah," I know she's not convinced. That familiar pressure settles on my shoulders, bearing down on me with what feels like the force of the entire universe. "Hermana, I'll be fine," I say again. "Things are going good here. I'll line up my next job soon. Just..." I taper off, unsure of how to phrase my next statement. "Just do me a favor and don't tell anyone, okay? I don't want Mom and Dad to worry, and if Mandie found out, she'd hound me about what I'm going to do—"

"Celia, don't worry," she interrupts. "Your secret is safe with me."

"Gracias." My voice sounds as small as I feel in this moment. Desperate for a subject change, I force my tone to brighten as I ask, "Everything in the apartment look good?"

"Oh, yeah, everything's fine. It's weird, though. I've never been here without you. It's too quiet."

"I know what you mean," I reply, my words thick with emotion. Despite all the time locked away in the studio with Oliver, plunking down chords and fiddling with various computer-generated instruments, life here in Maine is so *quiet*. There's no city noise here, no hum of AC units or rumble of delivery trucks, no one calling my name from the opposite end of my parents' home. I'm not exactly used to it, per se, but I've learned to live with it. As if the noisy, rambunctious hole in my heart—the one usually occupied by the energy of the city and the love of my family—is expanding, filling up with something or someone else.

I shake that thought out of my mind as I say, "Tell everyone I love and miss them."

"I will. Love you, hermana."

"Love you, too."

I end the call and close my eyes, pressing my phone against my chest. Rosa will *most likely* keep this secret, but there is no way she would have kept her mouth shut if I told her about Oliver. That one is too big and juicy for her to not tell Amanda. Plus, he and I aren't anything other than coworkers. Not officially.

Day by day. This must be the fortieth time I've said this to myself today.

It does little to calm my nerves. The conversation with Rosa was a stark reminder that there's a ticking clock hanging above my head. My rent goes up in just a few weeks. I do not have another job lined up. Not to mention the aggressive *Lineage* deadlines we're working toward.

I'm running out of time.

**FROM: Dr. David Kendrick
<david.kendrick@Juilliard.edu>
TO: Celia García
<celia.garcia@Juilliard.edu>
DATE: Thursday, August 13 at 2:27 PM
SUBJECT: Student comp collabs**

Hi Celia,

I hope you've had a great summer. I enjoyed seeing your performances in the summer concert series this year. The jazz ensemble was a particularly special show.

Now that you're a third year, it's time for you to start thinking about what you'd like to do for our student comp collaborations. The dance students love working with our composition students and the faculty finds this to be one of the most fruitful learning experiences. I was talking to Linnea, who heads up our modern dance division, and mentioned how you bring such a fresh perspective to the music you write. She is interested in learning more about what you envision for this. I suggest you set up a meeting with her as soon as you return to campus next week.

I look forward to seeing you again soon. Take care.

Best,

Dr. K

Chapter Twenty-Four

◈

ELEVEN YEARS AGO

I BRING MY BATON down to the music stand. Thirty-two musicians sit in front of me, tucked beneath the floor of the stage, and lower their instruments. Above us, the dancers beam at each other, then at me, before falling into a line to take their bow. The burst of applause from the audience swoops through me. I have to hold in tears.

This is the greatest moment of my life so far.

It's also the culmination of months of work that started on day one of my junior year. I met with Linnea just as Dr. Kendrick suggested; in her cozy, cramped office, we talked about Alvin Ailey, Martha Graham, Bob

Fosse, and how a composer might go about writing music for dancers who are suited to modern choreography. In the weeks that followed, I met with four dance students every week to discuss our ideas and work out motifs that we wanted to expand on. Under the guidance of Dr. Kendrick, I wrote a thirty-minute contemporary symphony in the vein of Philip Glass but rooted in my own musical upbringing, which is to say I utilized a lot of rhythms from salsa, merengue, and bachata. Tonight was the performance for the student comp collaborations. It could not have gone better.

Dr. Costa takes the stage to announce the intermission, which is our signal to get out of the pit so the next group can prepare. Everyone in the orchestra smiles and whispers their congrats to each other as we file up the short stairs into the backstage area. I'm met with a whirlwind of girls in pink tutus and guys in cream-colored leotards. They could not look more different from the funky, bright colors worn by my modern dancers.

This troupe is the next group to go, heralded by Oliver, who wrote a ballet for the dance program. He was given the closing slot, which has annoyed me since the day Dr. Costa posted the program outside the Peter Jay Sharp Theatre. But tonight, I find that I don't care, not after everything went so perfectly for my performance. Everyone in my group is buzzing with energy.

It's so busy and lively backstage that it takes me a while to find my way to the dressing rooms they reserved for our group. The series of interconnected rooms are filled with muted chaos: dancers and musicians everywhere, whispering their excitement to each other, some half dressed as they peel off their costumes and pull on their hoodies. There are instrument cases on the floor and ribbons strung up on lights and flower arrangements on every flat surface—gifts from parents, friends, partners.

In the center of it all sits the largest bouquet. There are so many flowers bursting out of the glass vase that it's like an explosion of color. This one is mine, and they're from Anthony.

I run my finger over the card and smile: *Celia—No one does it like you. Break a leg out there, gorgeous. Love, Anthony*

"Are those from your parents?"

I whirl around at the soft voice I've come to know well. Oliver is standing right behind me, dressed in his concert black suit, his white conductor baton tucked into the crook of his arm. When I tuck a stray curl behind my ear, his eyes track the movement.

"No, actually," I reply. "They're from Anthony."

Surprise flashes across his face, so brief I almost miss it. "Oh. Are you two...?"

"Something like that."

Anthony and I have been on a few dates at this point. The first time, when he invited me to go see an off-Broadway show that was generating a lot of buzz, I thought it had been a friendly thing. But then he held my hand when we walked into the theater together and all through the show. I liked the way his fingers felt in mine; I liked the rough calluses from his cello playing, the way they softly scraped against my skin.

It's too early to put a label on it, but it's clear that we like each other. Plus, Anthony is a *great* kisser.

Oliver's face settles back into that cool, familiar mask. "Ah. Well, I just came to say well done tonight."

"Thank you," I reply, ignoring the pleasant rush of warmth I feel at being on the receiving end of a rare Oliver Barlowe compliment. "Good luck. I know yours will be amazing."

He blinks. "We'll see."

The house lights flash, signaling the end of intermission. The volume in the dressing room picks up then drops dramatically, as Oliver nods to me once before disappearing through the door. I follow him and watch as he heads down the stairs into the pit. At least sixty of our peers trail after him with their instruments in hand.

Of course he wrote for a full orchestra.

I tuck myself away in the darkness of the backstage area to let the dancers take their places. It's a flurry of tulle and pink shoes and long, elegant limbs as they line up in the wings. There are at least ten of them on this side, a combination of girls and guys, and I can see there are even more on the other side.

For the next hour, I get to watch and listen as Oliver's creation is brought to life. The dancers are astounding, so much so that they take my breath away several times. There's one in particular—a ballerina named Anya in our year—who is simply devastating to watch. The way she moves with such emotion is otherworldly. From my place in the shadows, I know I'm watching a future superstar.

While my collaboration was a celebration of music and movement, Oliver's is the opposite. It's a tragedy. Anya's character dies in the climax of it all while her lover watches from upstage, unable to get to her in time. The swell of the music is hauntingly beautiful. For what must be the hundredth time since arriving at Juilliard, I have no choice but to admit to myself that Oliver is *very* good at what he does.

The audience bursts into applause as his show comes to a close. As the dancers line up for their bow, Dr. Costa appears at my side. I wipe a tear from my eye and clap with enthusiasm.

"It was beautiful, wasn't it?" he asks.

"It really was," I reply. "Like a contemporary Tchaikovsky."

He smiles down at me. "And yours was wonderful, too. Unlike anything I've seen in the student comp programs."

"Thank you. That means a lot to me."

"And here comes your counterpart," he says, just as Oliver emerges from the staircase. "Are you ready to take your bow?"

My heart skips a beat as I nod. Oliver jogs

over to us and even in the low lighting, I can see his face is flushed, his eyes bright. We're riding the same adrenaline high.

"Okay, you two—go!" Dr. Costa urges, then pushes us together and forward toward the stage.

We step forward together, but something in me urges me to stop, like my subconscious is telling me to slow down, to savor this moment. I grab Oliver's upper arm and pull him toward me. He freezes, then looks back at me, eyebrows raised in question.

In a flow of dancers and musicians, we remain still as we look at each other, forcing everyone to move around us. The audience is still clapping and backstage is still chaotic but this moment between us—it's peaceful and still. It's a blip in time for the two of us to relish our hard work over the last two semesters. Even more than that, if you count the years we spent practicing and studying and developing our craft.

When I smile at him, he does the same.

I reach down and thread my fingers through his. With his hand in mine, I pull him out to center stage. The lights are so blinding and hot that I can't pick out any faces in the audience, but I can *hear* them loud and clear when nine hundred or so people stand up and applaud us. I glance up at Oliver to find his smile has transformed into something wonderful. Like he can't believe that we're here, and all these people are cheering for us. I know this, because I'm feeling it, too.

We take our bow together. It's only when we run offstage and I spot Anthony in the wings that I let go of his hand. When I look back to say congratulations, Oliver is nowhere to be found.

**FROM: Chris Ross
<cr@eyeproductions.com>
TO: Celia García
<celia@celiagarcia.com>,
Oliver Barlowe <oliverb@gmail.com>
DATE: Saturday, October 3 at
5:52 AM
SUBJECT: post-prod**

hey—we are almost done shooting. we're on schedule if you can believe it. it's time we start thinking about orchestra recordings. NY phil maybe? whoever you want to work with, if you want to go to boston or wherever that's fine. when will you be ready for this? needs to be dec or jan

wrap party will be next week here in nyc which is mostly for cast and set crew. i always host a postproduction dinner when we shift gears and you're both invited. these dinners are always a little more civilized than the wrap party. good time to get away from computers and talk shop, etc. we're looking at november most likely. can you make it? i hear you're working up in maine so lmk. no rush. i'll have my assistant send the details once we confirm everything.

everything from you has been great so far but my schedule frees up a lot when shooting is done. if you want to talk through anything we can jump on a zoom

c

Chapter Twenty-Five

"¡FELIZ CUMPLEAÑOS!" THE words burst out of me as soon as my sister answers my FaceTime call. "Thirty freaking years old!"

On my phone's screen, Amanda's face lights up with a big grin. "Thank you!"

"What's the birthday girl up to today?" I ask as I flop onto one of the den chairs we never use, careful to hold my phone so she can still see me.

"Well, I'm off today," she replies, and then I'm being carried from one room to another as she moves around her apartment. "I'm going to a yoga class in a bit, and then we have dinner reservations at Carmino's."

"Oooo, fancy," I say with a wiggle of my

shoulders. "Then you're going up to Besos, right?"

"Yeah, probably."

"Rosa has your gift from me, by the way. She might have left it with Mom and Dad."

Amanda nods as she sets me on her bathroom counter. "She told me. She's bringing it to dinner tonight."

"Good." I watch as she brushes her long, wavy hair into a ponytail. My stomach sinks with guilt over not being there for this birthday, for missing such a big celebration in her life. My beautiful little sister, somehow thirty years old. "What else are you doing this weekend?"

"Well, I think I want— Oh!" Her eyes go wide as she looks down at the phone screen. "Who is *that*?"

"Sorry," Oliver says as I whip my head around. He's waving his hand as he backs away from the chair, hair askew, face already scarlet. "I didn't know it was a FaceTime, sorry—"

"It's fine!" I say, beckoning him closer with one hand. "Come here, come meet my sister. Again."

His forehead creases as he looks at me, eyes pleading for mercy, but I persist. He was rude to them once and apologized for it; it's time for a fresh start.

I hop off the chair so I can fit us both into the small phone screen with my hand extended. We're practically cheek to cheek. "Amanda, you remember Oliver, right?"

"I do now," she says, eyebrows raised so high they almost disappear into her hairline.

"Hi, Amanda," he says softly, while I sneak my free hand around his back to touch him. "Happy birthday."

She picks up her phone and brings it closer to her face. Her eyes dart between the two of us. "Thanks. How's it going up there? You two working hard?"

"Always," I say at the same time he says, "Great."

Oliver and I look at each other and smile.

"Uh-huh." Amanda's response pulls me back to my phone. "Seems like you're having some fun, too."

"We try, but mostly we sit in the studio all day," I reply with a shrug.

"Well, I can't wait to hear all about it when you get back," Amanda says, her tone carefully laced with something I can't name—sarcasm, maybe, or just shrewdness. "When is that, by the way?"

Chris's email hangs over me as I reply, "Not sure. I'll let you guys know as soon as we get it figured out."

"All right. Well, I gotta go to yoga. You two be good or whatever."

I cock my head at this weird goodbye. "We will. Happy birthday! I love you! Tell everyone I said hi!"

"Love you, too," Amanda says, and then the phone goes black.

Next to me, Oliver lets out a sigh as he adjusts his glasses. "I'm sorry. I didn't know it was a FaceTime. I didn't mean to interrupt your sister time."

"Oliver, it's *fine*," I say with a reassuring squeeze of my hand. "The more the merrier and all that."

Now that I'm looking at him, I can see how beat he is. We started early today, so for the last couple of hours, we've been taking turns transcribing our handwritten notes and scribbles into the notation software. This has been our life for the last week now that shooting has wrapped. The big brainstorming moments at the real piano—the fun parts—are all but gone. We're into the nitty-gritty of it now, writing out the music we've created so that a real orchestra can perform it in just a couple of months.

The pressure was immense before we got that email from Chris last night, which Oliver and I have yet to discuss, but now? Now I feel like I can barely breathe for all the directions I'm being pulled in. Finishing *Lineage* and doing it justice. Getting back to New York in time for the dinner. The fact that I'm missing my sister's birthday and tried to stave off my own guilt with a gift I couldn't afford.

Not to mention the fact that I've started sleeping in Oliver's bed every night.

I have no choice but to deal with all of this later. *Work comes first*, as I told Oliver a few weeks ago.

"I can take over," I say as I gesture to the studio door left open. "You've been at this for a while."

"I don't mind," he mumbles as he rubs his eyes under his glasses.

When he's done, I pull his hands into mine. He wrenches his gaze from the studio to me. My stomach does a little flip when his lips curl up into a small smile.

"Let me." It's basically a plea; I need something singular to focus on, something that will take all my brainpower. "I want to."

"Okay." He kisses me once, briefly, the kind of thing that feels so familiar that it's somehow just as intimate as the scorching ones we share when we're naked in bed together. "I'll make us some lunch. Or breakfast. Whatever time it is."

When he leaves, I shut myself into the studio. Here, it's just me and the music. All my anxious thoughts are out of sight and out of mind. At least, this is what I tell myself.

♪

When I wake up the next morning, the bed is empty. My hands stretch out instinctively to reach for him, only to be met with cold sheets. Confused, I sit up and look around the room. Oliver is nowhere to be found.

The temperatures are dropping dramatically now that we're into October, so it takes a great deal of effort to pull myself out of the comfort of the warm bed and stumble into the bathroom. I rush through my usual morning stuff, fueled in part by genuine concern for Oliver in addition to the constant companion of my nerves. Ever since I half moved into his bedroom, he's been sleeping through the night. If he did manage to escape and take himself on a field trip—well, then I guess I'm going to learn how to drive today.

Turns out, there's no need; I find him as soon as I enter the kitchen. He's already dressed in a black chunky cable-knit sweater with dark denim jeans. There are two to-go coffee mugs on the counter and some kind of insulated lunch bag next to them. I rub the sleep out of my eyes and pull at the T-shirt I slept in, feeling very underdressed.

"What's all this?" I croak.

He swerves around the kitchen island to wrap me in his arms. After working until well after midnight, I'm so tired my limbs feel like wet noodles but I do my best to hug him back. All I want to do is burrow into that sweater of his and go back to sleep.

"Good morning." His lips are warm and soft as he places a kiss on my forehead. "I planned something for us. We need to get out of the house."

My eyes close as I lean into his body heat. "Mm. Or we could stay here and go back to bed."

"Don't tempt me," he mutters darkly, and I smile against his chest. "I could tell that you were in the zone yesterday so I didn't want to pull you out of it, but I can also tell that you're tired. We both are. It's good to get out of here once in a while."

"But the work," I mumble just as my heart cinches in my chest. There's still so much left to do; I know he knows this because we're staring at the same screens day in and day out. Every day that passes is one closer to when we need to be fully finished. One closer to when this all comes to an end.

"The work won't get done if the maestros can't function," he chides. "It'll be here waiting for us when we get back."

I force myself to open my eyes. With a sigh, I reply, "Okay. Just for today."

"Great." He leans back enough that I can see how big his smile is, and suddenly I find that I don't care how much time we'll lose doing whatever it is he has planned. With the way he's looking at me now, I'd be willing to take a week vacation to a remote island where there is no internet or instruments. "Do you want to eat breakfast here, or take it to go?"

"To go?" I ask in question. "What are we doing?"

"It's a surprise." His eyes sparkle with excitement; I can feel the energy thrumming through him. "Wear some layers. It's a little cold out today."

He releases me, and I hurry upstairs to my old room to find something to wear. I throw on some jeans, my favorite tan leather boots, and a white sweater. A few minutes later, I've pulled my hair back into a ponytail, swiped on some mascara, and fished a flannel jacket out of the depths of my suitcase. When I return downstairs, he already has the SUV running to warm up.

Once we're buckled in and cruising down the driveway, I crack my window and sip my coffee. The air has that distinct autumn chill to it now; it smells both fresh and earthy, probably because the trees overhead are in the middle of transitioning from green to orange, red, and yellow, some of their leaves already on the ground. It's a gorgeous day with a cloudless blue sky.

"Okay, this was a good idea," I admit once the caffeine hits my system and Oliver turns down the highway. "It's really beautiful out."

He's swapped out his regular glasses for his black Wayfarer sunnies, a look that still does it for me apparently. When I look at him, I'm struck not just by how handsome he is, but how *cool* he looks. The high-neck black Moncler jacket he's got on frames his jawline in such a way that I wonder how it took me this long to notice how hot Oliver Barlowe is.

"Told you," he says with a playful smirk.

With one hand on the steering wheel, he slides the other down my thigh. There's a not-so-subtle grip to his touch, and that's all it takes for the spark to ignite low in my belly, but it's more than that needy desire this time. There's something else firing up inside of me, something that unfurls with hundreds of little tendrils, spreading everywhere through me, the feeling both delicate and persistent.

I don't have time to dissect whatever this is because the SUV slows to a stop as we pull into a parking lot. We're in the middle of Boothbay proper now, the harbor just steps away to the east, rows of multicolored businesses behind us to the west. It's clear that tourist season is basically over because the town has essentially emptied out. It's just our car and a few others in the big cement lot.

Oliver is out of the car and opening my door before I've even unbuckled my seat belt. The bag he packed is already slung over his shoulder as helps me out. The sun is warm on my face, the salty ocean breeze cool on my skin, and his hand sturdy in mine, so I'm content to let him lead me wherever. I don't even feel the need to badger him about what he has planned; I'm happy just to be here.

"This is good," he says as we approach one of the picnic tables set in a patch of lawn not far from a small playground, where a handful of kids are running around. "We can eat first."

I sit on one side while he settles in opposite me. He unloads the small bag and hands me something wrapped in foil. It's still warm and smells distinctly cheesy.

"My personal breakfast angel. Thank you." I unwrap my breakfast to find he made us scrambled-egg-and-cheese bagel sandwiches. The first bite is so good a moan slips out of me. He smiles sheepishly before taking a bite of his own—his way of saying, *You're welcome.*

For a while, we eat in companionable silence. We sip our coffee and listen to the calls of the seagulls circling the water and the bells from the boats. Every now and then, the laughter of the kids on the playground floats over on the breeze. It's all so perfect and easy that I don't think about anything else other than the two of us sitting here on a fresh fall morning, eating the food he woke up early to make, enjoying each other's company.

"Before, when I told you about Bea," Oliver says once he's finished his sandwich and wiped off his hands with a napkin. "This was where we spent most of our time in the summers. Right here, at that playground."

"Really? The same one?"

"They redid it years ago so the equipment is different, but yeah," he replies. "I know you want to know what I was like when I was a kid, so if you turn around, you can see it."

I pull my sunglasses off my face and look over my shoulder. My brows knit together as I scan the jungle gym, where a few children are clambering over each other. A girl shoots down a slide, her friend right after her. To the left of this is a swing set, where a little boy sits by himself, idly swinging with no real enthusiasm. He's far away from the other kids.

A lump forms in my throat. I force myself to swallow past it as I turn around and ask, "Do you mean that one boy off by himself?"

"How'd you know?" Oliver is smirking, but he's still wearing his sunglasses so I can't see his eyes, can't tell whether he finds this amusing or sad. "Yeah, that was basically me. I was a total loner. Still am, in some ways. The only child of two parents who probably shouldn't have had a kid, so I spent all my time with one adult who did her best, but I had no social skills when it came to people my age."

"You do now," I point out, because even though I'm grateful to hear about these parts of him that he keeps locked away so tight, I want him to know how I see him *now*. Passionate, clever, thoughtful—maybe a little aloof at times, sure—but the kind of person anyone would be happy to have in their life. Me included.

"That's debatable." He shrugs. "I spent all this time bouncing from place to place with my parents and Bea, and my mom and dad never really took an interest in me, to the point that I always wondered if something was wrong with me. Why have me if you don't want to spend time with me, you know? But I had everything I needed and more. When I showed an interest in music, they made sure I had the best of the best when it came to private teachers. And then, when I got older, people I met always wanted to know more about my parents—my mom's family money, or my dad for his work. What could the Barlowes do for them? What dollars could they squeeze out for a fundraiser or could they get Robert in for a special guest concert or whatever?"

I have to stop myself from holding my breath as he keeps going. I've never heard him talk this much about anything. Ever.

"It was that way all through college, too. Everyone wanting to know what my dad was up to, what wisdom he might have bestowed upon me, if he would make an appearance at school. He's the whole reason I *didn't* go to Harvard. I didn't want to be his literal legacy there. I wanted to try to be me somewhere else. Just me."

He pauses, so I reach for his hand. Even with the shield of his sunglasses, I can see his attention shift from the playground to where my fingers skate lightly over his skin. It's not unlike the way he comforted me at the restaurant weeks ago.

"All I ever wanted was for someone other than Bea to see *me*," he says softly. "To choose *me*. Not because of my family—whom I rarely talk to—but because they wanted me, whether as a friend, a colleague, whatever."

Us, I think. *Just us.*

"I see you, Oliver." I stand up, round the table, and sit back down right next to him. I can feel the tension in his body when I lay my head on his shoulder. "I choose you."

He slings an arm over my shoulder and tucks me underneath the crook of his arm. "I'm sorry. I didn't mean to dump all that on you. I think... it's just weird, being back here again. The last time I was here, I was alone and didn't really leave the house. I guess being here with you is stirring up all this bullshit or something. Or maybe it's the therapy finally working."

"Don't apologize. I meant what I said. I choose you, okay? I like getting to know you," I reply, then lighten my tone and add, "Especially this version of you that's been in therapy for a while."

He huffs out a laugh. I can feel his muscles relax as relief washes through me. I snake one arm around his back and hug him tighter to my side.

"Can I ask you something?" I ask cautiously.

"Go for it."

I bite my bottom lip as I consider how to phrase this. "Why this career, then? Why pursue music if you wanted to be separate from what your dad does?"

He leans back and pulls his sunglasses off his face. He scans my face as I do the same, searching for any signs of distress or anger—the clench of his jaw, the pursing of his lips. But there's none of that today, save for a hint of sadness in those green eyes, especially when he sighs and says, "Because I love it."

That—that I understand. For all the ways that Oliver and I are different, we share this in common. This fire that burns between us to build our entire lives around making music, sometimes at great cost to ourselves—that's what brought us together thirteen years ago, and what brought us together again now.

I have no way to say this with words, so instead I kiss him.

When we pull back from each other, a little breathless, he checks his phone and startles. "Shit. We're gonna be late."

"Late?" I blink, a little dazed as he jumps to his feet and starts dumping our trash into the bag he brought.

"Come on. We have a boat to catch."

TODAY 10:14 AM

Rebecca   *10:14 AM*

Omg. You have to go Chris's dinner!!!

10:20 AM

Seriously this is the networking opportunity of a lifetime. The first time I went to one of these dinner things, I got my next three gigs

10:22 AM

Let's grab a drink before!!

Chapter Twenty-Six

I DON'T HAVE TIME to ask any more questions, because we have to run. Literally. All the way back to the car, where Oliver chucks the bag in the back seat, and then down the sidewalk, straight onto the boardwalk. I'd be stressed if we weren't laughing the entire time, my hand in his as my short legs struggle to keep up with the length of his stride. All the heaviness of our conversation dissolves with every giggle that bursts out of me, every look back from him, both our faces flushed and smiles wide as we dodge people all along the pier.

When we slow to a stop near the end, I'm breathless and warm. We've arrived at what can only be called a red shack on stilts. There's a white sign dangling from the awning, bearing the words "A Whale of a Time Cruises" in loopy cursive blue paint. There's already a small group of ten or so people gathered near a docked double-decker boat. On the hull of the boat, the name *Moby Deck* is printed in more blue cursive lettering.

"We're doing a boat tour?" I ask as I unzip my jacket.

"Whale watching, yes," he replies lightly, but then his forehead scrunches as he looks at me. "Is that all right? We may not see anything because it's so late in the season, and I should have asked if you even like—"

"Oliver, it's more than okay." I put my hand on his arm and smile at him. "I don't even care if we don't see whales. I'm always down to get on a boat. I just have one question."

He cocks his head to the side. "Oh?"

"Is it a bad omen if the boat is named after a whale who kills a bunch of people?" I ask as we sidle up to the shack's window.

He smirks as he glances back at me.

"Would it make you feel better if I called you Ishmael during the trip?"

"What would that make you then? Ahab?" I wonder out loud. "I don't want you to die, either."

"I think we're safe. This company has been in business since I was a kid."

Oliver shows the man at the window something on his phone—tickets he already bought, I assume—and then we're ushered on board by a friendly staff member in a red T-shirt with a picture of a puffin riding a whale on it. We find a place to stand near the bow that provides an ample view of the harbor. The boat sways and bobs beneath our feet.

"I'm surprised you know so much about *Moby Dick*," Oliver says, his forearms propped against the railing of the boat. "I thought you weren't a big reader."

"We read it in college. I guess it stuck with me," I reply. "We were in the same lit class at Juilliard, remember?"

"I remember."

His voice is soft when he responds. I tear my gaze away from the sparkling water and turn to glance at him on my left. He's already looking at me, his gaze hidden behind those damn sunglasses, and I wonder what those memories look like for him, wonder how it feels when he thinks back on those four years we spent circling each other, if he ever thinks about what went down the last night we saw each other.

The questions are forming on my tongue when the boat pulls away from the pier and the captain's voice booms over the speaker system. Wind whips through my hair as the captain begins a safety lecture, providing instructions on where to find life jackets and flotation devices should things go south on our tour. This is followed by talk of refreshments and food available for purchase, as well as where to find the onboard bathrooms.

It's clear the moment is gone. I swallow all

questions I want to ask. Blink back the memories until they dissolve.

Our vessel picks up speed as we exit the crowded harbor. Despite the dazzling sun, the temperature drops dramatically once we're out in the open water. I zip up my jacket as cool wind laced with the brine of the ocean lashes at my exposed skin. Out here, I can feel the promise of winter, another stark reminder that we're hurtling toward the end of our time in Maine—when it will no longer be *just us*.

"Cold?" Oliver asks, cutting through the captain's spiel about the history and establishment of Boothbay Harbor.

"A little," I admit as a shiver runs through me.

"Take my jacket."

He's already unzipping his sleek black coat when I turn to face him, shaking my head in protest. "No, no, no. Then you'll freeze. I'm fine. The sun is shining. I'll warm up when we slow down."

I jam my hands into the pockets of my jacket and raise my eyebrows, as if to say, *See, it's not so bad*. He flattens his lips. Cold ocean water sprays us and we both startle, then laugh. I shake my head at how easy it was for nature to prove me wrong as Oliver steps behind me, caging me in with his warmth.

With our shared body heat, it's much easier to enjoy being out on the open water. My lungs expand with great gulping breaths in my chest as I relish the freedom of the outside world. The hum of the boat's engine, coupled with the chop of the waves against the hull, is loud. Finally, my life is loud again—I take great comfort in the noise and the rush of the wind. It almost feels like New York on a particularly gusty day.

"We received word from our friends up the coast that a pod of humpbacks was spotted about an hour ago," the captain says, his voice barely audible over all the water noise. "If we're lucky, we may come across their path as they move south."

To my right, a woman in a red coat lets out a little squeal of excitement. "Did you hear that, honey? We may actually see some whales this time!"

"Third time's a charm," the man to her right yells.

I crane my neck to look back at Oliver. "Have you seen whales before?"

"Twice," he replies. "Once when we went sailing here when I was a kid, and again when I was in Hawaii in my early twenties. You?"

"No. I've only ever seen dolphins in Florida. We tried to see whales in Puerto Rico once, but it didn't work out."

"Your family is from Puerto Rico, right?"

"My mom's side, yeah," I reply. "My dad's side is from Cuba."

"Hence the salsa club."

Surprised that he made the connection, I blink up at him. "You know about that?"

"Of course I do. You talked about it when we were at school."

A little stunned, I turn back around as

the boat slows to a stop. I know I told all my college friends about Besos; we even went up there a couple of times once we were old enough to legally drink. Oliver must have been around when I talked about it, but I don't remember him ever acknowledging it, let alone showing any interest in anyone's life outside of our schoolwork.

In my periphery, I can see the coast is simply a blurry line in the distance; we're really out in the open ocean now. The vessel jostles and sways in the water as everyone on deck tries to stabilize themselves. Without the roaring wind or the thrum of the engine, the waves and seabirds circling overhead sound impossibly loud.

The captain's voice crackles to life over the loudspeaker again. "All right, folks, we're going to drift here for a bit in hopes we see some whales. As a reminder, we have snacks, beer, wine, and nonalcoholic refreshments available for purchase in the interior lounge. We've also got some boat-friendly games available if your little ones get bored, but try to keep your eyes on the water!"

"Good thing neither of us gets seasick," I say as I grip the railing for support, my hands right next to his.

"No kidding, Ishmael," he replies wryly. "You want anything to eat or drink?"

"I'm okay for now. Thanks, though."

Around us, people mill about the boat, but I'm content just to stand there, leaning into Oliver's warm torso while I watch the gentle, glittering waves. Out here, it's easy to be with him, to take comfort in his quiet strength. To know that he sees me, just like I see him.

"Why are they doing that?" I ask as I point toward a cluster of birds circling the same spot some twenty yards away.

Before Oliver can answer, the surface of the water breaks. Directly underneath the gulls, a spout of water erupts, just before a humpback whale breaches the water in a magnificent twisting flip. It crashes back into the waves with enough force that our boat rocks from the impact.

"We've got whales, folks! Starboard side! Hurry!" the captain yells over the speaker.

There's a flurry of people behind us. In an effort to see, they push Oliver and me closer to the railing until his front side is completely flush with my back. The boat sways with the sudden movement, but Oliver's arms prevent me from being smashed.

Not that I care—I'm transfixed by the sight of two, three, then *four* humpback whales skimming the surface of the water less than a hundred feet away. One of them rockets out of the water again, impossibly fast and high for an animal so huge, before flopping back into the ocean on its back.

Awestruck, I murmur, "Just beautiful."

Oliver shifts behind me, dipping his head to the side so that his breath is warm against my temple. "Yes. Beautiful." When his hands grip the railing harder, I can't tell if he's referring to what we're witnessing, or me.

♪

When we get back to the house that afternoon, everything I'd shoved into the far corners of my mind comes rushing back: Chris's dinner invite, the orchestra sessions, Rebecca's latest texts.

I know she's right; private dinners like the one Chris is hosting are full of industry people who are all scouting their next creative partners. The number of doors that could open for me just by going to this thing and shaking hands with the right people—it's so staggering that I've been sweating since I first saw her messages hours ago. This is exactly what I've been hoping for, waiting for, *working toward* for years.

I have to assume that Oliver saw Chris's email; he seems like the type of person who is on top of those things when it comes to his work. But for some reason, I can't bring myself to broach this subject with him when we return to the studio to get in a few hours of work. It's easy enough to lie to myself and think that my focus is on the music in front of us.

When we call it a day and Oliver goes downstairs to work out, I have no choice but to be honest with myself. Chris hates production drama—Rebecca said as much to me two months ago over dinner. If Chris or any of the producers see Oliver and me at that dinner, what will they think? If we show up *together together*, will they be able to look past the fact that we're doing whatever this is? Will they be able to separate me, the composer and musician, from him, the one with the connections and history in the industry? Will they want to hire me—just me?

My stomach churns. I know the answer already: No, they won't.

To add insult to injury, I check my bank account on my phone. The news is not good. All my first-of-the-month bills hit, and I don't get paid again until we deliver a recorded soundtrack.

Curled up on the couch in the living room, I scroll through the various streaming services on the TV. I settle on one of my favorite reality dating shows that I'm way behind on since all I've done is work and fool around with Oliver for the last several weeks. The bright colors and loud contestants are a familiar comfort that helps to slow my mental spiral.

"*Battle for Love*, huh?" Oliver asks when he appears in the living room. His hair is wet from the shower and he's dressed in a white T-shirt and gray sweatpants. I gulp when I see those slung low on his hips.

"I love this show," I reply indignantly. "Nothing more romantic that people willing to physically fight each other for someone."

He smirks as he plops down at the end of the couch near my feet. "Very primitive. Let me guess—that huge guy with the shoulders the size of mountains wins, right?"

"No spoilers!" I toss a throw pillow at him and miss by a wide margin. "I'm not caught up yet."

"Oh, that short one is a former UFC fighter?" he asks as the show's plot unfolds. "I bet he wins."

"You can't underestimate the quiet ones, either," I reply. "A scientist won last season. He was really scrappy when it came down to it."

Oliver barks out a laugh, but I can tell he's enthralled by the show. For a while, we sit there and watch it together, with me sneaking glances at him to find him intensely focused. He's got a sort of amused expression on his face the entire time, and for the first time, I realize just how lighthearted and funny Oliver can be now that he trusts I won't misunderstand him. Those warm tendrils of feeling return, spreading out from my chest, and I have no choice but to admit how happy it makes me that he's showing an interest in what I like, that we can sit here together and bask in the silliness of it all.

My phone dings on the coffee table. A text from Rebecca lights up my screen. All of a sudden, that pleasant warmth evaporates. Cold trickles down my spine.

> **Rebecca**
> btw I did not text Oliver about meeting up in the city before the dinner. Figured it would be more fun if it was just us gals :)

I tap out of the message and pause the show. He looks over at me as I sit up straighter on the couch and tuck my legs under me. My heart races when I clear my throat.

"So, that email from Chris…" I start, but trail off, my confidence already losing steam.

"Yeah, I was thinking about that in the shower," he replies. "I think we should aim to record in January, right after the New Year. December will be pushing it, considering how much we have left to do, plus I think we'll have issues getting the talent in what with holiday concert programming and all that."

I'm nodding. "Right. Yeah. That makes sense. What about the other stuff—the post-prod dinner?"

He adjusts his glasses and shrugs. "I don't know. Might be hard to make it to New York by then. It's in—what, three weeks?"

"Yeah, something like that," I reply, as if I don't have the email committed to memory already. "I was thinking we could swing it if we finish the rest of the score from the city. We could do the rest of it from my place—or yours, if you're set up—since most of the heavy lifting is done. We can get by without the Maine studio."

He hums as he pulls his lips between his teeth.

"I feel like we should be there," I add, forcing a lightness into my tone.

"We still have a lot to do," he muses. "The work has to come first, right?"

Even though his question doesn't *sound* accusatory, I feel like I've been slapped in the face hearing my own words thrown back at me. This dinner invitation *is* work. The harsh reality is that this entire industry is built on relationships—how else am I supposed to build those if I'm not in the room where it happens?

"Right, but Chris is basically our boss," I manage. I can feel the heat of embarrassment climbing up my neck and cheeks.

"True." He runs a hand through his hair as he sighs. "He said we didn't have to RSVP right away. They didn't even have a date picked out, right? I think we can wait until we see how much progress we make over the next couple of weeks."

"Okay. Yeah."

Even though I nod and force myself to settle back into the couch, I can still feel my rapid heartbeat everywhere in my body. Oliver reaches for my feet and starts rubbing them when I resume the show. I'm so wound up that not even a foot massage can relax me.

Somewhere in the middle of our second episode, I text Rebecca back.

> **Celia**
> I'll be there, but don't tell anyone yet. Still have to figure out logistics.

BLOOM—
A SYMPHONY IN THREE PARTS

A coming-of-age story told over the course of three women's lives, exploring how time and age do not prevent us from rediscovery and joy.

Submission packet for comp competition

Music written and arranged by Celia García

Year Four

December 12

Chapter Twenty-Seven

TEN YEARS AGO

"CELIA, CAN I speak with you?"

Dr. Kendrick's question cuts through the noise of ten students packing up their belongings. His Composition Forum class just ended, and I know that he knows it marks the end of my day—aside from the mountain of homework I have to do. Senior year has proven to be no less brutal than all the semesters before it.

I can feel the eyes of my peers on me as they exit the classroom. Everyone is nosey as hell, including Oliver, who can't seem to help himself this time. He's basically avoided me since we took our bow together on stage at the end of our junior year. Fine by me. It's easier to ignore him than to tiptoe around each other awkwardly all the time.

Today, though, Oliver and I hold each other's stare for longer than necessary. A whole thirty seconds pass during which I raise one eyebrow—in question and defiance—while his face ices over completely. He's the first to break when he trails after the others. I don't watch him leave.

I pretend that my palms aren't sweating and that I don't know what this is about as I weave around chairs to where Dr. Kendrick half sits on a table near the front of the room in a green sweater and black dress pants. My throat dries out immediately as I try to fix my face into a calm, pleasant expression.

This is only our second week back after the winter recess, which means that it's been over a month since I submitted my packet for the student comp competition. All composition majors were required to submit a fully orchestrated work—for any group size, in any genre of music—intended to be performed by our dance program. During the last semester, I spent hours and hours and hours meeting with the dancer friends I made, getting their input on the kind of choreography they want to perform in their final year, writing and rewriting ninety minutes worth of music, and implementing Dr. Kendrick's feedback whenever he sent me notes. The prize of the competition is conducting your own work while the best of Juilliard's dancers perform at Lincoln Center. In a prime-time evening slot. For thousands of people, including industry scouts and talent agents.

There is only one winner.

"Did you have a nice break?" he asks, once the door to the classroom closes and we're alone.

I paste a smile on my face. "I did, thank you. Did you?"

"Yes, yes, thank you. Time always seems to pass too fast but too slow at the same time."

I nod slowly. As much as I genuinely like

Dr. Kendrick, I wish he'd skip the platitudes here. My skin is itchy and hot under my black sweater.

My heart starts racing just as he takes a deep breath and says, "I wanted to talk to you about the comp competition. One-on-one, before the email goes out and the announcement goes up in"—he pauses to look at the watch on his wrist, which I notice is a Rolex for the first time—"about ten minutes."

I hold my breath. I can't help it.

"You didn't get it, Celia," he says, and the gentle kindness in his voice does nothing to soften the enormous blow that hits me square in the gut. "It was a very tough decision this year. More than it ever has been. May I speak to you candidly, in confidence?"

It takes all my effort to squeak out a "Yes, sir."

"You're well aware that your entire cohort is very talented this year." He clears his throat and shifts his weight on the table. "Ultimately, it came down to two of you. The faculty committee was evenly split. For a while there, I didn't know if we'd ever make a decision. But my dance colleagues made some valid points regarding the talent of their students, and eventually convinced everyone that a more traditional ballet would be best for this performance."

"Who?" Even though I know the answer, I need to hear him say it. "Who won?"

"Oliver," he replies, and I could swear a glint of regret flashes in his blue eyes for a second.

The deepest breaths I can make myself take. The count of my pulse in my ears. The soft fabric of my jeans beneath my fingers. I focus on all of it so I don't cry.

"Thank you for telling me." My voice holds steady; no warbling yet. "I know—Oliver, he...well, yeah."

I can't bring myself to say he deserved it, even though it might be true. If he wrote a ballet, then he wrote it for Anya, the fourth-year ballerina who all the major companies are circling like hawks. Last year, when I saw her perform with him, I knew I was watching a future star. Apparently, he saw the same thing.

Then there's his dad. Rumor has it that the faculty is courting Robert Barlowe to do a special guest lecture at the end of the year. Anthony told me he heard Dr. Costa and Dr. Adams talking about it last week. Of course the school would give Oliver the big slot if it earned them brownie points with his famous father.

The disappointment is barreling through me so hard I can feel myself crumbling. All those dreams of me being in the pit at Lincoln Center, of being celebrated by New York's arts patrons and industry professionals, of my family seeing me *make it*—it's gone, all gone, just like that.

Dr. Kendrick's face softens into a sympathetic smile. "For what it's worth, Celia, I loved what you did with *Bloom*. The rhythm section alone was astounding. It was clear how you took the input of the dancers to create something just for them. You should be very proud."

"Thank you," I reply, even though what I want to say is—so what? So what if it was good? No one is going to see it now, because all the dancers are going to be cast in Oliver's dumb program where someone is probably going to die because he writes about sad, miserable people. All that work, all those sleepless nights of mine, all the missed dates with Anthony and parties I skipped at Rebecca's Upper West Side apartment, were for *nothing*.

"Chin up," Dr. Kendrick says lightly. "You know where to find me if you ever want to talk."

I think I mumble another "thank you" but I'm not sure. The frustration and disappointment are taking over my brain and I know I need to get out of there. I give an awkward little half-wave as I hustle out of the classroom. My eyes prickle and my nose burns. The tears are coming and I *refuse* to cry in front of my department head.

Out in the hall, I gulp down a shaky breath. I head straight for the stairs. My heart is beating so fast I'm afraid I might flatline. My vision is tunneling.

My dorm—I just have to make it back to my dorm.

The day gets even worse when I hit the lobby. Oliver is there. Standing with Anya—willowy, graceful, perfect ballerina Anya. She's smiling as he talks to her, but then his gaze finds me somehow, even though there are dozens of people in this big space. When we lock eyes and I have to register that cold face of his, my stomach bottoms out.

He smirks—actually fucking *smirks* at me—and I want nothing more than to evaporate into nothing, but I keep moving, putting a wide berth between us. If he tries to talk to me right now, I'll lose it.

I'm already losing it. My bottom lip quivers when I burst into a cold January afternoon. It's practically dark out, the exterior campus lights already on even though it's only

4:00 p.m., as I hustle across campus. By the time I make it into the dorm building and into the safety of the elevator, the hot tears are trickling down my cheeks. I wipe them away, afraid to be seen crying by any of my peers.

My phone dings in my back pocket. It's a text from Anthony: you ok? where are you?

He knows, then. That means everyone does. Even though Anthony and I are established as a couple, I don't want him around right now. I'm crushed that I didn't win the competition, but I'm also humiliated that I lost—to Oliver, of all people.

As soon as the elevator lets me out on my floor, I shove my phone in my pocket, his text unanswered. It's not until I'm in the privacy of my solo dorm room that I let the floodgates open. I throw myself on my bed and cry—because all that hard work was for nothing, because I lost, because this will disappoint my family even if they lie and say they're still proud.

I composed something original, something

true to me, something that I thought others could resonate with. It was a story of finding yourself over and over again in your life. Just like I saw my own family and community do; whenever they got knocked down, they picked themselves up and started over again. It was hopeful—*I* was hopeful—but I didn't play the game. I didn't write for a specific star; I wrote for the *whole* dance program.

Oliver played the game, and he won. Through ugly sobs and heaving breaths, I promise myself I'll never make that mistake twice. If I ever get the chance to play again.

FAMILIA GROUP CHAT

Today 1:45 pm

Madre   *1:45 PM*
Hi hija, any news on when you'll be home? We miss you

Rosa   *1:51 PM*
seriously it's been like 2 months

Amanda   *2:02 PM*
it takes as long as it takes you guys!

Padre   *2:17 PM*
Si si but we do miss you

SECOND CHANCE DUET ♪ 451

TODAY 6:11 PM

> **Celia** — *6:11 PM*
> i might get to come back in a couple of weeks

Madre — *6:15 PM*
Wepa!

Rosa — *6:18 PM*
for good??? omg

> **Celia** — *6:48 PM*
> yeah I think so, we can finish things up in the city

> *6:49 PM*
> there's a meeting I need to be in next month

♪ Ana Holguin

> **Amanda** — 6:56 PM
> well if it's for a MEETING then ok

> **Rosa** — 6:57 PM
> by 'meeting' she means she wants to sleep in her own bed and hang out w us
>
> she's tired of professor pendejo lololol

> **Padre** — 7:01 PM
> Girls

> **Celia** — 7:04 PM
> he's actually not a pendejo at all

Amanda *7:05 PM*

he really isn't. you should see him

Rosa *7:06 PM*

ok who kidnapped my sister? who is this?

Chapter Twenty-Eight

EVEN IN THE small Zoom square on my computer screen, Chris kind of looks like shit. There are dark circles under his eyes and his hair is much longer and shaggier than the last time I saw him in New York two months ago. It looks like he lost weight, too; his cheekbones are more pronounced than before.

Damian, however, looks about the same, with a shock of red hair and an alert gaze. I guess there is a stark difference when a person serves as showrunner *and* executive producer versus just producing. Chris must be exhausted after shooting nonstop for the last four months.

"I know our timeline is aggressive, but we really can't push back our streaming date,"

Chris says. "We're Limelight's big bet for spring. They're doing a promotional tie-in where Amex customers get three months free starting on our drop date, followed by a fifty percent discount for all other forms of payment the next month."

"They're eager to draw people away from their main competitors after their last big-budget show was panned by critics and audiences," Damian adds.

"It's not a problem," Oliver replies. In order to fit in the same Zoom box, we had to sit so close to each other that I can feel the warmth of him all the way up and down the left side of my body. "We'll be ready."

"We're thinking January for recording," I say. "Oliver made a good point that it'll be tough to schedule in December with all the holiday concert programming."

Chris nods. "Which orchestra?"

"New York Phil, most likely. I still have contacts there from my interning days. I already reached out to see if they can do it,"

Oliver replies, and both Chris's and Damian's faces light up.

"Can't wait to hear them with that drumbeat for the main theme." This from Damian.

My confidence soars internally at the mention of my individual contribution to this massive project. As much as I've loved collaborating with Oliver—much to my own surprise—it feels *so* good to hear someone call out my instrument. Especially someone who has the power to hire me in the future.

"Those drums were all Celia," Oliver says.

I can't help it; I smile, both at him when I glance over, and then at the screen when I see the look on Damian's face. It's one of admiration, if not surprise.

"Oh?" Damian asks.

"Yeah," I reply, forcing my tone to be nonchalant, as if these compliments aren't putting in extra work to fix all the times I've doubted myself. "I was a percussionist before I became a composer."

"I just have to say, it's been a real fucking treat working with you two," Chris says as he rubs a hand over his chin. "I was worried about hiring people who are so green, but you've been absolute professionals about it. Took everything in stride and just went heads down to put in the work. With this many people working on a project, something always goes wrong. There's always some drama of some kind, even though I do everything in my power to keep things running smoothly. When Gus dropped out, I thought we were totally fucked. Then you two showed up and helped me get this thing off the ground."

I nod my head and smile at Chris's little speech because this is everything I'd hoped to hear from a man who has the power to make or break a career. At the same time, there's a dark cloud hanging over my head, too. *He hates drama*—Rebecca's words of warning. She wasn't lying.

I have to tread so, so carefully here.

"It's our pleasure," I reply. "It's been an amazing experience working on this show with you."

"Agreed," Oliver adds.

"Great. I think we have what we need, right, Damian?" Chris asks. When Damian gives a thumbs-up, he continues, "Will we see you two in New York next month? We've got a private room booked at the Gramercy Tavern for the dinner."

Oliver and I haven't discussed this since we watched three episodes of *Battle for Love* three weeks ago. We've spent so much time in the studio, even more so now that the early episodes are considered picture lock, which I've learned means nothing in reality because the editing team is constantly changing things around. We've barely had time to come up for air.

There's a brief, awkward pause. I can't bring myself to look at Oliver. Instead, I make a split-second decision and say, "Yeah, we'll be there."

"Great. I'll have my assistant reach out with the details," Chris replies.

"Keep us posted on the New York Phil," Damian adds.

"Will do," I say, and then both Chris and Damian drop from the call. I close my laptop and take a deep breath. Time for me to face the music.

"We're going?" Oliver asks, clearly annoyed, as he pushes away from the studio desk.

I turn around to face him, immediately struck by how much he looks like the college version of himself. His face is back to that chilly mask, his expression dark and his jaw tense. The Oliver I've come to know over the last several weeks is nowhere to be found.

In that moment, I know I have two options. I can either play dumb and pretend like it's no big deal, or I can be honest with him—*really* honest about how much face time with decision-makers means for my career. How much is at stake for me.

For all the moments he's shared the truth

about himself with me, I know there really isn't a choice here. I owe him.

"Listen, I know that was a dick move. I'm sorry," I start, and I hope that he can hear how much I mean it. "I just—I can't miss that dinner. Do you remember when I told you about how much I need this job to go well?"

He crosses his arms over his chest, along with his legs. He could not be more closed off if he tried, but he does nod. I take it as a sign to continue.

"Well, that's true, but there's more to it. I'm, like, on the verge of having to quit and go do something else. All of my corporate gigs have basically dried up. AI is taking over commercial work. My rent is going up and I'm... scared." To my infuriating surprise, I can feel tears rising to the surface, the inevitable result of repressing this anxiety for as long as I have. "I have been working my ass off for so long, and for what? If I can't get another job after *Lineage* is done...I don't know. I have no skills except for this. What would I even do?"

As I wave around at the studio equipment surrounding us, Oliver's face softens. I blink back the tears threatening to fall, clinging to the final shreds of my pride.

"I have been knocking—no, *pounding*—at the door of the entertainment industry for years, basically begging to be let in," I say. "Someone finally opened it for me. If I don't go, it'll be the final nail in the coffin of my career. Chris and Damian now know I'm at least somewhat talented, but that's only half the battle. It's the relationships—those count even more."

What I don't say is that it's also the game—the one I once lost to the same man sitting in front of me. I'd think he remembers that because it's the last thing we talked about before we went our separate ways for nine years, but I don't know if he's making that connection. If I bring it up, I'll completely lose it.

A beat of silence passes between us after I finish talking. There's a tense moment where

I wonder if he'll say anything at all, but then he untangles all his limbs and lets out a heavy sigh. He scoots his chair closer and puts a hand on my knee.

"I know this industry is tough," he says, the ice from his earlier tone now gone. "It's okay. We'll go. Just…don't blindside me again, okay?"

Swallowing hard, I nod. I'm afraid if I open my mouth, I'll cry. It's hard enough letting him see just how dire things are for me when we're sitting in his family's beautiful custom home. Instead, I put my hand over his and force a smile.

Even though I got my way, I don't feel much better. Not for the rest of the night, and not in the days that follow, spent holed up in the studio, working away. Forcing Oliver to agree to go to this dinner was just one part of a difficult process. I still have to network my way into another paycheck. I still have to make this boys' club see that a person like me—a Latina from the Heights—belongs there.

**FROM: Celia García
<celia@celiagarcia.com>
TO: Ann Martin
<ann.martin@talentfirstagency.com>
DATE: Wednesday, October 14 at 9:52 PM
SUBJECT: Lineage contract installments**

Hi Ann,

Hope all is well with you! Just want to double check something—I'll get my next contract installment when we complete the score recording, correct?

Cheers,

Celia

FROM: Ann Martin <ann.martin@talentfirstagency.com>
TO: Celia García <celia@celiagarcia.com>
DATE: Thursday, October 15 at 8:12 AM
SUBJECT: RE: Lineage contract installments

Hi Celia,

Yes, that's correct. They were prompt to pay first installment on signing (rare for studios!) but I'll stay on top of them to ensure you get paid quickly. When are you recording?

Best,

Ann

FROM: Celia García <celia@celiagarcia.com>
TO: Ann Martin <ann.martin@talentfirstagency.com>
DATE: Thursday, October 15, at 8:14 a.m.
SUBJECT: RE: Lineage contract installments

January. I'll let you know as soon as it's done. Thank you!

Chapter Twenty-Nine

WINTER ARRIVES IN Maine. On our last full day, I wake up to a view of snow-laced treetops. It's the beautiful kind, too—fat, puffy flakes that cover the boughs in a sparkling blanket despite the sun hiding behind the clouds. It'd be idyllic if it weren't for the lump of dread in the pit of my stomach.

With every frantic day that passed in the last three weeks, I've grown more and more aware of the fact that our time here is coming to an end. Oliver and I have been working around the clock to finish the score as much as possible so that we can complete it with our own mini-studios in the city, which look like kindergarten business compared to what we've been working with here. He's also spent much of his spare time winterizing the house, something I've never had to think about as a city rat with a dad who took care of all that stuff, whatever it is. We've been packing and cleaning and repacking. Tomorrow morning at 7:00 a.m., a taxi is picking us up at the house and driving us to the Portland airport. We'll be back in New York by noon. The dinner is at 8:00 p.m.

For all the complaining I did when I sat on the stoop of my family's home nearly three months ago, I'm not ready to leave. I feel like I have one foot here, in Boothbay Harbor, and one foot in the life I left behind. I miss my family, my creature comforts of my own space, yes—but this quiet world I've inhabited with Oliver has grown on me so much that I don't want to let it go.

Just us, I think as I burrow under the covers. He's still fast asleep next to me, one heavy leg slung over my own. I nestle into his chest. Breathe him in. Let that clean smell of his soap and the remnants of his cologne fill my lungs.

For a while, I hover in that space between—awake and asleep, here and New York, the present and the future. *Day by day*, we've said before. If this is our last one in Maine, then we'll make it a good one.

Sleep is so precious for him that I don't want to wake him. I slip out of bed without incident and silently shut the bathroom door to tend to my morning routine. Once I make it to the kitchen, I can see that we got at least three inches of snow. It's still beautiful and untouched; the perks of a house so remote that you cannot see your neighbors.

While the coffee brews, I check my phone. There are a few automatic-bill-pay emails waiting for me—a reminder that the unfun parts of my life in New York are waiting for me—along with a bunch of unread messages in the family group chat. Everyone is so excited I'm coming home. I wish I shared the same enthusiasm.

I tap into Amanda's contact card. If there's one person I can talk to about my complicated feelings, it's her—the middle sister who is not only an early riser, but also the most reasonable and levelheaded of the three of us. My ears strain as I listen for any signs of movement upstairs, but I'm met with silence. I fix myself a cup of coffee and hit the call button.

Amanda picks up on the second ring. "What's wrong?"

"Nothing," I whisper through a smile. "Just wanted to say hi."

"Okay, well, hola," she replies. "I don't think you've ever called me at seven a.m.—no, wait, six forty-five."

"Well, I'm up now and wanted to talk to my sister. Is there something wrong with that?"

"No, but why are you so quiet?" she asks.

"Oh my god, you and Rosa," I mutter, rolling my eyes. "She asked me the same thing when we talked."

"My loud-ass sister calls me first thing in

the morning whispering like she's being held hostage and you expect me not to ask questions?" There's a bunch of noise on her end of the line, like dishes clattering in a sink, and I can picture her standing in the small kitchen of the apartment she shares with her roommate. "Be for real, Celia. What's up?"

I take a sip of my coffee. "I'm just trying to be *nice*. He's still asleep."

"But what's the real reason you called? I'm gonna see you in, like, thirty hours."

I take a deep breath and remind myself why I called this sister out of all people—she sees right through my bullshit. This is what I wanted when I picked up the phone.

"I guess I'm just feeling, like, weird about it all," I say, hyperaware of the fact that I have to be careful here; no one knows what's happened between Oliver and me. "When I first took this job and came up here, all I wanted to do was crush it so I could go back home. But now we're leaving tomorrow and I feel like...I don't know. Like I've changed or something."

"*We're* leaving," Amanda repeats.

I blink, confused at the direction she's taking. "Yeah, he's going back to the city, too."

"This weird feeling—it couldn't be because there's something going on between you and him, right?"

I almost drop my coffee. "What?" I ask, but when the question leaves my lips, I know that it won't fool her. Not for one second.

"Listen, hermana, I'm not trying to pry. If you don't want to tell me the details, that's fine, but you can't call me for advice or whatever and lie to me. I saw the way you two looked at each other when you FaceTimed me for my birthday. You're quiet in the group chats, too. I know you're a workhorse and this was a big job, but you're holding all of us at arm's length for a reason."

My heart is racing and it has nothing to do with the caffeine. I lean against the counter and bite my lip. Amanda is content to let the silence stretch out between us.

"Okay, so, what if that was true?" I finally

ask. "Hypothetically speaking—what if there was something going on between Oliver and me?"

"Then I'd laugh and say congrats," she replies. "He's hot now."

"Yeah, I'm aware," I mumble. "But what if... what if there are feelings involved?"

It's the first time I've said it out loud in any capacity. I still don't know what those feelings are, exactly, but I know they're *there*. All the memories of him from college, the reality of who he is now, the work we're doing, the uncertainty of my future, of *our* future—it's all tangled up in a hot mess inside me.

"What kind of feelings?" she asks.

"Amanda," I huff. "I don't know. That's why I called you."

"I think you do know." Her response is quick, her tone soft. "And that's why you called me instead of Rosa."

Because our baby sister would squeal and start planning our wedding. She'd demand every detail. She wouldn't care that Oliver and I are colleagues. It wouldn't even cross her mind that this could be an issue for me professionally.

I'm about to ask what I should do when I hear the water turn on upstairs. He's up and moving around. Panic ensues.

"Shit, I have to go," I whisper frantically. "Don't say anything, okay? Promise?"

Amanda scoffs. "Have I said anything to anyone yet? I got you."

"Love you. See you soon."

"Love you t—"

I end the call, set my phone on the counter, and breathe. It's totally normal for me to call my sister; there's no real reason for me to hide that from him. What I don't want him to know is why I called her.

When he appears in the kitchen, still in his flannel pajama bottoms and T-shirt, all that nervous energy coursing through me zeroes in on my chest. My heart feels like it's going to explode when I look at him. I feel hot all over, and not in a bad way.

"Good morning," he says with a lazy smile, clearly oblivious to the riot happening inside me. "You been up long?"

"No, haven't even finished my first cup." I raise my mug before pouring one for him. "Sleep well?"

"Like a baby," he replies, his arms winding around me until I'm tucked against him. "You?"

I press my cheek to his chest, relishing the way we fit together, the easy way our bodies mold for each other. "Yeah, good."

"Can't believe it snowed this much," he says. "I swear, I blinked and the seasons changed."

I swallow hard. "I know."

He pulls back and surveys me. His arms stay looped around me in a loose semicircle as we look at each other. I take in the depth of his green eyes behind his glasses, the fullness of his lips, the faint pillow line still etched across his left cheek. Not for the first time, I wonder if this is how he looks when he wakes up in New York. If it'll feel this way there. If I'll even get to see it.

"Our last day in Boothbay Harbor," he says softly. "Anything in particular you want to do?"

"I still need to figure out how to close my suitcase and double check I got everything out of my old rooms. We have some stuff to finish up in the studio but... I don't care what else we do, as long as I spend it with you."

When he kisses me, I taste him—the minty toothpaste, but also that essence that is undeniably Oliver. That spark low in my belly ignites, singeing away the ball of dread I woke up with. Here, in his arms, it's easy to forget everything waiting for us, everything riding on me showing up to that dinner.

So I do—I forget all that, and let it be just us.

BOSTON SYMPHONY ORCHESTRA
301 Massachusetts Avenue
Boston, MA 02115

Dear Ms. García:

Thank you for your interest in working with the Boston Symphony Orchestra. We regret to inform you that your application for the Conducting Internship was not selected for the forthcoming year.

Each year, we receive thousands of applications for a very limited number of spots. Our committee is tasked with making these difficult decisions, made even more challenging by the caliber of talent from musicians such as yourself. We are honored that you considered the Boston Symphony Orchestra as the next step in your career.

Please do not contact the administration or staff regarding feedback on your application. Our committee is unable to discuss materials once a decision has been made.

We wish you all the best in your future endeavors.

Sincerely,
The Boston
Symphony Orchestra

Chapter Thirty

TEN YEARS AGO

FROM MY PLACE on the floor, I flip the page in my history book and sigh. My phone sits next to me; the time reads 8:58 p.m. I've been waiting nearly an hour for Anthony's rehearsal to get out—the one for Oliver's ballet, which hits the Lincoln Center stage for one night only in just two months.

I'd be lying if I said I retained any of the information I need for my History of English Music class. Mostly I've been trying to hear what's going on in the room on the other side of the wall. All I've managed to catch are bits and pieces of the orchestra between all the stopping and starting they've been doing. If

I had to guess, I'd say it's been a frustrating rehearsal for all involved. The petty side of me takes a little pleasure in that.

With a sigh, I close my book, shove it in my backpack, and haul myself to my feet. I've been waiting long enough. As quietly as possible, I slip into the room. No one notices me tuck myself along the far wall.

"Okay, can we try it again?" Oliver asks from his place on the conductor's podium. "Woodwinds, pay attention to your dynamic markings this time."

Oof. I cringe at the terse way he speaks to everyone. Every time he's been in charge—whether in small ensembles or with a larger group like the Lab student orchestra—he's been like this. Demanding. Abrasive. Curt.

After a rehearsal with the Lab last year, I heard one of the freshman-year trumpet players ask if Oliver was always such a dick. The senior he was talking to didn't even hesitate when he said yes. Everyone else laughed.

That white button-down shirt and those

black slacks Oliver's wearing might make him think he looks like a grown-up, but I disagree. It mostly just makes him look unrelatable. Everyone else is comfortable and casual in their jeans and hoodies. One of the saxophone players might even be wearing pajamas.

He raps his baton on the music stand. The flutists at the edge of a row side-eye each other. Everyone lifts their instruments. With a wave of his hand, the music starts. I release a breath I didn't know I was holding when a haunting melody fills the room.

When the flutes come in, they're too loud. It's a crass juxtaposition with the low timbre of the strings. I notice it right away and it appears Oliver does, too. He waves his hands to stop everyone.

"No. Still not right. That's enough for tonight, I think." His shoulders heave with a sigh. "Practice, please. I'll see you on Sunday, three p.m. Do not be late."

While everyone starts packing up, I watch

as Oliver drops his baton on the stand and jams his hands into his hair. For the first time since Dr. Kendrick sat me down and told me that my piece wasn't chosen, I don't feel jealous. I'm not even pissed. I can see the weight of the world on Oliver's shoulders. I've heard through the grapevine how much time he's spending on this single performance, between orchestra practice and meetings with the dancers. The combined rehearsals haven't even started yet. This is on top of all our regular schoolwork and graduation prep. Every single person in our year is working fast and furious to secure a job, an internship, or a place in their graduate studies, all while keeping their grades up.

I might have lost the competition, but I also lost all the stress that comes along with it. I'm barely keeping up between auditions, internship-packet submissions, and everything else.

Could I have done it? Could I have taken this on, led seventy-some of my peers in this effort, all while keeping up with my full course load? I like to think that I could, but I don't know.

Oliver turns around, hops off the podium, and spots me. Surprise flashes across his face. I've barely looked at him since that day in the lobby, let alone spoken to him. Yet here I am, crashing his rehearsal, staring right at him.

When he beelines straight for me, it's my turn to look surprised. My brow flattens as I look behind me, as if there could be someone else he'd be walking toward, but it's just a blank wall. Sure enough, he stops right in front of me, careful to keep at least a foot of space between us.

"How much did you hear?" he asks.

No greeting, of course. I shrug with forced nonchalance. "Enough."

"How did we sound?"

This time, his question sounds so earnest that I don't know what to say. Never, in all my time at this school, has Oliver asked me what I thought. Nor have I seen him ask anyone else their opinion on anything he did.

I narrow my eyes. "Do you want my honest answer?"

"Yes," he huffs. "Why else would I ask?"

"Well, I didn't hear that much," I reply, choosing to give him a little grace for all the stress I know he's under. "But what I did hear—it seems like they're not responding to you. Maybe try a different approach?"

"Like what?" he fires back.

My train of thought is interrupted when Anthony appears at my side. The strap of his cello case is slung over his shoulder, his dark hair still styled into that artful swoop thing he does in the mornings. I smile at him as he slips his hand into mine.

"You're still staying the night?" Anthony asks, to which I nod. He's one of Rebecca's three roommates; I cherish my nights spent off campus in the company of my friends. "You ready to go?"

"Yeah, just a second." I turn my attention back to Oliver, who is staring at Anthony's profile so intently that I wonder what the hell that's about. "So, I was gonna say—try being a little nicer to them. Everyone's got a lot on their plate, you know? You barking orders at them isn't going to help them learn the music faster."

"Right," Oliver grits out as his gaze slides back to me. "I wouldn't say I *bark* at anyone, but I'll take that into consideration."

It takes all my effort not to roll my eyes. Oliver looks so annoyed that we're already on the brink of arguing. I swallow the resentment that's managed to resurface in the two minutes I spent talking to him. Oliver says nothing when Anthony and I leave with half-hearted waves.

I already know he won't take my advice, but I don't care. It's movie night at Rebecca, Anthony, Blake, and Chloe's place. We're watching my pick, *West Side Story*. I'm not going to let Oliver's arrogance ruin that.

On Sunday night, when Anthony gets out of rehearsal, he calls me to tell me that Oliver brought in pizza for the whole orchestra. I don't believe what I'm hearing until Anthony shows up at my dorm with two slices that he snagged for me. It's the good kind, too, from the little family joint down the street.

SISTER GROUP CHAT

Today 8:31 PM

Rosa — 8:31 PM
omg we get to see you!! like in a few hours!!

Amanda — 8:32 PM
omggg I can't wait!!

Celia — 8:48 PM
well I have to go straight to my apartment and get ready for that dinner, so it's really like two days

8:49 PM
but yes I'll see you once that's done

> **8:49 PM**
> friday!

Rosa *8:50 PM*
sure lmao

Amanda *8:51 PM*
;) ;) ;)

Chapter Thirty-One

MY BAGS ARE packed. All our files for *Lineage* have been uploaded into Dropbox. The house is, essentially, shut down for the foreseeable future. Aside from one last bag of trash to take out in the morning, it's almost like we were never even here.

I should be thrilled I'm going home tomorrow. I got my way; we're going to that dinner and I don't have to miss the holidays with my family. But for some reason, that's not at all what I feel when I tiptoe my way back downstairs, wearing one of his old T-shirts and a pair of sweats.

Oliver is showering in the owner's suite, which is where I should be, curled up in bed, waiting for him. Instead, I'm sitting at the piano in semidarkness. My fingers rest on the ivory keys, but I don't make a sound.

I'll miss this place—that much I've made peace with. After all the bitching I did when Oliver first sprang this on me, I've grown to like it here. The quiet expanse of it all doesn't freak me out anymore, doesn't make me feel like I don't belong. It's the opposite, actually. I like that it's so peaceful that I can hear myself think—something I've had to do a lot of in the last three months.

A soft knock at the door catches my attention. I'm already smiling when I turn around to find Oliver leaning against the doorframe with his arms crossed, hair still damp from the shower. He's wearing a clean white T-shirt, those gray sweats, and his glasses—the most lethal combination in human history. I force a swallow.

"Hey," he says softly.

"Hi." I scooch over on the piano bench and pat the empty spot next to me. "Sit?"

When he does, I'm enveloped by the smell of him. It's so intoxicating that it's almost dizzying. How he can smell so good, so clean but also expensive in a quiet luxury kind of way, I'll never understand. I found his cologne on the bathroom counter the other day and sprayed it in the air, but it doesn't smell like this when it's not on him, and I doubt he sprayed any on tonight after his shower. No, the good part—the part I can't get enough of—is all his own body chemistry.

"Needed one last go-around at the piano?" he asks, pulling me out of my reverie.

I lean my head against his shoulder and let my hands fall into my lap. "Something like that."

"It's weird, isn't it?" he asks quietly. "To leave here after all this time together?"

"Very." I blow out a breath of relief. "There were times where I felt like this would never end—like I would actually live in this house for the rest of my life or something. But now it's our last night and I'm thinking about going back to my tiny-ass apartment and I... I don't know. I guess maybe I took this for granted."

His fingers find my chin and, with a gentle tug, he turns me so we're face-to-face. There's a tiny pinch between his eyebrows, the action so small I would have missed it three months ago, but I see it now. He's sad, too.

"This is where it started for us," he replies. "At the piano."

I know what he means; even though we technically met at a café in the city, *this* is where things changed for us. But I'm not sure if he knows that's true of our first go-around, too, all those years ago. If he even remembers the first time we spoke to each other in that Juilliard practice room. If I affected him as much as he affected me, even if I couldn't or wouldn't admit it then.

He clears his throat gently. "Celia, I don't—I don't want this to end."

"I don't, either." The words come out of me in a rush, the relief palpable in my chest.

"I care about you so much. These feelings... they are a lot."

If I were braver, I'd tell him what I think those feelings are. I'd tell him that I feel tingly and warm whenever I look at him. That I understand every nice thing he's done for me has been to show me that he cares when he struggles to articulate it. That I think he's one of the only people in my life who understands my passion for this weird, difficult career I've worked so hard for, and I am so grateful for it.

His thumb skates along my jaw, grounding me in the here and now. I lean into him, drinking in those big green eyes and committing those faint freckles along his nose and cheeks to memory. When his lips meet mine, my eyes flutter closed, and I suspect he's feeling and thinking the same thing because there is no restraint or hesitation in the way his lips and tongue move over mine.

We're running out of time.

That thought—that reality—sends my heart spluttering and my stomach swooping. I grip his shoulders as I half lift myself off the bench and swing a leg over him until I'm straddling his lap. He doesn't miss a beat, not when his hands cup my ass to give me a little more support while my legs dangle over the other side of the bench, and especially not when those long fingers of his manage to grip my hips and grind me against him. Both of our pajama pants do little to hide how this is affecting him.

I cup his jaw while we kiss each other with a sort of reckless abandon, almost like it's a competition to see who can taste the most of each other. His hands keep controlling my hips, pushing and pulling me over his lap, and I start to wonder if I'm going to come like this by how fast the pleasure is building between my legs. I let out a moan when he shifts his hips under me and before I know what's happening, he's standing, lifting me with him while my legs wrap around his waist, his lips never once leaving mine.

My ass hits the piano keys in a jumbled, discordant mess of a sound. Oliver looms over me, a dazed sort of half-smile on his face, as we pull back from each other. My chest heaves as I take in his blown pupils, his puffy lips, his messed-up hair—but it's the *way* he's looking at me, like I'm all that he sees in this world, that forces me to put a name to that feeling currently blooming in my chest.

Love—I'm falling in love with him.

Does he know what I'm thinking? He might because he's watching me carefully, his focus dialed in on me so as not to miss a single thing, when one of his hands dips below the stretchy waistband of my pants. I'm not wearing any underwear. He shuts his eyes briefly and groans at this discovery.

I have no choice but to close my eyes when his fingers slide over me, then inside of me, my legs falling open as wide as they'll go. Every time I move or shift on the piano, I strike more keys, but it doesn't matter. It feels so good when he does that thing I like that someone could throw a drumstick at my head and I wouldn't notice. The way he makes me feel, so alive in my own skin, that's all I have right now, and I'm literally shaking for it.

"Turn around," he says, voice gruff and low, as his hand slips out of my pants.

I peel myself off the keys and do as I'm told, bracing my hands on the top of the piano for support. Maybe it's because we only have a few hours left here together, or maybe we both want to show each other how we feel, but there's a frenetic energy between us tonight. My pulse is going a million miles a minute and I can hear the labored breaths of Oliver behind me, especially when he pulls my pants to my knees. I rise up on my tiptoes in anticipation.

"Oliver." His name is a whisper, a plea, a prayer—I could write a hundred sonatas and vocalises and études for the way he's making me feel right now, the way his strong hands hold me in place to guide himself in. "Please."

He takes a shuddering breath before he asks, "You're close, aren't you?"

He knows the answer to this. Somehow, he

knows my body better than anyone I've ever slept with, including the boyfriends I dated for a lot longer. I push back into him to show him exactly what he's done.

He murmurs my name as he starts to move. It feels so good, all of it does, that I know it won't take long for me. I'm overwhelmed by him, in me and around me, our history in front of us and behind us, all of it culminating in the place we're joined together.

How I feel, those words—they're right there, on the tip of my tongue.

When he slips a hand around my front and touches me there, it's over for me, in a shuddering cry with my hands slapping the shiny wood of a Steinway piano. He's right behind me, muttering a stream of oh-gods and oh-fucks until everything slows to a languid stop. His warm chest presses against my back as he brushes the hair off my neck.

I never do say those words. Not when we help each other clean up, not when we inspect the piano and determine we did not damage it, only defiled it in theory. I think them, though, all through the fitful few hours of sleep I get next to him. But then our phone alarms beckon us out of bed much too early in the morning, and I know the moment has passed.

Our time in Maine has come to an end.

LINEAGE — EPISODE EIGHT, "ALL'S FAIR"

EXT. — MOORE FAMILY ROOFTOP   561

FADE IN on HARRISON. His back is to his brother and sister as he takes in the New York skyline. His hands clutch the glass partition.

                EMILY
You can't be serious, Harry.

                JAMES
              (laughing)
This is honestly the stu-pidest thing you've ever done. Ever.

HARRISON turns to face them.

                HARRISON
Well, it's done. She's your sister-in-law now.

                    EMILY
Maybe in the eyes of
the law, but she doesn't
belong here. She's not
family.

                    HARRISON
You're a fucking snob.

                    JAMES
                (laughing)
He gave it all up for a
bartender. Em, you owe me
two Gs, by the way. I told
you he would do it.

Chapter Thirty-Two

WHEN WE START our descent into Newark, I almost don't believe my eyes. It's been three long months since we left the city. That's two months and three weeks more than the longest stretch I'd been gone before this.

I can't even turn to Oliver and gush over the sight of the Empire State Building. We booked our tickets so late that there weren't any seats next to each other. He's two or three rows behind me on the other side of the plane.

Not that it matters—New York is a short ninety-minute flight from Portland, and we already spent an hour in the back of a taxi cab that smelled like cigars and coffee, plus we sat together at the airport in an exhausted daze.

Now that I'm here, that sense of elation that has been noticeably absent returns. After all this time, I'm *home*.

Well, almost home, as I'm starkly reminded when we taxi on the runway for half an hour. I crane my neck and try to catch a glimpse of Oliver, but he's either slouching or sleeping because I can't find him. Instead, I answer all the texts from my family, letting them know we made it back safe and sound.

When we're finally let off the plane, I want nothing more than to run to baggage claim and get my stuff, but I make myself wait for Oliver at the gate. It's strange to see him emerge from that tiny hallway, to see him in the flesh on home turf after everything that's happened between us. I wonder if he looks at me and sees a different version of me, too.

I watch as he approaches, his leather bag slung over his shoulder and his carry-on rolling behind him, and I feel somehow comforted and more anxious the longer I stand there. *Day by day*, we said back in Maine. In reality, we've only been doing whatever this is for—what, six weeks? Maybe two months since our first kiss? That's not a long time, but it all felt so intense, so inevitable with the two of us in that house, making our music together.

Now here we are, back in the big city, a world of options at our fingertips. What happens to us now?

But then Oliver breaks into a wide grin when he's a few feet away from me. That warm, tingly feeling zips all through me, stronger than it ever was before. I smile back at him without having to think about it.

"It's good to be back, isn't it?" he asks, and just hearing his soothing voice calms my nerves a little.

"So good."

Between my tote bag and carry-on, plus his own stuff, our hands are full as we make our way down a series of long airport hallways. We're at that part of a trip where I'm eager to get back to my own place but constantly deterred by everything else. Too many people.

Slow walkers. A baggage claim carousel that hasn't started moving yet.

I check the time on my phone. It's well after noon now. Even though the dinner isn't until 8:00 p.m., I can't help but feel the pressure of time running out cloaking my shoulders.

Our bags do show up eventually—that I had to pay fifty dollars for, this morning's stark reminder that I need to get *paid*—and Oliver hoists them off the carousel. I'm hit with a cold blast of winter air when we head outside for the taxi stand. I didn't pack my real winter jacket when I left the city in the height of summer, and my little lightweight coat is *not* cutting it.

"You're in Midtown, right?" he asks as we queue up behind the short line of travelers waiting for a car.

I shiver. "Yeah. Where are you?"

"West Village," he replies. "Here, take my gloves."

He's already stripping them off his hands but I shake my head to stop him. "I'm okay. I guess it doesn't make sense for us to share a cab, right? Mine will take the Lincoln Tunnel but you'll take the Holland."

"Right." The line is getting shorter; it's almost our turn. "I guess this is it, then."

"Until tonight," I offer with a smile.

"Yeah. Tonight," he replies with a weak smile of his own. It doesn't reach his eyes.

"About that," I start, but suddenly my heart is beating so fast I have to take a deep breath to calm myself. "I think we should keep it professional. Between us. At the dinner."

Then it's my turn to get into a cab. The driver hops out, puts my luggage in the back, and opens my door for me. For a long beat, Oliver and I stare at each other, the cacophony of the airport our soundtrack.

As his expression shutters, effectively cutting me off, my stomach drops.

"Just for tonight," I explain quickly, my tone bordering on desperate. "I don't want to give them the wrong impression."

There was that moment back inside, when he smiled at me and I thought everything would be okay. Our little whatever-this-is that started between us would survive the transition from quiet, coastal Maine to the hustle and bustle of the city. But now, when I look at him, closed off and cool, I'm not sure.

"Just for tonight?" he asks, so low I almost don't hear it.

"Yes. I promise."

He doesn't respond, but his head does dip the tiniest amount. It's *almost* a nod.

This does nothing to help my anxiety, nor does the loud, abrupt honk from my driver. My heart jumps into my throat and I think, *Fuck it.* I grab the front of Oliver's sleek black jacket and pull him toward me until our lips collide.

It's no different to kiss him here. He still feels the same against me, still smells just as good even after a long morning of traveling. When we pull back from each other, a smile breaks him open, slowly but surely.

"I'll see you later," I say, then hop in my cab to go *home.*

Ana Holguin

TODAY 1:44 PM

Celia — 1:44 PM
Made it back! We're still on for tonight?

Rebecca — 2:02 PM
Yes!!!! 6:45 at the Old Town Bar. Right down the street from Gramercy Tavern. We'll walk over together

Celia — 2:05 PM
Perfect. What's the dress code tonight?

Rebecca — 2:07 PM
Hmmm professional chic? The guys are pretty casual but you know how it is for women. Double standards and all that

Celia *2:08 PM*

yep sure do

Rebecca *2:10 PM*

can't wait to catch up!!!

see you later :) :) :)

Chapter Thirty-Three

THE SECOND I walk through my door, I go into prep mode. I wish I had time to enjoy being back in my own space, but traffic was crawling and now I only have three hours to pick an outfit, shower, and do full hair and makeup before I meet Rebecca for a pre-dinner drink. When I toss my bags into a pile next to my bed, I pray that I have some clean underwear somewhere.

The nerves hit me in full force about halfway through my shower. Everything I've been working toward—for the last three months and also every minute since my first drum lesson twenty-some years ago—rides on the connections I make tonight. Even this apartment

I've called home for the last two years depends on me securing a job that pays well enough that I can keep it.

The pressure chokes me. I'm so out of sorts that I fumble through my bathroom routine; I even nick both of my knees with my razor, something I haven't done in years. Standing in front of my closet wrapped in a towel with two tissue dots to soak up the blood, I decide that I hate everything I own. I don't have anything that says *professional chic* and also *nice enough to impress a bunch of rich gatekeepers*.

I make it as far as putting on a bra and underwear when I hear footsteps outside my door, followed by the key turning in the lock. My heart leaps into my throat and, like an idiot, I freeze. If I'm about to burglarized, it's going to happen while I'm almost naked.

My front door bursts open and a tornado of hair, arms, and screams barrels through my apartment. Amanda and Rosa descend on me while I stand there, paralyzed first by fear and then by surprise. It takes them a good five minutes to calm down enough that they can laugh at me.

"Hermana, what the *hell* is going on?" Rosa exclaims as she takes in all the clothes that have been ripped out of my closet and are now strewn around the floor.

"Hold up," I say, hands up in front of me in a sign of defeat. "What are you two doing here?"

Amanda flops on my bed, still in her blue winter coat, right on top of a pile of shirts I just deemed ugly five minutes ago. "You didn't think we'd wait until tomorrow or the next day to see you, did you?"

I sigh and let my hands fall to my side. "Well, yeah. You know I have to go to that dinner tonight."

Rosa smirks as she takes a step back and eyes what I'm wearing. "Speaking of—nice outfit."

"That's why we're here," Amanda adds. "We knew you'd freak out about what to wear, so we brought options."

It's then that I notice two things: first, that I'm still in my underwear, and second, that Rosa draped a black garment bag over my computer chair. I grab my towel off the floor where I dropped it and wrap it around me so it's tucked under my arms. Rosa sheds her pink coat and tosses it on my bed before picking up the garment bag and unzipping it with a dramatic flair.

"We know how much you love that dress Amanda bought in that Nordstrom sale last year," she says.

Amanda nods. "And that one sweater Rosa got last winter. The boatneck one with the gray stripes."

The flurry of fear, surprise, and anxiety dissipates as my sisters start pulling clothing options out of the bag. Of course they showed up for me. They knew I'd panic, knew that I'd want to put my best possible foot forward tonight.

As Rosa holds up different options against my body, I think of Oliver—how he has no siblings, no one who barges in to help when he needs it the most. I think about that conversation by the bay, where he all but told me how lonely he was, and all the ways he's tried to become the kind of friend a friend would like to have.

"I think the black sweater with the silk skirt," Rosa proclaims.

"Agreed," Amanda adds.

I look down at the garments that Rosa pinned against my towel-clad body. It's a lovely black sweater with a V-neckline that shows just a little bit of my chest without being too risqué. The fluidity of the skirt adds a touch of refinement without being too formal. I know both clothing items well; I've borrowed them before, separately, for different occasions.

I blow out a sigh of relief. "Oh my god, thank you."

"Don't sweat it," Amanda replies. At some point during Rosa's game of pin-the-outfit-on-the-sister, she took off her own jacket and is now lying on my bed in jeans and a sweater. "How long till you have to leave?"

"Hour and a half," I reply after glancing at my phone.

"Great. Sit down," Rosa demands as she clears the clothes and junk off my computer chair. "I'll do your hair." My sister shoves me into the seat and starts combing through my damp curls with her fingers. "Jesus, it's gotten long."

"And you can catch us up on everything," Amanda adds, with a wink just for me.

As much as I'm steamrolled by the two of them, I'm incredibly grateful—not just because they knew to show up with the best of their clothes or that both are keeping different secrets of mine, but because they're my sisters.

♪

When I walk into the Old Town Bar at 6:45 sharp, I feel as confident as possible given how much is at stake for me. My outfit looks great after Amanda steamed it and Rosa managed to style my curls into an elegant low twist that somehow looks effortless even though I have about ten bobby pins jammed into my hair.

The two of them even stayed behind to put all my clothes back into my closet so I don't return home to a disaster. Hopefully not alone.

The low-lit space is hopping, so I have to squeeze through crowds before I even make it to the bar. Rebecca is already there, a martini in front of her, her black coat draped over a chair next to her to save me a spot. Her hair is different; it's grown out enough that she now has curtain bangs to frame her green eyes. Otherwise, she looks about the same.

"You made it back in one piece!" she exclaims when she sees me.

She hops off her stool so we can give each other a quick hug. I do a brief pass of her outfit to compare it against my own, then sigh with relief when I see she's wearing a soft-gray turtleneck tucked into wide-leg black trousers. Totally comparable to my own 'fit.

"That's debatable," I reply as we each slide onto our barstools. "What a whirlwind couple of months."

"No kidding. When you told me you were

on your way to Maine for this, I was shocked. Of all places! Maine!"

I nod and shrug at the same time. "Right? Turns out that was exactly what we needed. But how are *you*? Did that superhero movie of yours finally wrap?

The bartender drops by then, so after a quick glance at their drink menu, I order a winter Aperol spritz to keep the alcohol content low. I can't let myself get too muddled before meeting the people with the power to hire me.

"Yes! Fuck, thank *god*," Rebecca mutters before taking a generous drink of her martini. "This was my first time working with this director and he's very old-school, so Barlowe didn't even get a glimpse of the movie until the first picture lock was done. Which means that *my* job is insanely rushed and difficult, even when I'm working with a legend like that. I literally cried tears of relief when my director approved the musical cut." She pauses to shudder. "Don't get me wrong, it was a great experience, but I am so glad I have some time off before I'm needed for *Lineage*. That's why I'm in New York. I'm spending the holidays with my family here."

"Barlowe?" I ask. "As in, *Robert* Barlowe?" When she nods, I continue on. "What's it like, working with Oliver's dad?"

A look of surprise registers on her face. "You've never met him?"

"No."

Her expression turns thoughtful as she considers my response. "I guess that shouldn't surprise me," she says. "You know he never once came to Juilliard to see Oliver? Not even at graduation. I looked for him everywhere because I wanted to introduce myself like the nosey bitch I am, and ... nada."

I think of everything Oliver's shared with me—about how he felt like little more than baggage to his parents, how *not* close his family is—and find myself nodding. "I know," I say. "I remember."

"Anyway, to answer your question: Robert is just like Oliver was ten years ago, but more of an asshole," she says with a breezy air. "He is absolutely married to the job and only speaks when he has something very important to say, which means you'd better be listening, because he is *not* going to repeat himself. He will only record at Abbey Road Studios, so I had to haul my ass to London for a few days while they laid everything down. The weeks that followed were the most stressful experience of my life."

My spritz arrives then. I buy myself some time when I take a drink. Hearing about Oliver's dad through Rebecca, after everything I learned in Maine, feels like taking a knife to the gut.

"Well, you did it! And now you have a big superhero credit to your name," I manage with enough cheerfulness that it comes out sounding authentic.

"True." There's a triumphant gleam in her eyes while she considers her own hard-won success. "Speaking of Oliver—how has it been, working with him?"

"Good. Really good, actually."

"Really?" she asks, the skepticism in her voice made all the more obvious by the way her eyebrows raise.

"Yeah, *really*," I reply with a laugh. "We had kind of a bumpy start, but once we found our groove, we were in it."

She blows out a breath as she leans back. "Whew, that's good news. I have to admit, I was a little worried you two might kill each other given the way you were at each other's throats in college."

"We weren't *at each other's throats*." I cringe at the description and take another drink. "We just...didn't understand each other," I finish lamely.

"That's not how I remember it," she replies with a smirk.

I choose to ignore that, the need to defend Oliver too strong to resist. "He's a remarkable musician. Always has been, but he's even better now. There were times where I felt, like, overwhelmed by the work, but he pulled me out of it. He's super generous, too. I mean, he moved both of us almost four hundred miles at the drop of a hat. That's something, right?"

Rebecca's eyes narrow. When I finish my little speech, she says nothing, the jazz music from the bar filling the space between us. Eventually she leans forward, her eyes little more than slits, and asks, "What exactly happened up north?"

I blink, surprised. I open my mouth to stammer out a response, but she cuts me off by saying, "Actually, don't answer that. Not until post-prod is over."

"Rebecca, I—"

"Can I give you some advice?" The urgency in her voice sends a surge of fear through me. "Woman to woman?"

I nod.

"Tonight, when you talk to everyone at dinner, do *not* give them any reason to think that there's any kind of funny business going on. And I mean anything—like arguments, romantic shit, whatever. Everyone in this industry is dispensable because there are a million people vying for the same gig." She pauses for a second, then adds, "Okay, in our case, maybe there's hundreds of thousands of people gunning for our jobs, but the sentiment is the same: Until you're so established that you're turning down work, you can't afford a misstep."

At my horrified expression, Rebecca softens her tone and places a hand on my shoulder. "The same thing goes for me, babe. You know how hard it is to make it in this industry. I had my dad's help, but even then, I have to be extra careful about how I present myself. Part of it is that our niche is such a boys' club, but it's also a Hollywood-movie thing in general. Every connection you make is transactional. The second these people think you're going to cost them something, you're out—unless you have the safety of a super famous parent or something."

I know this is true, but it's somehow harder to hear it coming from Rebecca, the same girl whose hair I held back while she puked up jungle juice in her apartment bathroom. We're no longer stressed-out college students who have each other's backs; we're now stressed-out working professionals, still trying to keep an eye out for each other.

"You're right, I know," I reply after a hard swallow. "No funny business tonight. I promise."

She smiles. "It'll be fine. Just be your usual charming self, and I'm sure you'll walk out of there with a few coveted email addresses."

"I sure fucking hope so," I mutter.

"Shall we?" she asks as she glances at the time on her phone.

As we wait for the bartender to run our cards, I force myself to take deep breaths. *Chris hates drama*, Rebecca warned me months ago. Even though Oliver and I have personal things to figure out, we've made it this far without any kind of major problem. What's one more night in the grand scheme of it all?

The bartender sets our credit card slips

in front of us. After I scribble a tip, I turn to Rebecca and say, "Hey, before the night gets away from us, I just wanted to say thank you. It's not lost on me that I wouldn't be here if it weren't for you."

"First of all, it's your talent that got you this far, not me," she replies as she slips off her stool and shrugs on her coat. "Secondly, you know I love to help a sister out in this business, but I can't take full credit for that, either."

"What do you mean?"

"It was Oliver who suggested I reach out to you. I mean, once he said your name, I knew you'd be great at it so I texted you right away, but technically, it was his idea," she says. "Did he not tell you that?"

My breath whooshes out of me. I'm so stunned that I momentarily freeze while putting on my jacket.

"No, he...he never mentioned that," I reply quietly as I struggle to find my zipper.

"Huh." Rebecca cocks her head to the side and shrugs. "I was a little surprised when he suggested you since, well—the whole college thing, but it all worked out, right?"

"Right." I force a placid smile on my face. "It all worked out."

Rebecca leads the way out of the bar and into the cold, wintry night. When her back is to me, I pull my phone out of my purse and hammer out a text to Oliver at lightning speed.

> **Celia**
>
> you put me up for the lineage job? why didn't you tell me that?

The restaurant is only a five-minute walk away, so I have no choice but to forget about this until later. After all, the work comes first.

DEADLINE EXCLUSIVE:

See the First Teaser Trailer for Chris Ross's New TV Show *Lineage*

BY LISA MORRISON, TV EDITOR
NOVEMBER 5TH

DEADLINE has the exclusive first look at Chris Ross's new TV show *Lineage*. Check out the first official teaser trailer HERE!

Best known for his hefty drama films, which have garnered him multiple awards, Ross brings his directorial and producing talents to the small screen for the first time ever in partnership with Limelight and A24. The prestige drama about a wealthy New York media family stars Golden Globe winner Luke Tudor and three-time Emmy nominee Erica Stewart. Details about the show have remained under lock and key throughout production, leaving both industry professionals and fans speculating on what we can expect from Ross's first foray into television.

Speaking exclusively to *DEADLINE*, Limelight President & CEO Greg Baros said, "*Lineage* is the kind of show that every service would kill to have on their roster. It's storytelling at its highest form. We couldn't be more thrilled to welcome Chris Ross and team to the Limelight family."

Lineage is slated to stream exclusively on Limelight April 2nd.

Chapter Thirty-Four

GRAMERCY TAVERN IS one of those New York dining institutions I've heard of but never had a reason to go to. It's all rich, dark woods, sexy lighting, and white linens from the second Rebecca and I walk in the door. They already have their holiday decor up around the space, with tasteful touches like evergreen boughs that are draped across wooden beams and shelves. We're greeted by a lovely hostess immediately, our coats whisked away by a porter as soon as she hears we're there for Chris Ross's dinner.

We're led through a full dining room to a private room tucked in the back. My heart races as I take it all in: the long table running through the middle, the candles, the handful of people milling about with drinks in hand. My brain is in work-mode overdrive, so Chris is the first person I register. He's talking with the white-haired man I met at the Limelight office months ago—John, the director of photography. Chris looks better than he did on the Zoom just a few weeks ago; he's less gaunt and tired looking and his sandy blond hair has been tamed into submission.

I feel Oliver before I find him. A warm sensation zings up my spine. My eyes scan the room, unseeing all the other faces until they settle on the far corner. There he is, looking devastating in a bespoke gray suit and black sweater, head bent slightly as he talks with a short brown-haired man I've never seen before.

Oliver's eyes are already on me. A current passes between us, electric when it runs all the way through me. He put me up for this job—but why? With the way we left things before graduation and all the years after when we didn't speak, *why?*

"May I get you something to drink?"

My attention snaps to the tray-bearing waiter that appeared in front of Rebecca and me. She orders a dirty martini; I ask for the same. When the server leaves with a polite nod, he's replaced by Damian, the producer we met with just last month.

"Welcome!" he says, and I notice the reddish tinge to his cheeks that matches the ginger hair. "So glad you could both join us."

I smile and avoid looking at the empty drink in his hand. Chris had said this dinner was more civilized than the wrap party; I can only imagine how rowdy an all-cast-and-crew event gets.

"Good to see you, Damian," Rebecca says.

"Happy to be here," I reply. "Thanks so much for the invite."

"Come, come, let me introduce you to some people."

With a jerk of his head in the general direction of the room, Damian leads Rebecca and me around the space. First, we meet the only other woman in the room, a tall, athletic-looking person named Michelle, who I learn was the unit production manager for the show. Chris and John break away from their conversation to greet us with handshakes and hellos. We make our way to the corner, where Oliver and the stranger are still talking quietly with each other.

"Adam, please meet Celia and Rebecca," Damian says as he waves his empty drink around us. "Rebecca here is our music supervisor, and Celia cowrote the music with Oliver."

Adam is about my height, with a wiry build and watery eyes. He smiles at us, exposing straight teeth already stained a pale shade of purple thanks to the glass of red wine in his hand.

"Are you going to tell them what I do, or are you going to make me say it?" Adam asks of Damian, who laughs and claps a hand on Adam's shoulder.

"Sorry, sorry—Adam is our head writer. The best in the business, honestly."

We all exchange nice-to-meet-yous and quick how-are-yous. A martini appears in my hand just as Damian looks to Oliver and says, "I heard you two went all the way up to Maine to write the score."

Oliver nods. "We did. My family has a studio up there."

"How did that work?" Adam asks, his gaze bouncing between Oliver and me. "Did you two have to live together and work together?"

"Yep. Roommates and coconspirators," I reply with a smile. I can't bring myself to look at Oliver when I add, "It was pretty easy, actually. He's a great collaborator."

Not the truth, exactly, but not a lie, either.

Adam shakes his head, flabbergasted by this. "I could never. I can't speak to anyone when I'm in the middle of writing. Even my wife knows to leave me alone."

"We know," Damian smirks.

The clinking of metal on glass turns everyone's attention to the middle of the room. Chris stands at the head of the table, fork in one hand, glass of what looks like whiskey in the other. It hits me then, all at once—I'm here, in this room, surrounded by people who have decades of experience in the industry I've been gunning for all my life. They're Oscar winners, studio favorites, the people who are responsible for making some of the most beloved movies of the last ten years.

And I'm *here*. My heart jumps into my throat. Now I just have to convince them to let me stay.

"Before we sit down to eat, I just wanted to take a second to say thank you," Chris says. "We all know it takes a huge crew to get a show off the ground, and every one of you played an integral part in that. You read Adam's words, saw my vision, and ran with it—so a moment of gratitude for all of you, for helping me to build this plane while flying it."

"To building the plane," Michelle replies as she raises her champagne flute.

The rest of us raise our glasses as Adam adds, "And to safe landings."

A chorus of chuckles rumbles around the room while everyone clinks their glasses together and drinks. A group of servers descends on our table to pull out chairs. I make my way toward it, a little uncertain of where I should sit, when I feel a light tug at my elbow.

I glance behind me to find Oliver much closer than I expected. His scent finds me, cutting through the savory smells coming from the kitchen. When I take a deep breath through my nose, his pupils dilate.

"I got your text," he whispers. "We'll talk after dinner."

My cheeks heat and my mind reels. I need an explanation from him, but this is not the time or the place. There's no way anyone can hear us, but the people in this room cannot even *see* this exchange; I can't risk them getting the wrong idea. I smile as brightly as I can when I step away, hoping this will look like an easy conversation between friends to anyone who might be watching.

The table is set for ten, but there are only nine of us here, including a man I haven't met yet. Everyone is settling into chairs, and there are three open spots left: two next to each other to the right of where Chris sits at the head, and one on the other side, between John and Rebecca.

I make a game-time decision to sit between Rebecca and John. I have to put some distance between Oliver and me. If I sit next to him, I won't be able to focus at all.

This means he takes the seat directly across from me. As we both settle into our chairs, my eyes look to him, but he's quick to fall into conversation with Damian. I take a deep breath and remind myself that it'll all be fine—just yesterday, we sat at the piano and told each other we weren't ready for this to be over. I'll get some answers, and we'll get through it together.

Dinner is served as a series of plated courses. It's rich, hearty food dished up in tiny, elegant portions, the kind of fine dining

I can never afford on my own. Between bites of steak tartare, roasted squash, and tortellini, I manage to learn a lot about John. He's been married four times, divorced three, and has two kids, one of whom is working as a cinematographer, just like him. When he makes a sarcastic joke about how hard it must be to be a nepo baby, I force myself to laugh.

Conversation weaves around the table. Sometimes, the whole group talks about *Lineage*; other times, they talk about Chris's last movie, which they all worked on together. I contribute as much as I can, but it's obvious that I'm the least experienced person at this table. I'm introduced to Tom, the last person for me to meet, and learn he's also a producer. All the while, I nurse my martini, intent on maintaining some control over myself despite how overwhelmed I am.

Not that it would matter—everyone here is drinking plenty. The wine flows through every course. Voices grow louder and faces grow splotchy and red as the evening wears on. Everyone's lips seem to be loosening, too. We shift from industry chat to industry gossip by the time the desserts arrive.

When Tom starts telling a story about a book adaptation they had to kill because they discovered the author had a semisecret identity dedicated to harassing women online, I let my attention wander to Oliver for the first time since sitting down. I'm surprised to find he's already looking at me, that singular focus of his locked in despite the empty wineglass next to him. I feel hot all over, all the way down to my bones.

"You said you went to Juilliard, right?" John asks, effectively snapping that tether between Oliver and me.

"Yes! I did my undergrad there in music."

He sighs as he runs a hand over the gray five o'clock shadow on his jaw. "My youngest is talking about going there for acting. She graduates next year, but my ex-wife is trying to talk her into staying in LA where they live. Would you be open to talking to her about it? Telling her what campus life is like and all that?"

John looks like he's in his sixties, and he has a daughter that's seventeen? Ignoring the mental math, I say, "Yeah, of course. Happy to help. I'll give you my number?"

When John and I exchange digits, I can't help but think—*One down, five more to go.*

Once all the plates are cleared, Michelle is the first to depart. She cites an early morning and waves off the protests that she stay and have another. Tom goes not long after she does, and I hate how disappointed I am to see them both go. They might know my name now, but I barely got to speak to either of them. Some first impression.

This begins a game of musical chairs. Chris has to take a call, so he steps out; John takes his seat and starts talking to Oliver in a low voice. Rebecca turns to me and plops an elbow on the table with a loud thud. Her eyes are glassy.

"So, having fun?" she asks quietly.

I sneak a glance at Oliver, Damian, and John to make sure they're not listening to us. "I wouldn't say *fun* is the right word, but I'm here."

"It's stressful, right?" she whispers. "Being the new person, I mean."

"So stressful." I blow out a breath.

"I think I'm gonna go." The way she says it sounds like she's trying to convince herself it's a good idea. "Chris talked to me about the next thing he's thinking about doing and made it abundantly clear hiring me for it depends on how well *Lineage* does. I think I've hit my limit."

"Okay, well, thanks again. For everything. Text me when you get home?"

She nods as she stands. Without her next to me, I feel even more uncertain of myself than I did in the days leading up to this dinner. I hadn't realized how much of a comfort her presence was—my old college friend, whose opinion mattered enough that I got this job.

While she says her goodbyes, I sneak away

from the table and head for the bathroom. I don't even need to pee; I just need time to collect myself, to turn it off while I swipe some lip gloss on and breathe.

When I exit the restroom a few minutes later, Damian is there, either going in or coming from the men's room. The little alcove is semidark but I can still tell he's surprised to see me. His eyes widen for a second before they narrow, his expression suddenly thoughtful, maybe even calculating.

"Celia, hey. I wanted to ask you something."

My heart slams into my chest. I aim for pleasantly curious and wind up with a small smile and lifted brows. I might just look deranged. I don't know. "Oh? What's up?"

"Is there... something going on? Between you and Oliver?"

My stomach bottoms out. It's a bold question that comes out in a bold voice. I know he's at least a little drunk because I saw how much wine he consumed at dinner, but I don't know if he's asking this because he's trying to protect the show, or for something more nefarious.

No funny business—Rebecca's words from earlier ring out in my ears.

"Oh! No. Not at all." The lie slips out of me at a fast clip. Almost manic. I try to save face by forcing a bigger smile. "I mean, we're close after living under the same roof for weeks, but that's it. Just creative partners for this. And former roommates," I add with a laugh that sounds a little like I'm choking.

He folds his arms over his chest. "So you work alone, too."

It's not a question, but I still answer. "Yes."

"Are you familiar with the works of Debra Cain?" he asks.

Of course I've heard of Debra Cain; everyone who is even the tiniest bit media savvy knows her for her soapy network drama that is well into its tenth or eleventh season. She's also written and produced a handful of movies, most of which are critical indie darlings.

As a Black woman in film and television with a strong tenure, Debra is a true glass-ceiling breaker, and someone whose work I admire deeply.

"Who isn't?" I ask in response to this conversational pivot.

"Fair enough. Well, the reason I'm asking is I was talking to your creative partner earlier, and he reminded me that both Dahlia's theme and the percussion parts were all you." He tilts his head. "Is that true?"

Inside me there are two wolves: one who is grateful that Oliver gave me credit, and one who feels like shit for denying he's more to me than a former roommate. Damian can't know any of this, so I simply nod and say, "Yeah, that's true."

"I'm producing her next movie. It's a Limelight original. When I heard that sound for *Lineage*, I thought—Debra would love this, so I sent it to her and she gushed. Really, just raved about it. We can't afford the both of you, but we can afford one. Would you be interested in reading the script? Seeing if it's something you'd want to work on?"

That funny feeling comes over me, just like it did back at the restaurant in Hell's Kitchen. A chill—as reassuring as it is unnerving—spreads over me as I realize: *This is it, again.* The reason I came to this dinner, the reason I've worked my ass off for so long, the reason I needed Damian to see me as an artist, independent of Oliver...it was for this. To work with Debra Cain, a force and a trailblazer in her own right.

"I'd love to read it." Somehow, the words come out normally.

"Perfect. I'll send it over this weekend. Let me know when you're done with it. If you're interested, I'll set up a call with you, me, and Deb to talk vision."

"Sounds great. I appreciate you thinking of me, Damian."

His free hand pats my shoulder in a friendly pseudo-hug. "Good to see you, Celia. Glad you were able to join us tonight."

Damian disappears into the restroom just as Oliver exits. There's no time for me to celebrate this professional development—a meeting with *Debra fucking Cain*—because there he is. The man I just denied any feelings for. And boy, he is *pissed*.

SECOND CHANCE DUET ♪ 543

**FROM: Dr. David Kendrick
<david.kendrick@Juilliard.edu>
TO: Celia García
<celia.garcia@Juilliard.edu>
DATE: Wednesday, May 10 at 3:26 PM
SUBJECT: Congrats**

Hi Celia,

Before the semester gets away from me completely, I wanted to personally congratulate you on your time here at Juilliard. You are a remarkable student. It's been such a pleasure to watch you grow, both as a musician and a person.

I know you were disappointed that you didn't get the internships with Boston or the New York Philharmonic, but I know you are in great hands with Gio at the Eastern Symphony. He and I overlapped at Oberlin and have kept in touch over the years. You'll get a lot of hands-on time with the ensembles there and Gio has a bold vision for contemporary classical. He'll take great care of you.

I look forward to following your career. Please don't hesitate to get in touch if I can ever be of assistance in the future. I plan to retire here, which is still many years away, so you know where to find me.

Best,

Dr. K

Chapter Thirty-Five

NINE YEARS AGO

JUST LIKE THAT—it's over. Four years of college are behind me.

It's the Wednesday before commencement, in that weird period where all of us seniors are done with finals and performances, but we haven't been granted our degrees yet. I moved out of my dorm over a week ago, and my internship doesn't start until June, so I'm back with my parents for now. Once I see my first paycheck, I'll start the roommate/apartment search for real. Amanda is still living at home while she completes her nursing degree, so all three of us sisters are constantly on top of each other. We're one bad morning away from throwing hands.

That's why it was easy to say yes to Rebecca's invite tonight. A sort of pre-grad party at her apartment, though in all honesty Rebecca has thrown a lot of parties in the last few weeks. Still, it doesn't take much to convince me to leave the room I share with my baby sister, so that's where I am, riding the elevator up to the eighth floor of her Upper West Side building at 9:00 p.m. on a weekday.

As soon as the elevator door opens to her floor, I know this party is different than the others. I can hear the bass of music from the hallway and it seems like half the senior acting students are loitering outside her front door. This is new; the drama studio didn't interact with us as much as the dancers did. It seems everyone just wants to party together until all of this is gone.

We exchange waves and heys and what's-ups as I pick my way through the group. I wonder what the neighbors must think of all the noise as I pull open the door, not bothering to knock. Immediately I'm assaulted with the pungent aroma of weed smoke and a thumping Zedd song. The apartment is full of people.

"Celia! You made it!"

Rebecca maneuvers through a crowd of people to hug me. She's wearing a skintight black minidress and a little sequin shrug. The dark lipstick she has on pops against her fair skin and black hair that she clearly curled earlier today but is deflating in the heat of all the bodies. I feel appropriately dressed in my bright-blue strapless dress I bought at H&M last week.

"Holy shit, did you invite the *entire* graduating class?" I ask over the music.

She grins as she releases me. "Word got around. I think everyone wants to hang out together one last time before the family stuff starts this weekend. Come on, let's get you a drink."

She grabs my hand and pulls me through

the living room I barely recognize. It looks so different with all the people squished in here. All the nights I spent on the lumpy gray couch, curled up with Anthony and some variation of the roommates, watching a movie or studying, feel a million miles away.

Speaking of… "Where's Anthony?" I ask once we squeeze our way into the small kitchen.

He and I broke up two weeks ago in the most civil, adult way. It was clear things weren't going to be forever for us, not with him going to do his masters in Los Angeles at USC and me staying in New York for my internship. On a bench in Central Park, we shared one last kiss and promised each other we'd stay friends. The fact that it was so easy to walk away from him after over a year together only solidified my most private thought—that I would never love Anthony and never did. Which is fine because we never did end up saying those three little words to each other.

"Around here somewhere," she replies. She

stops us in front of a counter that's covered in half-empty bottles of all different shapes and sizes. "Okay, what do you want? Beer? Screwdriver? Cosmo? I don't know if we have Grand Marnier but we could make do with something else."

I spy a bottle of Ketel One and a bunch of limes. "Vodka soda?"

Chloe comes stumbling into the kitchen then. She's definitely not on her first drink judging by the smear of mascara under her eyes and the uncharacteristic frizz to her blond hair. The second she sees me, she throws her arms around me and screams.

"Ceeeeelllliiiiaaaaa!!! Can you even *believe* we're done with school?! Like, forever!"

Anthony slides into the kitchen behind her, a beer bottle dangling from his fingertips as he says, "Speak for yourself."

After a full minute of hugging Chloe, it becomes clear that we're not just hugging, I'm actually holding her up. I help her get her feet underneath her and keep an eye on her as she releases me and leans against the wall. She fixes her sparkly tank top as she says, "I think I need some water."

I pull a bottle of water out of the fridge and hand it to her, my eyes finally sliding to Anthony. My heart does a funny little twist in my chest, not because I regret breaking up with him, but because that's what happens when you let go of someone you care about. Also when that someone saw you naked. That can't be erased with a polite goodbye.

"Here," Rebecca says as she hands me a drink, complete with a straw. "Enjoy! I have to go check on Mrs. Norbet. Last time I saw her, some of the actors had convinced her to try a beer bong."

"You invited your neighbor? The old lady with the corgi?" I ask.

Rebecca grins and flips her hair. "I invited *all* the neighbors. That's why no one is complaining about the noise. They're all here somewhere."

Anthony and I share a look of combined

disbelief and admiration as Rebecca leaves us. I take a sip of my drink and nearly choke. It must be 80 percent vodka.

"Incredible move on her part," Anthony says as he shakes his head. "How are you, by the way? Ready for graduation?"

I manage to get the sip down without coughing. "I'm good, yeah. Ready as I'll ever be, I guess. You?"

"Good. Feeling a little overwhelmed by the move and my entire family coming into town tomorrow, but it'll be fine."

He takes a sip of beer, then pauses with the bottle still at his lips. His eyes shift to me; my brows flatten at the weird look he's giving me. He proceeds to chug the rest of the beer in three enormous gulps.

"You sure you're okay?" I ask.

He rubs the back of his neck with one hand. "Yeah, but I should probably tell you—I'm here with someone tonight."

A shocked laugh escapes me before I can stop it. It's been *two weeks* since we broke up.

I haven't had time to do anything except wrap up everything with school, move out of the dorm, and try to put my life together uptown. "Are you serious? *Who?*"

"Marie, from the drama studio," he replies sheepishly. "She's moving out to LA, too. She's got an agent and everything."

"Wow. Okay." I blink and stir my drink just to do something with my hands. "Congrats?"

He smiles with relief even though my sentiment was clearly a question. "Thanks. I'll see you later, yeah?"

When he leaves me in the kitchen, I say nothing. Suddenly, the drink that was way too strong seconds ago is the perfect cocktail. I suck most of it through my straw when two very drunk clarinetists stumble into the kitchen and nearly knock me over. I top off my drink with more vodka and a splash of soda before squeezing my way out of the small space.

It's not that I'm mad or upset he found someone new. I think I'm just surprised at how fast it all happened. Fifteen days ago, we were making out in his bedroom just two doors down, hands all over each other, bodies slick with sweat. Now he's planning a move across the country with a girl I only met in passing a handful of times.

I down half my drink. There's a dance floor developing in the middle of the living room. Rebecca is in the center of it all, hands in the air. I slide in to join her. Let Pitbull carry my worries away.

This works for a while. I'm dancing with my friends while the alcohol works its way through my system. I'm graduating in three days from the best music school in the country! I have an internship lined up! Who cares that it's with a small regional symphony! I got a job in my field! Sort of!

But then I see Anthony and Marie join the fray and I know it's time for me to get the hell out of that room. Rebecca grabs my arm in protest when I try to slip away, so I rattle my empty drink cup and wiggle my eyebrows.

She gives me a lazy, drunk smile when she releases me. She never stops swaying her hips to the rhythm of the song.

Once I'm free, I don't go to the kitchen. Instead, I head down the dark hallway to the bedrooms, past Anthony's, Chloe's, and Blake's rooms. When I get to Rebecca's at the end, I wrench open the door, slam it behind me, and shut my eyes as I throw myself against it.

"Oh. Celia. Hi."

Even over the muffled music and the voices of all those people, I know exactly who that is. My stomach drops at the sound of his voice. I don't bother to open my eyes because he's the last person I want to see.

"Please don't," I mutter. "I can't do this right now."

"Do what?" he asks quietly.

He sounds closer than before. The room tilts beneath my feet. My eyes fly open to orient myself. Sure enough, Oliver is standing next to her unmade bed, wearing some kind of dark dress pants and a button-down shirt. I can't tell what color anything is because Rebecca has a pink silk scarf draped over the lamp next to her bed. The whole room looks like we're inside of a heart.

"What are you doing here?" The question comes out harsh, the alcohol swirling through me loosening all my filters.

His lips purse together as he takes me in. I hate it. Hate that he's seeing me in yet another vulnerable moment. Hate that this guy beat me—for the comp competition, for the internship with the New York Philharmonic, for all the jobs we'll compete for that he'll ultimately get because he's Robert Barlowe's prodigal son.

"I'm graduating, too, you know." He steps closer; I slide along the wall to put more distance between us. "Are you...okay?"

"I'm fine." My hip bumps Rebecca's dresser, rattling the perfume bottles and jewelry on top of it. "Why are you hiding in here?"

His eyes narrow. "Why are *you* hiding in here?"

"Rebecca is my best friend. I'm allowed to be in here."

With the help of the dresser, I leverage myself off the wall to stand. He inches closer when I sway a little, but I right myself. The world evens out when I stand on my own two feet.

"You didn't answer my question," he says, his gaze focused and intense as he stares at me.

I put my hands on my hips and look to the ceiling—anywhere but at him. It's uncomfortable being in such close proximity, even after four years of sitting in the same performance halls, classrooms, and orchestra pits together. My skin prickles with awareness, but that could also be the Ketel One heating me up from the inside.

The vodka—it has to be the vodka that's making my heart race, forcing my head down to look at him square in the eyes, pulling all the things I never dared to say before to the tip of my tongue.

"I'm hiding because I *lost*, Oliver." My

words are laced with an undeniable anger. "I didn't play the fucking game and I lost."

He scoffs—literally scoffs at me. "What are you talking about?"

"I'm talking about *you*." My finger finds its way to the middle of his chest. "I lost to you, over and over again."

It's not just him. I'm sober enough to know that, even if I won't say it. Part of this is because my ex-boyfriend of two weeks is grinding on another girl about fifty feet away. Oliver isn't responsible for all the rejection letters that I accumulated over the last semester; those nos are because I wasn't good enough. Maybe I never will be.

His gaze trails down to where my finger is pressed against his chest, right on top of his heart. When he pulls his gaze up, that cold, unreadable mask is gone. His brows are pulled together and his eyes are so charged with an emotion I can't name that I take a step back, my hand falling to my side.

"It was never a game for me," he says, so quiet I almost can't hear it over the Killers blasting from the living room.

"Like hell it wasn't," I snap.

"Did we compete with each other? Yes." He steps closer, so I fold my arms across my chest. "But that's how this goes."

A dry laugh shoots out of me. "That's the literal definition of a game."

"Fine." He scowls. "Maybe it was a competition."

"Yeah, and you fucking *beat me*, over and over again. Congratulations. I'm sure you'll be the best intern the New York Phil has ever had. I'm sure all these wins have nothing to do with the fact that you're Robert Barlowe's son, right?"

Even in my tipsy haze, I know that's a low blow. It lands with as much impact as I intended. Anger flashes in his eyes as he sucks in a sharp breath.

"Or maybe I'm just better than you," he grits out.

"There it is," I say with triumphant sarcasm. "I always knew you felt that way. Now you finally have the balls to say it."

My pulse is pounding in my ears as I try to move past him, but the room is so small that my right side collides with his left. I sneer up at him in indignation. His lips part as he glares down at me.

For a second, it looks like he's going to say something, but I'm done. I'm done losing to him. I'm done avoiding Anthony at this party. I'm done with all the bullshit of college.

Oliver doesn't try to stop me when I pull open the bedroom door. He lets me go without another word.

FAMILIA GROUP CHAT

Today 9:16 PM

Madre — 9:16 PM
Hija what time was the dinner today?

Amanda — 9:19 PM
8 so she she's probably still there

Madre — 9:25 PM
ok let us know how it goes por favor

Rosa — 9:30 PM
literally the second you're done we wanna hear all about it!!

SECOND CHANCE DUET ♪ 561

Padre   *9:33 PM*

Girls. Let her focus

9:35 PM

But sí please please let us know hija

Chapter Thirty-Six

MY DAD HAS a phrase that he uses all the time. Whenever one of us finds ourselves in a pickle, he'll sigh, put his hands on his hips, and say, "Well, aren't you a rock in a hard place." I was in high school when I learned he'd been saying it wrong all those years. The actual saying is "stuck between a rock and a hard place," but English wasn't my dad's first language, and so the García family phrase is a little different.

As I say my goodbyes to Chris, Damian, and John, I am just that—a rock in a hard place.

I'm trying not to make it obvious that I'm rushing to get out of there, but I'm desperate to catch Oliver before he's gone. He didn't speak to me at all after we ran into each other outside the bathrooms. All I got from him was a stare so icy I felt the chill in my bones. By the time I took a few deep breaths to calm myself down, he was already shaking hands with Chris, one foot practically out the door.

Eventually I manage to excuse myself while still maintaining the facade of being totally fine, when in reality I'm freaking out. Oliver overheard me talking to Damian. I don't know what exactly he heard or what part he's pissed about—that I denied being involved with him, or that Damian came to me about the Debra Cain project and not him.

If it's the former, I have to apologize, have to make him see why I had to do what I did. If it's the latter, well—he can fucking deal with it. He's beaten me at this game for *years*. It was time for me to win one round.

No matter what, I have to salvage this. We still have work together, even if minimally, for another six weeks.

He's not at the front of the restaurant, where

I'm handed my coat by the same friendly porter from earlier. I dig around in my purse for some stray cash and hand him a crumpled-up bill. That might have been a twenty I just forked over, but I don't care even though I'm verging on broke. I'm out the front door and into the freezing New York night before the hostess has a chance to open it for me.

I whirl around so fast I almost hit a stranger with my arms. Panic fuels me as I scan the sidewalk, praying he hasn't already grabbed a cab or started walking, when I see him—maybe twenty feet away, bathed in the dramatic orangey glow of a streetlight, he stands alone, head bent as he stares down at his phone.

I jog over to him and curse the heeled boots I wore with every step. "Oliver!"

He looks up when I call his name, frowns, and then returns to his phone. I slow to a stop when I'm less than a foot away. It's clear he's refusing to look at me.

"Hey," I try, breathless, but that does not work. "Just—talk to me. Please?"

"Why?" he asks, eyes still trained on his phone screen. He's watching his Uber make slow progress toward him; I only have a few minutes.

"You heard me talking to Damian." I watch his face for his reaction. If I didn't know him so well now, I might have missed the tiny tick of his jaw and the hitch of his breath. "You're upset."

He doesn't respond, but he does pull his lips between his teeth. Just like before.

"Can you tell me what's going on in your head?" I ask, more desperate than before. "I can't talk to you if you don't tell me what you're feeling."

That does it. He finally looks at me, that closed, cold mask firmly in place. This is Oliver at his most unreachable.

I wince.

"What's the point, Celia?" The question is

so quiet that I have to inch closer just to hear him. "The work comes first, right?"

I feel like he just shot me in the chest. My hot breath forms little clouds in front of my face as I struggle to form words. Tears pool at the corners of my eyes and threaten to spill over with every frustrated blink.

"I told you how much was riding on this dinner." My voice is wavering and breaking with every word. "I—I told you we needed to keep it professional tonight. You know how much I need to find work."

"Enough that you would lie to our producer?" he asks, returning his gaze to the Uber app.

I clear my throat and wipe the stray tear that slips out. "It's none of his business. We haven't even defined what we're doing. What we are."

He pinches the bridge of his nose beneath his glasses, face screwed up like he's in pain. "Thirteen years. *Thirteen years.* That's how long I've had a crush on you. Fucking *pined* for you. I finally get my chance with you, make it clear that I'll do this on your terms, and you drop me the first chance you get."

The sidewalk beneath my feet feels like it's made of quicksand, like no matter what I do I won't be steady. My knees buckle; I lock them just to stay upright. What he's saying can't be true.

A Honda Civic with an Uber sticker in the window pulls up to the curb. He shoves his phone into his coat pocket and wrenches open the door. He's already got one foot in the car when I cry out, "Wait!"

When he looks at me, I can see the tears shimmering in his eyes. I don't know what to say, how to fix this, where to even start. Those tendrils of warmth—all that love I feel for him—swirl around inside me so fast I'm nearly nauseous.

"Please don't go," I whimper. "Please."

"That morning, by the water. What you said...I believed you. But I can't be your dirty little secret." He shakes his head, brows pinched together. "I have to choose me here, Celia. All that time in therapy can't be for nothing."

And then he's gone, tucked into the back of a stranger's car, and I'm left standing by myself, tears streaming down my face. No one pays any mind to the crying woman on the street, not for the entire twenty-five-block walk back to my apartment.

Welcome home: Someone is always crying in public somewhere in New York.

SECOND CHANCE DUET ♪

Today 10:01 PM

Celia — 10:01 PM
can we please talk about this

what do you mean 13 years?

10:05 PM

i didn't lie but i see how it looks that way. i was afraid if damian knew we were together in some way that he would judge me or blacklist me or just wouldn't be able to see me separate from you. you know there's like 3 women working in film composition right now? there's only 1 latina

10:10 PM

it was a judgment call in the moment. i don't know if it was the right one.

> **10:11 PM**
> i'm sorry. i really am

> **10:13 PM**
> i meant everything i said in maine. still do

Chapter Thirty-Seven

TWO WEEKS PASS. I don't hear from him at all. Not a single text back, nor an email. I'd be afraid for his safety if I didn't see him working in the Dropbox folder. He's alive, at least, and well enough to work.

The same goes for me, but that's about it. Before we left Maine, we divvied up the remaining things to do for the score and made a promise that we'd help each other out if we ever got stuck in the tiny details of orchestration. It seems that particular promise is cooked, but he's holding up the rest of the deal, just like I am. Everything will be fully written and ready come January.

Every time I see his edits in a file, or a note he left for himself on our to-do list document, my skin grows hot and my stomach somersaults. Does he feel the same way when he sees my name all over the work we share? Does he ever look back at the texts I sent him that night, like I do? Is he having trouble sleeping, too?

This is what I think about when I lie in bed at night, unable to sleep.

For the most part, the *Lineage* work occupies my days, but Damian does send over the script for Debra Cain's project like he said he would. I read the whole thing in one afternoon and am immediately obsessed with it. It's a multigenerational saga about a family of El Salvadoran immigrants who wind up in Chicago. My brain buzzes with ideas for how to tell the story with music.

It takes me forty-five minutes to craft an email response with the right ratio of enthusiasm to professionalism and the correct amount of exclamation points. Damian's response is simply, "ok more soon."

So, I wait. I rot in my apartment and try to block out my neighbors' noises; the upstairs guy replaced his treadmill with a weight bench while I was gone, so that's a fun new development. The temperature outside drops, Christmas trees go up in department stores, and menorahs are placed in windows. I buy some earplugs to help me sleep; it doesn't work. Occasionally I drag myself up to the Heights to have dinner with my parents and whichever sister is free that night, which is usually Rosa, since Amanda is on an overtime kick with hospital staffing shortages.

It's a Tuesday, or maybe a Thursday, when there's a knock at my door. I'm lying in bed watching an old season of *Battle for Love* while also pretending that I'm not thinking of the night Oliver was entranced by this silly show. Confused, I look to my door but don't bother to get up. I'm not expecting anyone and didn't buzz anyone up. This must be a mistake.

They knock again. I ignore it.

The key turns in the lock. This time, I don't panic. I know it's a sister or two. I stay where I am in my bed, curled up under a blanket.

It takes them a while, but eventually they get my lock to cooperate, and soon Amanda is stepping over my threshold and taking off her winter jacket. My brows flatten as I look at her. I thought she was working today.

"What are you doing here?" I ask.

"Nice to see you, too," she mutters, kicking off her shoes. "I came to hang out with you. Duh."

I look at my phone. It's actually Wednesday night, which explains why she's still in her scrubs. "Did we have plans?"

"No." She rolls her eyes, pads over to my bed, and crawls in next to me. "Do I need to preschedule time with you? Are you, like, super busy right now?" Her tone is laced with sarcasm as she looks from me to the TV.

"Shut up. I'm taking a break, okay?"

Amanda does shut up; that's the difference between her and Rosa. She also steals half my blanket as she burrows underneath it. I'd complain, but I appreciate the warmth.

For a while, we watch six men mud wrestle

each other for the chance to go on a date with a twenty-seven-year-old marketing manager from Des Moines.

"I love this show," Amanda says with a sigh. "This is absolutely insane."

I snort. She's not wrong, but I know she didn't come all this way to watch a show that streamed three years ago. I turn on my side, prop my head on my hand, and ask, "Why are you here?"

She sighs and takes the claw clip out of her hair before turning to me. "I'm worried about you."

"What? Why?"

"I *know* you, hermana," Amanda chides. Her wavy hair is a frizzy cloud around her head. "I know things are looking up for you with that script you got to read and all that, but I could tell something was off at dinner last week. When Rosa tried to poke fun at Oliver, you got all quiet and sad."

My lungs deflate. I thought I'd deflected well enough that night. Guess I was wrong.

"And since I don't think you told anyone else about him, I figured I'd come here in case you wanted to talk or something. You tend to, like, shoulder your problems on your own. I think it's a big-sister thing, because I do it with Rosa, but not as bad as you. But you can talk to me, you know."

"There's not really much to say," I reply, then flop back into the pillow and proceed to talk for almost an hour.

I tell Amanda everything about Oliver—from the day we left for Boothbay Harbor, up until the night of Chris's dinner. The only parts I keep to myself are the horny moments and the specifics of what Oliver told me that morning by the water. That confession of his feels too big, too precious to share, even with my sister.

I've had enough time to stew on all this now that I understand why he's so hurt. How it must have felt for him to hear me say those things to Damian after everything we said and did together. Oliver did what he had to do in response—he chose himself, to protect all that hard-won growth.

For her part, Amanda is an engaged listener, her eyes going wide for every dramatic moment in the story, her gasps like little dynamic flourishes.

"Do you think I did the right thing?" I ask, once I've caught her up to speed.

She blows out a breath and rubs her forehead. "I don't know, hermana. Your situation fucking sucked. Here's the big shot Hollywood dude asking you about your love life, but you don't want him to think you're messy, so what are you supposed to do? I would have said the same thing you did, for what it's worth. Doesn't mean it's right, but it's true."

"I just wish Oliver hadn't overheard it." I groan.

"Even if he hadn't, he probably would have found out." She bites her bottom lip as she considers this. "These movie people sound like real gossip queens to me, and that's saying something, coming from a nurse."

I huff out a laugh as I stretch; my body is going stiff from being horizontal for so long. "Maybe you're right. I don't know. I just hate how it went down. I hate that I hurt him. I hate that I was a rock in a hard place, just trying to get a job doing what I love."

"A rock in a hard place!" She cackles and slaps the blanket. "I love our dad. But yeah, you're right. You're just trying to get by. This has been your dream for so long."

"I wish it wasn't like this," I mumble. "It shouldn't be this way. I always felt like I didn't understand this game that everyone was always playing. Like there was no transparency and the decisions were already made but if you guessed right or something, you might still get to keep playing?" I shake my head, aware this won't really make sense to her. "I don't know, I thought I'd get better at it as I got older, but I still feel like I'm losing."

"Then change it," Amanda says simply.

I blink, confused. "What do you mean?"

She looks at me with one eyebrow raised.

"You're on the verge of making it, Celia. When you do, change things up. Do it differently. *Your* way."

As soon as she says it, I know that's what I want—to not only make a name for myself, but to also change things once I do. I don't know how I'll do that, but that's a problem for future me. The present me still has to get through the next few weeks without falling apart.

**FROM: Oliver Barlowe
<oliverb@gmail.com>
TO: Celia Garcia
<celia@celiagarcia.com>,
Rebecca Eagan
<rebecca.eagan16@gmail.com>
CC: Chris Ross
<cr@eyeproductions.com>,
DATE: Wednesday, December 2 at 4:47 PM
SUBJECT: Lineage recording sessions—NY Philharmonic, January 12**

All,

Our date with the New York Philharmonic is set for Tuesday, January 12. We'll record at Trio Studios in Midtown. Call time TBD.

Rebecca—are you able to join us?

Chris—we'll come in under budget for this. The orchestra cut us a deal.

Oliver

FROM: Rebecca Eagan <rebecca.eagan16@gmail.com>
TO: Oliver Barlowe <oliverb@gmail.com>
CC: Celia Garcia <celia@celiagarcia.com>, Chris Ross <cr@eyeproductions.com>
DATE: Wednesday, December 2 at 5:02 PM
SUBJECT: RE: Lineage recording sessions—NY Philharmonic, January 12

I'll be there! Can't wait.

Chapter Thirty-Eight

OF COURSE, THIS email from Oliver comes in minutes before my meeting with Damian and Debra. The first time I hear from him directly in almost a month and I'm trying to prepare myself for an interview with an icon. It's been rescheduled so many times over the last two weeks that part of me believes it's not going to happen at all.

That didn't stop me from doing a full face of makeup, styling my hair, and steaming my white button-down shirt. It's a Zoom meeting, so I look outstanding from the waist up; I'm wearing ratty old leggings on the bottom. I even went so far as to get special wipes meant for computer screens at the Duane Read down the block, so my computer's camera is sparkling clean. Let Debra see me in the best possible light. *Please.*

I don't have time to deal with all the emotions swirling through me as I read through Oliver's email, once, twice, then a third time. I take that guilt, the love that has no place to go, all of it, and shove it into the far corners of my mind. Instead, I focus on the script printed out next to my computer and all the notes I scribbled into the margins.

As I close out of his email and fight against a new tingle of nerves working its way through me, I think of the morning I visited my father at his club. Maybe it's the delirium of not sleeping well lately, or maybe the memory is just that visceral, but I swear I can smell the fresh café con leche in front of me as his words echo in my mind: *Life isn't a dress rehearsal, hija. It's the real performance. This is the moment you've been waiting for.*

When I tap Damian's Zoom link, a sense of *home* settles over me, as warm and comforting as the feel of drumsticks in my hands.

Two hours later, I shut my laptop with deliberate slowness. Halfway through the call, the lady who lives next door to me started playing "In the Arms of an Angel" by Sarah McLachlan on repeat and she's still going. I don't care. I just got the fucking job of a lifetime.

Debra Cain is *everything*. She is poised, thoughtful, and enigmatic, with a kind of graceful command of herself that makes it easy to see how she handles production teams. We clicked immediately, even with the added challenge of being locked in a small computer screen. Our visions for the score aligned. Production on the film is scheduled to start in February, which means my job picks up in March or April. We discussed budget at a high level; the pay Damian and Debra quoted is more than enough to keep me afloat. Contract details will be sent to my agent right after the New Year.

I will be *employed*.

After almost ten long, hard years, full of

unanswered emails and nos from every direction, I finally got a win. I don't have to move. I don't have to search for a second job, at least not for a while. I rise from my chair on stiff legs and let out a scream—of excitement *and* relief.

Sarah McLachlan starts playing a little bit louder.

As my heart rate slows to a more normal rhythm, I throw on some jeans, boots, and my jacket. I don't even check to make sure I have everything in my purse when I bolt out the door and run down the stairs. There's one person I need to see immediately.

Well, two people. But one of them isn't speaking to me outside of work emails.

For the entire A-train ride, I think about Oliver, about all the years we've known each other. *Thirteen years*, he told me, his eyes sparking with hurt, and it's clear to me now that we view those thirteen years with very different perspectives. All this time, I knew him to be an uppity asshole—and he was, in some ways, but because he walled himself in, terrified of being rejected after being cast aside by his own parents. The same parents that people asked him about constantly. He must have hated all those questions about his dad.

I was stubborn then. Naïve, too. I marched into Juilliard thinking it would be the key to the future I'd planned out in daydreams, only to be met with some harsh truths, chief among them that talent and drive are not enough. There's always going to be someone more connected, someone who has a leg up. It *is* a game, and it's so hard to play.

On a whim, I Google "Anthony Amato." I haven't thought of my college boyfriend in years; after graduation, we never kept in touch. His LinkedIn profile is the first result to pop up. I click on it and discover he's got some administrative job at a hospital in San Diego. He hasn't worked in the arts for years.

Persistence and tenacity, my agent said back in August, and she was right. My stubbornness paid off in some ways. I refused to give up. Still do.

It's snowing in earnest by the time I emerge at the usual 181st Street station. Cold flakes kiss my cheeks and dot my hair as I hoof it down the block. When I round the corner and spot the neon red Besos sign, I can hear the music floating in the air, the familiar rhythms filling me up, comforting me with the sounds of my childhood.

I let myself in the side door using my key, not wanting to make small talk with all the front-of-house staff. The house band is playing tonight and the club is already half full of guests parked at small tables that fan out from the stage. Dinner service is usually the slower part of the night; things really pick up once people have had a few cocktails. That's when the dance floor fills up and things start to get loud.

No one pays me any mind as I slip into the back. My stomach rumbles at the smell of all that good food in the kitchen. I peer around, looking for my father, but don't see him anywhere. It's only the usual back-of-house people—the cooks in their white coats and hairnets who have worked here for as long as I can remember, servers in their all-blacks flitting in and out, the dishwasher grinding away with stacks of plates and trays of glassware. He looks up and nods to me when I pass by him. I wave in return.

Tucked away in the very back of the building is the office door. It's little more than a repurposed closet, but it does have a computer, a bunch of filing cabinets, and a desk jammed in there. The door is cracked open, light spilling out onto the tile floor, and I know instantly that's where he is.

Knocking softly, I peer inside. "Papi?"

"Hija?" My dad's eyes widen as he looks up at me. He's seated at the desk with a pile of yellow and pink carbon-copy papers spread out in front of him. "What are you doing here?"

I scooch my way inside and sit down on

a red plastic crate that's been turned upside down. "I have some news."

He gasps and grabs his phone. "Did I miss it?!"

"No, I haven't told everyone yet. I wanted to tell you first." I pause to relish that look he's giving me—dark eyes shining, all excited anticipation. "I got the gig. The Debra Cain movie."

"¡Wepa!" he shouts, jumping from his chair in triumph. "I knew you'd get it!"

He pulls me up with rough hands so we can jump and shout and hug together. The metal filing cabinets rattle around us. As good as it feels to make my dad proud—to know that I'm escaping destitution for a little while longer—there's a dark cloud hanging over my head, keeping me from truly soaring.

My dad clocks this as soon as we calm down. His thick eyebrows furrow as he looks at me, the telltale line of concern splitting his forehead nearly in two. "What's wrong, hija? Isn't this what you wanted?"

"It is!" I let my hands drop to my side as I sigh. "I just—I think I fucked things up. With Oliver."

It's a testament to his genuine concern that he doesn't scold me for my choice of language. "What do you mean? I thought things went great with the show."

That's what my parents believe because that's what I've told them—through the group chat, over dinner, anytime the topic of my work comes up, which is often. Only Amanda knows the truth about it. As close as I am with my dad, the subject of who I'm sleeping with is not something I've ever wanted to broach, so I bite my lip, unsure of how to explain what I'm feeling, what I've done.

"They did, for the most part. The music itself is good," I start. "But I said some things behind his back that he overheard, and now he won't talk to me."

He clicks his tongue and shakes his head. "Aye, hija."

"It's—well, it's complicated. You know he

was a jerk when we were in college, but we hashed all that out and things were good between us." A gross oversimplification of the last four months of my life, but it'll have to do. "And then he heard me say some things that weren't true, and I tried to apologize to him right after, and again in a text message, but he won't respond. It's fine if he's done with me after this job is wrapped up. I just...I need him to know the truth."

My lip trembles. It's the first time I've let myself acknowledge that Oliver may want nothing to do with me once *Lineage* is finished. Even with all the uncertainty around us, before that cursed conversation with Damian, I thought that Oliver would be in my life in some way. That if we couldn't make it work as a couple, I'd at least get to call him a friend.

"A text message?" my dad asks, clearly offended. "Celia, I raised you better than that."

"He won't answer my calls."

Dad puts a warm hand on my shoulder and looks me square in the eyes when he says, "Words aren't always the answer, hija. You have to *show* people how you feel."

There's a big lump in my throat when I nod. He's right. I just have to figure out how to do that.

SECOND CHANCE DUET ♪ 593

**FROM: Celia Garcia
<celia@celiagarcia.com>
TO: Oliver Barlowe
<oliverb@gmail.com>
DATE: Wednesday, December 2 at 7:57 PM
SUBJECT: (no subject)**

I got your email about the recording session. Thanks for setting that up. Do you want to conduct? Or we can split it?

I'll get the score printed and bound. I have a guy uptown who does a great job. I can drop them off to the NY Phil's admin offices. Are your parts done? If so, I can handle that this week so everyone has a chance to practice their parts.

I think about you all the time. I hope you're doing well.

**FROM: Oliver Barlowe
<oliverb@gmail.com>
TO: Celia Garcia
<celia@celiagarcia.com>
DATE: Thursday, December 3 at 3:23 AM
SUBJECT: RE: (no subject)**

Chapter Thirty-Nine

THE HOLIDAYS PASS in a blur of food, drinks, and people. Once I print, bind, and hand deliver the *Lineage* parts to a nice lady named Kathy at the David Geffen Hall administration office, I throw myself into prep mode. With my father's recent advice fresh in my ears, I spend almost all my time with my mom, helping her to cook, bake, and wrap gifts.

The biggest day for the Garcías is always Christmas Eve. My parents' place is a revolving door of people—the titis and tíos who come in from Jersey and Long Island, my mom's piano students and their families, my dad's employees and theirs. So many cousins.

So many neighbors. It's a holly-jolly chaos fueled by coquitos and food.

The sheer number of people I have to talk to keeps me occupied, but after a few rum-saturated cocktails, I sneak into my old bedroom and pull out my phone. I'm seconds away from texting Oliver—just to say happy holidays, to ask if he's in Florida with Bea—when Amanda appears in front of me. Her sisterly sixth sense must have gone off, because she puts a hand on my phone and shakes her head.

"Not a good idea," she says gently. I don't argue with her.

A few days after the New Year—which I spent at a party hosted by Rosa and Hector—I'm curled up in my desk chair in front of my computer, updating my website with my new *Lineage* credit. It's a quiet, snowy afternoon, that weird period of time where half the country is back to the grind while the other half is still in a holiday daze. Just as I click Save on the web page, an email notification flashes in the corner of my screen. The subject line reads: "FW: SIGNATURE REQUESTED, final contract - C. Garcia, Cain Productions, Limelight Studios."

My heart jumps into my throat. I knew this email was coming, but it doesn't make the moment any less emotional for me. My agent and I have swapped messages a few times, hammering out some final details while she negotiated on my behalf. But to actually see my *own name*, sans anyone else's, attached to a project like this? With that many zeroes in the compensation column? It's more than a relief—it's a milestone, marked only by the wild drumming of my pulse.

This moment, this feeling of security and stability all wrapped up in the promise of creative exploration, passes without much fanfare. It's just me, my damp palms, and an electronic signature box. A few clicks and some typing. Just like that, it's done: I'm a TV *and* film composer now.

The days of scraping by with advertising

jingles are gone. No more losing jobs to AI just so a packaged-goods company can save a buck. After nearly ten years of hustling, I'm finally here. I made it.

♪

The morning of our first recording session, I wake up way before my alarm. Every single part of me is alive in a way that I've never been before. My senses feel heightened somehow, as if my brain is determined to turn this into a core memory. Dressed in my best business casual chic—only half of which is borrowed from Rosa—I set out for the day earlier than necessary. Trio Studios is not that far from my apartment, so I brave the cold and salt-covered sidewalks to clear my head as the city rouses itself from slumber.

For the first time in nearly two months, I get to see Oliver today. It's not healthy how much I've thought about this, which is to say that's basically *all* I've thought about. Every time I washed a dish over the last month, I remembered the way it felt to watch him clean the kitchen of the Maine house, how happy it made me to be so domestic with him. Every time I tossed and turned in bed, I remembered how easy it was to sleep next to him. The first time I saw cinnamon rolls in a bakery, I nearly cried. Every time I had to haul grocery bags upstairs, I remembered all the times he opened doors for me, carried bags for me, went and got something for me just because he could. Not just during this whole *Lineage* experience, but thirteen years ago, too.

I love Oliver Barlowe; I have for months now. Now it's up to me to show him that.

And if he doesn't feel the same way... well, my sisters will be there for me.

When I press the buzzer next to the nondescript glass door of the recording studio, my stomach somersaults.

I've beaten our 8:30 a.m. call time by half an hour, but there are a few audio professionals and studio techs here. Trio Studios was always way out of my budget for all the ad work I did, so I've never been here before. James, the friendly studio manager, shows me around the huge space, with walls decorated in album covers of various musicians and groups that have recorded here. When I see one of Celia Cruz's albums—one of the last recorded in her storied career—I fake a cough to cover a mini-sob. As I peruse the relics of a history littered with awards and game-changing artists, James trails after me at a respectable distance. There's a current of understanding that passes through us. This place is sacred. We've come here to make history of our own.

By the time we reach the fourth and largest studio space, more people have filed into the mixing suite, separated by a wall of glass much like the Barlowe studio in Maine. Except this studio is *enormous*, with high wooden walls built to acoustical perfection, the floor filled with sleek black chairs and music stands to accommodate eighty-five musicians. In one corner, there's a full drum set and a Steinway full concert grand. Countless cords run along the floor and walls like veins, all of them leading to a small platform at the head of the room, where a complicated assortment of plugs feed into a small monitor. It's both the heart and brain of the operation.

The conductor's stage.

"Celia! Hey!" I whip around at the sound of Rebecca's voice. She's standing at the door to the studio, her eyes bright as she waves at me. "Come and meet your concertmaster."

I already know who that is; he's a legend and a fellow Juilliard alum, though he was several years ahead of me, so we never crossed paths. Still, I recognize the black hair, dark eyes, and warm disposition that resonates even in photos when I exit the studio and finally meet the man.

"Qiang Chen." He's quick to smile as we shake hands.

"Celia García," I reply. "So nice to meet you."

"Likewise," he says, as he adjusts his grip on his violin case. "Are we still aiming for a nine a.m. start time?"

Both Rebecca and I reply with a quick "Yes."

"I'll make sure everyone is warmed up and tuned by then. Let me know if you need anything," he replies. "I'm used to being the intermediary between the conductor and the orchestra."

"Perfect. Thank you."

With a quick nod, he edges around us to enter the studio. Rebecca links her arm with mine and leads me down the hall, which is now full of various people discarding coats, chatting in small groups, and unloading instrument cases from tired backs. "Who's conducting today?" she asks.

"We're splitting it," I say.

"Okay, who's first?"

"Oh. I don't—I'm not sure." This is something I would have figured out earlier if Oliver had replied to my email with anything more than a thumbs-up. "He can go first, if he wants."

"Speak of the devil," Rebecca says, drawing my attention to the end of the hall.

I thought I had prepared myself for this moment. I was wrong.

My chest burns with a sense of yearning so acute I stop in my tracks. Rebecca's arm falls from mine in the process, but she doesn't seem to notice; she's being pulled away by one of the audio technicians who is rattling off tech specifications. Oliver's face is tilted down toward his phone, his baton case tucked under one arm, so he doesn't notice me at first. It gives me ample time to drink in the sight of him—to admire the slim cut of his tailored navy trousers on his long legs, to smile at the way the matching suit jacket fits the curves and swells of his strong shoulders.

Holy shit. I miss him so much.

He doesn't even look up as he starts to move with ground-eating strides. When he almost gets knocked sideways by a man hefting a standing bass, he finally does. Our eyes meet. His face remains expressionless but it's his throat that gives him away. It bobs with a hard swallow. I'm warm and tingly all over.

He slides his phone into his pocket as he closes the distance between us. When there's still a good foot of space left, he gives me a flat "Hey."

"Hi." The singular word is breathless and high-pitched. "How are you?"

"Fine. You?"

"A lot," I reply honestly. "I'm...a lot of things."

His eyes are assessing as they roam over my face, snagging briefly on an errant lock of hair that escaped my low bun. His hand twitches at his side. I forget how to breathe.

James, the studio manager, pokes his head out of the mixing booth. "You two ready? I want to go over a few things with you while everyone gets set up."

We both nod before filing into the small room, which is filled with endless sound mixers covered in knobs and buttons and sliders. James's appearance should have broken the spell that came over me—really, all the people here should be enough to distract me—but it didn't. It won't. I'm going to be hyperaware of Oliver's presence every single second of this day.

James unloads advice and instructions about acoustics and sound quality. Rebecca joins the conversation, chiming in with her own thoughts on how to best achieve the results we're looking for. All the while, the studio fills with sounds of an orchestra coming to life. Flutes run scales. Trumpets soar. Percussionists test bells while the pianist practices the main theme. I catch snippets of the cellists rehearsing Dahlia's piece.

"Celia can go first," Oliver says to Rebecca. "If she wants."

He's not looking at me when he says this, but I take it as a good sign. Here he is, letting me have this moment, so different from our Juilliard days when he was demanding and heavy-handed with a group. Now he's showing me he was listening when I said how important this was to me. I can only hope that it means he still cares.

"I do want to go first," I say.

I make my way toward the conductor's podium just as Qiang finishes the final tuning of the orchestra. The sound is warm, rich, and nearly overwhelming in a studio built to capture even the most pianissimo notes. Everyone falls silent as I step onto the platform. Under the soft recessed lighting, I catch the gleam of Qiang's Stradivarius violin out of the corner of my eye.

Looking out at eighty-some expectant faces, the same orchestra that rejected me almost a decade ago, I allow myself a moment to just exist. To be present. To think about nothing other than the fact that I have fought for my entire life to get to this point. I *deserve* this.

"Thank you for being here," I say. "On behalf of myself and Oliver, it is a privilege to do this with you."

The musicians murmur their assent as they pull on the headphones provided to them. I do the same as I flip open the full score that's been laid out on a flat music stand. When I lift my baton, there's a flurry of movement as the musicians ready their instruments. "Let's start at the beginning. Section one point one A, Title Sequence."

I glance over at the window of the mixing booth and give a tiny nod to James, who gives me a thumbs-up in return. With my free hand, I press the Play button on the screen in front of my score. On the black screen, I watch the Limelight Studios countdown pass from ten, nine, eight, seven, six, five, four, three, two...

At *one*, I lock eyes with the percussionist at the drum set and my baton swings down. The cue is seamless. The beat floats through the room, filling the space, all the way up to the highest crevices of the ceiling, echoing the rhythm of my own heart.

I am here, it beats. *I am here, and I am worthy.*

LINEAGE — EPISODE EIGHT, "ALL'S FAIR"

INT. — JFK AIRPORT, FIRST-CLASS LOUNGE 572

We open on the big diamond ring on DAHLIA's finger. She's looking at her bank app on her phone. She transfers $9,999 from one account to another. She repeats this process four times before she's interrupted by HARRISON. She closes her phone and smiles up at her new husband.

> HARRISON
> Our flight is boarding.

> DAHLIA
> (teasing)
> Look at how quickly you've adjusted to flying commercial.

> HARRISON
> I'm not as spoiled as you
> thought I was.

DAHLIA stands up and kisses him on the cheek.

> DAHLIA
> Oh, I know you're spoiled,
> but I love you anyway.

Chapter Forty

IT TURNS OUT to be a very long day.

It's after 8:00 p.m. by the time Oliver lowers his baton for the final time. From my place in the mixing suite, I watch as James hits a series of buttons, then flashes him a thumbs-up. All at once, nearly a hundred people clap in celebration. Pure, unadulterated pride surges through me as Rebecca claps a hand on my shoulder.

"Great work," she says, beaming. "Now it's my turn."

"Thank god," I mutter, which makes her laugh.

As the orchestra begins the process of packing up, Oliver makes his way to the mixing suite, his eyes bright and his face a little pink from the rush of it all. There's a quick conversation with James, Oliver, Rebecca, and me in which we congratulate one another before James outlines next steps. He'll have the tracks available to Rebecca within a week. It really is out of my hands now.

"So!" Rebecca says as she claps her hands. "It's a bit of a tradition for everyone to go out for drinks after. Qiang mentioned the Kerryman around the corner. You wanna go?"

I'm bent over my tote, gathering up my stuff, so I wait to hear Oliver's response. I'll go wherever he does.

"I'm in," he says.

So I add, "Me, too."

James hits a button on his panel and leans in to a microphone. "Drinks at the Kerryman. Everyone is invited."

There's a rumble of recognition from the orchestra members packing up in the studio.

"I can head over there and get some tables?" I offer.

"Sure, that'd be great," Rebecca replies.

"It's a big place, so it shouldn't be too hard. I'm gonna wrap up here and then I'll be over."

I try to catch Oliver's eye, but he's got his phone to his ear as he steps out. Deep breaths. I'll catch him at the bar.

The Kerryman is, quite literally, around the corner, less than two minutes from the studio. It's a classic Irish pub with lots of wood and deep-green accents. U2 is playing from a speaker somewhere. This late on a weeknight, it's sparse in terms of customers, with only a few guys in beanies parked at the long bar, eyes trained on the hockey game on the TVs.

Orchestra members trickle in. I greet them all, acting as a sort of de facto hostess until Rebecca arrives and takes over, while the bartender looks on at us, confused. It's clear she was not expecting to see dozens of people with bulky cases take over the space.

I order a beer and sip it slowly. I try to partake in the conversations bouncing all around, but I've got one eye trained on the front door. Every time it opens and a cold gust of winter wind bursts in the room, my heart skips a beat. This happens no less than ten times before I start to get worried.

If Oliver doesn't show up tonight...

Someone asks me about the Debra Cain movie; I smile and answer the best I can. Inside, I'm dying. Today was my last shot with him. He's already proven that he's strong enough to ignore my texts. He may have blocked me altogether. I don't even know where he lives.

Another cold breeze blows through the room and I swear I feel him before I see him. All those tendrils of warmth shoot through me when I tear my eyes from the group in front of me to the door. Of course it's him this time, looking just as handsome as earlier, sleek and fine in a black wool jacket.

"Sorry, one second," I mutter as I peel myself away from the bar.

He's heading in my general direction—not *to* me, but to where people are gathering to order drinks—and I manage to catch him in the middle of the room. His eyes widen when he sees me beeline straight for him. He freezes.

"Hey. Um. I..." My breath catches as he looks down at me. Everything I want to say clogs my throat. I'm acutely aware that there are at least sixty people in this bar now. This could not be less private.

But that's the point, right? Oliver needs to be *chosen*, needs to believe that he's loved for who he is on his own. I fucked this all up when Damian put me on the spot. I may never know if I made the right call that night, but I can at least show Oliver what he means to me—by putting my heart on the line in front of all these people.

I clear my throat, straighten my spine, and look right at him. "Sorry, I'm a little tongue-tied. I have been all day, actually. I just—I knew that I missed you, but seeing you today made me realize how *much* I miss you."

His lips part. A chair drags across the wood floors. People are starting to look at us, but I keep going.

"I fucked up that night of the dinner and I'm sorry. I'm *so* sorry I said what I did. If I could go back in time, I would have done so many things differently, but...that's not an option, so all I can do is tell you this and hope you hear me." I take a deep, shaky breath. "I love you, Oliver. I chose you that morning by the water, and I still choose you now. Even if"—my voice cracks—"you don't feel the same way, I needed you to know."

My little speech is greeted with silence from him. It's just me, U2, and the eyes of about twenty people who are pretending not to watch this unfold but definitely are. His face scrunches up as he closes his eyes.

"It's okay," I say softly, bravely, because I half expected this, even if I hoped for something different. "You can reject me. Walk away, if that's what you want."

I give him a watery smile when he finally looks at me.

"I was so pissed that night," he admits quietly. "I know you said you wanted to keep it professional, but after everything, I couldn't believe you'd—well, yeah." He runs a hand through his hair as he shakes his head. "But then I went down to Florida for the holidays and talked to Bea."

"Oh?" I ask, my heart twisting, writhing with hope.

"You were in an impossible situation," he says. "One I've never been in and probably never will be. Would I have done things any differently if I were in your shoes? Honestly, I don't know. By the time I talked to Bea about it, I'd already figured that out on my own. But you should have seen the way she looked at me when I told her what happened. Like *I* was the idiot for shutting you out."

I struggle to swallow. "You weren't—aren't—an idiot."

His eyes drop down to the floor. "I was. This is how I've been all my life. The whole rejection thing—you know." He glances around at the crowd, clearly uncomfortable rehashing those particulars in front of people who may know his family. "I thought I was doing the smart thing putting myself first that night, but once the anger faded, I realized I was doing what I always did. Closing myself off. I put those walls up so high in college that you had no idea how much I liked and respected you."

"I really didn't. That night of the graduation party, when you said you thought you were better than me—I believed it," I choke out. "I believed you."

His eyes cut to me, focused and intense. "I didn't mean that. I said that because..."

"Because I insulted you first," I finish for him. "I got so much wrong back then. I'm sorry. I thought you hated me."

"Never," he says, barely more than a whisper. "Not then, and not now."

"Oh." I reach for him, my hand landing on his upper arm, fingers curling into the soft wool of his coat to keep them from trembling. "I never hated you, either. There were times when I was jealous, and maybe times when I resented you, but that's what happens at a place like Juilliard. We were made to compete with each other. By design. I know that now."

"We don't have to compete anymore," he says, lips curling into the barest hint of a smile. "I never wanted that—I always respected you. That's why I mentioned you for this gig."

"And it changed my life. Thank you."

There's a moment where I think this might be it. This is as far as he'll go when it comes to clearing the air and accepting my apology. My "I love you" hangs in the air above us like an anvil, ready to drop.

But then he pulls me into him, his eyes full of questions, like he's not sure if I'm okay with this even though I just publicly apologized and confessed my love to him. There's a shimmering feeling in my veins as I look up at him and smile—my way to tell him, *Yes, this is what I want.*

"I'm sorry," he says. "I love you so much, and I'm sorry it took me this long to get here."

I've heard enough. My arms loop around

his neck. I pull him down to kiss me, my eyes fluttering closed.

It's not like it is in my TV shows, when two people have their big romantic moment in a crowd of onlookers. There's no big applause, no whoops and cheers. I do hear one guy go "Nice!" and the distinct voice of Rebecca saying, "Holy shit."

But I don't care. All that matters is my body melting into his, the smell of him winding through me, the feel of his lips stretching into a smile against my own. His hands are on my hips as he clutches me against him. I hold on to him as tightly as I can—for as long as he'll let me.

**FROM: Dr. David Kendrick
<david.kendrick@Juilliard.edu>
TO: Celia García
<celia@celiagarcia.com>
DATE: Thursday, March 4 at 9:02 AM
SUBJECT: RE: Internship idea**

Hi Celia,

What a pleasure to hear from you. Yes of course I remember you. I'm so glad to hear you are well.

I'm still at Juilliard as you can see. I will probably die here. I would be happy to talk with you about this internship idea of yours. Agree that it's very difficult to navigate the industry when you graduate. Job placements in the arts are never easy but don't tell my current students that. We always need more people who are willing to help students navigate life after graduation.

Would you like to meet for coffee? I'm at the Lincoln Center campus most

days but could meet you wherever.
My cell is 212-402-9221 if easier.

Best,

David

Dean of the Music Division

Epilogue

FIVE YEARS LATER

THE GOLDEN GLOW of a perfect summer sunset settles over me. It's warm out, the breeze off the Hudson a welcome reprieve from the oppressive humidity. The pier is bustling with people just like us.

Oliver leads me to the metal railing along the water. I can already tell the tension has lifted from his shoulders, that easy, elegant grace back in his limbs. To this day, I'm still floored by how handsome he looks in those black Wayfarer sunglasses of his. They did it for me all those years ago, and they still do it for me now.

"Can I ask for your opinion on something?" he asks as he pulls his phone out of his pocket.

I smile at him. "Of course."

I clamber onto the railing to sit, mindful not to flash the world in the dress I'm wearing. "Here, listen to this," he says as he hands me a corded earbud.

"How can I convince you to join this century and switch to Bluetooth?" I ask as I pop it into my ear.

"You can't." He slides closer to me so we can share the pair.

I sigh in mock frustration. This is one of those funny things I've learned about Oliver in the five years we've been together. In some ways, he's surprisingly old-school; he prefers his corded headphones despite having a newer smartphone. He resisted the pair of electronic toothbrushes I got for us, only relenting when I showed him an article on how much better they clean your teeth. To this day, he's never ordered anything off Amazon, not once. He says he likes going to a store to pick out exactly what he wants.

But that's my husband for you. Deeply loving, always thoughtful, and not without his quirks. I love him all the more for it.

He's also talented, only getting better with age, as evidenced by the music pouring into my ear. I've never heard anything quite like this from him before. It's all bare strings and stripped percussion. Haunting in that signature Oliver way, but distinctly contemporary.

"This is for that movie about the ghost, right?" I ask. "The family that thinks they're haunted but it's actually the trauma they never dealt with?"

He nods as he places a hand on my bare knee.

"It's beautiful," I say, and I mean it.

"Do you think it sounds *too* ghosty?" he asks as he takes the earbud from me.

"Not at all. If it were all violins, maybe, but

you focus on the viola so much that it mostly just feels threatening."

He smiles. "Good."

This is how our days look now that we've been married for two years. Long hours spent at the piano, in front of the computer, or in a studio, followed by walks along the Hudson River Park, hand in hand, while we talk about everything or nothing at all. Today was my idea; it was obvious to me he needed to clear his head when I saw him hunched over the computer, lips pulled tight between his teeth. I dragged him out of the West Village apartment we share to get some fresh air.

No one in the industry bats an eye at this. They never did, not after our very public reunion, but I think that partially has to do with the fact that *Lineage* was a hit by all accounts. To this day, I still get royalty checks from the first season's soundtrack, which earned both Oliver and me our first Emmy nominations.

Our individual careers really took off after

we co-won one for *Lineage*'s second season three years ago, and then again when we won for season three. Chris already called to ask us about season four; for the first time in my life, I had to tell him I want to come back, but it'll depend on schedules. Debra Cain and I have worked together on four more projects since our first, and I just agreed to do her next TV show, plus my agent and I are in the middle of contract negotiations to join one of the big sci-fi franchises for their next film.

Oliver continues to do it all—TV, movies, even a video game. He did that last one because it's something his dad has never done, but said later it was the hardest he'd ever worked for the least amount of money. He swears he'll never do it again.

He helps me down from the railing and slips his hand in mine. "Did you pick your summer interns yet?"

"Not yet." I blow out a breath. "I got *two hundred* applicants this year."

The internship program I started with the help of Dr. Kendrick is in its third year. For the first go-around, we started small, offering up one spot to fourth-year students at universities in New York. The first one came from Juilliard—an obvious choice, considering it's my alma mater and Dr. Kendrick has become a sort of mentor to me—and the second came from Columbia. I expanded and added another slot in the second year. That semester, one came from Juilliard, the other from the Ohio State University.

When word started to get around that my interns got hands-on, *paid* experience working in film and TV thanks to a nice endowment from Juilliard, I saw my application numbers rise. Especially since all of my interns secured jobs in the field afterward—that's the thing I'm most proud of, even more than the awards that sit on the bookshelf at home.

"That's incredible," Oliver says. "Let me know if I can help."

"Don't tempt me," I mutter, but I know that if I asked, he would.

This is what we do; we help each other. When one of us is drowning, the other makes sure we come up for air. When one of us is stuck, the other helps talk or play it through. When one is exhausted, the other makes sure we eat and get some rest.

When we're not working, we're up in the Heights with my family. Oliver even speaks enough conversational Spanish now that he can hold his own with my dad when they have drinks—just the two of them, usually once every couple of months. We make it down to Florida to stay with Bea and her family at least once a year. Whenever Oliver's parents blow through town, I follow Oliver's lead on whether he wants to see them.

Most of all, we're happy. Because I get to wake up every day and see the man I love. Because he knows I have his back. That I'd choose him over and over again, just like he would choose me.

Because he is my person, and I am his—it'll always be *us*, whether we're curled up in the bed together or rushing out the door to spend our days apart. We got a second chance with each other. This time, we're never letting go.

Acknowledgments

First, I want to thank my agent, Laura Crockett—both your advocacy and friendship are *so* appreciated. I know I have great people in my corner because of you and the Triada team.

To Sam Brody, my lovely editor, who saw the potential in this book and helped me strip it down to the studs so we could rebuild it—thank you. I'm particularly proud of this one and hope you are, too. I also want to thank the wonderful team at Forever for all the support throughout this publication process: Estelle Hallick, Carolina Martin, Daniela Medina, Jeff Holt, and Leah Hultenschmidt. To Nicole Medina, who created another stunner of a cover for my novel—thank you for bringing Oliver and Celia to life with your talent.

There are a few people who I leaned on for the research that went into this book. Ida, Karen P., Daniel M., CJ—you may not even remember me hitting you up with random questions over the last four years, but I'll never forget your willingness to help. Thank you.

To Callan, who read an early version of this book several years ago—thank you for believing in me and for always offering such thoughtful, helpful notes. To Adrienne T.—I can't say thank you enough for the friendship and candor on the various topics we meander through all day long. To Adrienne G.—thank you for agreeing to be a conversation partner to a stranger and for showing up prepared, fabulous, and fun as hell. Your friendship means so much to me.

To Patty, Amanda, and Stove—you didn't get the dedication this time, but that doesn't mean I love you any less. To Elyse and Fitzy—thank you for being my friends. I know I am the lucky one because you are all in my life. Not a day goes by when I don't think about that.

To the teachers who have made such an impact on me over the years, especially Mr. K—thank you for everything.

To my sister and my mom—I would be so lost without you. I love you. Thank you for all of it.

To Sheldon and George, the most perfect writing companions—thank you for always keeping my spot on the couch warm. I love you with all my heart.

Last, but certainly not least, to all the readers, librarians, and booksellers—I am so full of gratitude for each and every one of you. Having my books published is a lifelong dream realized that wouldn't be possible without you. Thank you for your support.

Reading Group Guide

1. Celia faces financial, creative, and career problems all at the same time but decides not to tell her family. This is partly because she doesn't want to worry them, but there's also some pride at play here. Did you agree with Celia's decision not to tell her family? Why or why not?
2. Celia and Oliver are opposites in many ways. She's mostly an extrovert who forms connections with others easily, while he's a shy introvert who requires more time to open up to people. Do you relate to Celia or Oliver more? Do you consider their differences complementary to each other?

3. Oliver acknowledges that his family connection helps him in the industry and that Celia has it harder as a woman of color in their chosen career. Do you think he understands her struggle? Why or why not?
4. When Rebecca tells Celia that Oliver is the one who put her up for the *Lineage* job, Celia is shocked. Were you surprised by this? Why or why not?
5. For most of the book, Celia remembers Oliver as a jerk during their college years. If you had been in Celia's shoes, would you have thought of Oliver this way? Why or why not?
6. When Oliver looks back on their time at Juilliard together, what do you think his memories look like? How do they differ from Celia's?
7. Celia is very close with her family, especially her sisters, Rosa and Amanda. Was there a member of the García family you connected with more than the others?

8. When Damian asks Celia about her relationship with Oliver, she lies. Do you agree with Celia's decision not to tell Damian the truth? If you had been in her situation, would you have responded differently?
9. If Celia hadn't managed to find another composing job after *Lineage*, she would have had to pivot to a different line of work to stay afloat. What kind of job could you see Celia doing?
10. Celia and Oliver get married between the final chapter and the epilogue five years later. What do you think their wedding was like? Was it a huge party or a smaller, more intimate affair?

About the Author

Ana Holguin grew up in the American Southwest and eventually made her way to the other side of the Mississippi, where she landed in Chicago. She now lives in the City of Broad Shoulders, where she writes about connection, joy, and love in its many forms.

You can learn more at:
AnaHolguinWrites.com
Instagram @AnaHolguinWrites

RAISING READERS
Books Build Bright Futures

Thank you for reading this book and for being a reader of books in general. We are so grateful to share being part of a community of readers with you, and we hope you will join us in passing our love of books on to the next generation of readers.

Did you know that reading for enjoyment is the single biggest predictor of a child's future happiness and success?

More than family circumstances, parents' educational background, or income, reading impacts a child's future academic performance, emotional well-being, communication skills, economic security, ambition, and happiness.

Studies show that kids reading for enjoyment in the US is in rapid decline:
- In 2012, 53% of 9-year-olds read almost every day. Just 10 years later, in 2022, the number had fallen to 39%.
- In 2012, 27% of 13-year-olds read for fun daily. By 2023, that number was just 14%.

Together, we can commit to **Raising Readers** and change this trend. How?

- Read to children in your life daily.
- Model reading as a fun activity.
- Reduce screen time.
- Start a family, school, or community book club.
- Visit bookstores and libraries regularly.
- Listen to audiobooks.
- Read the book before you see the movie.
- Encourage your child to read aloud to a pet or stuffed animal.
- Give books as gifts.
- Donate books to families and communities in need.

Books build bright futures, and **Raising Readers** is our shared responsibility.

For more information, visit **JoinRaisingReaders.com**

Sources: National Endowment for the Arts, National Assessment of Educational Progress, WorldBookDay.com, Nielsen BookData's 2023 "Understanding the Children's Book Consumer"

www.ingramcontent.com/pod-product-compliance
Lightning Source LLC
LaVergne TN
LVHW031534060526
838200LV00056B/4486